THE TAKEN GIRLS

Glenn Cooper

An Aries Book

THE TAKEN GIRLS

First published in the United Kingdom in 2021 by Aries,
an imprint of Head of Zeus Ltd

9 7 5 3 1 2 4 6 8

A CIP catalogue record for this book is available from the
British Library.

ISBN (PB): 9781800246348
ISBN (E): 9781800242227

Cover design © Lisa Brewster

Typeset by Siliconchips Services Ltd UK

Printed and bound in Great Britain by
CPI Group (UK) Ltd, Croydon CR0 4YY

MIX
Paper from
responsible sources
FSC® C020471

Aries
c/o Head of Zeus
5–8 Hardwick Street
London EC1R 4RG

www.headofzeus.com

Victoria and Elizabeth's Story

Villa Shibui.

No one in these parts knew the meaning of *shibui*. Most of the residents of Filarete who saw the sign on the gate assumed the American who lived in the villa was linguistically confused. Others were aware that the American's wife was Italian, and others still, knew that Elena was a native Calabrian, so they were able to debunk theories about a language muddle.

Jesper and Elena Andreason had purchased the dilapidated villa three years earlier when Victoria was two and Elizabeth was five. At the time, it was known Villa Del Mare, a bland appellation that traced back to nineteenth-century deeds. The previous owners had let the rambling residence go to seed, but Jesper and Elena saw a house with decent bones, some fine period touches, and a spectacular view of the sea from its perch on a coastal plateau.

Still, Elena had not been keen on shouldering a project of this magnitude because, in part, of the logistical challenges of supervising construction from five thousand miles away. But Jesper got very excited about the property—as he did about many things. He persuaded Elena that it could be spectacular and opened his checkbook wide to make sure he was proved right. He hired an award-winning architect from Milan, an experienced construction management firm from Catanzaro, and commissioned Elena's mother, Leonora, an artist, to do the interior design. Elena's parents lived just up the coast, one of the reasons for the purchase.

Years before, when Jesper made the old-school gesture of asking her father's permission to marry, he promised that one day they would buy a vacation house in Calabria so that Elena's parents could have front-row seats to grandchildren. Leonora grafted Jesper's spare and modernist sensibilities onto the Mediterranean roots of the house to create something sunny and minimalist and altogether unique.

The first time Jesper jetted in to see the finished project he fell to his knees and bowed to Leonora.

"You like it?" she said, laughing.

"No, I love it. You're a genius."

"It's a European house, but I was guided by a Japanese concept. I think it's very *shibui*."

"What is that?"

"It's an aesthetic of simple, subtle, unobtrusive beauty that comes together in a timeless sort of tranquility."

"Then that's what we'll call it. Villa Shibui."

The girls were now five and eight and this was their first summer at the house. Elena was planning on staying the full season; she assumed that Jesper would make good on his vow to spend the first two weeks of July and the last week of August in Calabria. He'd assured her (and himself) that with high-speed Internet and an encrypted video link he could conduct office business from the house, but shortly after their arrival, he learned of a Pentagon procurement meeting that he needed to attend.

"You promised," she said, pushing the button to retract the patio awning.

A blood-orange sun was setting over a calm sea, and the expanse of lush, green lawn where the girls were playing was darkening. A high Lucite fence at the boundary of the property protected them from the cliff without interrupting the sublime views.

"I know," he said. "I'm sorry."

"Why you? I'm sure your father can handle the meeting."

"He made me CEO. It's my responsibility."

He poured himself more red wine. Elena put a hand over her glass.

"Mickey will do anything for the girls. Tell him they'll be sad to see their father leave."

"Dad should stay at the lake with Mom. He's been doing these meetings his whole life. It's my turn."

"When do you have to go?"

"I'll drive up to Rome in the afternoon and stay in an airport hotel. I'm on an early flight Thursday morning."

"Mickey won't send the company plane?"

"I don't want to act like a prima donna. I can fly commercial. First class, of course."

She gave no indication she was listening anymore. "Look how much they love it here," she said.

They were kicking a ball up and down the lawn, but the younger girl, Victoria, decided to see if she could loft it over the fence. Her first attempt bounced off the Lucite.

"Stop it!" Elizabeth cried. "We'll lose it."

"It'll float," Victoria said. "It'll float all the way to America and we can get it when we go home."

"It won't," her sister insisted with the wisdom of age. "You're just being silly. Do it again and I'll tell."

Everyone who saw the girls raved about their beauty. Victoria, ever-exuberant, still had baby fat and possessed a fuller face than her sister. Elizabeth was demonstrating a new-found grace as her body elongated into that of a dancer. With parents as tall and chiseled as Jesper, and as striking as Elena, who could have been surprised at their looks? Jesper liked to joke, "What do you get when you cross a Danish guy and an Italian girl? Brown hair." Actually, their hair was more of a golden brown, and Elena had them wear it long so that their fine features were framed in Botticelli curls.

Elena called to them, "Girls, come in now, it's late."

"I'll tuck them in," he said.

She began to clear the dessert from the patio table. "It should come from you that you're going."

The girls' room was immaculate. In Villa Shibui clutter was a dirty word. Their toys were deposited nightly into a white chest decorated with small yellow Teddy bears.

Jesper sat on Elizabeth's bed and spoke to both of them. "Daddy's going to America for a few days."

There was a collective "No!"

"The time will pass quickly, and when I come back, what shall I bring?"

"Presents?" Victoria asked.

"What a ridiculous question. Of course, presents. Now, mind your mother, you hear? And remember, your daddy loves both of you."

Later, under white bedding, in a bedroom of white

furniture, a white rug laid over bleached floorboards, and French doors overlooking the dark sea, Jesper reached for his wife.

"I'll be back before you know it."

"You'd better be."

"How about one last poke and moan?"

"My God, you're such a romantic."

2

Jesper and Elena took pains to ingratiate themselves to the town of Filarete by retaining the gardener who had tended the property for many years and the housekeepers who had worked for the previous owners. The husband-and-wife housekeepers, Giuseppe and Noemi Pennestrì, were particularly important to the couple because they knew everyone in town and could put in a good word about the Americans. Their duties involved cooking, cleaning, and food-shopping while the Andreasons were in residence, and looking after the empty property the rest of the year. According to his in-laws, Jesper paid them more than the going rate and he liked to push a folded twenty-euro note into Giuseppe's shirt pocket as an extra something whenever he saw him. Giuseppe told his wife he found the gesture somewhat demeaning, but he said nothing because, after all, twenty euros was twenty euros.

When they arrived for work this morning, Giuseppe drove through the open gate.

"Why's the gate open?" he asked his wife.

"Maybe they forgot to close it last night."

"Jesper is leaving today for America, you know," he said.

"I know," Noemi replied. "Elena told me. She's not happy."

"Wives are always disappointed in their husbands."

She chortled at the comment. They'd been married for forty years. "You're right, for once in your life."

They drove down the white-pebbled drive lined by tall cypresses, past mini-groves of olive, fig, and lemon trees taken from elsewhere on the estate and artistically replanted by a renowned landscape architect from Florence who had further interrupted the two-hectare expanse of meadows with dry-laid walls of dolomite limestone. As a paean to Elena, the architects maintained the original Mediterranean character of the house together with its master-suite addition, although the white stucco was redone smoother and more refined, and the new, energy-efficient windows had modern white frames. The new shutters were the palest of greens, redolent of the first leaves of spring, and a new red-tiled roof was done in the ancient Roman design of imbrex and tegula overlapping ceramics. From its traditional exterior, it would be impossible to know that the interior design favored Jesper's wholly different California-modern aesthetic.

Noemi rang the bell while Giuseppe, grumbling at the threshold as he always did, removed his shoes. "One little speck of dirt on the floor and Jesper goes crazy," he groused, "and it's me who's got to clean it anyway."

She rang the bell again, and then a third time.

"See if they're in the back garden," she said, sending her husband into fits because now he had to re-lace his shoes.

He came back and told her that no one was there.

Jesper's Mercedes and Elena's Fiat were parked in the usual spots outside the barn.

"Maybe her parents picked them up."

"Probably," Giuseppe said. "Just use your key and let's get on with it."

Inside, she called out, "*Buongiorno!*" Then, "Elena, Jesper?"

"They're not here," Giuseppe said, walking into the living room. "The girls always come yelling when they are."

"Your shoes!" she scolded.

"Christ, woman, do you ever stop?"

The two of them got to work, Noemi in the kitchen and Giuseppe in the lounge, pushing the vacuum cleaner. She called out to him, and he just about heard her over the machine. He switched it off and yelled, "How in God's name am I supposed to hear you with the Hoover on?" he shouted.

"Something's strange," she said. "Come here."

He appeared in his stockinged feet. "What?"

"They didn't have any breakfast, not even a coffee."

"You made me come for that? Her parents probably took them out for breakfast."

"But not even a coffee?"

He waved her off with both arms. "Would you let me get back to work? I'm supposed to wash the cars today."

An hour later, Noemi called Giuseppe to the master bedroom. With lunch simmering on the stove, she had gone upstairs to make the beds.

"Both their phones are charging on their night tables. Who goes out without their phones?"

"I do," Giuseppe said.

"You don't have a mobile phone," she said. "The only person on the planet. I'm worried. Something's not right. I'm calling Senora Cutrì."

Giuseppe watched his wife make the call and he saw her face darken.

"They're not with her," she said, sitting on the bed. "She has no idea where they are, but she is terribly worried."

"So, what do we do?"

"She's coming over right now. She asked if we looked on the beach."

"I'll do that right now."

Leonora Cutrì arrived a few minutes before her husband, Armando, who drove separately from his law office in Palmi. The Cutrìs, like the housekeepers, were in their late fifties, but their wealth had them looking much younger. Leonora was regal in appearance, her long black hair elegantly streaked with gray. Her posture was erect, even in a state of alarm. Her husband had been scheduled to appear in court and he was wearing one of his good suits, tailored to obscure his ample belly. In a similar trick, a well-trimmed beard did its job of concealing the extra roll of flesh under his jaw. The only thing askew was his thinning hair; his left hand was greasy from nervously ruffling it while he drove to the villa.

Both of them tore through the house, searching every room and closet, while the housekeepers were dispatched to search the barn and smaller outbuildings.

"Maybe one of their friends picked them up for breakfast," Armando said.

"Elena would have told me of the plan," Leonora said. "We spoke last night. And have you ever seen them without their phones?"

"Never. Their noses are always in their phones."

"Dear Lord!" Leonora said, opening the drawer of Jesper's bedside table. "His billfold is here. He would never go out without it. And look, his watch!"

"All right," Armando declared. "I don't need more convincing. I'm calling the Carabinieri."

Leonora was crying now. "Then call Mickey. You must call Mickey."

"In Chicago? It's the middle of the night!"

"You know how he is," Leonora said. "He has to know immediately."

3

The two men received VIP treatment at the Reggio di Calabria Airport, clearing customs on board, then deplaning the Gulfstream G550 straight into a Mercedes idling for them on the tarmac. Their time of arrival was approximately twelve hours after Armando Cutrì placed his first call to the United States.

"Ever been here before?" Mikkel Andreason asked Marcus Handler.

"You mean this part? Toe of the boot? No."

Until an hour before touchdown, Marcus hadn't been aware they were going directly to the house. No hotel, no shower, no sobering up from the *ad libitum* Scotch on board. In the aft lavatory, the best he could do was run a comb through his wire-bristle hair, splash water on his haggard face, pop breath mints, and cinch up his necktie. At the best of times, he avoided mirrors. He preferred the delusion that he was his thirty-year-old self, not fifty, although women told him he was still a remarkable specimen. Tonight, was not the best of times. Mickey had caught him in the middle of the night at a casino in East Chicago ahead of a planned day off. Now, everything about Marcus was tinged gray—his skin, his stubble—even the blue in his irises seemed to have drained away.

His boss, however, had the appearance of someone who had just emerged, fresh and crisp, from a walk-in refrigerator. Mickey was the youngest-looking seventy-two Marcus had ever met. His skin was tight and shiny and his eyes were a proper, vivid blue. His full head of silky hair was only a shade or two lighter than his son Jesper's yellow locks. And he moved with the loose-jointed fluidity of a youngster.

"I never liked it here," Mickey said. "Especially now."

"I imagine," Marcus said, innocently enough.

"Do you? Imagine?" His voice rose in anger. Mickey had been bottling it up, Marcus thought, and now he was going to be on the receiving end. "I didn't want them to have a house here. The area is crawling with the Mafia."

"In Calabria, it's the 'Ndrangheta mostly." As soon as Marcus issued his correction, he regretted it, because it gave Mickey an excuse to get even angrier.

The louder he got, the stronger his Danish accent. Even when he swore, he sounded refined. "I don't care what the fuck they're called! For God's sake! Jesper put his family and my company at risk. And why? Because he's pussy-whipped by my daughter-in-law! If her parents need to see my granddaughters, they could damn well spend their summers in Chicago."

The sea was to their left, invisible in the darkness. Marcus didn't have a chance to light a cigarette on the tarmac and he was feeling the chemical void.

"What was the name of the policeman we spoke to?" Mickey demanded.

"Lumaga. Major Roberto Lumaga."

"Lumaga said the house had a security system, but it wasn't engaged. Did you talk to Jesper about arming his system every night?"

"I don't believe we had that specific conversation."

"Lumaga said there were no cameras inside the house or on the grounds. Why not? Lumaga said there was no panic room built into the remodel. Why not?"

"I offered to review his construction plans, but Jesper didn't take me up on it."

"You offered. Why didn't you insist? He's the company CEO for fuck's sake!"

"I believe I offered on more than one occasion. He's my boss. I couldn't force him."

"I'm your fucking boss!"

The driver glanced hard into his rearview mirror.

Mickey had hired Marcus, but when he relinquished the CEO title to his son, all of Mickey's direct reports transferred over. Apparently, to Mickey's state of mind, this was merely on paper.

"I smell booze on your breath."

Marcus wheezed a sigh and went for his breath mints. "I assumed we'd be going to our hotel first."

"You assumed."

They drove in silence the rest of the way until Marcus asked the driver to let him know when they were about five kilometers from the house.

"About here," the driver said at a certain point.

Marcus was already working, scanning the dark road for CCTV cameras. A few minutes later, the driver announced that they had arrived. Through the open gates of Villa

Shibui, the headlights bounced off white gravel. Apart from the lights of the villa, the grounds were pitch dark.

The house is isolated as hell, Marcus thought. *A lot of shit could've gone down and neighbors wouldn't have been any the wiser*. Outside the house, he counted eight vehicles, including two marked Carabinieri cars.

Mickey got out first and barged in without knocking. Marcus lagged for a few moments, shining a penlight onto the gravel behind the Mercedes. Coming inside, he saw a veritable cast of thousands—well, not quite. He counted four uniformed officers and six civilians. Mickey was holding himself stiffly as an elegant woman cried and hugged him and said with an Italian accent, "Oh, Mickey, what shall we do?" He assumed this was Elena's mother and that the man who then solemnly and wordlessly shook Mickey's hand was her father. They asked Mickey how his wife, Freja, was holding up, and he replied that she was not doing well, not well at all.

Marcus noticed that family photos had been removed from frames and scattered on the coffee table, presumably rephotographed by the police for missing-persons purposes. They were certainly a handsome family. He knew Elena and the kids from company social events and from the times he went to their suburban Chicago Lake Forest estate for the occasional meeting with Jesper. He always found Elena to be personable and charming, not to mention stunning. The little girls were bold and sassy, not the least bit shy, and Marcus thought that they lacked the unpleasant traits that so often afflicted the offspring of the privileged. He was less fond of Jesper. He found him too excitable for a good leader and prone to treat his employees with a lack of respect, a trait learned at his old man's knee.

A florid young man with peach fuzz, whom Marcus doubted had ever shaved, rushed forward to be next in line to kiss the ring. Before he opened his mouth, Marcus had him pegged as an American.

"Dr. Andreason," the fellow said. "I'm Mitch O'Connor from the American Embassy in Rome. The ambassador wanted me to personally let you know that any resources you require will be forthcoming."

One of Mickey's first calls in the middle of the night had been to the American ambassador to make sure that the best people in Italian law enforcement were going to be working on the case. Mickey had considerable pull. Andreason Engineering Corp was the largest private defense contractor in America, supplying mission-critical electronic systems to companies like Lockheed Martin, Boeing, and Raytheon. Mickey, a Danish national born in Copenhagen, had designed an innovative gyroscope as a PhD student at MIT. After graduation, he licensed the patents from the university and started Andreason Engineering in his garage.

To say that it became a success would be a mammoth understatement. In the last fiscal year, the company had thirteen billion dollars in revenue and customers in seventy countries. Jesper, an only child, followed in his father's footsteps, got his degree at MIT in electrical engineering, and joined the company in the R&D department. From there, he began his inevitable rise to the C-suite.

"You came all the way from Rome to tell me that?" Mickey asked O'Connor, ladling irritation over the young man like gravy. Marcus had seen this behavior in spades during his six years with the company. Mickey Andreason did not suffer fools.

"And to monitor the investigation—yes, sir."

"Good, monitor away," Mickey said, turning his back.

The next in line was a short, balding Italian who had rushed to find his suit jacket when Mickey entered. He was a representative of the Italian Ministry of Defense. Andreason Engineering was a major supplier of missile guidance systems to the Italian Navy.

Mickey said, "You're here to monitor the investigation too, I assume."

"Precisely," was the reply.

"Well, who the hell is doing the investigating?" Mickey bellowed.

"That would be me."

The reply came in English from a tall Carabinieri officer in his forties who had been watching the proceedings with a square-jawed, poker face. From the moment he laid eyes on him, Marcus figured he was the big dog on the porch.

"And you are?" Mickey asked.

"Major Roberto Lumaga, the commanding officer of the Carabinieri station at Reggio Calabria." His English was polished and refined.

"Yes, we spoke on the phone," Mickey said.

"Indeed, we did. And this is your security chief, Mr. Handler?"

Marcus nodded and offered a clipped wave.

The room was warm and everyone who had been waiting seemed to be wilting except for Lumaga. He appeared completely comfortable in a black jacket trimmed with silver braid and scarlet piping and perfectly creased black trousers. He was the only one in the room who was deeply tanned. Marcus figured he was just coming off a vacation or liked his tanning beds.

Before Mickey could demand an update, Lumaga provided one.

"First of all, you will want to hear that we have not yet received a ransom demand or indeed any communication from kidnappers. We have officers monitoring the fixed telephone lines at the Cutrìs' residence and Dottore Cutrì's law office, as well as the telephone line here at the villa. I am assuming that if a call came into your company offices in America or your Italian affiliate in Rome, that the information would have reached you."

"We checked before we landed," Marcus said. "It's radio silence on our end."

"Well, that doesn't mean that we won't hear demands tomorrow or in the coming days," Lumaga said, "but that is where we presently stand. Next, I can tell you that our forensics squad was at the house until only a few hours ago and they have fully processed the crime scene. There were no signs of struggle, no blood, no broken objects. According to the housekeepers, the Pennestrìs, nothing seems to have been stolen. Isn't that correct?"

Giuseppe and Noemi were sitting apart from everyone else. They nodded sadly.

"The Cutrìs were good enough to scrutinize the wardrobes and bureaus of the children and the parents to try to decide what clothes they might have been wearing when they left the house, but they were unable to make a determination."

Leonora raised her hands in exasperation. "They all have so many clothes and shoes. It's impossible to say."

Lumaga continued, "As I told you on the telephone, Mr. Andreason and Mr. Handler, we found Jesper's and Elena's wallets and purses with their credit cards and driving licenses, family passports, and their mobile phones. Elena's phone was unlocked and we examined it for any evidence of unusual communications. There were none. Jesper's phone was locked and we have not been able to access its contents."

"I should hope not," Mickey said. "It's going to contain all sorts of sensitive corporate data."

From Lumaga's expression, Marcus thought that the policeman was about to say something like: *Excuse me, but your son's been kidnapped, and your first concern is your corporate secrets?* Marcus preempted him and said, "All our executives use encrypted phones. I can get into it tonight and give you a read-out of relevant information."

Lumaga smiled and said, "That would be excellent. Now, I must say, our forensics technicians encountered some challenges. The housekeepers cooked and cleaned for approximately one hour before becoming alarmed and calling the Cutrìs. The house had been thoroughly dusted and vacuumed."

Giuseppe shrugged. Guilty as charged.

"Of course, we found many, many fingerprints around the house, and we have taken the prints of the Pennestrìs and the Cutrìs for exclusion, but we do not have prints of the Andreason family."

"I figured this would be an issue," Marcus said. "I have Jesper's fingerprints on file from his federal security clearances and I took the liberty of sending someone over to their house in Chicago to dust all the rooms. I'll forward you the files. Except for Jesper, I won't be able to tell you who belongs to which prints, but they'll be useful for exclusionary purposes."

"That will be most helpful," Lumaga said. "There was no sign of forced entry and, as you know, the alarm system had not been armed. We checked the log and it seems they only activated the system when they were away from the villa for extended times."

"But they always locked the doors," Noemi said, by way of defense for her employers. "They were good about that."

Lumaga said, "We can only assume that the intruders rang the bell and were permitted to enter sometime between 10 p.m. when Elena telephoned her mother for a call of routine pleasantries, and 8 a.m. when the housekeepers arrived. We had hoped that for a magnificent house such as this, we might find security cameras, but unfortunately, that is not the case."

"Don't even get me started," Mickey fumed.

"We arrived from the south," Marcus said. "It's nighttime, but I didn't see any CCTV cameras within five kilometers of here."

"We are making checks," Lumaga said, "but it seems that is the case. From the north, as well. This is a rural area. We don't have the kind of camera coverage here that you see on highways and cities."

"And you're not going to get any tire tracks from the gravel driveway."

"You are also correct about that, Mr. Handler."

"So that's it?" Mickey said. "You're saying you've got nothing? A family of four vanishes and you've got nothing?"

"Frankly, Mr. Andreason," Lumaga said, "that is precisely what I am saying, but please, do not lose faith. This investigation is only getting started."

"Right now, from where I'm sitting, I can't say I've got any faith whatsoever in your operation, Major. Go ahead and surprise me. I like some surprises, not others." He rose, looking disgusted, and said, "Armando, do you know where Jesper keeps his liquor? I'll need a drink before I call Freja."

"Come with me," Armando said, looking pleased to be of help. "I'll take care of you."

Lumaga went straight for Marcus and said, "Let me get you Jesper's phone."

He spoke to one of his men in Italian and a plastic evidence bag was produced.

"I'll take care of it," Marcus said.

"Good, but perhaps you could come outside with me for a moment while I have a cigarette.'

"Thank God," Marcus said.

"You also have the filthy habit? Fine, let's go."

The summer had started hot and had remained unseasonably warm. The air was heavy. The moon was somewhere up there, but a thick layer of clouds kept the night black as India ink. Although the villa was isolated and well off the road, it was far from quiet outdoors. Waves were pulsing against the cliffs and there was a much louder racket, a high-pitched, rhythmic clicking.

Marcus offered Lumaga one of his cigarettes and lit it for him.

"One always knows that summer has come to the south of Italy when the cicadas start banging their drums,"

Lumaga said. "The females make their presence known at well over a hundred decibels. That's a fact."

"I prefer it when a lady whispers," Marcus said in Italian.

"Me too. Where did you learn your Italian?"

As they walked, the gravel crunched under their shoes.

"I was stationed in Rome years ago."

"The military?"

"Me? No. I was with the CIA."

"Is that so? How fascinating."

"There were some fascinating moments, but they were few and far between."

"You were based in America?"

"Some of the time. Mostly Europe."

"May I ask what kind of work you did?"

Marcus chuckled. "You can ask, but don't expect much of an answer."

"Ah. If you told me, you'd have to kill me."

"Tired old joke. I was in counterintelligence."

"And this is a background that is desirable for a company like Andreason?"

Marcus flipped back to English. It was easier. "Mickey— Mikkel Andreason—thought so. We do defense contracting. A number of state actors, some unfriendly, and even some so-called friendly ones, are always interested in getting their hands on our technology. If your systems aren't hardened, your lifespan won't be much longer than these cicadas."

"I assume you are the person I'll need to communicate with about the investigation?"

"That's right."

"You see, Mr. Handler—"

"How about Marcus?"

"Certainly, and please, call me Roberto—what I must say is that there has already been considerable political pressure put upon me and my department from the highest levels in the Italian government. Wealthy American couple. High-profile company that deals in military technology. Two beautiful, young girls whose faces will sell many newspapers, presumably kidnapped, vanishing without a trace into our infamous Calabrian countryside. Once the media finds out about the story—which should happen in a matter of hours—you won't be able to get a hotel room within thirty kilometers of here. They will descend on us like the proverbial locusts. This will be a difficult, and possibly unpleasant case."

"I'm sure you're right, Roberto. So, what about the elephant in the room?"

Lumaga stubbed out his cigarette, picked the cool stub off the gravel, and put it in his pocket lest someone from forensics pick it up for testing. Marcus did the same, and this time, they lit Lumaga's cigarettes.

"I assume you mean the 'Ndrangheta," Lumaga said. "Look, this has to be the most likely theory, even before we get a ransom demand. This family could be thought of as a fat goose to be plucked. The 'Ndrangheta have spread all over the world—Europe, North America, South America, even Australia—but this region is their home. It's true that their roots are in kidnapping and protection, but this is relatively minor these days. It's drugs, drugs, drugs. This is their main business."

"But it's not like there's a central command and control, right? They have lots of autonomous cells, some of them small."

"Yes, for sure. These cells, as you call them, are based on family units. Some of the smaller ones still might find this kidnapping to be a tasty piece of trade. There are other possibilities, including the unfriendly state actors you spoke of, but for me, the 'Ndrangheta must be high on the list. I also have to say that Armando Cutrì is someone to think about. To be sure, not him as the perpetrator, but he is a prominent lawyer in this area, and he may have represented some members of the 'Ndrangheta. Who knows if there could be a—what's the word—a disgruntled client?"

"Tell you what. You work on your angles. I'll work on the corporate angle. We'll share everything. Okay?"

"It's a deal, Marcus. We'll help each other. Now, we'd better go inside before your boss gets me demoted several ranks."

"There's one more thing," Marcus said. "Andreason wants to make a statement to the media."

"And what would this statement be?" Lumaga asked.

"That he wants his family back and is willing to pay to make sure it happens."

Lumaga erupted. "That's crazy! We haven't even gotten a ransom demand yet. If he does this, we'll be buried in fake demands."

"I know. I told him."

"How much does he wish to offer?"

"A million euros."

"A fortune, but if he offers a million, the kidnappers will demand twenty. Don't you see?"

"I do see. Here's the problem. Mickey Andreason's a billionaire. He owns a big company. He plays golf with presidents and kings. Nobody tells him what to do."

4

That night, Mickey told Marcus he wanted to stay in the house instead of the hotel. There were two guest bedrooms and they'd be closer to the action, he said. When everyone else had departed, Marcus sat on the minimalist sofa in the minimalist living room, going through Jesper's phone while Mickey roamed the house.

"Everything is white, white, white," Mickey complained. "Even the fucking flowers."

Mickey had stopped by the house while it was under renovation, but he'd never seen the finished product.

"Anything on his phone?" he asked.

"Strictly business—and nothing we don't know about. No threats, no blackmail, no sign of hacking or phishing attempts."

"Nothing personal? Was he having affairs?"

"From what's on his phone, it looks like he's been a good boy."

"Remind me not to let you into my phone."

Even in his eighth decade, Mickey had a reputation as a player. Marcus knew all the rumors and more. A year ago, Mickey tasked him with delivering a nondisclosure agreement and a payoff check to a cocktail waitress in Las Vegas. It was an unpleasant piece of business. Freja Andreason was a very lovely woman with a very bad heart—some genetic condition, apparently. Marcus didn't know the details, but he heard she'd had at least two heart attacks, even though she was considerably younger than Mickey.

"I'll be done with the phone in a few minutes. Want to see it after me?"

"I'll take your word," Mickey said. "I'm going to bed."

"Do you want me to set the alarm?"

"Yes, of course. My son was stupid. I am not. Did you bring your gun?"

"I left it on the plane. I'm not licensed here."

Mickey grunted his disapproval.

Marcus finished trawling through Jesper's mobile, then found the stash of Scotch. He poured himself a large neat one and went onto the patio for the last cigarette of the night. The cicadas had wrapped up their annoying serenade and the waves had the stage for a solo. The gentle lashing of the shore made him drowsy and he synchronized his drinking and smoking to finish both at the same time. It was early evening in Chicago, but there wasn't anyone to call. He had come to appreciate the lightness that came with no attachments, but on this night, high over a black sea, the emptiness got to him.

He washed out his glass, armed the panel with the code Giuseppe had given him, then went upstairs, pausing briefly at the forlorn thresholds of the family bedrooms.

The next morning Mickey put out the word to the media who were beginning to assemble at the gates of Villa

Shibui that he wanted to make a public statement at noon. At the appointed time, he trudged down the gravel drive and opened the gate. The Carabinieri officers struggled to maintain order as TV and newspaper reporters rushed forward. Marcus and Lumaga tried to stay out of view of the cameras.

"My name is Mikkel Andreason," he started, but he was immediately interrupted by "Spell it, please!" He shot off a sourball look but complied. "This will be in English. I'm sorry I don't speak Italian. I am the father of Jesper Andreason, the father-in-law of Elena Andreason, and the grandfather of Elizabeth and Victoria Andreason. My beloved family was taken from their holiday home here in Reggio Calabria. All of them are missing. We don't know who took them or why. What I do know is that I want them back immediately. I assume that some group of criminals knows that we are a family of some resources. I know how negotiations work. I'm a businessman. We will receive a ransom demand for a big number and the practice is to reply with a small number. Eventually, over days, weeks, or months, a number will be agreed upon. I don't want to subject my family to a lengthy time in captivity. I want them back now. Accordingly, I am going to short-circuit the negotiation process with my best and final offer. I will pay—no questions asked—five million euros in cash for the return of Jesper, Elena, Elizabeth, and Victoria—all of them—within forty-eight hours."

"Did he say five million?" Lumaga whispered to Marcus.

"I guess he slept on it and bumped his offer," Marcus said. "He does shit like this."

Mickey continued, "I'm speaking directly to the people who took my family. Think about it. You can spend weeks and months hiding from the authorities, trying to squeeze a few more euros out of me, or take a huge pile of cash now. Think about it and call this number." He took a paper from his pocket and read it out.

"He just gave the number of my Carabinieri station," Lumaga exclaimed. "I didn't give him permission. Is he going to hire more people for me to answer the phones?"

"Like I said, Roberto," Marcus said, "he does shit like this."

Years of middle-of-the-night, duty-officer wakeups had trained Marcus to get alert rapidly. Six years removed from the Agency, he could still come-to fast, and when Mickey opened his door at four in the morning, his feet hit the floor before Mickey uttered the first word.

"I've got to scramble the plane," Mickey said.

"What's going on?"

"Freja's had a stroke. They just called. She was too ill to come with me and too worried to be alone. I'm fucking cursed."

Marcus couldn't say what he was thinking. You didn't tell your billionaire boss that not everything was about him.

"You want me to stay or come?" he said instead.

"You stay. Keep me up to date with every detail. If this wraps up fast, fine. The office in Rome has the ransom ready. If it drags on, give me a written summary every week."

"Will do. I'll call the pilots and your driver. I'll move to the hotel in the morning."

"I want you at the house. Stay until they're found. Alive or dead."

Mickey delivered the last words without emotion. *He's a tough son of a bitch*, Marcus thought. He told Mickey he'd be able to perform his usual corporate duties remotely.

"No, I want you on this exclusively," Mickey said. "I'll have Mayhew pick up the slack."

Mayhew was Marcus's second-in-command in security. He was an ambitious prick who'd be giddy at the news.

"He'll do an excellent job," Marcus said.

Lumaga came by the house early that morning and was pleasantly surprised to hear of Mickey's departure, but he said, "He drops a bomb on us then leaves. We've already had a hundred calls claiming the ransom. It's a madhouse."

"I'm sorry," Marcus said. "There was nothing I could do. Nothing that's credible, I suppose."

Lumaga said, "Not one. All of them crazy people or opportunists. Okay, look, the calls will drop off. With Andreason gone, maybe we'll be able to work in peace," he said.

"There's something vitally important you can do for me," Marcus said.

"Of course, anything."

"See if you can make this coffee machine work."

Over cigarettes and coffee on the patio, Lumaga said, "You probably haven't seen the mess up on the road."

"Mess?"

"Satellite trucks from every important TV channel in the country, camera crews trying to climb the fence, photographers with lenses so long they can see a mosquito on the moon. They're multiplying like rabbits. Andreason's reward was fuel to the fire. We've had to bring in the municipal police to keep order and prevent an invasion of the property. And I can tell you, Marcus, this is only the beginning. So, would you like to come with me to Reggio Calabria to see what a Carabinieri station looks like?"

"Sure."

"I'll show you our war room."

"I'll bet it's very impressive."

"Impressive, no, but you'll like it because I permit smoking."

To: M. Andreason

From: M. Handler

Re: Investigation Summary—Week 1

To date there have been no contacts from any individuals or groups claiming to be holding Jesper and the family. In Major Lumaga's experience, 'Ndrangheta kidnappers usually deliver their demands within the first few days. Going a full week without a call to family or a media outlet is unusual, especially in light of your large ransom offer.

The forensic analysis of the villa is complete. All of the fingerprints are attributable to family members and the housekeepers. The kidnappers likely wore gloves. There were a number of human hairs recovered, but they all match those on hairbrushes and combs belonging to Jesper, Elena, Victoria, and Elizabeth.

Lumaga and his people have been working their informants in Calabria and have been liaising with colleagues in Rome, Naples, and Sicily about any leads emanating from other organized crime groups. So far, nothing to report.

Armando Cutrì has been completely cooperative with the Carabinieri. They have been reviewing his case files going back a decade to see if anyone had a motive. So far, nothing to report.

Lumaga has subjected the gardener and the housekeepers, Giuseppe and Noemi Pennestrì, to detailed background checks and polygraph testing. Nothing of interest has come of these investigations. Their banks have agreed to notify the Carabinieri if any unusual deposits are made into their accounts.

On our end, I have been reaching out to intelligence services in the US, UK, Germany, France, Italy, the Netherlands, Spain, Turkey, Israel, Saudi Arabia, UAE, Australia, New Zealand, Malaysia, Philippines, and South Korea to see if there has been any chatter from Russia, Iran, China, North Korea, etc. about the crime. So far, nothing to report.

I am also having Jesper's emails, letters, texts, and social media messages going back a decade analyzed, looking for anyone with a motive to do him harm. Ditto for any disgruntled past Andreason employees. This effort is being run out of Chicago.

Two of the most popular crime shows in Italy have begun nightly coverage, this in addition to extensive newspaper and magazine coverage.

To: M. Andreason

From: M. Handler

Re: Investigation Summary—Week 2

There was a potential lead from Palermo, Sicily. A local police informant reported overhearing a conversation between two known Mafiosi about the kidnapping. Upon further investigation, the conversation related only to what these individuals had seen on TV. They were cleared of any involvement. There continue to be no leads referable to the 'Ndrangheta and there have been no ransom demands.

The Armando Cutrì inquiry generated one lead. Armando has never represented a gangster in a criminal case because he is exclusively a civil lawyer. However, two years ago, he represented an 'Ndrangheta member in a civil matter. A Mario Foti was arrested for a variety of racketeering charges and in the course of the police inquiry, the investigating magistrate sought to examine the bank accounts of several of Foti's relatives, looking for surrogate money flows. Armando sought to block access to the account of a distant cousin, arguing that the woman had only a peripheral relationship with Foti. The court ruled against Armando's motions and sure enough, the cousin was Foti's money-laundering conduit. Foti was convicted of racketeering and has been serving an eight-year prison term.

Lumaga interviewed Foti at the high-security Panzera prison in Reggio Calabria. Foti told him that Armando did good work for him and he bore no grudges. Lumaga was of the opinion that he was being truthful. Nevertheless, he's checked the whereabouts of all the known members of Foti's cell, primarily family members in a Calabrian mountain village. All potential suspects had good alibis in the days before and after the abduction. For the moment, this appears to be a dead end. Armando told me he was distressed that he was even remotely connected to the investigation and that he was going to reach out to you directly.

The Pennestrìs have also been investigated. I've gotten to know them since they come by every day to take care of the house. They seem like genuinely nice, concerned folks. For reasons unclear to me, Lumaga seemed to have a high level of suspicion and sweated them hard during interviews and searched their house for cash. They got upset and told me they'd considered quitting. Lumaga hasn't found anything to connect them to the abductions.

They have one son, Andrea, in his twenties. Lumaga got interested in him because he used to date the sister of an 'Ndrangheta member from his town. Lumaga also leaned hard on Andrea, but there was nothing there. For now, all of the Pennestrìs are in the clear.

Lumaga also investigated all the workmen involved with the Villa Shibui renovation project. So far, nothing to report.

As far as we can determine, Jesper was not always the most popular colleague or boss, but there was no one in his orbit who seems to have had enough animosity to commit this crime.

Your reward continues to generate an avalanche of publicity. All the Italian crime shows post the new call-in number every time they air. The private company we hired to take the calls had to put on extra operators to handle the volume. As you can imagine, there have been a tremendous number of kook calls, but every credible lead is being passed to the Carabinieri.

There continues to be no human intelligence or signal intelligence referable to potential state actors.

To: M. Andreason

From: M. Handler

Re: Investigation Summary—Week 3

This has been a quiet week.

The number of hotline calls has decreased to a trickle and nothing that's come in has been credible.

The Carabinieri have run through all their lines of inquiry and have begun re-looking at data to see if they might have missed anything.

There has been zero chatter flowing into my network of intelligence agencies.

Major Lumaga tells me that at this point, he does not believe this was a kidnapping.

I'd like to discuss with you whether it makes sense for me to return to Chicago.

Some nights, Marcus got drunk enough that he'd forget to go outside to smoke. When Giuseppe and Noemi arrived in the morning, they would sniff at the odor and throw the windows open. Marcus was using Jesper's car to buy cigarettes and booze and he had to dodge Noemi's reproachful looks when she peered into the trash bags at his empties. There was less and less to do locally, and he was getting copied on fewer and fewer emails and memos from headquarters on day-to-day corporate security matters. He confronted Mayhew about this, but his underling denied he was being iced out and told him that things were quiet over the summer, didn't he know?

Sometimes he'd drive to Reggio Calabria and drop by the Carabinieri war room, which of late had lost its intensity and was now more of a peace room. Major Lumaga was ever attentive and solicitous, but he was given to presenting a very Italian shrug each time they discussed a dead-end theory.

At night he roamed the white house that had been polluted with his black thoughts and bad habits. He rifled through Jesper and Elena's papers and personal effects, looking for something, anything, he might have missed. And while he drank, he stared at the photos of the girls, that had been reinserted into their silver picture frames.

Victoria and Elizabeth.

Named after queens, treated like princesses.

Something happened late at night or early in the morning and their glittering lives of grace and plenty had changed in an instant.

Were they alive or dead? Comfortable or under duress?

He drank as if the answers were hidden at the bottom of a bottle.

He was in bed one morning when Mickey rang.

"Marcus, I've been thinking about what you wrote in your last memo."

His head was pounding, his mouth full of sand. He took a quick swig of water.

"About coming back?"

"Yeah, that. Look, I think you might as well return to

the States, but here's the thing. Don't bother coming to Chicago, or at least to the company."

"I'm sorry, what?"

Mickey dialed up his Danish accent. "I'm bitterly disappointed. It's thirty-two days since they disappeared and you and your investigation have accomplished nothing. Nothing! Not a single clue, not a single credible scenario of what happened. I have succeeded in business because I do not accept failure. You, my friend, are a failure. You are a failure professionally. You are a failure personally. Don't think I don't know about your drinking. Who do you think pays the housekeepers? You are terminated as of today. You will vacate the villa as of today. HR will email you the details of your termination. Please take particular note that you are bound in perpetuity by the terms of your nondisclosure agreement. Publicly talk about any aspects of the investigation or the company, and I will sue you for whatever you're worth, which I imagine is not a lot. Any questions?"

He wasn't angry. He wasn't disappointed. He was tired and numb.

"No questions, just a comment," he said. "I hope Victoria and Elizabeth come home one day."

5

Four years later

When Marcus opened his apartment door with his shopping, he pretty much knew what he would find. Still, the mess in the kitchen, the remains of last night's dinner on the coffee table, and the clothes and towels strewn in the bedroom and bathroom, set him off big-time. At least Sarah had removed herself—he had no idea where and had little interest. It was Saturday, so she probably went on a lunch date with one of her girlfriends he refused to meet. Couldn't she at least have spent half an hour lifting a finger?

This relationship of all of six weeks was already in decline. When it looked like he and Sarah might be heading toward cohabitation, he warned her not to give up the lease on her own apartment in haste. He hoped that when the time came, she would thank him for his sage advice.

They met, unsurprisingly, in a casino bar in Atlantic City. After he was shown the door at Andreason, he'd had to decide where to live. He had no affinity to Chicago, didn't have the slightest interest in returning to Europe, and the

Washington, DC area, where he had lived the longest, came with unpleasant flashbacks. Moving to New York City seemed like a good enough idea. He wasn't a suburbia guy, a country guy, a small-town guy, and most definitely not a California or Florida guy. If he got bored in New York, it was going to be his own damn fault. It was far and away the costliest option, but with his pension, he was able to manage a small one-bedroom apartment in a less-than-desirable building.

Sarah was a legal secretary, almost twenty years his junior. She looked a lot older than thirty-five and the first time she spent the night, he snuck a look at her driver's license. She was telling the truth. He chalked up his misperception to the woman's fondness for vodka tonics and Marlboro Lights. Why, he had wondered, was she interested in a man his age who didn't have much money?

"Because, look at you," she had said waving a cigarette and two nicotine-stained fingers in his direction. "You're a very sexy man. Your butt's tighter than my boyfriend's in high school. And wait till I tell my friends you used to be a spy. They're going to go apeshit."

He had just finished cleaning up the place when his mobile rang. It was from a blocked number, so he ignored it. A minute later, there was a similar call and he let that one go too.

The third time, he answered with a "Stop calling me."

"Hello? Marcus?"

There was some distortion on the line, but he recognized the voice immediately. He wasn't going to make it easy for him.

"Yeah, who's this?"

"It's Mickey Andreason. Am I catching you at a bad time?"

He thought about saying something like, *Any day I hear from the likes of you, is, by definition, a bad time*, but he only said, "What can I do for you?"

"I'm on my jet. We just took off from Chicago. I wanted to see if I could pick you up in New York."

"Oh yeah, why's that?"

The conversation lasted under a minute.

When he hung up, he placed a call to a locksmith to change his locks and left a note for Sarah telling her that all good things must come to an end.

This was the one place to which Marcus had been certain he would never return.

Yet, here he was, driving through the gates of Villa Shibui, seated beside the one man he was certain he would never see again.

Mickey had caught up to his age. He looked sallow and puffy and thicker around the middle, every inch a man pushing eighty. Marcus had Googled him from time to time. He learned that following her stroke, his wife, Freja, had lingered in a rehab hospital for a year before she died. Mickey had soured on retirement and stepped back into the CEO job on a permanent basis. The company was still a significant player in the defense sector, but its growth had faltered. The view on Wall Street was that Mickey had lost his mojo, and it was only a matter of time before he dropped dead in the saddle or sold out.

When they pulled up to the house, Marcus said, "There're only two cars here."

"I told Leonora and Armando to keep their mouths

shut—no police—and not to let the housekeepers leave. We need to keep a lid on this until we know what the hell we're dealing with."

The Cutrìs were standing in the hall, ashen. The Pennestrìs were sitting at the kitchen table, too drained to rise to greet them.

"Mickey," Leonora said. "I don't know what to say."

"Where are they?" Mickey asked, hardly making eye contact.

Armando pointed. "Upstairs."

"You didn't talk to anyone right?" Mickey asked.

The lawyer said, "Not a soul. What would we say?"

Marcus didn't wait for Mickey. He didn't work for him anymore. He didn't care about being deferential. He took the stairs two at a time and rushed down the hall where he paused at the closed door. He could hear Mickey taking the stairs slowly and deliberately, but he didn't hold back. He pressed the handle and pushed the door open.

They were sitting next to each other on the same bed.

He had stared at their photos every day for four years. When he moved to Manhattan, he clipped their pictures from a magazine and put them into silver frames, just like the ones their parents had chosen. Sometimes, he tried to imagine how they would look if they had survived and grown older, but he wasn't good at this feat of mental gymnastics.

He didn't need to be.

Victoria's feet were dangling in the air.

Elizabeth's were just brushing the floor.

Victoria was still five and Elizabeth was still eight.

Neither girl had aged a day.

6

Mickey elbowed past Marcus and threw his hands to his head.

"It can't be possible," he said. "What the hell is happening?"

The girls warily stared at him and shifted closer to one another. They were barefoot, dressed identically in white. White T-shirts without logos or designs. Plain white shorts. Their clothes were streaked and spotted with reddish-brown stains. Both of them had the palest of complexions, without a tinge of pink. Their hallmark curls were gone. Both had short, pudding-basin cuts.

Mickey raised his voice. "Where is your father? Where's your mother? Do you hear me? Say something." Now he was shouting, "Where is my son?"

They started to cry and Marcus stepped into the room, blocking their grandfather.

"Mickey, stop, just stop. You're scaring them." He dropped to a knee, making his six-foot frame as small as he could. "I know you," he said brightly, pointing at the youngest. "You're Victoria. Am I right?"

Victoria stopped crying and nodded.

"And I know you too. You're Elizabeth, aren't you?"

A small, barely audible yes came out of her mouth.

"My name is Marcus. We've met before, a long time ago. Do you remember me?"

They both said they didn't.

"That's okay. You can call me Uncle Marcus. Would you like to do that?"

They nodded in unison.

Marcus tried not to stare at the stains on their clothes. He knew what dried blood looked like. "I've got pictures of you in America where I live," he said. "I look at them all the time. Do you know why I look at them?"

They replied with tandem headshakes.

"Because I've been worried about you. You've been away from home for a very long time. Your grandfather Mickey's been worried. Haven't you, Grandpa Mickey?"

Mickey played along. "Yes, of course. I've been worried sick."

"And your Grandma Leonora and Grandpa Armando downstairs have been worried. Do you remember your grandparents?"

"No," Victoria said.

But Elizabeth said, "I do."

"Of course, you do. You're a big girl. Are you guys hungry?"

They said they weren't.

"Because if you are, Noemi is in the kitchen and she'll make anything you want. She's a really good cook. Hey, is it okay if Uncle Marcus sits on the other bed? When I was a lot younger, I used to play baseball. I was a catcher, the guy who crouches down behind home plate. Now I get a pain when I kneel down."

His knee popped when he got up. He sat opposite them, and to make Mickey come off as less threatening, he told him to sit by his side.

The girls' eyes darted from one man to the other.

"So, Elizabeth and Victoria," Marcus said. "Your Grandpa Mickey and I were having an argument. He said you walked back home. I said you flapped your arms and flew home like birds. Which one of us is right?"

"Neither!" Victoria said, animated for the first time. "You're both wrong!"

"Really? I could have sworn you flew."

"We just arrived," Elizabeth said. "We were somewhere else and then we were here."

"I see," Marcus said. "Did you arrive on your own, or did someone come with you?"

"Gray Man said he was taking us home," Victoria said.

Mickey emitted a loud syllable, but Marcus shut him down with an elbow. He had never interrogated children, never even spent much time around children, but the technique he had stumbled into seemed to be working.

"I had a feeling it was Gray Man, didn't I, Grandpa Mickey? Here's something I was confused about. Is Gray Man your father? Is Gray Man Jesper?"

"No, silly," Victoria said. "Gray Man's not our father."

Marcus palmed his forehead. "Oh. Silly me! Say, where is your father? Have you seen him?"

"No," Elizabeth said.

"Have you seen your mother?"

Another simple, emphatic no.

"When did you see them last?"

They looked at each other and both shrugged.

"Was it a long time ago?"

Elizabeth said, "We don't remember when. I was wondering if they would be here. They aren't here, are they?"

"Unfortunately, they're not," Marcus said. "Here's another question I had about Gray Man. Did he speak English? Or did he speak Italian?"

"English," Elizabeth said.

"Gray Woman too," Victoria added.

Marcus said, "I see, there's also a Gray Woman. I imagine that Gray Man would have been lonely without Gray Woman."

Victoria agreed with a nod.

"So, they both spoke English. Did they sound just like me when I talk?"

"No, silly," Victoria said.

"How did they sound?"

"Funny," Elizabeth said.

"Can you show me?"

The girls giggled and poked each other. It seemed like this was a shared joke.

"Who can do the sound the best?" Marcus asked.

"I can," Victoria said. "They sound like this." As she said it she pinched her nose and produced a nasal, vibratory growl.

"That sounds really funny," Marcus said. "That's the way they sounded all the time?"

"Yes."

"Why do you call them Gray Man and Gray Woman?"

They exchanged glances that seemed to speak volumes. Apparently, Marcus's question was the dumbest in the history.

"Because they are gray!" Elizabeth said in exasperation.

"Their faces are gray?" Marcus said.

Yes, he was told. Their hands too.

"What color are their eyes?"

"They have giant black eyes," Elizabeth said.

"How giant?"

Victoria balled one of her hands into a fist. "This giant."

"Those are very big eyes," Marcus said. "What do their clothes look like? Like mine?"

"Oh, no," Elizabeth said. "They dress all in white."

"Like you?"

"We're in shorts!" Victoria said. "They don't wear shorts."

Mickey's patience wore out. He whispered directly into Marcus's ear, "Ask them where they were, for God's sake."

Marcus was going to get there eventually, but to keep Mickey happy he asked the question. "You've been away from home for a long while. Do you know where you were all that time?"

"In a white room," Victoria said.

"Could you see out the windows?"

"There weren't any," she answered.

"Okay. Did the Gray Man or the Gray Woman tell you where you were?" Marcus asked.

They both nodded vigorously.

"Where?"

"On a spaceship," Elizabeth said earnestly.

Out of the corner of his eye, Marcus saw that Mickey was about to erupt. "Easy," he said to him. "Be cool."

"Yes, yes," Mickey muttered.

"Did the spaceship land anywhere?"

"I don't think it landed," Elizabeth said.

Marcus tried a bit of logic. "But it must have landed, because here you are. You came home."

The girls looked at each other and then something happened.

A single drop of blood fell from one of Elizabeth's nostrils. She noticed it when it slid onto her top lip and she began to cry. That's when blood began to briskly flow from both nostrils, making a fresh red streak on her white shirt. As Marcus rose to fish a handkerchief from his pocket, Victoria's nose also started to bleed and she too began to cry.

"My God!" Mickey said. "They're bleeding!"

"Lean forward and pinch your noses," Marcus said, rushing into the bathroom for wads of tissues. "Mickey, go downstairs and get someone to call an ambulance. Now!"

7

Major Lumaga was too impatient to wait for the slow elevator to take him to the pediatric floor of the Morelli Hospital in Reggio Calabria. He bounded up six flights and was well out of breath when he came upon Marcus outside the girls' room.

"Is it true?" he panted.

"It's true."

"How can it be?"

"Damned good question, Roberto."

"Can I see them?"

"The doctor's in with them. I think she's going to be a while."

Lumaga smiled. "Hello, by the way. Let's have a smoke for the sake of old times. You still have the filthy habit?"

"Is the Pope still Catholic?"

It was a sweltering early-September day. It had drizzled earlier, and the narrow, car-lined streets surrounding the hospital were wet and steaming.

Lumaga took a deep drag and said, "When you were fired four years ago, you left without saying goodbye."

"I didn't know we were a couple."

Lumaga laughed. "Don't worry, I didn't suffer. And now, here you are."

"Seeing is believing."

"You've been re-hired?"

"I'd say my status is unclear. It's not the most pressing issue on the table."

"Indeed not."

"You're still a major, I see."

He performed the gesture that Marcus had come to call, the Lumaga shrug, a deep, sustained shoulder elevation accompanied by a sour pucker. "Well, if not for this case and its unsatisfying lack of resolution, I'm quite certain I would be a lieutenant colonel by now. At least I wasn't demoted."

A RAI satellite truck slowly drove past them on Via Giuseppe Melacrino, looking for a place to park.

"And so, it begins again," Lumaga said.

"Didn't take long. I wonder who leaked?"

Another Lumaga shrug. "Ambulance drivers, admissions' clerks, nurses, blood technicians, who knows? If this was the case of the century before, now it's the case of the millennium. We should be prepared. Tell me, Marcus, are you certain it's them?"

"Ninety-nine percent. Different haircuts, thinner, paler, but they look the same. Mickey and the Cutrìs know the kids a lot better than me. They're certain. We're going to need to get fingerprints and DNA."

"How does someone not age?"

"Do I look like someone whose answer you'd take to the bank?"

"Well, maybe not, but you've had slightly longer than me to think about it. Where do they say they were?"

"On a spaceship."

Lumaga didn't bother to look at him. "A spaceship. Of course. Were the parents in space too?"

"Nope. They're lost in space."

"Sorry?"

"There was a TV show. Forget it."

"You must tell me everything they said, because I'm the one who's going to be on the hot seat very soon. It's a pity, really."

"What is?"

"I quite liked my job."

The head of the pediatric hematology department, an unsmiling middle-aged woman, briefed the grandparents inside an empty patient room. Marcus stood near the door, feeling like an interloper. Had Mickey not insisted he be present, he would have preferred waiting in the hall with Lumaga.

"My diagnosis is preliminary," she said, "and is based on only a cursory review of their blood smears. We have many specific blood tests pending and we will have to perform a needle biopsy of their bone marrows. However, I don't think the diagnosis will change. It appears they both have the same disorder called CML. Chronic myeloid leukemia."

"Oh, my God," Leonora gasped, reaching for her husband's hand.

"They both have leukemia?" Mickey said. "How can they both have it?"

The doctor looked over her half-glasses. "This is hardly the most surprising aspect of their case."

Armando said, "Tell us, Dottoressa, can this type of leukemia be cured?"

"CML is not a common leukemia. In children it is extremely rare. So, what I would say is that there are no good statistics on outcomes for children. Certainly, they will require immediate transfusions. They have profound anemias, requiring red blood cells. Their platelets are low, hence their nosebleeds, and they will need platelet transfusions. Once we have confirmed the diagnosis and done a variety of genetic tests, we can discuss treatments. But in general, they will need chemotherapy, and perhaps, eventually, bone marrow transplantation. We should test the three of you to see if you are good matches. I understand that there has been a request to validate that they are who you think they are, so we will want to take swabs from you for DNA testing as well."

"Of course," Mickey said, "but I certainly don't want them treated here. I'm taking them to America. I'm going to get them the top people in the field."

"Signor Andreason," the doctor said, acidly, "I don't care where you take them. We are perfectly qualified to treat them here. I, myself, did part of my specialty training at Johns Hopkins. I have thirty scientific publications in leukemia. But it is for you to decide. However, they should not be moved before they are stabilized. Their blood counts are dangerously low. Now, please excuse me. I have work to do."

Marcus looked at the floor in embarrassment. *Mickey, you really know how to win friends and influence people*, he thought.

When the doctor was gone, Mickey said, "Well, she was

rude. I'm going to make some calls about the best pediatric leukemia centers."

Armando tried to argue that this was an excellent hospital, but Mickey didn't want to discuss it. He stormed from the room with his cell phone to his ear.

"They match," Lumaga said. "The fingerprints are a perfect match."

He and Marcus were having a coffee in the hospital cafeteria. Marcus told him he wasn't the least bit surprised and asked how long it would take to get the DNA results.

"I've discussed it with my superiors. We're sending duplicate samples to the best laboratory in Milan and to Europol at the Hague. We can't tolerate the smallest doubt. We'll have the results in forty-eight hours."

"Andreason wants them out of here. He's got his plane standing by."

Lumaga was adamant. "That's not going to happen."

"How're you going to stop him?"

"A serious crime has been committed on Italian soil. Two kidnapped girls have been returned in an enigmatic state. Their parents remain unaccounted for. An investigation that had gone cold is now extremely hot. As you know, the Carabinieri are under the direction of the Ministry of Defense. However, the Ministry of the Interior also has a role in this case as a referral was previously made to the *Commissario Straordinario per le Persone Scomparse*, the special commission for missing persons. I have already received instructions from both responsible cabinet ministers. They have ordered me to block the takeoff of Andreason's jet and as a last option, to arrest him for obstruction of a Carabinieri investigation."

"You'd arrest a grandfather trying to help his sick granddaughters? How's that going to play in the papers?"

"It may not play well in America, but the Italian people will support it. The crime happened here. Our system of justice must be respected."

"He's going to go around you. He's got a lot of pull with the US government. He'll get senators, generals, the US ambassador to cry foul. There's going to be a lot of pressure on your government."

"I am assured that we are prepared for this. Your ambassador has already been informed of the decision to keep the girls in Italy."

"They have leukemia, Roberto. And he doesn't have confidence in a provincial hospital."

"Then we will permit them to receive their treatment in Rome. I am assured that the children's hospital, the Bambino Gesù Hospital, is one of the best in the world for their condition. Please help him become comfortable with this option."

"I can try."

A minor commotion at the cafeteria entrance got both men's attention. A TV cameraman and a reporter were being turned away by a hospital security guard. The reporter who was not easily cowed, called out to Lumaga by name to answer her questions.

"There's a rumor that there has been a development in the case of the missing girls. Can you confirm it?"

"I don't have anything to say," Lumaga shot back.

When the crew had been shooed away, Lumaga told

Marcus that they'd have to hold a press conference. "There's no holding back the tides," he said.

"When?"

"This afternoon. We'll do it at the Carabinieri headquarters. I've let the doctors know that I'll need to interview the girls soon."

"Can I sit in?"

He responded with a Lumaga shrug.

"Look, Roberto. You want my help with Andreason. It'll be easier handling him if I know what's going on."

"Okay. But please let me ask the questions."

"I'll just observe. Did your forensics people come up with anything?"

"Nothing helpful. The girls entered the villa via a rear door that was forced open. The housekeepers hadn't armed the security system after their last visit. They come every day to check on the property and they haven't felt the need."

"But the gate was closed, right?"

"It's possible that someone climbed the fence, entered the house, activated the gate with the button by the front door, and returned to a waiting car that held the girls. Once again, we have been handicapped by the lack of cameras."

"Don't look at me. I was fired, remember?"

"How could I forget? There were two sets of fingerprints from the house that did not belong to the Cutrìs, the housekeepers, or the girls. I am willing to bet my salary for September that they belong to you and Signor Andreason but we will need to fingerprint you as soon as possible."

"Of course."

"We got the results from the facial recognition software. The way the girls appear now is identical to photographs from shortly before they disappeared. Still, we'll wait for the DNA."

"It's them, Roberto."

"Personally, I'm completely with you on this, Marcus, but I don't plan on being definitive with the journalists. The white shirts, shorts, and undergarments the girls were wearing were plain cotton with no labels. I'm told they could have come from anywhere in the world."

"How about anywhere in the universe?"

"Very amusing. Anyway, that's where we presently stand."

"I'm glad it's not me facing the press."

Marcus took Mickey into the empty patient room to avoid a public scene when he told him about Lumaga banning the girls from leaving the country. Predictably, he raged at the news.

"Does he think I'll lie down and let some fucking nonentity of a policeman prevent me from doing what needs to be done for my family?"

"No, he's expecting a fight. But he's got his political ducks in a row. He's confident he's going to win."

"We'll see about that."

"I think you should cooperate," Marcus said.

"Why should I care what you think?"

It was hard to control himself, but he did. "Tell you what, Mickey," he said calmly. "You can forget I might have an informed opinion and I can forget that I'm an idiot for letting myself be persuaded to come back here."

"Fine," Mickey said. His tone carried a whiff of apology. "Tell me what you think."

"You've got your granddaughters back and that's a very good thing. Now you want Jesper and Elena. And I imagine you want whoever did this to be captured and punished. Once the girls leave Italy, the pressure to solve the case evaporates. Maybe it shouldn't, but believe me, it will."

Mickey went to the window and looked down onto the convoy of satellite trucks partially blocking the street.

"They need treatment. I'll be damned if it's going to be here."

"Lumaga tells me there's a world-class children's hospital in Rome they can go to."

Mickey turned to face him again. He looked like a very old man.

"Write down its name. I'll make some calls. I'll fly my own people over if I need to."

"You're making the right decision," Marcus said. "Ready for the next subject?"

"Go on."

"Why am I here? What do you want me for?"

"You're here because Victoria and Elizabeth are here. I imagined you'd want to see this through. You were involved at the beginning. It's logical you'd want to be involved at the end."

"So, this is for my benefit?"

"Partly, yes."

"Tell me about the other part?"

"All right, Marcus, partly for me. Is that what you want to hear? You want me to grovel? Still steamed that I fired you? Well, here's a newsflash: I'd fire you again for the same reason. I lost Jesper and the kids. There was no progress. Goddamn it, I believe in accountability and I fired you. Now, I need you. I need someone I can trust over here. I need someone to have a seat at the table, shadowing the Italians. For the first time in years, I have hope about Jesper. I need you to find Jesper. And Elena. You know the case. You know Lumaga. If I bring in a new man he'll have to start from scratch and he might never get to your level of knowledge and access. Don't tell me you're not interested. And don't tell me you don't need the job."

"What, you've been snooping around my finances?"

"I was curious. I had someone make some checks, maybe a year ago. You live in a shitty apartment in a relatively shitty neighborhood of Manhattan. You're still gambling. You're up to your eyeballs in debt."

"Eyeballs, no. My debts have never gotten higher than my waist. But here's my biggest problem, Mickey. If I stay here, I'm going to have a bunch of overdue library books."

"Yes, I can see that. Maybe this will help defray your fines."

Mickey reached into his jacket pocket for an envelope. Marcus took it and had a look inside. It was an Andreason Engineering contract with enough digits that it took a second look to register, and a check for a ten percent advance on it. He smirked.

"What's the matter?" Mickey said. "Not enough?"

It was a great deal of money, money he needed. What made him laugh was this: the guy was a billionaire and he still wanted to run the payment as a corporate expense.

"The money's fine."

56

"Then, do we have a deal?"

It was Marcus's turn to look out the window. He made Mickey wait a bit for his answer. He didn't want to seem too eager, but he was eager. The money was a factor, but not the deciding one. He wanted to use his mind again. He wanted to be relevant. There were two sick girls on the other side of the wall who were four years' younger than they should have been and he had a chance to be the guy to figure out why.

A photographer with a long lens spotted him at the window, pointed, and began shooting.

"Yeah, Mickey, we have a deal."

8

Lumaga peeled off his black jacket to make himself less threatening and positioned a chair between each of their beds. Although Marcus sat behind him, he was the one the girls mainly looked at, and he rewarded each reply they gave Lumaga with a small nod of encouragement. They didn't pay attention to the video camera on a tripod.

It was Elizabeth who gave the most substantive answers, but Lumaga frequently turned to the younger girl for confirmation. Following their blood transfusions, they had more energy and they were more animated.

"This white room," Lumaga said. "Was this the first place you were taken to?"

They both said they thought so, but neither exactly remembered.

"Did you stay anywhere else or was this the only place?"

"Just the white room," Elizabeth said.

"What was in the room?"

"We each had a bed. We each had a chair. We each had a chest of drawers."

"What was in the drawers?"

"Our clothes."

"What kind of clothes?"

"Shorts, tees, underpants, socks."

"All white?"

"Yes!" an exasperated Victoria said.

"So, everything was white," Lumaga said. "The walls, the floor, the bed covers."

"Not everything," Victoria said, continuing her impatience. "Our toys and our books were different colors."

"Ah, toys! What kinds of toys?"

There were board games, and puzzles, and Legos, and picture books for Victoria, chapter books for Elizabeth.

Lumaga posed the question that Marcus almost called out despite his promise to observe only. How did the spacemen have games from Earth?

"I asked," Elizabeth said proudly. "They said that they could make anything that we wanted from our planet."

"Did you have television? Videos? Video games?"

"We had videos and video games from Earth. They got those for us."

"And what about food? Did you have Earth food?"

"Yes, silly," Victoria said. "We weren't going to eat space food, were we?"

"I'm sorry. I was being silly, wasn't I?" Lumaga said. "So, you had chicken and fish and eggs and hamburgers and pasta and ice cream?"

They both nodded and Elizabeth said, "I know what you're going to ask next. You're going to ask if they had farm animals in space."

"That's precisely what I was going to ask."

"They said they didn't need animals. They had machines that could make any food we liked."

"Was the food good?"

"It was yummy," Victoria said.

"Now what about toilets? Where were your toilets?"

"In a bathroom, silly," Victoria said.

"In the same white room?"

"Through a door," Elizabeth said.

He asked if the bathroom was the same as on Earth. They were. Did the spacemen ever use the bathroom? The girls thought the question was hilarious. Of course not, they said.

"Gray Man and Gray Woman don't use toilets!" Elizabeth exclaimed.

"They built them for us because we're human beings, silly," Victoria added.

"Okay, then, I'd like to ask you some more things about the Gray Man and the Gray Woman now. You told Uncle Marcus that they spoke English. How did they know how to do that?"

"They can speak any language on any planet," Elizabeth said. She added proudly, "I know because I asked."

"Well, that was clever of you. Did you test them?"

"Oh, yes. Gray Man was very clever. He could say things in Italian, like our mother."

"Like what?"

"Anything. He could speak fast. I couldn't understand him. I only remember a few Italian words."

"Tell me, how could you tell that one of them was a woman and one was a man?"

"The woman's voice was higher," Elizabeth said.

"The funny voice you told Uncle Marcus about."

She nodded.

"For the camera, can you make the voices again?"

They both produced their versions of the vibrating, raspy tones.

"My goodness. They certainly are funny voices. The Gray Woman. Was there anything else that made you think she was a woman? Did she have, you know—?" With his hands over his chest, he made the universal sign for breasts.

Victoria giggled and said she didn't know and Elizabeth explained that their white jumpsuits were too baggy to tell.

"Were Gray Man and Gray Woman the only spacemen you ever saw?"

"It was just those two."

"Okay. Now I'm interested to know if they told you why they took you."

"They wanted to study us," Elizabeth said.

"Why?"

"They said they liked Earth."

Had they visited Earth before?

The girls didn't know.

"How did they study you?"

"They stuck needles into us."

"That must have hurt."

Victoria said it often made her cry.

"Did they just take out blood or did they put things into your body?"

"Both."

"Were you sick at all? Besides these nosebleeds, I mean."

Elizabeth said, "We were sick when we first got there, but then we got better."

"What kind of sickness?"

"We were tired and our tummies were bad."

"Did they give you medicine?"

They couldn't remember.

"Did they take you to their planet?"

"We only stayed on the spaceship," Elizabeth said.

"Did they tell you why they didn't let your parents stay with you?"

"We asked about them at first," Elizabeth said, "but they didn't tell us anything. We stopped asking."

"Okay, now this is a very important question," Lumaga said, leaning forward.

Go on, ask it, Marcus thought. *Ask the damned question.*

"You've been gone for four whole years. When did you notice you weren't getting any older?"

Bingo, Marcus thought.

Elizabeth leaned forward too, imitating the policeman. She had been propped on two pillows and one of them slipped behind her back.

"I didn't notice for the longest time," she said. "And then, one day, all of a sudden, I remember telling Vicky, 'You're still a little girl!'"

"And, Victoria, do you remember what you said to your sister?"

"I think I told her she looked the same too."

"You did," Elizabeth said. "That's exactly what you said."

"Did you mention this to the gray people?"

"I did," Elizabeth said. "Vicky didn't."

"What did they say?"

"They said that's what happens in space."

"I see. That's what happens in space. Did it seem like you were gone for four whole years?"

Elizabeth got her pillows squared away and said, "It seemed like a long, long time. I got bored a lot."

Victoria didn't offer her perception. She yawned and sank beneath her covers.

"You're getting tired," Lumaga said. "Last questions. When did you start feeling ill with these nosebleeds?"

"Not long ago," Elizabeth said.

"Days, weeks?"

"Days."

"Did they tell you they were taking you home?"

Elizabeth said, "One night, Gray Man told us we were going home. The lights went out, and we fell asleep like usual, but we didn't wake up in the white room. We woke up in our old house. Gray Man wasn't there. We haven't seen him again. Then the old man and old woman came."

"The housekeepers," Lumaga said helpfully.

"They called Grandma Leonora and Grandpa Armando."

"Okay, my dears. You've been so very, very helpful. We're going to let you rest now. I'm sure your grandparents will be coming to see you later."

Outside their room, Lumaga said, "You were very well behaved, Marcus."

"Only because you did a nice job. In fact, I couldn't have done it any better myself."

"My God! High praise from my American colleague."

"I'll even buy you a drink tonight," Marcus said.

"Tonight, I'll be with my beloved."

"She hasn't divorced you yet?"

"Not yet. The city only has two hundred thousand residents. It would be quite difficult for her to find a better husband."

*

Later on, Lumaga gave Marcus a ride to the Carabinieri station. The old war room with its large whiteboard was long gone, replaced by a warren of cubicles and desks. In a small conference room, Lumaga summoned his sub-lieutenant for an update on pending items.

The woman, a young Carabinieri officer named Fabiana Odorico who had been transferred to Reggio Calabria from Naples to shore up Lumaga's squad of 'Ndrangheta hunters, flipped open her notebook and eyed Marcus suspiciously. She had severe, angular features and a short, mannish hairstyle.

"It's okay," Lumaga said. "Signor Handler represents the Andreason family interests. He's someone we can trust. We're scratching each other's backs."

"Very well," Odorico said. "We have the full analysis of the fingerprints from Villa Shibui. The ones we couldn't identify did belong to Signore Handler and Signore Andreason. So, unfortunately, there are no unidentified prints. We can presume that whoever brought the girls back to the villa wore gloves."

Marcus said, "Either that or the girls were beamed into the house from space."

"Is that supposed to be a joke?" Odorico asked.

"On the contrary," Lumaga said, supporting his colleague with a wink. "It's a theory that we have not yet been able to exclude."

She looked at them as if they had been drinking and said, "Fine. We won't exclude that possibility, despite the forced rear door. I called the DNA laboratories in Milan and the Hague. We'll receive the final reports tomorrow, but they told me that it appears the girls' DNA will match the grandparents with a 99.99 percent certainty. So, we can be confident that based on their fingerprints, facial characteristics, and now DNA, that Elizabeth and Victoria are the girls who disappeared four years ago."

Lumaga said. "Now that we have the proof, we need to find experts who can advise us on the scope of rational possibilities for this phenomenon."

"Besides aliens," Odorico said.

"Now, the sub-lieutenant mocks me," Lumaga said.

"I'll make some calls," Marcus said, "but I doubt we'll find anyone who's seen anything like this before."

"That's probably true, but my superiors will ask the question. I'd like to be able to hide behind a so-called expert. Anything else, Fabiana?" Lumaga asked.

"Your order to analyze CCTV files in the areas surrounding Villa Shibui is doomed to failure, I'm afraid. We don't have any ideas about the vehicle that might have transported the girls. The team are looking for images of girls in the windows of cars or vans, but I'm afraid it's going to be a big waste of time."

"Also, probably true," Lumaga said, "but it's still necessary. Anything else?"

"Only this," she said, pulling her tablet computer from its case. "The artist spent time this morning with the girls. We have her sketches of the Gray Man and the Gray Woman."

"The best for last," Lumaga grunted.

Marcus and Lumaga stared at the sketches, swiping through the images.

To Marcus, they were caricatures of the gray men

from outer space that had been burned into the collective unconscious ever since the days of Roswell, New Mexico. Their bumpy skin was slate-gray. Their eyes were huge, dark ovals. Their ears and noses were nothing but membranous holes, their mouths, perfectly black spheres, no bigger than a golf ball with no visible teeth. Gray hands poked from white tunics, with four long fingers and a shorter thumb. It wasn't possible to say which one was male, which was female.

An aide knocked and informed Lumaga that the press was assembled and waiting.

"What's your plan?" Marcus asked.

Lumaga stood and adjusted his uniform. "I intend to lie a lot."

9

Because of the large number of journalists, the press conference had to be done al fresco in the golden sunshine. The majority were from Italian media outlets, but there was a contingent of reporters from elsewhere in Europe and North and South America. Lumaga took to the podium set up in front of the entrance to the headquarters. He squinted into the afternoon glare and tapped his microphone to start the proceedings.

Marcus was standing off to one side next to Sub-Lieutenant Odorico.

He whispered to her, "Is he good at this?"

"Speaking to the media or lying?" she asked.

"Both."

"He's a good speaker," she said. "I've never seen him lie."

"My name is Major Roberto Lumaga, the commanding officer of the Carabinieri station in Reggio Calabria. I'd like to make a statement and then I will take a few questions. We can confirm that there has been a significant development in the case of the Andreasons, the American family who disappeared four years ago from their holiday villa in Filarete. The two girls, Victoria and Elizabeth Andreason, have been returned to the villa. Both of them are being evaluated by medical doctors at the Morelli Hospital. At this time, we have no information about the location or the fate of their parents, Jesper and Elena. The girls have obviously been traumatized and we are interviewing them slowly, in stages, so as not to put them under unnecessary stress. Their Italian grandparents and American grandfather are with them and are assisting in their recovery."

So far, no lies, Marcus thought.

"We do not know where the girls have been these past years," Lumaga said. "We do not know who abducted them. We do not know who returned them. This new phase of the investigation is at its earliest stages. We have a dedicated group of investigators, and I have been assured by my superiors and by the relevant ministers that we will have every resource we require to find Jesper and Elena Andreason, find the perpetrators, and bring them to justice.

"Please do not expect to hear from me like clockwork. When there are important developments, I will make myself available. Until then, I will be devoting myself to solving this case. Also, we insist you respect the privacy of the family. The girls, of course, are strictly off-limits and we anticipate that they will remain under the care of doctors for the foreseeable future. Their grandparents have told me that they have no intention of appearing before the media. Now, I will take a limited number of questions."

Let the lies begin, Marcus thought.

There was a cacophony of shouts and hands.

"You there, in the blue shirt," Lumaga said.

A florid reporter in the front held his pocket recorder on high and said, "I've just been told by a source in the hospital that the girls look exactly the same as when they were taken. Is this true?"

Marcus knew that Lumaga must have been anticipating the question. The case was as leaky as a colander. But the policeman seemed to be searching the clouds for his answer.

"I don't know where you heard this. All I can say is that they are thin and their nutrition has, perhaps, been lacking. The doctors are paying a lot of attention to this."

The reporter snuck in his follow-on before Lumaga could call on someone else.

"No, no, I'm sorry, but this is more than being thin. I have heard that they appear to be the same exact age as they were before."

"I've already answered," Lumaga said, pointing to a woman whose name he knew—a journalist at a local paper.

"Thank you, Major," she said. "Have the girls said where they've been for the past four years?"

"They have made some preliminary statements, yes. However, since this is an active investigation, I won't be commenting about that subject at this time."

"Was a ransom paid?" he was asked.

"I can't comment on that."

A journalist from a popular true-crime television show based in Milan shouted over a newspaper reporter to say, "We have a source who says that both girls have an identical rare type of cancer that is often fatal. This seems very strange. Can you confirm this report?"

Lumaga shook his head emphatically and wagged a finger at the man. "I don't know who you've been speaking to. Even if I knew the answer, I wouldn't talk publicly about the health of children. In my opinion, you shouldn't ask this kind of question. Do you have children?"

"You're asking me?" the journalist said.

"Yes, I'm asking you."

"Well, I'm not going to talk about my family."

Lumaga said, "You've made my point. Next question."

A woman asked whether the girls had provided a description of their kidnappers.

"I can't possibly comment on that," Lumaga said.

A man asked, "Are the girls staying in Italy or are they going back to the United States?"

"There are no plans for them to leave Italy at this time."

Lumaga seemed to be purposely avoiding taking a question from a man in the front of the scrum who kept his hand in the air while others were speaking and who kept saying, "Hey, Major, why don't you call on me?" whenever Lumaga pointed to someone else. Marcus would later learn that the guy was Gino Forconi, a reporter for a major paper in Naples who was known for his aggressive style and someone Lumaga considered to be an agent provocateur, a real troublemaker.

Lumaga finally relented and said, "Okay, Gino, go ahead."

"Thank you, Major. I thought you didn't love me anymore. Can you tell me why an American private security specialist hired by the family has been given unprecedented access to the Carabinieri investigation, including witness interviews?"

Lumaga shot him a caustic look. "You shouldn't believe everything you're told."

"You're denying it?" the reporter asked.

"I'm not going to comment on this kind of gossip."

"But why not? He's standing right over there," Forconi said, pointing at Marcus, and soon, most of the cameras were pointed in his direction.

Lumaga leaned into the microphone and said, "Ladies and gentlemen, this concludes the press conference."

Marcus ducked back inside the headquarters with Odorico where Lumaga caught up with them. He was red in the face angry.

"The hospital staff talk to the media. The police staff talk to the media. The whole fucking world talks to the media. How am I supposed to conduct an investigation? And this guy, Forconi, he's the worst. Every time we've got a sensitive case in Calabria, he slithers south to make things difficult. A few years ago, the 'Ndrangheta kidnapped the son of a businessman, and Forconi convinced the family to stop cooperating with the police. He wanted to be the intermediary with the gangsters. We got the boy back, but because of his interference, I'm convinced it took much longer. I wanted to arrest the bastard, but the judge didn't want to charge a journalist. Fabiana, you're from Naples. You must know him."

"Sure. Everyone knows Gino," she said.

Marcus asked, "Is this going to cause you any problems, Roberto?"

He replied with a Lumaga shrug and said, "As long as you're helpful to this investigation, you're on the team. The second you're a dead weight, I'm sorry, you're off."

Marcus's phone chirped with a text. He glanced at it and said, "I've got to go back to the hotel."

"What's going on?" Lumaga asked.

"Just trying not to be a dead weight."

Mickey was holed up at the Excelsior Hotel, a short walk from the girls' hospital, working his phone. He had put out feelers among his circle of Chicago movers and shakers, looking for the best pediatric hematologist-oncologist in the city. The unanimous opinion was that it was Jessica Bingham, the head of the department at the Lurie Children's Hospital.

When he finally got through to her, Bingham started by telling him that in addition to his call, she had been contacted by both US senators from Illinois, three congressmen, and the governor.

"You must be an important fellow," she said.

"I'm not feeling all that important. I'm feeling like a scared grandfather."

"Why don't you let me know what's going on?"

He started by telling her that both his granddaughters were in a hospital in the south of Italy, diagnosed with chronic myeloid leukemia.

"I'm sorry, did you say both of them? Two simultaneous cases?"

"That's correct, Doctor."

"I've never heard of anything like that. How old are they?"

The question caught him flat-footed. Should he tell her they were eight and twelve or four and eight? He opted for this: "You may have heard about them. Victoria and Elizabeth disappeared four years ago with their parents."

"Wait, of course!" Bingham said. "I'm sorry, I didn't put two and two together."

"That's all right. Anyway, they were four and eight when they were abducted. We've just gotten them back but they are ill. The doctors at the Morelli Hospital here in Reggio Calabria made the diagnosis."

"I see. Do you have any of their records for me to review?"

"I'm sure I can get them."

"In the interim, how can I help you?"

"Well, my druthers would be to bundle them up on my private plane and get them to your hospital, but for a variety of reasons, they can't leave Italy. So, I'm looking for a couple of things from you. I'd like your opinion about the treatment and prognosis for this kind of leukemia. And I'd like your recommendation on the best CML doctors in Italy."

"Please understand, Mr. Andreason, that without seeing your granddaughters and reviewing their labs, I can only speak in generalities. For children, particularly young children, this is a rare cancer. Only one child their age out of two million will get CML each year. To see two simultaneous cases among siblings would be astronomically rare and would point, in my mind, to a specific environmental exposure, such as an unknown toxin. To your knowledge, have they been exposed to something?"

"I'd say that's unclear at this point," Mickey said.

"All right. Well, in general, kids with CML have more aggressive disease than adults. Patients with CML have an abnormal gene called BCR-ABL that makes a tyrosine kinase protein by the same name. Sorry for being technical."

"It's all right. Go on."

"The BCR-ABL protein causes the abnormal CML cells to grow and reproduce in an out-of-control way. Eventually, they crowd out the regular cells in the bone marrow like normal myeloid, or white cells, red blood cells, and platelets."

"They have low blood counts and they're getting transfusions," Mickey said.

"I see. Have they been started on chemotherapy yet?"

"Not yet."

"Okay, well the standard drugs to treat CML are called TKIs, or tyrosine kinase inhibitors. They can be quite effective in achieving remissions, even cures. However, the experience in children is far more limited than in adults, and TKIs are less effective in kids. I'd say that the majority of pediatric CML patients that I see go on to receive bone marrow transplants, many with excellent results. But please understand that transplants are only done in patients in remission. Your granddaughters are certainly in an acute phase, so they'll need to get TKIs as first-line treatment."

"These drugs—they have side effects?"

"They do, and whoever will be treating them will explain these in detail. Again, the experience using them in children is quite limited, so the long-term effects are not as well understood as we'd like."

"Who would you recommend to treat them in Italy?"

"Well, my first, second, and third choice would be Bruno Spara at the Bambino Gesù Hospital in Rome. Bruno and I have collaborated on research projects in the past. He's really top-notch."

"Would you send one of your relatives to him?"

"I absolutely would. I'll pass along his contact info and if you like, I can give him a heads-up that you'll be in touch."

"I'm grateful, Doctor. Your hospital can expect to receive a generous donation from my foundation."

"Always appreciated," she said.

When Marcus knocked on the door to Mickey's hotel room, he found him with his phone to his ear. He had booked himself the largest suite, and Marcus cooled his heels in the living room while Mickey finished up his call in the bedroom.

"How'd the press conference go?" Mickey asked when he was done.

"You didn't watch?"

"Yeah, but it was only in Italian, so I have no idea."

"CNN was there."

"Well, they weren't broadcasting it live," Mickey said with fierce irritation. "Would you mind just telling me?"

This was the Mickey that Marcus knew and didn't love. He eyed the full bottles of liquor laid out on a sideboard and said, "The Italian press has been getting leaks from everywhere. They knew that something funny was going on about the girls' ages; they knew they were both sick. They even knew that you'd hired an American security guy—me—and that the Carabinieri were giving me a lot of access."

"How'd Lumaga handle it?"

"He's good at the art of non-statements and dissembling."

"When this is over, he should come work for me in corporate communications."

"How're the kids?"

"They're okay. We're going to be moving them to Rome."

"When?"

"As soon as possible. I've got to make some calls. When

it's locked down, we're going to need good security at the new hospital."

"Just let me know the details and I'll coordinate with Lumaga. Is that why you had me come?"

"No, something else. My office put through a call from a French lady. It was quite something."

"How so?"

"She's a psychic and—"

He used the absurdity to get up and help himself to a Scotch. "Come on, Mickey," he said, breaking the seal.

"Hear me out, damn it. And help yourself to a drink, why don't you?"

Marcus poured a stiff one. "Thank you, I will."

"This gal—I forget her name—she says she had a vision, or whatever the hell psychics have. It was about the girls."

Marcus tugged at the drink and muttered, "Oh brother."

"Well, oh brother this: she said that Jesper, Elena, and the girls were abducted by aliens. She said they were taken to a spaceship. She said they had medical probes."

"Good for her," Marcus said.

"Did anyone at the press conference know that's what the girls said?"

"None of that came up, no. But it's just going to be some random kind of bullshit assertion. The so-called psychic got lucky. Why are we even talking about it?"

"Because she knew some details that only you, me, and the police know."

"Maybe she knows someone in the Carabinieri who's been leaking."

"Maybe so, but were they leaking about it almost four years ago?"

"What the hell are you talking about?"

"She says she sent me a letter almost four years ago. She sent me a photocopy. Here, read it."

Marcus took Mickey's phone and opened the text attachment sent from a French mobile number. The letter was composed on pink stationery with a feminine sort of handwriting and was dated four years ago, as Mickey said.

My Dear Mr. Andreason,

I have been following with sadness the tragedy that has befallen your loved ones in Italy and I would like to offer my services (at no cost, of course). You see, I have had certain psychic abilities ever since I was young and I have had a vision about what happened to your family. I do not know why they were taken but they were abducted and transported onto a spaceship by a race of aliens who have been studying them to understand our species. In my vision, the two young girls were in a pure white chamber. The alien creatures have gray skin and large dark eyes. If you would accept my offer of help, perhaps I will be able to gain further insights into their fates.

Sincerely yours,

Celeste Bobier

Marcus gave Mickey his phone back and reestablished contact with his Scotch glass.

"Look, I don't know how she got these details about what the girls said, but she obviously did and she's backdated the letter to give it credence."

"That's what I thought too. Maybe you don't know, because I fired you, but I received sacks of letters sent to the company from all over the world about sightings and the like. Every one of them was read in case they contained real tips, and we had them archived by date. Don't look at me that way. I'm an engineer and engineers are organized by nature. I had the office see if they could find the original. I received this scan and that's why I called this woman back." He checked his phone for her name. "Celeste Bobier."

He punched up an email from his executive assistant and showed Marcus the phone again. The embedded scan was the exact same letter on pink stationery.

"What do you say about that?" Mickey asked him.

"I don't have a fucking clue, Mickey. I really don't."

"That makes two of us. I was on the phone with this lady when you showed up. She's willing to help find Jesper."

"Please, Mickey, it's going to be a colossal waste of time and a big distraction."

Mickey was aging before his eyes. His shoulders were slouched, his eyeballs were shrinking into their sockets. It was hard to feel sorry for the guy, but Marcus was getting there. He knew something about loss himself.

"I can't take the risk of dismissing her, even if psychics don't fit into our neat little belief system," Mickey said. "I've got two little girls who haven't aged a day in four years. I've got two little girls who've got the same leukemia at the same time, which my expert in Chicago tells me is impossibly rare. We're stumbling around in the dark, and if this Celeste Bobier can shine some light, we're going to listen to her. So, get used to it, Marcus, because she'll be here in the morning and she's going to be your new best friend."

10

Celeste Bobier blew in like Le Mistral, the northerly wind that roars across the Rhône Valley, driving people mad.

She was in her thirties, Marcus thought, physically imposing, tall with deeply olive skin and prominent features. If one of them—the nose, lips, cheekbones, chin—had been smaller or out of proportion to the rest, the entire concoction would have failed, but in harmony, she was attractive. It was her coloration that especially dazzled from across the room. She had intensely green eyes, vividly red hair that cascaded down her back like a waterfall, and she wore a sexed-up red sausage-skin of a dress and green tights. Marcus might have forgiven what he took to be an obvious shout-out for attention, but her mannerisms were also over the top. Her letter had been modest and reserved. She was not. When Marcus and Mickey entered the hotel lobby to greet her, she threw herself onto Mickey, their height disparity leaving her breasts squeezed high onto his chest. While she embraced him, she said in a light French accent, "My poor man. The ordeal you have suffered."

Mickey disentangled himself, thanked her, and introduced Marcus as his security consultant. While Celeste towered over the comparatively diminutive Mickey, Marcus had several inches on her. He thought she wouldn't be as effusive with him, but to be safe, he kept her at bay with an extended hand. Her palm was dry and warm, almost hot, and he released it after a short pump.

"I am pleased to meet both you gentlemen," she said. "Where are the precious girls?"

Marcus was about to choose between, *Not so fast, lady*, and *Hold your horses*, when Mickey told her they were in a local hospital.

"May I see them?" she asked.

"Why don't we have a little talk?" Marcus interjected.

Mickey told her he had a room reserved for her and that perhaps she wanted to freshen up, but she said she was ready to talk immediately.

She left her case at reception and they went across the lobby to the restaurant. As she stirred her coffee, Marcus noticed a tattoo on her left wrist—the stars of the Big Dipper. He hated tattoos, especially on women, and wondered how much ink there was underneath her slinky red dress.

"So, you're French," Mickey said apropos of nothing.

"Yes, although I am not pure-bred. My mother is French, from Lyon. My father, who is no longer with us, was Lebanese."

Mickey asked whether Celeste was her real name or one she had chosen given her psychic abilities.

"My father used to say that one often grows into one's name," she said. "It is absolutely my given name. Your name, Mikkel—I believe it means he who is like God."

"Yes, you're right," he said, "but in my case, I most certainly did not grow into that."

Marcus wondered if she'd looked that up before coming,

anticipating the obvious question about her own name. He set a challenge. "How about Marcus? Any ideas on me?"

Without skipping a beat, she said, "Now yours is an interesting name with more than one meaning. From the Latin, it means warlike, referring to Mars, the god of war. Are you warlike, Marcus?"

"When I have to be. I'm not aware of other meanings."

"Well, then, you are not a student of Etruscan," she purred. "In Etruscan, the word mar means to harvest. So, Marcus, you are also a harvester, perhaps."

"Neither literally nor metaphorically," he said. "I'll go with warlike."

"You said you were flying from Marseille," Mickey said. "Do you live there?"

"Near Marseille. I don't like big cities. I prefer the tranquility of the countryside. It is far more conducive to the kind of work I do."

"And that is?" Marcus asked.

"Well, I think you know. I am a psychic."

"You make a living doing that?"

"A living. An interesting expression. I live. I work. Sometimes they are the same, sometimes they are different. But if your question is, do people pay me for my psychic abilities, then the answer is, yes. Am I a billionaire like Mikkel? No, nor a millionaire. But I am comfortable living and working as I do. May I ask you, Marcus, do you make a living being a security consultant?"

He grinned. "Recently, no, but things are looking up." It was his turn to serve and Mickey would just have to turn his head like a spectator at a tennis match. "How do people find you? To hire you as a psychic, I mean?"

"Basically, it is word of mouth. One client tells a prospective client and so on, and so on. How do people find you? To hire you as a security consultant."

"They don't. I'm retired. I used to work for Mickey. I came out of retirement a few days ago."

"Because of the girls," she said.

"Because of the girls," he said. "Before we move forward, I think we should get an idea about your fees."

"My fees are variable," she said with a broad smile. "They vary between zero and zero. When it is a matter of life and death, I do not charge for my services."

Mickey seemed embarrassed. "If we have good results, I will want to pay you."

"You are a gentleman, Mikkel. I don't need psychic abilities to see this. When someone wants my help to make money or find love, I will ask for a fee. But in a case such as yours, where your granddaughters were missing and where your son and his wife are still missing, I won't take money. If you can simply cover my expenses, I will be more than happy."

Marcus was half-expecting her to ask him about his own fees, but she sipped her coffee, adding more red to the stain on the rim.

"You are a gracious woman," Mickey said.

Marcus wasn't as convinced. She had to have an angle. Everybody had an angle. "How do you suggest we proceed?" he asked.

"Please take me to the girls," she said.

"They're not well," Marcus said. "They've been through a lot and they need their rest. They've answered a lot of questions already."

"I don't need to ask them anything," she said. "I simply need to be in their presence. Perhaps hold their hands."

"And what happens?" Marcus asked testily. "You weren't in their presence years ago when you wrote to Mickey about spaceships and gray men."

"I don't know the hows and whys of my visions," she said matter-of-factly. "I'll tell you how it happened. During breakfast, I was watching a news show about the abductions—a short time after they occurred. Suddenly, I was no longer aware of the television. I was no longer aware of my kitchen, my flat, or any earthly space. I was floating above the dear girls. I remember how lovely and curly their hair looked. My mother used to keep my hair like their mother kept theirs. I saw them in a room that was as white and clean as a fresh snowstorm. I felt cold. Then I became very scared when two gray figures entered this white room. My mind told me that these were alien beings and that the girls were no longer on Earth, but in a spacecraft somewhere extremely far away. I couldn't hear what the beings or the girls were saying but I saw the girls were frightened. The parents were not there. Then one of the aliens approached them with a long needle and the vision abruptly stopped. I had this vision only once. The next day I looked for Mikkel's address online and wrote the letter. You never responded."

Marcus continued drilling. "I don't understand. If you had this vision by watching TV, why do you need to see them now?"

Her eagerness to answer suggested she wasn't offended by his prickly tone. "Frankly, it's quite unusual for me to have visions at a distance. Usually, my clients are in the same room. I feed off their energy and the visions come."

Aliens, Marcus thought. *More like bullshit*. He didn't know what the hell happened to Mickey's family, but psychics going on about aliens wasn't going to solve the mystery. He wanted to discredit—no, demolish her in front of Mickey and send her packing back to France.

"All right, let's do a little test," he said.

She responded with serenity. "I am completely at your service."

Mickey fiddled with a small spoon, but didn't intervene.

"Use your psychic powers to tell me about me," Marcus said. "What do you see?"

She made no objection. She didn't say she needed to be in a more private or quieter space. She simply nodded, slowly closed her eyes, and sat for an uncomfortably long time, gently rocking herself.

Finally, she opened her eyes and said to Marcus, "Now? In public?"

Marcus said, "I'm an open book."

"Perhaps. Perhaps not. But as you wish. An image came to me, very powerfully. You were standing at a place I couldn't quite fathom. There was some sort of a ceremony. You were surrounded by many, many people who were crying. There was a deep hole in the ground and you were staring into it. You were wishing you were in that hole. That's what I saw."

Anger welled up. He knew that image. He had looked into that grave. He had wanted to fling himself into it. He said nothing. As the seconds passed, he was aware that Mickey was staring at him, waiting for some kind of response, so he said, "Was that parlor trick supposed to impress me?"

"It wasn't a parlor trick," she said, evenly.

"So what? I've been to funerals. Who hasn't? Let's talk about the girls, Miss Bobier."

"Celeste," she said, her lips pressed into a wry little smile.

"You can't see them right away. Their doctors are getting them ready to be moved."

"Moved? Where?"

"To Rome," Mickey said. "I'm having them sent to a specialist hospital tomorrow morning."

"They are very sick?" she asked. "What that journalist said at the press conference is true?"

"I'm afraid so," Mickey said. "You're welcome to come with us to Rome. I'll have a hotel room reserved for you."

"Then, please, take me to the house where they were abducted."

"Why?" Marcus asked.

"You do want to find Mikkel's son and daughter, don't you?"

Marcus derided it as a field trip, but Mickey insisted that he take Celeste to Villa Shibui while he went to the hospital.

On the coastal road to Filarete, Marcus deflected her small talk and after a time, she gave up and looked to the sea. Arriving at the villa, he opened the gate and drove to the house. The housekeepers were there, doing their dusting and airing-out routine and Marcus explained to them that he would be giving this exotic woman a free rein to look around.

"Go ahead," he told Celeste. "I'll be in the kitchen."

Noemi was quick to make him a coffee. He always got

along well with the Pennestrìs, especially Noemi. She took a dim view of his drinking, but he stirred up her maternal instincts, and during the month he lived at the villa, he never refused her tender mercies.

"So, tell me, how have you been?" she asked.

"Surviving," he said.

"Only surviving? Are you eating properly?"

He took that to be a veiled question about booze, not food. "No shortage of good food in New York," he said.

"Ah, New York! No longer Chicago?"

"I moved on."

She poured the coffee from the Bialetti. "Tell me, are the girls very sick?" she asked.

"They are. Mickey is taking them to Rome tomorrow. To the Bambino Gesù Hospital."

"A very strong hospital," she said. "The Pope's hospital. I am praying for them. Even Giuseppe is lighting candles. How can it be that they haven't changed? This seems impossible."

"We don't know," he said. "I wish we did."

"Who is this woman?"

"She's a psychic. She wrote to Mickey. He thinks she can help."

"A psychic? Like a gypsy?"

"She has visions."

She crossed herself. "I don't believe in this."

"Neither do I."

Giuseppe came in and complained that he saw Celeste opening drawers in the bedrooms.

"Mickey wants her to be here. There's nothing I can do."

"What if she steals something?" Giuseppe asked.

"That's about the only thing I'm not worried about."

He drank his coffee and chatted until Giuseppe pointed out the window. "She's outside."

Marcus joined her in sea-gazing by the Lucite fence.

"It's a lovely family house. A friendly house," she said.

"Until someone came for them."

"Yes, until then. Look how beautiful it is here."

He didn't want to talk about the view. "Well? Have you solved the mystery?"

"No solution, but in the parents' bedroom I had a brief vision."

He wanted to hit her with a choice bit of snark but said only, "I'm all ears."

"I sat on their bed and that's when I saw Jesper and Elena. They were in the white room. They were alone. They were serene. That is all I saw."

He made no effort to hide his scorn for her. "So, you think they're in space too."

"Very far away. I'll tell you what I think, Marcus. I think the girls were returned to their house because they were sick. I think the beings who took them could not help them."

"So, they showed compassion, but not enough of it to return their parents with them."

"It's my opinion, nothing more."

"Noted."

"You were uncomfortable with my vision about you, no?"

"No comment."

"Was I correct?"

It had turned overcast. A front was advancing and the sea was a froth of white caps.

He refused to look at her. "You weren't wrong."

II

Marcus was back at the hotel when Mickey called to find out about Celeste's experience at the villa. He gave him a just-the-facts debriefing.

"I don't know what to say about that," Mickey said.

"Neither do I."

Mickey asked what he thought about her.

"You really want to know?"

"I asked, didn't I?"

"I think she's a bullshitter."

"A bullshitter," Mickey repeated. "I'm an engineer. I'm a businessman. I deal in facts. Here's a fact: she was right about the girls' version of what happened to them. Here's another: I know your history. Years ago, I checked you out before I hired you. She was right about you."

Marcus felt like hitting him for that. "My opinion stands."

"She was right about the things the girls described."

"I'll give her an asterisk for that."

"An asterisk?"

"It's a footnote that says: Marcus Handler doesn't understand something but he damn well is going to figure it out."

"Where is she?" Mickey asked.

"At the hotel having a rest. These visions are tiring, apparently."

"I've got another assignment that's going to piss you off. Elena's parents tell me that the Bishop of Catanzaro wants to see them. He's got some theories about the girls. I want you to go with them. In case he's also not a bullshitter."

They traveled in Armando's large Audi. Catanzaro was almost a two-hour drive from Reggio Calabria. The Cutrìs had heard about Celeste from Mickey and now, Armando demanded to know what she had to say about their daughter. Leonora cried in the back seat when he told them about her vision, then she closed her eyes for the rest of the journey. Marcus and Armando had little else in common, so they traveled in silence.

The bishop's palazzo was in the city center, adjacent to the Santa Maria Assunta Cathedral. They were shown into the reception room where they waited for an uncomfortably long interval until Archbishop Taricco arrived, looking heavenwards and apologizing for the delay. He was elderly, a towering mountain of lard with a damp handkerchief in his hand to mop his sweaty forehead and bushy eyebrows. It seemed that the bishop and the Cutrìs knew each other because they exchanged lengthy pleasantries before Armando asked if they might switch to English for Mr. Handler's benefit.

"And who is Mr. Handler?" the archbishop asked.

"An American investigator."

"Italian is fine," Marcus said.

"Good, because my English is weak. Welcome to

Catanzaro," Taricco said, shaking his hand. "Please, sit, sit. I am glad you made the journey."

Marcus detected a whiff of alcohol on the cleric's breath. He knew the syndrome.

A nun entered with a tray of orange juice and biscuits and the archbishop slid several onto his plate.

"Tell me," he said, "how are the dear girls?"

"They are quite weak," Armando said, "but the blood transfusions have improved their strength. Tomorrow, they go to Rome for specialist treatment at the Bambino Gesù Hospital."

"Ah, good, good. I will make a call to the Vatican to make sure they have the very best care."

"Thank you, Eminence," Leonora said.

"Now, let me tell you why I wanted to see you. It involves the profound mystery of the appearance of the girls, the fact that they have not aged since their disappearance."

Marcus was fully aware that leaks abounded, but he was determined that the family not be a conduit. He said, "Somebody told a journalist something about their appearance. We're not confirming or denying anything at this stage. I'm sure you'll appreciate the sensitivity."

"Of course, of course, Mr. Handler. However, my information comes not from a journalist, but from the family priest who visited them at their hospital in Reggio Calabria."

Marcus turned to Armando. "You let a priest in?"

"It was Father Leuti," Armando said apologetically. "He's known my family forever."

Marcus could only shake his head at the casual way his no visitors rule had been ignored.

"Don't worry," Taricco said. "My discretion is absolute. The fact remains that we have a significant mystery on our hands and I can tell you that high officials at the Vatican have already reached out to me, seeking my opinion."

"Did you confirm the lack of aging to these officials?" Marcus asked.

"Yes, but you shouldn't have any concerns. Their discretion is also absolute."

"I'm certain it is," Marcus said, his face showing nothing of the sort.

"Their interest can only be helpful," the archbishop said. "The Vatican has many resources."

Leonora said, "We would be grateful for anything the Vatican can do to help find our daughter and her husband."

"Certainly, certainly, Signora. They have opened a file on the matter. It is not a strong concern at this time, but proper contemporaneous documentation would be quite useful if, in the future, far in the future, an investigation is made concerning the possible beatification of the dear girls."

Leonora silently crossed herself and Marcus wondered if anyone noticed his disgust.

Taricco continued, "I wanted to share with you some of my thoughts on this matter. I understand that the police are correctly focused on the earthly explanations involving kidnapping and the like, but I believe there are spiritual considerations that deserve a place at the table."

"Please, go on," Armando said earnestly.

Marcus thought: *is Armando just an ass-kisser or is he prepared to believe the nonsense that was bound to be spewed? If it's the latter, remind me never to use him as a lawyer.*

When Taricco leaned back in his chair, his cassock stretched and accentuated his girth. "Well, the facts point to the conclusion that the girls have been in a state of suspended animation," he said. "What do the Bible or the compendium of Christian writings have to offer us about their condition? Nothing. Nothing at all. The closest concepts are the states of purgatory and limbo. Of course, these refer to aspects of death."

"Surely, Eminence," Leonora cried, "you aren't suggesting that Victoria and Elizabeth have died."

"No, no, my dear lady! There has only been one resurrection! Your granddaughters have not died. They have been paused. They have spent these past years within a certain white room and—"

"How do you know about that?" Marcus asked.

"Oh, the girls told Father Leuti about that and also the spacemen. It's charming what children are led to believe."

Marcus sputtered, "Again, I must say—"

"Yes, yes," Taricco said, biscuit crumbs falling onto his cassock. "Absolute discretion. The point I was making is that we might be treading on some new theological ground. Now, I will be the first to admit that as a seminarian, I was not at the top of my class in matters of eschatology, but it is important that I share with you my thoughts on the matter before I propose them to the Vatican. It is only proper that you hear from me what might become an important matter for the Church."

"We appreciate that," Armando said.

"I should ask, Mr. Handler, are you Catholic?" the archbishop said.

"Not even close."

"Very well. Perhaps I should define eschatology."

"It's the part of theology that talks about the end times, the ultimate destiny of mankind," Marcus said.

"Ah, you are aware of this."

"I get around." He didn't really. He hadn't "gotten around" in years. What he did have, despite the drinking, was a good memory. He'd taken a couple of religious studies courses a lifetime ago as an undergraduate at Georgetown University and the spaghetti was still sticking to the wall.

"What I am proposing," Taricco said, "is that the girls, and perhaps their parents, entered into a state of Divine suspended animation, a sort of waiting room where ordinary reality was put on hold in a prelude to a reunion with God. In this white room that they perceived, they were neither alive nor dead. The passage of time did not occur and thus, they did not age. We experienced four years. For them, it was, perhaps, the blink of an eye. My proposition is that they were chosen by God as a kind of prelude to what one day, we all will come to experience at the Eschaton, the end time, when Christ will come again and usher us into His Kingdom of glory. Thy Kingdom come! I will raise my interpretation with my superiors. They will be able to put it to greater theological scholars than myself. And then, we shall see."

The archbishop seemed pleased with himself and reached for the biscuit tray. Marcus looked over at the Cutrìs. Both of them seemed to be interested in their shoes, so Marcus decided to lead the charge.

"What about the gray men?" he asked.

"Ah, them," Taricco said. "I would suggest that they

were angels of some sort. Who are we to know about the appearance of angelic beings?"

"And what about their illnesses?" Marcus said.

"Perhaps this state of suspended animation causes some harm to the body."

"And why do you think the parents are still missing?"

"This remains a mystery, but we can pray that they too will be returned soon, hopefully in good health."

Marcus lightly slapped one of his legs and said, "Well, I'm sure I speak for the Cutrìs when I say that we are fascinated by your theory."

"Certainly," Armando mumbled. "Your Eminence has honored us with your observations and opinions. We seek your prayers and blessings for the return of our Elena and Jesper."

As the archbishop rose, crumbs showered the floor. "I will pray for them," he said.

They were half an hour into their return trip when Marcus said, "That was a complete waste of time."

Armando raised one hand in a gesture of futility. "We had no choice. He is an influential man who deserves our respect, even if he has become a little absurd in old age."

"More than a little."

"Look, Marcus, I understand your contempt, but we live here. This is our community; this is our Church. If it became known that we refused an audience with Taricco, my law practice would suffer even more than it has. There are many other lawyers in Palmi for people to choose."

"Why is your business down?" Marcus asked.

"Surely you must understand the answer to that. It's well known that the police investigated me and my clients after the disappearance. To the best of my knowledge, I have represented only a single 'Ndrangheta in all my years, and it was for a civil banking matter. I do not do criminal work. In any event, the theory of the police was weak—what if Cutrì got in trouble with a mob client who exacted some sort of revenge? As it happened, this client of mine was cleared of any involvement to the kidnapping. However, it doesn't take much to get people talking and to stain a reputation I have spent decades establishing."

Leonora sobbed. "It's been a nightmare. At first people were supportive, but then they turned on us and became suspicious. I don't even like to leave the house anymore. I can't paint. I can't do anything. I just want my daughter back."

"Yes, yes," Armando said, "and our granddaughters healthy."

"I'm sorry," Marcus said. "I feel for what you folks are going through."

"Will you find our Elena and Jesper?" Leonora asked.

"I'll try my hardest."

"We're happy Mickey brought you back," Armando said. "If you thought the archbishop was a waste of time, what about this French psychic?"

"I'll tell you what I told Mickey. I think she's a bullshitter with an asterisk."

Armando furrowed his brow and said, "By which you mean that you think she's lying, but you can't understand how she knows certain things."

Mickey smiled. This lawyer had gone up a few pegs in his estimation. "Armando, you're a smart fellow. You should be chasing away new clients with a stick."

*

Major Lumaga invited Marcus for dinner that night to a small, family-owned restaurant off the beaten trail, not far from the hotel. He was out of uniform, but the owner and waiters treated him with the full respect of his office. Marcus had two glasses going, one whiskey, one wine. Even though the food was delicious, he picked at it. The case was killing his appetite.

Lumaga asked, "So, what are your theories about Celeste Bobier?"

"I've been telling everyone she's full of shit."

"But is that what you truly believe?"

"Belief is a funny thing, Roberto. I believe in verifiable facts. I only believe in things I can understand."

"What about religion? What about God? What about Heaven and Hell?"

"I don't understand them and I don't believe in them."

"We differ here," Lumaga said, spearing some of the restaurant's specialty, maccheroni col ferretto, with his fork. "I can be a pragmatic policeman, dealing in verifiable facts, but also a person of faith who is able to trust in that which I cannot fully comprehend."

"More power to you. I'm not putting you down."

"Look, the fact of the matter is that Victoria and Elizabeth, despite their youth, give credible accounts of their time in detention. They are sober girls. They are intelligent. And then we have this Bobier woman who offers, in a way, a collaborating story, committed to writing years ago."

Marcus tried to get the waiter's attention to bring

him another Scotch. Failing, Lumaga stepped in and accomplished the task with a subtle gesture.

"Do you want me to start believing in alien abduction?" Marcus asked.

"I think this case forces us to maintain an open mind to every possibility until facts arise that cause them to be excluded. The girls do not seem to have aged. That is a fact. Once someone has provided a plausible explanation that does not involve alien abduction, then I will happily exclude the possibility. Until then, everything is on the table. I presume you analyzed data at your CIA job. I'm sure you utilized the same methodology."

"There were times I got caught in a web of lies," he said, christening his new glass. "These days, it takes a lot to convince me of anything."

Lumaga's phone played a tune. He excused himself and stepped outside then returned a minute later, looking sour.

"Fabiana Odorico—you remember her, my sub-lieutenant—she's on her way over here with something to show me."

"What?"

"I didn't ask because, from her voice, it's definitely not good news. I wanted to finish my pasta before my stomach begins to churn. My revenge for her spoiling my dinner will be spoiling her night when she sees that I'm with you."

"Oh, yeah?"

"No one in my department is happy about my cooperation with you. She was undoubtedly the source of the leak about you to the journalist from Naples."

"It was her? Why didn't you take her down a few notches?"

"Two reasons. First, she's good at her job. Excellent, actually. Before the girls returned and sucked all of our resources back into the case, she was making some big 'Ndrangheta arrests up in the mountains. Second, she's not wrong about you. It's bad for morale for me to include an outsider in the investigation. Frankly, I don't have a choice. The shit rolls downhill from the US ambassador to the Ministry of Foreign Affairs and from there to the Interior Ministry and the Ministry of Defense and from there to my poor Carabinieri station. Besides, I like you, so Fabiana has to deal with it."

She arrived during dessert. Lumaga was halfway through a huge portion of pitta di San Martino and Marcus was on his fourth Scotch. As soon as Odorico saw him, Marcus knew that Lumaga was right about her being the leaker. She looked like she was an inch away from tipping him backward out of his chair.

"Have a seat, Fabiana," Lumaga said. "You want a bite, a coffee?"

"No, thank you. I just need to show you this."

She tapped a link on her phone and passed it to him.

"*Oh, Madonna!*" he hissed, as he read on. "Unbelievable. How can we get anything done in this country when everyone leaks!"

When he was done reading, he passed the phone across the table to Marcus.

They Have Not Aged—Before and After Photos Of The Missing Girls
We Were Abducted By Aliens—Kept On A Spaceship By Gray Men

Marcus finished his drink and said to Odorico, "Can you email this to me? I've got to let Mr. Andreason know right away."

"Give me your address," she said, coolly.

His phone dinged with the email and he said, "This is from a local paper, right? Has this hit the streets yet?"

"In the morning," she said. "But they've already tweeted it."

"Some piece of shit took their pictures in their hospital beds," Marcus said. "Where was the security?"

"Right outside their door," Lumaga said. "I'm quite sure they were taken by someone on the staff of the hospital who had a legitimate reason for being in the room. Everyone with a phone has a camera. Fabiana, we'll need to at least make a show of investigating the leak, but I don't want to divert people from critical tasks."

"I understand," she said.

Marcus kept looking at Victoria and Elizabeth's "after" photos. The photographer had asked them to pose and the results were two sad little smiles.

"We're going to be ass-deep in alligators tomorrow," he said, and by Odorico's short, sharp laugh, he wondered if it was the first time she'd heard the expression.

12

With the extensive police escort, members of the public might have assumed that an important politician or maybe a Mafia judge was riding in one of the black SUVs. But the police had good cause for accompanying the girls from their hospital to the airport because paparazzi in cars, motorcycles, and scooters jockeyed dangerously for position on the narrow roads. Marcus rode with Mickey and Celeste in the lead SUV and the Cutrìs accompanied the girls and a nurse in the second.

From the back seat, Marcus was looking into the driver's wing mirror when he saw a motorcycle with a photographer on the back trying to overtake the convoy and pull alongside. An oncoming car forced it to regain its lane and it almost collided with one of the police cars.

"It's a fucking zoo," he said.

Celeste was wearing another form-hugging dress, this one black with a demure neckline. She had asked whether she could ride with Victoria and Elizabeth, but Marcus told her she'd have a chance to see them on the plane. Left unsaid was his insistence on supervising her interactions. He didn't trust her and he didn't want her planting false memories to burnish her psychic claims.

Marcus's phone rang.

"Roberto," he answered. "What's going on?"

Lumaga said, "There's a new leak, I'm afraid. It's gotten out that the girls are heading to the Bambino Gesù Hospital. You can expect crazy scenes when you arrive."

"I wish you were coming to Rome," Marcus said.

"There's important work to be done here, but don't worry, I've notified the chief of the main Carabinieri station in Rome. You'll have excellent security protocols in place for the transport from the airport and while they are at the hospital. You've got my number. Call if you need anything. I'll contact you if we learn anything new down here."

"What did he say?" Mickey asked.

"The world knows which hospital we're heading to."

"For Christ's sake," Mickey said. "Are people selling information, or can't they keep their lips from flapping?"

"I'll take that as a rhetorical question," Marcus mumbled.

When the convoy pulled onto the tarmac and parked beside Mickey's jet, one of the policemen bounded up the stairs and asked the pilot if they were ready. The officer flashed a thumbs-up and Mickey boarded first to organize the seating. He placed the girls in adjacent, cross-aisle seats with Celeste and Marcus facing them. Leonora and Armando settled in the aft with the nurse, and Mickey took his favorite oversized chair nearest the cockpit.

"Wheels up," he told the pilots, pulling his laptop from his briefcase, preparing to catch up on company emails.

Elizabeth eyed Celeste suspiciously. "Who are you?" she asked.

"My name is Celeste. I'm so happy to meet both of you."

"Are you a nurse?" Victoria asked, playing with the hide-away tray.

"No, I'm not a nurse, but I like to help people."

"How?" the little girl asked.

"By telling them things about themselves."

The plane began to taxi. Both girls tensed.

Marcus reassured them. "Flying is fun. Do you remember flying on airplanes?"

Elizabeth said she did; Victoria said she didn't.

No one spoke again until the jet pierced the cloud cover and sunlight flooded the cabin.

Elizabeth clearly had been mulling over Celeste's statement. "What do you tell people about themselves?"

Marcus turned to watch Celeste's response. Lips that seemed glued together by red lipstick peeled apart at the tug of a smile.

"I tell people about things from their past that they have forgotten or perhaps never knew. I tell people about their future."

"How?" the girls asked.

"I see things."

"Like what?"

"Sometimes I see people. They might be talking. They might be silent. They might be kissing."

Victoria sniggered and said, "Ewww."

"Usually when they kiss, it's nice," Celeste said. "Sometimes I see the places where people have been, or where they are going."

Marcus could see that Celeste interested the older girl. The younger one had figured out how to retract the tray table and she dipped into her fun bag for a coloring book and crayons.

"Like where?" Elizabeth asked.

Celeste's tone was lilting and soft. Marcus fought its attraction, but it was mesmerizing.

"Maybe it's a green, green forest shaded by tall trees. Maybe the person I'm helping is there. Maybe something good will happen to her in the forest."

"Like what?"

"Maybe she will find someone who is lost in the forest."

"A little girl?"

"Yes, perhaps a little girl. Then another time, maybe I'll see a lovely beach with seagulls riding the wind, calling from above. Maybe a man and a woman are walking on the beach and they are splashing in the warm water with their bare feet. And maybe the man will ask the woman to be his wife making her very happy. And maybe they'll have children, like you."

"Are they our mommy and daddy?"

Victoria took notice, looking up from her coloring.

"Perhaps. Do you remember them?"

"I don't," Victoria said.

Elizabeth said, "I do."

"Tell me what you remember?" Celeste asked.

"Daddy was tall and he talked on the telephone with a loud voice."

"I remember that," Victoria said, unconvincingly.

"Mommy was very kind," Elizabeth said. "She made us yummy meals and read to us in bed and sang songs."

Victoria claimed to remember that too.

"Do you remember when you last saw them?" Celeste asked.

Marcus watched Elizabeth bear down in thought and her sister aping her.

"I don't remember," Elizabeth finally said.

"Me neither," Victoria said.

Celeste pressed on. "When you were in the white room on the spaceship, did you see your parents there?"

They both said no.

"Did the gray men ever talk to you about them?"

Elizabeth corrected her. "There weren't gray men. There was Gray Man and Gray Woman."

"Ah, I'm sorry," Celeste said. "Did Gray Man or Gray Woman talk about them?"

After a very long pause, Elizabeth said yes. "I remember once, a long time ago. Gray Woman told us not to cry and that if we were good, we would see our parents again."

"What did being good mean?"

"We had to eat all our Earth food, we had to brush our teeth, and we had to let them poke us and take our blood."

"And were you good?"

"Not always. Sometimes."

"But you didn't get to see your parents again."

"No." Elizabeth fidgeted and said she was tired.

"You can rest, child," Celeste said. "Thank you for speaking with me. I think both of you girls are very sweet and very special."

Suddenly, Victoria looked at her and said, "I love you."

Marcus didn't know what to make of this burst of affection, but Celeste didn't seem surprised. She replied, "I love you too."

The flight time was only just over an hour, but halfway into it, both girls were asleep. Leonora came forward with pillows for them. Marcus leaned into the aisle and, in a low voice, asked Celeste if she found her conversation with them helpful. His question had an edge he couldn't entirely disguise and she immediately picked up on it.

"You distrust me," she said quietly.

"It's not a matter of trust."

"What then?"

"I just can't figure out your angle."

"Angle. I think I know what this means. It's like, what I want? My intentions?"

"That's exactly what it means."

"I want to help them find their parents. I want to help Mikkel find his son and daughter-in-law. I want to help Armando and Leonora find their daughter. I even want to help you, although you don't want my help."

"What help do I need?"

"You want to succeed in your job. I believe that is important to you."

"So, you're driven by altruism. Is that it?"

"Mostly."

"Mostly? What else?"

She changed the direction of her gaze just enough to avoid his eyes. "My number of clients has been down lately. If it became known that I helped find Jesper and Elena, my business would be much better."

"I'm relieved," he said.

"You are?"

"I am. That's a motivation I can understand. You're not a saint."

"No, Marcus, you're wrong," she said. "A part of me is, well, not saintly, but altruistic. If I don't increase my wealth by a single euro, I will still be content and serene. Why? Because doing good things for people is far more important than making money."

Their conversation ended, Marcus would have been left to his own thoughts for the rest of the ride had not Elizabeth jolted awake and asked him if he wanted to do a puzzle book with him. He dove in obediently, and soon, Victoria, perhaps attuned to her sister's wavelength, was awake too and wanting to play. Until they touched down in Rome, the girls were lost in their own kind of space, doing puzzles with Uncle Marcus.

Lumaga was true to his word. A contingent of Carabinieri was waiting for them at Ciampino Airport. They were needed. The media presence at the airport and at the hospital dwarfed what they had experienced in Calabria. The trip was only ten miles, but at every traffic signal, photographers on motorbikes tried to land their money shots. Marcus used his sports coat to drape Victoria, and Armando covered Elizabeth with his. Marcus knew they were about to arrive when they crossed the Tiber and he saw the dome of St. Peter's Basilica.

Pulling through the hospital gates, the van driver told Marcus that he would wait for them to return and take them to the nearby Gran Meliá Hotel. The paparazzi were not allowed into the hospital forecourt and the entourage was whisked through the entrance of a modern, glass-fronted building that complemented the older parts of the hospital complex. In the lobby, some staff had been alerted to their arrival and a billing clerk tried to usher them into her offices. An imposing, white-coated physician with gray, buzz-topped hair and the mannerisms of a field marshal blocked her.

"No, no," he complained in English, sternly wagging a finger. "This can be done later. I want these girls taken upstairs to my department immediately." He must have recognized Mickey from his press photos, because he went straight for him with an outstretched hand. "Bruno Spara, at your service. I'm the chairman of the Onco-Hematology Department."

Mickey introduced himself and added, "It's good to be here. Jessica Bingham speaks highly of you."

"Well, Jessica is a dear colleague." He dropped to a knee in front of Victoria and Elizabeth, his expression softening, and said, "Welcome, dear girls. My nurses can't wait to meet you. A small bird told me you were a little sick. Do you feel a little sick?"

They shook their heads shyly.

"Well good, because you look nice and strong to me. Come on, I'll let you push the buttons on the elevator."

Mickey told Marcus to check into the hotel with Celeste while he and the Cutrìs stayed with the girls. Just then, a heavyset man with a blue chambray shirt and red suspenders emerged from the café and came trotting toward them across the lobby. A Carabinieri officer stepped in his path and held up his hand.

"Mr. Andreason! Sir!" he called out in an American accent. "My name is Virgil Carter. I just flew in from Washington. I've got vital information for you about the abduction. I know where they were held. I know a man who was held there at the same time."

13

Virgil Carter was in his seventies. His hair and bushy beard used to be redder, but he favored the color, and along with his suspenders, his belt and the monogram on his shirt pocket were red. After he was stopped by the policeman, he waited patiently while Mickey and Marcus had a word.

"See what this guy's going on about," Mickey said.

"Why do all the nut jobs like red?" Marcus said.

When Mickey turned his back, Carter called after him, "Mr. Andreason, you really ought to speak with me."

Mickey walked on and said, "My security man will talk to you."

With that, Mickey headed for the elevators with Dr. Spara, the Cutrìs, the girls, and their nurse.

Marcus told the policeman that he'd handle this Carter fellow and introduced himself.

"I'm Marcus Handler. What can I do for you?"

Carter said, "I know that important men like to delegate. Here's my card, Mr. Handler."

**Virgil M. Carter, Lt. Colonel, US Airforce (Retired),
Silver Springs, Maryland, www.u_an.org**

Celeste drew near enough that Marcus felt compelled to introduce her.

"Do you work for Mr. Andreason as well, Ms. Bobier?" Carter asked.

"I don't, no. Perhaps, like you, I came to Italy to help him find his son and daughter-in-law."

"Are you in the alien-abduction field like me?" he asked.

"Not at all. I'm a psychic."

"Well, different strokes for different folks," he said with a loud chuckle. "Far be it from me to judge."

Marcus's patience was nonexistent at this point. "No, I'll do the judging," he said. "Look, Colonel Carter, we need to get situated in our hotel. You've got thirty seconds to tell me what you want."

"Going to take more time than that."

"Starting now."

"Well, be like that. Okay. I run one of the largest citizens' networks in the States on UFOs and alien abductions. A year ago, I interviewed a fellow named Ruben Sanchez from Arizona who disappeared for five months."

Marcus looked at his watch.

"Now, I told you it was going to take more time. Just hang in there. You won't be disappointed. Sanchez told me he was abducted from his truck one night by Grays."

"What are Grays?" Celeste asked.

"Aliens with gray skins—sound familiar? Well, he was kept on board their craft—more on that later—and while he was there, he communicated by tapping on the wall of his—get this—his white room, with an Earth woman by the name of Helen, he said. I understand the girls' mother's name is Elena. Do I have your attention yet?"

Celeste sucked air through her red lips and nodded emphatically.

Another nut job, Marcus thought, but Mickey was going to be livid if he didn't at least talk to him. "Why don't you come with us to our hotel?"

Some of the media broke off and followed Marcus's van to the hotel. It was a very short ride to the five-star resort adjacent to the Vatican. Once the photographers saw that the girls weren't there, they took off. Carter followed Marcus and Celeste into the lobby, a study in cool, white marble, and gave out a whistle.

"I saw this one on Booking.com," he said, "but it was way out of my price range. Air Force pension, you know, and not a lot of money in the alien-abduction game."

"I'm not surprised," Marcus said. "I've got to deal with the bags. Be right back."

"You really a psychic?" Carter asked Celeste when they were alone.

"I really am."

"Well, you're the prettiest psychic I've ever met."

"Have you met many?"

"You're the absolute first."

"And you're my first alien-abduction gentleman."

He seemed delighted by the innuendo. "Know what they say," he said. "You never forget your first. So, what's a psychic doing here, if I may ask?"

"It seems we have a confluence of interests, Mr. Carter. I'm here because shortly after the abduction, I had a vision of the girls on a spaceship with gray beings."

He sprouted the widest of grins. "You want to know something? I am liking you more and more."

When Marcus returned, the three of them repaired to a shaded terrace that overlooked the Vatican walls and the Castel Sant'Angelo. Carter asked if it was okay if he had lunch and Marcus told him that Mr. Andreason would spring for it. The fellow ordered half the items on the menu, while Marcus and Celeste contented themselves with coffees.

Munching on a breadstick, Carter said, "Marcus, no offense, but you seem a tad on the old side for a bodyguard. Am I missing some mad kung fu skills you possess?"

"I'm a security consultant, not a bodyguard."

"Oh yeah, what kind of a background does a fellow need to get into that line of work?"

"I worked for the government."

Carter drew out the words, "I see," and laughed at himself. "In my experience, when a guy says that, he worked in Langley."

"Something like that."

"What is Langley?" Celeste asked.

"CIA headquarters in Virginia," Carter said, helpfully. "Mr. Handler, it seems, was a spook. We've got a bunch of you guys who're members of U-AN."

"And that is?" Marcus asked.

"UFO Abduction Network. I founded it the day I retired from the Air Force. Want to hear my story?"

"My guess is it would take a bullet to stop you."

"Well, you're right about that. I spent fifteen of my twenty-two years in the Air Force at the Pentagon. I've always been in logistics. I was never a pilot—hell, I don't even like to fly. Logistics isn't sexy, but if the Air Force needed to get X materials to Y place, I was their guy. I was always vaguely aware of the subject of alien abductions—I mean, who doesn't know about the famous cases like the Betty and Barney Hill abduction?"

"I don't," Celeste said.

Carter's caprese salad arrived and after admiring it, he said, "You're kidding, right? New Hampshire? 1961?" Working off her blank stare, he asked Marcus if he was similarly ill-informed.

"Please go on, Colonel."

"Only if you call me Virgil. Okay, forget the Hills. So, years ago, I met a flyboy from Idaho who was doing a Pentagon tour of duty, and he told me about a buddy of his, a civilian, who was a truck driver, who was abducted one night, right out of his rig. He was transported up into a spaceship, a sausage-shaped affair, which was why the poor bastard, to the day he killed himself, was cruelly called Hot Dog. The aliens who did all manner of experiments on him over about a week's time before returning him to Idaho—well, they were Grays. These are far and away the most common types of aliens abductees describe. You've got your Grays— they've got gray skin, large, elongated heads, big eyes, tend not to have ears, noses—they're the classic Roswell-type of aliens. Then, you've got your Reptilians. They're green, of course, with lizard or snake-type heads. Then, you've got your Nordics. They're a heck of a lot taller than the Grays or Reptilians, usually with fair skin, blue eyes, blond hair— basically Swedes in space."

Marcus muttered under his breath.

"Sorry, didn't catch that," Carter said.

"I said I can't believe I'm listening to this."

"Well, listen and learn, my friend. Shit, lost my train." He took advantage of his memory lapse to pop a glob of cheese into his mouth. "Okay, got it back, so, let me fast-forward, 'cause I can see I'm in danger of losing you. After hearing about Hot Dog, I began compiling cases of abductions, at first as a kind of a hobby, and after a while I began doing some shoe-leather research, interviewing abductees and their friends and families. My employer took a dim view of such undertakings, so I waited till I hung up my spurs before starting U-AN with an online data dump of all my research. Currently, we are the biggest network of abduction documentation, bar none. Which brings us to Ruben Sanchez. Ruben Sanchez, a fellow who drives an Uber in Phoenix, dropped a post on U-AN a year ago. Now, after doing this long enough, I can separate the wheat from the chaff, and I could tell right off that he was a legitimate abductee."

"How?" Celeste asked.

"Well, because all the assholes—excuse my French; shit, you are French; that's pretty dumbass of me—they can't help themselves from engaging in a-nod-and-a-wink BS, showing how clever and funny they are. Ruben was earnest and his account was pure, so I contacted him, then went to Phoenix to interview him in person. In a lot of ways, his abduction story had typical elements, but it was also unusual, because he was missing for a long time. Five months was one of the longest disappearances on record. At the time. Now we know it was small beer compared to the Andreason girls. So, his family filed a missing person's report. The police had an active investigation ongoing. And then he shows up, five months later, walking along the very road he disappeared from with a helluva story. Anyway, with Ruben's permission, I posted all his details and documentation and you can find it on my website with the date I posted it."

"What about this woman named Helen?" Marcus asked.

"Well, Ruben is kept in this all-white room, and the Grays are doing all manner of experiments on him, when one day, he kicks one of the walls in frustration. And guess what? Someone thumps back at him. The two of them have a lot of time to kill, as one does in the stir, and before long, they work out the simplest form of code to communicate. It's an alphabetic knuckle rap. A is one rap. C is three raps. N is fifteen raps, and so on. It's not fast, but like I said, what else did they have to do?"

"He said her name was Helen? You sure?"

"That's what he told me. Now, it took them some time to figure out how to use their code and to ask each other some basic questions, and shortly after they exchanged names, Ruben goes to sleep one night and wakes up on the highway. His five months is up."

A large steak arrived and Carter asked for steak sauce. He grumbled when the waiter told him they had none, but he tucked a napkin into his shirt, sampled the meat, and declared that it was tasty enough, dry.

"Mr. Andreason's daughter-in-law's name is Elena, not Helen," Marcus said.

"I'm aware of that. Ruben told me she said it was Helen."

"Could he have made a mistake?" Celeste asked.

"An E is five taps, and H is eight," Carter said. "Maybe he got it wrong, maybe she was using some variation of Elena."

"Do you have his number?" Marcus asked. "Could I speak to him?"

"It'll be a very long-distance call," he answered. "Ruben passed away two months ago. When he came back, he had headaches and they found a tumor."

"Oh, my God," Celeste gasped.

"That what the girls have?" Carter asked. "Brain tumors?"

Marcus shut that down. "We're not discussing their health. Did Ruben mention communicating with anyone else? In space?"

"Just Helen, and as far as I'm concerned, that's close enough for government work. So, there I was, having a sandwich in my condo yesterday, minding my own business, when I saw the reports on Twitter coming out of Italy about the girls being abducted by Grays and returning the same age as when they were taken. Now, it's entirely possible that Ruben didn't age during his ordeal, but he was forty-seven and he was only gone for under half a year, so there was no way to tell. And it's possible that other abductees didn't age either, but their abductions were even shorter. Anyway, I could tell that this is, by far, the most important case I'll ever see, so I bought a ticket and got my ass to Dulles. And here I am, eating an Italian steak, without sauce." He wiped his mouth and said to Marcus, "So, when can I see the girls?"

Bruno Spara brought the grandparents to a family consultation room on the Hematology ward. He had large hands, and when he laid them, palms-down on the table, they seemed as big as dinner plates.

"How are they, Professore?" Armando asked.

"I examined them and reviewed the medical reports and laboratory tests from the Morelli Hospital, where I must tell you, they received excellent care. I concur with the diagnosis of chronic myeloid leukemia. I believe that Jessica Bingham already told you how unusual this leukemia is in young children, but we know how to treat it, and I can reassure you that the prognosis is quite good with appropriate and aggressive therapy."

"Thank God," Leonora said.

"What's your explanation for the way they look?" Mickey asked.

"Are you asking about the fact they appear to be the same age as when they went missing?"

"I am."

Spara finally lifted his hands off the table and slowly turned them palms upwards. "I have no explanation. There is a very rare genetic disease in children called progeria, which is an accelerated aging. These progeria kids are born with abnormal proteins that make the cells age and die prematurely. By the time they're eight, nine, ten years old, they have the appearance and the bodies of ancient men and women and they usually die of old age before they are teenagers. If anything, Victoria and Elizabeth have the opposite condition. Here, we are confronted with the absence of the expected changes that young children would experience over five years. But there are no functional ways to measure age other than the calendar. People aren't like trees. We can't count our growth rings. I can say with complete certainty that there are no reports in the medical literature of a slowing or cessation of the aging process. It's better that I stick with something I know about and that is the treatment of leukemias."

"We're in your hands," Armando said. "Tell us what must be done."

"I'm starting them today on a drug called Tasigna. It's a fairly recently approved drug, a so-called second-generation tyrosine kinase inhibitor. The anticipated side effects are not so profound, and even if they occur, we can manage them quite easily. I'll be giving you a brochure with all the safety information."

"What's the prognosis?" Mickey asked.

"I expect to see a deep molecular remission in about a fortnight."

"That fast," Mickey said.

"Yes, children can respond very quickly. They will need to stay on the drug for a year or maybe considerably longer. However, given their age, we want to be aggressive. We want to go for a cure, not just control. So, once we get them into remission, we will wipe out all of their blood-forming stem cells with strong chemotherapy, then perform bone marrow transplantations to give them new, healthy cells that will continue to grow inside their bone marrow. The hospital in Reggio Calabria never had the chance to do the testing, so I'd like to test the three of you to see who is the best genetic match. If all goes as well as I hope, I feel very good about their prognosis."

Carter was on dessert when Mickey called. Marcus excused himself and took a walk through the lush hotel gardens. Mickey wanted to know if Carter was on the level. Marcus played back the conversation and let Mickey form his own judgment.

"Brain cancer, you say. Not leukemia."

"That's right. Sanchez had brain cancer," Marcus said.

"And it was Helen, not Elena," Mickey said. "I don't know what to say about that?"

"I do," Marcus said. "If we keep collecting them, we're going to have enough crazies to play doubles tennis."

"Then I'll be the umpire and I'll keep an open mind," Mickey said.

"Carter wants to speak to the girls. He wants to cross-reference things that came out of his interviews with this Sanchez guy."

"Maybe later. Not right away," Mickey said. "They're starting their treatment today. Dr. Spara seems good. I trust him. If all goes well, they'll get curative bone marrow transplants in a couple of weeks. I hope Armando or Leonora are a better match so the poor girls won't have to get my old-man cells. So, let's keep Colonel Carter close by. Put him up at our hotel."

"He won't say no," Marcus said. "He likes the restaurant."

After lunch, Carter went off to his first hotel to get his things and Marcus gave Celeste her room key.

"How are the children?" she asked.

"Fine, I think. Mickey's happy with their doctor, seems upbeat. They'll be getting bone marrow transplants soon. He mentioned the C-word. Cures."

Marcus checked into his room and before long, drank his way through the three little bottles of Scotch in the minibar.

He rang room service to bring up a full-size bottle and had them take cash, so it wouldn't appear on the bill. He paced himself as the afternoon drifted along in case Mickey wanted him for something and managed to stay on a knife-edge of mild inebriation. When the hotel phone rang, he expected to hear Mickey's voice, but it was Celeste and she sounded distressed.

"What's the matter?" he asked.

"I was sitting quietly with the curtains drawn," she said. "I had a vision."

There was a little bit of drink left in his glass. He swallowed it. "Oh, yeah? What kind of vision?"

"It was their doctor, Dr. Spara. He came into a room to speak with Mickey. He looked very grave indeed."

Marcus poured another measure. "And what did our Dr. Spara say?"

"He said, 'I'm sorry, Mr. Andreason, but the bone marrow transplantation has gone horribly wrong. Victoria and Elizabeth are going to die.'"

14

The man's English wasn't good; he just about got by with it. He slathered his tortured linguistic constructions and neologisms with a thick Eastern European accent that made it especially difficult to understand him. This evening, the difficulty was compounded by poor cell-phone coverage.

"You cannot hear?" he said.

The fellow on the other end of the line sounded exasperated. "You're cutting in and out."

"I should be moving?"

"Where are you?"

"I can move."

"I can hear you now. Where are you?"

"Only one bar but I can move."

"Just talk to me. Where are you?"

"In rental car on a street. You can't hear?"

"What town?"

"Town called Vibo Valentia."

"Wait. Let me check a map."

The Eastern European was a large, powerfully built man, with long blond hair and a wispy, yellow moustache. He lit a cigarette and rolled down the window a little.

"Okay, Vibo Valentia. I see it. Did you find him?"

"Not sure. I think maybe."

"You either found him or you didn't. Which is it?"

"Maybe found him. Not see him yet, but I think he inside flat I looking at."

"Sorry, Gunar, I lost you for a second. Did you say you looked inside the flat?"

"No. Am in car."

"Then why do you think he's there?"

"Not sure. Maybe he there. Yesterday I go to where he from. Village called Cessaniti. His mama live there. I wait till she shopping and I break in. No sign him. Last night, guy in bar says he know him but he no see him for years. I give him hundred euros and he tell me he has old girlfriend in Vibo Valentia. I find where she live. From car I look up in window now. Guy is there who look like him but not sure. I need go inside, I think."

"All right. Find out and let me know."

"Sure, sure, no problem. I let you know. You want I take care of it, if it him?"

At that, the man on the phone completely lost his cool. "That's why I sent you there! Was I not clear?"

"Sure, sure. I take care."

"This is the last thing we needed," Lumaga told his sub-lieutenant at the door to the apartment building. He had parked his car on the sidewalk and had ducked under the crime-scene tape stretched across the narrow street. Knots of neighbors milled around, watching him with suspicion. Not everyone in this area loved the Carabinieri.

"It's a pain in you know where," Odorico said.

GLENN COOPER

"You know the last time we had something like this in Vibo Valentia?" he asked. He knew she didn't know the answer as she was from Naples, so he answered it himself. "Three years and that was a domestic situation. A wife killed her drunk husband with a kitchen knife."

"What happened to her?"

"The judge took pity. The husband was a violent bastard. He spared her jail. This one's not domestic, I take it."

"Not unless one of them was able to shoot themselves twice in the head then make the gun disappear."

"So, we've got a murderer on the loose."

On the landing outside the flat, they put on booties and gloves. Inside, they kept out of the way of the forensic people and squeezed into the bedroom.

Lumaga was a tough guy with a strong stomach, but this was bad. One victim, a man who looked to be in his thirties was on the floor. The second victim, a woman of a similar age lay on the bed, her eyes open wide. Blood and brain matter were everywhere—on the floor, the bed, the walls, even the ceiling.

"She's like the *Mona Lisa*," Lumaga said.

"How do you mean?" Odorico asked.

"Wherever I stand, she seems to be looking at me."

The *medico legale*, a crusty old doctor who wore her gray hair piled into a messy bun was photographing the woman.

"Anything here beyond the obvious, Lidia?" Lumaga asked.

"Each with a double-tap to the brain," she said with a smoker's rasp. "Small caliber, I'd say, maybe a twenty-two or twenty-five. They didn't find the casings so the killer used

122

a revolver or picked them up. I'll buy you dinner if he left fingerprints. Very professional, all around."

"A classic hit," Lumaga said.

"One or both of them were probably into some seriously bad business," Odorico said.

"Not my department," the doctor said. "There was a small bag of marijuana in the living room, but that doesn't make them drug barons."

"Who are they?" Lumaga asked.

Odorico referred to her moleskin notepad. "The woman is Cinzia Rondinelli. This is her apartment. She teaches chemistry at the local secondary school."

"Maybe she's the Walter White of the operation," Lumaga said, sending the *medico legale* into a coughing fit.

"Who is he?" Odorico asked.

"*Breaking Bad?*" Lumaga said. "Chemistry teacher? Methamphetamines? You don't watch television? Lidia knows who I'm talking about."

"I don't own a television," Odorico said. "Shall I continue?"

"Please do."

"The male victim is Ferruccio Gressani, age thirty-six, a resident of Madrid, Spain with a Spanish driving license. At this point, that's all the information we have."

"Was there a mobile phone?"

"Hers, not his."

"Everyone has a mobile. I wonder if the killer took it."

"It's possible," she said.

"Who found the bodies?"

"A friend of the woman. Cinzia wasn't answering

her phone this morning, so she stopped in. She had a key because she waters her plants when Cinzia's on holiday. She's traumatized by what she saw and had to be taken to hospital to be sedated. I haven't been able to speak to her yet."

"Lidia, what time were they killed?"

"I'd say about twelve hours ago. Between 10 p.m. and 2 a.m. I'll know better after the autopsies. I'll be going now, Roberto. You know how to find me."

Lumaga said, "Indeed I do. Fabiana, what about the neighbors? Did they hear anything?"

"They've all been interviewed. There was nothing. No screams, no gunshots. Nothing out of the ordinary."

"He must have used a silencer. Any cameras on the street?"

"No, I'm sorry to say."

"Okay, let's find out who Cinzia and Ferruccio are and who might have been angry enough at one or both of them to do this. Talk to her friend in hospital. See if Ferruccio has any local connections. Get the police in Madrid involved. See if either of them has a police record here or abroad. Take the lead on this and try to wrap it up as soon as possible. I need your full attention on the Andreason case."

"It done," the man said.

"Any complications?"

"There was girl."

"And?"

"She done."

"Any other complications?"

"None. Quick job. Easy job."

"What about his car? Did you find his car?"

"I find. I burn it."

"His phone?"

"I have phone."

"Excellent. I need you in Rome now."

"Where you think I am?"

He was on Piazza di Sant'Onofrio, smoking a cigarette and looking up at the Bambino Gesù Hospital.

"You're at the hospital?"

"Yes."

"Good man. How many helpers do you have?"

"Two guys."

"They're in the dark, right?"

"Not worry. They don't know nothing."

"I'll worry until this is finished. You know what to do."

"I know, I know," he said dismissively.

His flippancy wasn't appreciated. "Listen to me. These girls are vitally important. They are more important than you. They are more important than me. They are the two most important people on Earth."

Odorico visited Marta Di Marino in the Emergency Ward of the Jazzolino Hospital in Vibo Valentia where she was being held for observation.

"We gave her a tranquilizer," the nurse told her. "She's been sleeping, but she just woke up and we gave her some tea. When you're done with her, the doctor will decide if she can go home."

The policewoman parted the curtain and introduced herself.

"I was wondering when the police would come."

She was about the same age as the victim. Her hand was lightly shaking and Odorico saw where she had spilled some tea on her hospital gown.

"I know you've had a big shock, but I need to ask you some questions while everything is still fresh in your mind."

"Yes, yes. Please."

"Why did you go to Cinzia's apartment this morning?"

"We often go out together for a coffee on Saturdays. I rang and texted last night to confirm and when I didn't get a response, I rang a few more times. This morning, I was worried, so I went over. I don't live far. It was the most horrible thing I've ever seen. I don't want to see anything like that again, as long as I live."

"I know. It was terrible. It must have been a big shock. Tell me, how did you know Cinzia?"

"We teach at the same school."

"Chemistry?"

"I teach mathematics."

"How long have you known her?"

"Maybe thirteen years. We started at the school the same year."

"Has she ever been in trouble with the police?"

"Cinzia? My God, no, she's a good girl." She teared up and reached for a tissue. "She was a good girl."

"No drugs? No Walter White?" Odorico had consulted Google to atone for her ignorance of pop culture.

"I never saw her use drugs. Both of us watched *Breaking Bad* together and used to laugh about crazy chemistry teachers."

"Did she have any enemies?"

"Cinzia? Only friends. Everyone loved her. She was like sunshine."

"Did you also know the male victim, Ferruccio Gressani?"

"I met him a couple of times, years ago when they were together."

"When was that?"

"They broke up at least ten years ago. I didn't see him since then."

"You didn't know they were back together? That he was with her?"

"I didn't know he was here, that's for sure. I'm certain they weren't back together. She would have told me."

"But she didn't tell you he was here."

She shook her head sadly.

"Where did Ferruccio go after they split up?"

"He went to Spain, I think. He got a job there."

"Where in Spain? Doing what?"

"I don't know. She never talked about him."

"Did she have boyfriends since then?"

"Some relationships, sure, but nothing too serious. This is a small town. The fishermen of Vibo Valentia catch plenty of fish, but on land, there aren't so many good catches."

Odorico snorted knowingly. "So, no boyfriend now or recently?"

"Not for at least two years."

"Where did she meet Ferruccio? Years ago, I mean."

"At a party, I think. He was a local boy."

"From Vibo Valentia?"

"No, from Cessaniti."

"Why did they break up?"

"They broke up because she didn't love him. A good

reason. It wasn't a big, bad breakup. It just ended. He was sad, but that's life."

"When you knew him, was he into any bad shit? Drugs? The mob?"

"I wouldn't know. He seemed like a nice enough boy."

"Did he have a job?"

"He was a laboratory technician."

"Do you know where he worked?"

"Here, I think. This hospital."

"Do you know why he went to Spain?"

"I don't know, sorry."

Odorico's questions were exhausted and she seemed satisfied. "Okay. I think that's it, for now. Here's my card. If you remember anything else that you think could help the investigation, call me."

The woman took her card and said, "Whoever did this, Ferruccio must have been the target. Cinzia was just there. No one would want to hurt dear, sweet Cinzia."

Odorico tucked her notebook into her pocket. "You could be right."

"You've seen these things before, I'm sure. Will I ever be able to forget what I saw?"

Odorico reached for the woman's hand. "I'll be honest with you. With time, the memory will fade, but it will never completely go away."

It could not have been more convenient. Odorico's next stop was the personnel office of the hospital where she asked to review the employment records of Ferruccio Gressani. It was a thin file. Gressani had a degree in medical laboratory science and had been hired by the pathology lab at the Jazzolino Hospital fourteen years earlier. He was employed there for four years. He had a good work history with top assessments from his superior. Seven years ago, he gave his notice, telling his boss that he was taking a job in Madrid. That was it—there was nothing illuminating, except for an address in Cessaniti that, when she checked it, was a house in the name of a Manuela Gressani.

Cessaniti was a village of about three thousand residents ten kilometers from Vibo Valentia. Halfway there, it occurred to Odorico that this was going to be more than an interview—it was going to be a next-of-kin notification. The house was small and pretty with red shutters and flower boxes in the windows. A woman in her seventies answered the door, bent over with scoliosis, and she appeared baffled as to why a Carabinieri was calling.

"Are you Manuela Gressani?" Odorico asked.

"Yes, what do you want from me?"

"Is Ferruccio Gressani your son?"

The woman choked on a swallow and nodded.

"May I come in?"

The sitting room was clean and tidy. There was a photograph of Ferruccio on the mantel. Signora Gressani stood in the middle of the room. Because of her curved spine, she couldn't look the officer in the eye.

"Why don't you sit?" Odorico said.

She did, saying, "What is it? Is something the matter?"

Odorico took the lowest chair to be at the woman's eye level.

"When did you last see your son?"

"Not for a few years, but we speak all the time. Why?"

"And when did you last speak with him?"

"He called maybe two weeks ago."

"Where was he calling from?"

"He lives in Spain. In Madrid."

"Did you know that he was in Italy, in Calabria?"

"When?"

"Yesterday."

"I don't think so. He would have come to see me."

"Signora, I'm afraid I have to give you some terrible news. Ferruccio was killed last night in Vibo Valentia."

The woman said no, a few times, before asking the policewoman to repeat what she said. When it sunk in, she didn't scream, or even cry. She began to shake uncontrollably.

"Can I get you some water?" Odorico asked.

"Yes, some water."

Returning from the kitchen, Odorico saw her partially slumped over and thought she might have passed out, but she righted herself and took the glass.

"Are you sure it was my Ferruccio?"

"Yes. I'm sorry. Is there someone I can call to be with you? A friend, a relative?"

She ignored the question and asked, "Who would want to hurt him?"

"We don't know. The investigation has just begun."

"He was in Vibo Valentia?"

"Yes."

"Was he staying there?"

"He was with a woman who lives there. Her name is Cinzia Rondinelli."

"His old girlfriend. What does she say?"

"She was killed too."

"Oh, my God! Both of them? Who would do such a thing? Ferruccio is a beautiful boy. Such a good son. I didn't see him, but we talked and he sent me money all the time. He would say, 'Momma, go buy yourself something nice. Buy yourself a new television, a new radio. Anything you like.' He bought me jewelry. Do you see this bracelet? He sent me this for my birthday."

Odorico looked at the bracelet. It didn't look inexpensive. "It seems he was a good son. Do you know if there was anyone who might have wanted to harm Ferruccio?"

"Of course not."

"No one from when he was living in Italy?"

"No!"

"Did he say if he had gotten into any trouble in Spain?"

"Nothing like that. He had a good life in Spain."

"Doing what?"

"He worked in a hospital for the first few years."

"Which hospital?"

"I wrote it down on a piece of paper. I'm sure I can find it for you."

"After the hospital—then what?"

"I don't think he had another job. He won the lottery, you know. He made a lot of money from that. That's why he always had money for me."

"So, he retired in his thirties? Is that what he said?"

"When you win the lottery, you retire. Are you sure it was him? I don't believe it could have been my Ferruccio."

"Unfortunately, it's true, Signora. I'm sorry to ask, but it's my job to ask such questions. Is it possible that Ferruccio was involved with drugs? Selling illegal drugs?"

The woman sputtered and tried to rise, but she didn't

have the strength. "Don't you dare say something like that again. Ferruccio was never involved with drugs. He was a good boy!"

"I'm sure he was, but I had to ask. When he used to live in Calabria, were any of his friends into drugs? Were any involved with the mob, the 'Ndrangheta?"

"Do you mean Marco?"

"Who is Marco?"

"He was a boy Ferruccio knew from when he was young. Marco Zuliani. His whole family were criminals. I didn't like him and I told Ferruccio not to be his friend. I was happy when he and his people moved to Canada."

"When was that?"

"Oh, my God, it was a long time ago. Ferruccio was still living in Italy."

"So, more than ten years ago."

"I'd say so." She began to shake again. "Tell me, how can you be sure it was my son who got killed?"

15

When Marcus came down for breakfast, he spied Mickey at a table with Celeste and Colonel Carter. He was hung over and couldn't imagine a better way to kill off his brittle appetite than joining them. He was about to turn tail and order room service, when Mickey noticed him and called him over.

"The three of you solve all our mysteries?" Marcus asked, taking a chair.

"Still a few left," Mickey said.

Marcus ordered coffee only. He could tell by the way Mickey was moving his jaw that he was agitated.

"Do you know what Celeste just told me?"

Marcus had a pretty good idea. He stirred his coffee and waited for the reveal.

"She had one of her visions," Mickey said. "It was about the girls and their bone marrow transplants. Their doctor told them they were going to die. It's very troubling. However, I do have confidence in Dr. Spara."

"With all due respect to Celeste's legendary psychic abilities, don't believe every bit of bull flung at you."

Celeste smiled sweetly and Carter said, "Damn, that's one helluva burn."

"I'll tell you what's legendary," Mickey said, pointing a fork at him. "Her vision about the spacecraft and the Grays. Don't be so dismissive of things you don't understand."

Marcus missed the center of the saucer and almost tipped his cup. "Grays. I see you've been talking to the colonel."

"We met at the bar last night," Carter said. "Over some Roman libations, I gave Mr. Andreason a primer on alien abductions."

"And what are Roman libations?" Marcus asked.

"They had bourbon and they had ice and this is Rome," Carter replied.

"That's very good." Mickey chuckled. "Honestly, I learned a lot from the colonel. I've been involved with the military my entire career. Of course, I've heard about and read about UFO sightings—and, I've been dismissive. I recall asking an Air Force general about UFOs one night—another bar-room conversation—and he laughed off the subject. He told me that the Air Force program to document pilot sightings of UFOs that started up in the 1950s—Project Blue Book—was terminated in 1970 because it was, to use your term, bull. But the colonel tells me that the Pentagon was so inundated with credible pilot reports that in the early 2000s, they began a successor program called—what the hell was it called?"

"AATIP," Carter said. "Advanced Aerospace Threat Identification Program. The Navy owns it, owing to the fact that Navy pilots have become the largest group of reporters. It's a classified program, that was said to be shut down in 2012, but I'm assured by insiders that it's very much alive and well."

"He also told me all about his own database, U-AN. I was on the site half the night. Fascinating stuff, really fascinating. And then you consider, this Ruben Sanchez report about the white rooms, Grays, and an abductee named Helen. Then add it to Celeste's documented, contemporaneous vision and the statements from Victoria and Elizabeth's own mouths and what do we have? I'll tell you what we have. We have a very compelling case that my granddaughters were abducted by aliens and that their static ages and their illnesses are the result."

Poor guy, Marcus thought. *He's so desperate for answers that he's buying into this shit.* "Helen," Marcus said. "Not Elena."

"Nitpicking," Mickey replied.

Marcus finished his Americano and asked for a refill by pointing to a waiter and then his cup. "Why am I even here, Mickey? I mean, you've got this all figured out. Maybe I ought to get on a plane and head back to New York to see if my hot girlfriend will have me back. Wait. Never mind. I was the one who kicked her out, and she wasn't hot."

"You're here because we have to find Jesper and Elena. Until I have them back, I want all bases covered. You're a conventional base, I'll give you that, but you're still a base. With that in mind, please see what Major Lumaga's been up to. And after that, the girls asked after you. They want Uncle Marcus to come and play with them."

"When can I see them?" Carter asked.

"I don't know," Mickey said. "They'll be getting a battery of tests this afternoon. I'll get back to you."

"In that case," Carter said, his plate groaning under eggs, potatoes, and ham from the buffet, "I'll be off to the

Vatican. It's been on my bucket list for a dog's age. Want to come with me, Celeste?"

"I had a vision you would ask," she said.

"You're joking, right?" Carter said.

"Yes, Virgil, I'm joking. What time shall we go?"

"Okay, what do you have?" Lumaga asked Odorico.

"We received Cinzia's phone records," she said, passing the papers across his desk. "A Spanish mobile number we presume is Ferruccio's, begins calling Cinzia's mobile phone just over a week ago. Going back three years, there's not a single call from him and then he's calling every day until the day before the murders. We got his carrier to provide us with his locations. The first call was from Zaragoza, Spain, about one hundred kilometers from the French border. The next call was from Girona, near Barcelona. Then he's in France, in Montpelier. Then he's in Italy and he rings from Genoa, Pisa, Fiumicino, Salerno, then Vibo Valentia."

Lumaga shrugged. "So, he's like a lovesick puppy calling his ex-girlfriend as he drives across southern Europe to her doorstep. Where's his car, I wonder?"

"We found it. The night of the murder, residents around the corner from Cinzia reported a vehicle in flames. It had Spanish tags. We checked with the Spaniards. It was his car. The petrol cap was off, so we think someone stuck a rag in and lit it. It's down to bare metal."

"Kill the man, kill the car. What does that tell us?" Lumaga asked.

"There was possible evidence about the killer's identity in the car."

"Probably," Lumaga said. "Ferruccio's phone? Anything?"

"We've tried to geo-locate it, but it's turned off or it's destroyed."

"Have the Spanish police been helpful?"

"Quite helpful. They gained entry to Ferruccio's apartment in Madrid. It didn't look like he'd been living there for a while. They're still going through the place, but so far, there was nothing of an illegal nature."

"What about what his mother told you?"

"The police checked on his story. It's true that he left his job in Madrid about five years ago. He was working in a hospital as a technician and apparently, he was a good employee. He didn't provide a reason for his resignation. The hospital didn't know where he went and didn't provide any references. For the last five years, he didn't pay anything into the Spanish social security system and wasn't signed on for healthcare."

"But he maintained an apartment. How'd he pay his rent?"

"The landlord got his rent in cash every three months in advance by mail."

Lumaga raised an eyebrow. "That's unusual, wouldn't you say?"

"Quite unusual. What he told his mother about winning the lottery seems to be a lie. There's no record of a Ferruccio Gressani winning anything."

Lumaga furiously tapped his pen on a pad. "This guy's got to be up to something and that something has to be drugs. He leaves a good job, drops off the grid, keeps his apartment although he lives somewhere else and pays his rent in cash, gives his mother expensive gifts, and—oh yeah, he's murdered in a professional hit. Drugs, drugs, drugs."

"And let's not forget his old friend, Marco Zuliani," Odorico said. "His nickname was Zulio. We've got a file on him and his family as thick as the Naples phonebook. They were significant heroin traffickers in their day. Unless they found God or joined the circus, they're probably still in the business."

"A good number of 'Ndrangheta set up shop in Canada, especially Toronto. You need to contact the authorities there."

"Already did. I'm expecting a call-back from Toronto."

"Very nice work, Fabiana."

She looked pleased. "Thank you, Major."

He shooed her away by waving the back of his hand. "Now solve these murders quickly and get back onto the Andreason case, all right?"

The Carabinieri officers guarding the door checked Marcus's identification against the approved visitor list before allowing him into the room. As soon as they saw him, the girls sprang from their beds for hugs. They both had butterfly ports in their hands for their latest transfusions. Their color was good and it seemed their energy had improved.

"Uncle Marcus!" Victoria said. "You came!"

"You called and here I am."

"Are you going to play with us?" Elizabeth asked.

"That's why I'm here. Pick your game."

Victoria ran to a table and picked a board game from a stack. Mickey had finally found something the American

Embassy could do for him: staffers somehow got their hands on English versions of children's games, new in the box.

"Candyland!" she exclaimed, holding it up.

"It's been a good while since I played," he said, "but I don't expect to lose."

"No, I'm going to win," Victoria said.

"No, me," Elizabeth insisted.

With the two girls cross-legged on one of the beds and Marcus in a pulled-up chair, Elizabeth took home game number one, much to Victoria's consternation. Marcus waited until the next game to ask them questions.

"How're you guys feeling?"

"Good," they both said.

"Did you see Dr. Spara today?"

"You mean Bruno Bear?" Elizabeth said.

"Is that what you call him?"

"It's what he calls himself, silly," Victoria said.

"He came while we were having our cereal," Elizabeth said. "He's really nice."

"That's good," Marcus said. "Did he give you any medicine yet?"

"Oh, yes," Elizabeth said. "Bruno Bear calls them magic beans. I can swallow them, but Victoria can't."

"You can't?" Marcus asked her playfully.

The girl made a gagging sound, making Elizabeth laugh.

"They crushed mine in gelato," Victoria said.

"I got jealous and they gave me a scoop of gelato too," Elizabeth said.

"Well, I hope the medicine makes you completely better."

"Are you married to Celeste?" Victoria asked suddenly.

"No, I'm not married to her."

The little girl seemed awfully curious about him and she kept drilling. "Where do you live?"

"In America."

"Were your children sad when you left them to come see us?"

"I don't have children."

"Why?"

What was he going to say? That his wife wanted children, but he didn't? That if he had it all to do over again, he'd make different choices? That now he was pretty much all alone?

"I don't know, honey," he said. "If I knew that kids could be as special as you two, I might have had some."

"You can be our daddy," Victoria said innocently, and Elizabeth concurred.

That brought out a handkerchief. He wiped his eyes and told them that was far and away the nicest thing he'd ever been told.

16

Marcus walked back to the hotel blowing cigarette smoke into the bright blue sky. The grounds of the hospital were off-limits to the media, but outside the gate to the main entrance, the satellite trucks were massed, jamming traffic. He made it through a scrum of smoking and vaping reporters who, unaware of his connection, let him pass unimpeded. He reached for his phone and called Lumaga.

"How goes it in Rome?" Lumaga asked.

"You were right about the media. It's crazy."

"Most of the parasites clung to your fur and left with you. It's good for us. The girls? How are they?"

"They're getting medicine. They look better."

"Good, good."

"Anything new on the investigation?"

"I wish the answer was yes," Lumaga said. Marcus visualized the deep shrug that probably accompanied the statement. "Frankly, I'm getting the same feeling as four years ago. No leads, no positive energy. There are no CCTV images that capture pictures of our girls riding in cars near Filarete, no eyewitnesses who saw the girls arrive at the gates of the villa, or, I might add, only half-joking, no reports of

UFOs hovering over the villa, no fingerprints at the villa other than people we know, no calls to our confidential hotline, nothing. We don't know who returned them, how they were returned and we have nothing to add to our large pile of previous nothingness about the fate of the parents. Then, on top of this, a new difficult case has landed in my lap, and my life—domestic and professional—can best be characterized as shit."

"What's the new case?"

"Double murder. A young couple. Probably related to drugs, possibly related to the 'Ndrangheta."

"Sucks to be you, Roberto."

"And I believe it also sucks to be you, Marcus."

Determined to avoid his constant companions, Marcus decided to flee the hotel at 7 p.m. His plan was to honor his promise to call in on the girls for another game of Candyland before visiting hours lapsed, then find a secluded café for a solo dinner and as much Scotch as he could put away without falling over. Predictably, the plan got scuppered almost before it began when he ran into Celeste and Carter entering the lobby, toting bags from the Vatican Gift Shop.

"Where you off to?" Carter asked cheerily.

"Out," he replied.

"We can see that," Celeste said. "We had the most enjoyable day, didn't we, Virgil?"

"That we did. My wristwatch tells me that my feet are aching for a damned good reason. We walked fourteen thousand steps, give or take. That museum goes on forever. Good collectors, the Catholics."

"The only thing we didn't see was the Holy Father," Celeste said.

"Someone probably neglected to tell him you'd be coming," Marcus said. "Look, I've got to run."

"Not joining us for dinner?" the colonel asked. "Mickey's invited us out to someplace great. We got texts. Did you get a text?"

He had. He'd ignored it. "I don't think I did," he lied. "Give him my regrets when you see him. I've got an appointment."

"Any developments?" Celeste asked.

"Nothing on my end."

"Well, I've got a development," Carter said. "I let my followers on social media know that I was in Italy working on the Andreason return. I got an email from CUFOM this afternoon and they are mobilizing like crazy to help us." Carter searched Marcus's blank face and said, "Hell, you probably don't know what CUFOM is."

"I probably don't," Marcus said.

"Now, I'm probably going to make a hash of the Italian pronunciation, but it's the Centro Ufologico Mediterraneo. It's a sister organization to mine. It runs the leading Italian and southern Mediterranean site for UFO sightings. They've got members all over the country who report on UFO phenomenology and alien abductions. Their president, a very good guy named Antonio, is someone I've been seeing at conferences for years. Well, he's agreed to put out an alert to his whole membership soliciting any and all reports of unusual activity in the skies over Calabria and Filarete the night the girls returned. I was emailing him in the Sistine Chapel of all places. I can tell you that Antonio is a guy who can get shit done. My guess is, by tomorrow, we're going to have a ton of photos and videos to review."

Marcus sighed and said, "That's very exciting but you're going to have to excuse me. I've really got to get going. Have a nice time tonight."

Outside the hospital, the media presence had melted away for the night. Marcus breezed in, not relishing another turn at a childish board game, but looking forward to seeing the girls. He never supposed he'd bond with a couple of young kids, but then again, there was a lot about his life he never anticipated.

When he got off the elevator at the Hematology ward and looked down the hall, he noticed something was off. The Carabinieri guard wasn't stationed outside their room. If the policeman had to take a lavatory break or needed a coffee, the correct procedure would be to radio for a colleague to come up from the lobby. Maybe they were getting lax. He made a mental note to complain.

As he pushed the door open, he prepared himself for an onslaught of cuteness and cuddles, but that didn't happen.

He processed things fast, a holdover from his Agency days.

The Carabinieri officer, laid out on the floor, zip-tied and gagged, bleeding from a head wound.

Two men, both in hospital scrubs, lab coats, and surgical masks, one blond with long hair, one brown-haired, each hunched over a girl, taping their mouths shut.

He didn't have a plan. He was an unarmed fifty-four-year-old about to confront two much younger adversaries.

He heard himself shout, "Hey!"

The blond turned first, dropping his roll of tape. A flick

knife appeared from the pocket of his jacket so quickly it seemed like magic.

"Out. Get out," the blond man said with a Slavic accent. To Marcus, the most unnerving part of it was the quiet, professional tone.

The brown-haired guy turned too and emptied his hands.

Elizabeth gave out a muffled cry.

"Girls, stay where you are!" Marcus shouted.

"Okay, mister," the blond man said. "Time to die."

Marcus did what anyone would do. He screamed at the top of his lungs. "Help!"

For all the potential scrapes and dodgy situations he'd encountered in life, he'd only been in one fight where there was the actual threat of grievous bodily harm. It was when he was a college freshman and it involved defending the honor of a girl he didn't even know when he drunkenly waded into a group of boozed-up idiots wielding beer bottles. He gave a spirited showing of himself, charging them with an aluminum trash can before getting the crap beat out of him and spending a day in the infirmary with a broken nose and a cracked rib. During his induction training at CIA, he was schooled in various self-defense techniques, but as an operations officer he had never used his fists, his feet, or a weapon, and besides, the training was half a lifetime ago.

Brown-haired man was closer and made contact first, a two-armed tackle around his waist, bringing him to the floor. The guy was strong and he was able to work his hands up from Marcus's torso to his neck. At the first squeeze, Marcus felt the terror of air-hunger. He reacted by violently bringing his right knee into his attacker's groin. The man's grip loosened and Marcus was able to roll away, but just then, he felt an excruciating pain in his left shoulder, near the tip of his collarbone, where blond man managed to plant his flick knife.

It came as a surprise to him that he didn't cry out. Instead, the sharp pain seemed to infuse him with a raging burst of strength. He found himself on his feet, his fists balled up, a moment before brown-haired man tackled him to the floor again. This time, he didn't let the brute get anywhere near his neck or face. He pummeled him in the temples with alternating rights and lefts, while out of the corner of his eye, he saw blond man preparing another knife assault.

Both girls must have peeled off their mouth tape, because he heard them screaming and crying. He felt something hard against his leg, the policeman's leather holster. He reached for it, found the snap, and when the Beretta Cougar was in his right hand, he got his thumb on the rear-mounted safety and clicked it down. While he was fumbling, brown-haired man was capitalizing on his wandering arm by getting hands around his neck again.

He didn't know if there was a round in the chamber, but the blast was the answer to his prayer.

The slug entered brown-haired man's side, tearing through his liver and intestines. Impossibly, he managed to crush his thumbs down even harder onto Marcus's larynx, but before he could choke him out, Marcus fired three more times into the same spot.

The pressure dissipated and the man's body went slack.

The room was hazy and fouled with gunpowder.

The girls were hysterical.

The door to the room opened and a nurse appeared, recoiling in terror.

Marcus raised the Beretta, but blond man, with a cat-like move, got one arm looped around the nurse's neck and put his knife-hand to her throat, positioning her as a shield.

The nurse screamed and blond man calmly said, "Shh-shh," and backed her out the door.

Marcus told the girls to stay in the room and followed blond man into the hall, leaking blood from his shoulder.

The hall was filling with hospital staff. Marcus shouted at them to get back and call the police.

Blond man kept dragging his hostage backwards at a fast clip until he was at the elevator. He pressed the down button with the bloody tip of his knife.

Marcus followed along the corridor and kept the man's head in the pistol sights, but even an expert marksman wouldn't have contemplated the shot. The elevator doors slid open and blond man backed himself and the nurse inside.

Staff reappeared from inside the rooms where they had fled.

"Go help the girls!" Marcus shouted. "Did anyone call the police?"

No one had. He ran for the stairwell and clicked the Beretta's safety in case he tripped up on the way down.

The elevator stopped on the first floor where blond man roughly ejected the nurse, sending her to her knees.

When the doors opened again in the lobby, the white lab coat and mask were on the ground, the knife was in the breast pocket of his scrubs, and blond man slowly exited with a benign smile on his face, after pressing a button and sending the elevator back up.

The Carabinieri must have gotten the alert, because as blond man casually sauntered across the lobby, two officers passed him running toward the elevators. One of the descending elevators reached the lobby and the policemen scrambled in, punching in the girls' floor.

By the time Marcus exited the stairway at the lobby level, he was feeling the pain from his stabbing. He pressed forward. There was no sign of unusual activity in the lobby, so he ran out the sliding doors into the hospital forecourt where an ambulance was speeding away. As it turned right out of the gate, he saw a shock of blond hair in the passenger seat.

A man had just dropped off a passenger at the front doors when Marcus approached him, waving the Beretta.

"I'm sorry," he said, pulling the driver's side door open. "I'm taking your car."

One look at a bleeding man with a gun convinced him to abandon his Hyundai and flee into the hospital. Marcus put the car into gear and took off after the ambulance.

The Passeggiata del Gianicolo that hugged the hospital grounds was a tight, winding road lined by ancient stone walls. Marcus redlined the small engine uphill and just when he thought the chase was going to be futile, he entered a stretch of extreme hairpin turns, requiring heavy braking to stay on the pavement. He glanced to his left in the direction of the Tiber and saw the white ambulance with its orange side-stripe. The switchback was so extreme that it almost seemed he could have thrown the Hyundai owner's can of soda out the window and hit the ambulance.

He honked his horn aggressively to let the ambulance know that it was being pursued and that's when he saw blond man gesticulating to the driver and pointing straight at him.

"That's right, asshole," Marcus said in a rant powered by adrenaline. He lowered his window and raised the gun as a symbol of his rage. "That's right. I'm coming for you."

He accelerated and then immediately had to brake when he entered the chicane. The ambulance did the same, but when it came to the next chicane, its high center of gravity defeated the driver's best efforts and it skidded hard into the side of a parked car.

Marcus saw the accident ahead and aggressively accelerated until he was alongside, then slammed on his brakes, pinning the ambulance against the caved-in Volkswagen.

He leapt out of the Hyundai, swearing and shouting and tried getting the Beretta into a proper two-handed firing position, but his left arm was too painful.

The driver had no such problem. He flung open his door and did a barrel roll onto the road, expertly landing belly-down, and with both hands he aimed a semi-automatic pistol at Marcus at a distance of under half a car length.

Marcus started squeezing rounds off with his unbraced right hand. He made up for lack of accuracy by rapidly emptying the Beretta's clip. His second or third round caught the driver on the top of his head, eliminating the threat before a single shot came his way.

In the fog of the moment, Marcus forgot about blond man.

He didn't know he had exited the ambulance from the rear doors.

He didn't see him come up behind him holding an oxygen cylinder.

He didn't process the heavy blow he took to the back of his head or hear the other drivers shouting at blond man who calmly got into the Hyundai and drove off.

He wasn't aware of the drivers and pedestrians yelling at each other to call the police.

And he didn't hear a couple of dog-walkers standing over him and asking, "Is he alive?"

Marcus's Story

17

Washington DC, twelve years earlier

"You came," Alice said.

His wife was in a bed on the thoracic surgery floor of the George Washington University Hospital. Marcus put his bag down. He was clutching a small bouquet from the hospital florist. He had thought the larger ones would give the impression he was trying too hard.

"I wasn't sure I'd make it before you were discharged," he said. That's when he noticed a tube running into a collection bag hanging off one of the bed rails. "What's that?"

"That's why I'm still here. It's a chest tube. They had to put it in to keep my lung inflated."

He thought she looked wilted and drained of color, like an unwatered house plant kept too long in the shade. He, on the other hand, was the strongest and fittest he had been in years. He'd been on a healthy eating kick and had joined a gym in Paris, near the Embassy.

He put the flowers on her bed tray. "Does that mean there was a complication?"

She used the bed controls to raise the head higher. "I was told it might be something they had to do. It's not good; it's not bad."

He leaned over and gave her a peck on the cheek and looked around for a vase. She hit the call bell and when a nurse came in, she asked for one.

"Aren't those pretty?" the nurse said, using her bandage scissors to cut away the cellophane.

"I'm the husband," Marcus said. "How's she doing?"

"Hello, husband. She's a star patient. Need more pain meds, hon?"

"I'm all right for now," Alice said.

Alone again, Marcus pulled up a chair.

"You going to take your coat off?" she said.

It was a week before the winter solstice—it was as cold in Washington as it was in Paris. He removed his wet overcoat and draped it over his chair. Through the window, the darkening sky reminded Marcus of a poorly erased, streaky chalkboard.

"The weather sucks," he said.

"You came right from the airport?"

"Yeah. Do they have the results of the biopsy yet?"

"I'm expecting the doctor to tell me on his evening rounds."

"I'll wait, if you don't mind."

"Why would I mind? You're the husband."

The husband. A statement of fact. It was, perhaps, the best way to describe him with respect to her. He wasn't an attentive husband, or a loving husband. Their marriage, their relationship, had become transactional and flying four thousand miles to visit her on her sickbed was a transaction, something required.

"That would make you, the wife," he said, instantly regretting it. He detected a flicker of a grimace, but wasn't sure if it was a reaction to him or physical pain.

"How long will you be here?" she asked.

Before he could answer, she had a painful coughing fit. He rose and she pointed to a plastic box with an attached tube.

"What is it?" he asked.

She took it from him and breathed into it hard, lifting a row of four balls on columns of air.

"I'm supposed to use it every hour," she said. "It keeps my airways open."

"A week," he said. "I'm on leave for a week."

"That's not very long."

"It's as much as I could get. There's something going down."

She didn't ask anything about it. She was well trained.

"I'll take the week. I could use some help at the house. I was thinking of moving a bed into your study so I could avoid the stairs. Bill's got a bad back, but Janie could help you."

"Is that necessary?"

"I'm just making contingency plans."

"How are they?"

Janie and Bill—her sister and brother-in-law. Not his biggest fans.

"They've been great. They'll be in later."

They talked about banal, household matters for a while

before Alice made an offhanded comment about craving a cigarette.

"Really?" he said with equal measures of amazement and anger. "You're not planning on kicking the habit?"

"It depends," she said. "If it's good news, I'll quit. I'm not stupid. If it's bad news—fuck it—why deprive myself of my few pleasures?"

His typical response would have been to tell her that she was stupid for smoking all those years, but he censored himself. "Well, hopefully, you'll be quitting. It's about time."

"You should talk," she said.

The surgeon swept in, accompanied by his surgical residents and medical students. He was big and tall with hands the size of beavers' tails. Marcus would have bet the farm that he had played college ball.

"Brought the whole team," Marcus said.

The surgeon winked but otherwise ignored him and went straight to Alice's bedside.

"How're you feeling?" he asked.

"The tube's a little uncomfortable."

He checked the drainage bag. "The x-ray looked good. We'll plan on getting it out tomorrow morning."

"Can I leave then?"

"Probably. We'll make the call in the afternoon. So, you're probably on pins and needles about what we found."

"More like swords and daggers," she said.

"Good one," the surgeon said. "I might steal that. Look, it shouldn't be a shock as we talked about this pre-op. The MRI was very suggestive of a malignancy, especially with your smoking history. The biopsy has confirmed that it's lung cancer. It's a type called non-small cell cancer, which is the most common one in smokers."

"Did you remove it?" Marcus said.

The surgeon half-turned to include him in the conversation. "Are you Mr. Handler?" he asked. "If we've met, I apologize."

"I just got here. I work in France."

"I see. I did remove the mass. It was fairly large."

"Did you get it all?" Marcus asked.

"Ninety-plus percent. We call that de-bulking. We'll treat the rest with radiation and chemo."

"Can it be cured?" Marcus asked.

The surgeon turned back to the bed and didn't answer him. Marcus felt vestigial. He wondered if his wife had given the impression that she was functionally single.

"Alice, we biopsied a number of lymph nodes in your mediastinum—the central core of the chest—and we had a colleague from the abdominal surgery team come in and do a needle biopsy of that suspicious area in your liver. All the biopsies were positive for non-small cell cancer originating from the lung. The chances are overwhelming that the mass in your brain is the same."

Marcus felt wobbly. He steadied himself with the chair-back. She hadn't told him anything about masses in the liver and brain.

Alice simply said, "Oh."

"The medical oncologist is going to see you, hopefully tonight," the surgeon said. "I expect that you'll be started on an aggressive cocktail of chemotherapy and targeted radiation therapy to the lesions in the chest, liver, and brain.

I'll see you in the surgery clinic in a week, but the oncologists are going to take over from here. Okay?"

"What's the prognosis here?" Marcus demanded.

The surgeon showed some white teeth, put one of his huge hands on Marcus's shoulder—Marcus wondered how he could do his job with those paws—and said, "Let's see what the oncologist says. Those folks have all the stats at their fingertips."

They had their answer a few hours later. Marcus almost missed the visit. He had gone down to the cafeteria for a bite and when he returned, the oncology attending, a bird-like woman with clipped and precise speech, was already there.

The outlook was grim. She didn't sugar-coat it. The surgeon hadn't mentioned that her bone scan was also positive. The cancer was pretty much everywhere.

"Yours is a very extensive malignancy," she said. "We'll know fairly soon whether your tumor is chemo-responsive. If it is, you've got months. If it isn't—weeks. I wish I had better news. I recommend starting your infusions before you're discharged."

Neither of them asked many questions and the doctor acknowledged that as she was leaving. She gave them both her card and told them that she was sure the questions would come. She closed the door behind her.

"Looks like I haven't had my last cigarette," Alice said.

His boss's, boss's, boss kept him waiting for over half an hour in his anteroom with nothing to do but trying not to stare at his perfumed administrative assistant. Every time he came back to Langley, he was reminded why he hated working there and why he never intended to return for a permanent posting. The sea of eager faces and dark suits, the frenetic display as people race-walked through the complex to make themselves appear to be hurrying to meetings of great import, the mind-numbing paperwork and bureaucracy. His appointment was with Dennis Correia, the Assistant Director, Europe Division of the NCS, the clandestine service. How Correia knew he was in town was a very minor mystery; Marcus figured there was some sort of HR-sourced alert within the NCS when a field officer was stateside on leave. He had been in plenty of in-person and video-link meetings with Correia, but had never had a one-on-one. He knew what the agenda was going to be. It was patently obvious.

Correia was appropriately apologetic when he finally arrived. He was about the same age as Marcus, a forty-something lawyer by training, Ivy-League polished, with a helping of smarminess. He had his assistant bring in a pot of coffee that he poured himself into weirdly dainty china cups.

"How's your wife?" was his first question. "Alice."

"How'd you know about her?"

"Jim told me."

Jim Alicante was his immediate superior, the station chief in Paris.

"She's home. Recovering."

"Cancer, right?"

"Yeah."

"I'm sorry. Must be rough. She stayed in Virginia for your deployment, I understand."

There were a lot of secrets rattling around the Agency. His personal life wasn't one of them.

"When we came back from Bonn, I promised her she wouldn't have to do it again."

"We didn't make the same promise to you, I imagine."

"I knew I'd probably get posted again."

"You're twenty-two years in, right?"

"Correct."

"Came right in after college."

"Correct."

Correia pointed to his own head. "There's a lot of institutional knowledge in that noggin."

"I suppose there is."

"And they're hyper-aware of that."

They was the FSB. The meeting had just pivoted.

"They know a lot about me, yes."

"Is that his angle—Burakov? That he's courting you—trying to take you to the prom?"

"That's what he's telling his people."

"And what are you telling your people?"

Marcus felt his face flush. "Excuse me?"

He repeated the question, sipping from his dainty cup.

"I'm telling my people that I'm recruiting him. Want to know why I'm telling them that? Because it's what I'm doing."

Correia smiled. "Okay, take it easy. It's my job to worry. FSB first-rank captains come around once in a career—ten-carat, flawless diamonds. Everyone in the building, right up to the director, knows you've got a big fish on the line. I get questions. Who's recruiting who, I'm asked? Everyone's scared shitless about every outcome but one—a nice clean deal where Vasily Burakov takes the leap, is exfiled to Maryland, and over the ensuing months, spills enough beans to compete with Starbucks. We don't want blowback. Seeing as you were in town, I wanted to get briefed—horse's mouth."

Marcus didn't like the guy, but there was nothing to be gained by making it obvious. He let his anger dissipate like steam from the release-valve on a pressure cooker and said, "Burakov is using the cover of grooming me to meet at FSB's safe houses in Versailles, Saint-Cloud, other suburbs."

"Purpose-built?"

"We think so. They aren't properties we were aware of. Short-term rentals, probably."

"How do you get to them?"

"Different every time. I take a taxi to this hotel or that hotel, have a drink in the bar and a cruiser puts a few eurocents on my table. The number of coins corresponds to a stall in the lobby men's room—numbered left to right. Taped to the bottom of the tank is an envelope with a parking ticket for a nearby lot and car keys. Inside the car's glovebox is an address and the location of a public parking lot. I drive, park, and hoof it to the house."

"And Burakov's the only one there?"

"He's the only one who shows himself. Could be mice, though."

"But everything that transpires is recorded on brilliant HD video and Dolby audio."

"Every syllable, I'm sure."

"And you feed him intel during these sessions."

"The stuff that your people feed me, a mixture of noise mixed with a few nuggets. The nuggets are feeding the habit."

"When do you do the real business with Burakov?"

"When we're done at the house, he walks me to the nearest taxi rank. We exchange memory sticks. Mine has info, like on how we're going to exfil him, his wife, and his sons who're all with him in Paris, proposals on upfront cash and ongoing stipends, living arrangements in the States—the usual housekeeping. His contains the open-the-kimono intel he's giving us to prove his bona fides. You've seen it. It's mostly gold."

"There's some good stuff. It's not the 1849 strike, but Burakov knows his way around the FSB. He knows where the bodies are buried because he's buried a lot of them. When does his exfil happen?"

"About a month from now."

"What about your wife?"

"What about her?"

"Come on, Marcus, you know what I mean."

"I'll deliver Burakov. Then I'll request compassionate leave to tend the home fires."

"I'm sure it'll be granted."

"Thank you."

"How do you know he's not going to double up?"

"I don't. That's going to be your job to figure out once he's in Maryland."

"And how do we know you won't be the one to take thirty pieces of silver?"

He barely stopped himself from telling Correia to fuck himself and said, "You don't. Want to polygraph me?"

More teeth. "I'm glad you offered. The lab boys can take you this morning."

18

Marcus had never been particularly friendly with Alice's sister and now, in the wake of her diagnosis, their relationship had entered a zone of borderline hostility. With Alice in his study and Janie and her husband in the guest bedroom, he felt like a stranger in his own house. After a restless night with a bottle of Scotch on his bedside table, Marcus found himself alone with Janie in the kitchen. Alice was sleeping late, Bill was off jogging around their Reston, Virginia, neighborhood.

"It's not true, is it?" she asked as he installed a new coffee filter.

"What's not true?"

"That you're going back to France."

"Just for a short while."

"How long is a short while?"

"A month, tops."

Her arms were folded across her chest so tightly, it looked like she was wearing a straitjacket. "She's got terminal cancer, Marcus."

"I'm acutely aware of that. I've got some urgent business to tidy up. When I'm done, I'll be asking for an extended leave."

"The chemo's going to make her sick. Bill and I can only stay another week. We've got jobs."

"I'm going to arrange for her to have a nurse who'll stay with her if it's necessary. She's got a lot of friends in Reston who've been calling to help."

The woman couldn't contain her fury. "Your vows, Marcus. For richer, for poorer, in sickness and in health."

"I remember them."

"Do you?"

"Yeah, Janie, I do. I'm sure you mean well, but you're an outside observer trying to figure out another couple's marriage."

"I've had a bird's-eye view for over twenty years. Alice has told me everything. Everything. Your drinking. Your affairs. Your emotional abuse. Everything."

He listened while watching the coffee drip into the pot. "Then you know about her affairs too, right?"

"What did you expect her to do? She was looking for some comfort in the face of a barren relationship."

"I guess we were both looking for something."

"Why didn't you just bugger off? Go off and do whatever you do and let her find herself?"

"I don't know, Janie, I just didn't. You'd have to ask Alice that question too."

"I have. She was in love with you, the poor thing. She still is."

His study smelled like a sick room—a sick room with cigarettes. She stuck with her vow to keep smoking and he didn't give her any grief about it. The night before his departure, he pulled his desk chair up to her bedside and sipped a Scotch. They shared a cigarette. The chemo was making her weak and she'd been puking her guts out. The first visiting nurse scolded her so much about the smoking that they had to get the agency to send a more tolerant one. Janie and Bill had left for Tennessee, timing their departure to a slot when Marcus was out shopping. He counted it as a win-win.

"This is important, right?" she asked. "What you're doing."

"It's important."

"Preventing the world from ending important? Or America's going to kick Russia's ass important?"

"The latter."

"Do we still need to kick their ass?"

"Beats me," he said. "I'm not a policy guy."

She accidentally blew smoke toward him and used her hand to dissipate the cloud. "Maybe we should stop trying to kick each other's asses," she said.

"A damn fine idea."

"If I survive this thing—"

"You'll beat it."

"I appreciate the sentiment. *If* I survive it, then I was thinking, maybe we can try to make a go of it. For the sake of the water under the bridge."

There was a lot of water under the bridge. They had met at Georgetown when he was getting his master's in political science. She was only a freshman, a literature major. He'd already been contacted by a recruiter when they met, so it was fair to say that their entire life together was overshadowed by the Agency. He did his training at

Camp Peary, the infamous CIA Farm, while she was still an undergraduate. There, he took a fair bit of stick for his name. "So, what are you, born to the fucking job, Handler? Going to be a spy Handler? Good thing your name wasn't Asswiper."

His first assignment was to Langley as a counterintelligence analyst and he rode a desk until Alice graduated. As soon as she was relocatable, he got a transfer to the National Clandestine Service. His initial posting was to the US Embassy in Ankara where he got his feet wet in tradecraft and playing possum with the Soviets. Alice was fluent in Spanish and French and she got jobs in Turkey as a freelance translator for American publishers. Thus, they began their lives, shuttling back and forth between foreign and domestic appointments. During one extended stretch at Langley, they bought their house in Reston and Alice landed an editorial job at a publishing company based in Washington. She was well liked and they let her work remotely when she returned to foreign postings with Marcus—Rome, Lisbon, Madrid, Bonn.

Three years earlier, she'd balked at Paris. She just couldn't do another one, at least, not with him. They didn't call it a separation. They didn't call it anything. He went and she stayed. He started seeing a woman, a neighbor in his building. He assumed Alice was seeing someone at her company. Don't ask, don't tell.

"Yeah, for the sake of the water," he said. "Definitely."

"You'll come back? Permanently?"

"Why not?" he said. "Time to let the younger guys save the world."

"Will they let you?"

"I'm not a slave. I'll leave if they don't. Must be someone out there who'll hire me to do something."

"Promise?" she asked.

"Yeah, I promise. Can I ask you something?"

"That's a silly question. I hope your real question is better."

"Why'd you stay married to me?"

"I thought about it. You know I did. Every time I got close, I pulled back from the edge."

"Why?"

"Because I remembered the way we were together in the early days. We were good. And I always said to myself, Alice, maybe we can be good again. Also, I didn't have the energy to plan another wedding."

He snorted half a laugh, half a cry.

"We should have had kids," she said.

"You think?"

She lit a new cigarette from the dying stub of the last one.

"It makes me sad," she said, "Who's going to worry about you when I'm gone?"

Marcus liked Jim Alicante better than any of the station chiefs he'd worked for. He was a guy's guy who didn't act like most of the stick-up-the-ass preppy types who got promoted to management jobs. He was blunt, a little rough around the edges, and he had a wicked sense of humor. And he wasn't the least bit ashamed of letting his blue-collar roots show. Marcus found it refreshing. When he was younger, he hadn't been as comfortable with his own less-than exalted pedigree. His father had been an accountant at a small, strip-mall tax firm, his mother a kindergarten teacher. He always resented the rich kids at Georgetown, and at CIA he despised the Ivy-League types who pranced around the director's suite on the seventh floor at Langley like they were the chosen ones.

The Chancery of the US Embassy in Paris was a neoclassical fortress on the Avenue Gabriel. From his fourth-floor office, Alicante had a good view over the gardens of the Champs-Élysées. The sunlight that morning was impossibly bright. Others might have adjusted the blinds or pulled the curtains. Not Alicante. He put on his sunglasses and said, "Nice day for a defection."

"That it is," Marcus agreed.

"Run me through the logistics."

"I'll be leaving in two hours for the Grand Hôtel du Palais Royal. As per usual, I'll be picking up a car nearby and I'll drive to the designated meet point. We'll have two follow teams. When Burakov leaves the meet house with me, Team One will take both of us to the safe house in Montreuil. Team Two will pick up his wife and kids at the Galeries Lafayette where they'll be shopping. Once everyone's assembled in Montreuil, we'll move out to 123 Airbase Orléans-Bricy, where a Learjet is fueled and ready."

Alicante grinned. "If I asked you what could possibly go wrong, would you have time to get to the meet?"

"We'd still be talking at midnight."

"Figured as much. You flying out with him?"

"That's the plan."

"One-way ticket?"

Marcus nodded.

"I'll miss you. All I'll have left are the guys with positive attitudes."

"You know I've got to go."

"How's she doing?"

"The chemo's a rough ride. I should have left a week ago."

"She's not on her own, is she?"

"Her sister's there again."

"Well, Godspeed, man. I'll light a candle for you and one for her."

He needed a clear head, but one lousy Scotch on the rocks wasn't going to be clouding anything. Before settling into the hotel bar, he checked out the lobby men's room and saw three stalls. He resisted the urge to search all of them for the envelope, and simply splashed his face with cold water. While he waited, he got a text from Janie. Alice had a fever and she was taking her to George Washington Hospital. She finished with: When the hell are you going to be here? He texted back: Tomorrow. For good.

The wait was longer than usual and he broke down and ordered a second drink. A youngish fellow in a dark suit flashed by and dropped two coins onto his table. He paid the tab and retrieved the envelope from the second stall.

It was a new meet house in Saclay, about twenty kilometers from the hotel, near the University of Paris-Saclay. He parked the car on the periphery of the university and found the property hidden by a high hedge, a modest post-war house on a narrow residential road.

Burakov answered the door, dressed casually in a cardigan and dark slacks. He seemed too relaxed. If the shoe were on the other foot, he'd be amped up.

"Marcus, did you hit much traffic? I wondered where you were."

"The traffic was ridiculous. It took twice as long as I thought."

"Come, come, it's not the nicest house we've had, but it's well stocked. My colleagues made sure to put in your favorite Scotch. You want one?"

Marcus looked around the living room for the cameras. He didn't spot any right away, but they were there.

"Yeah, just a small one."

"A small one!" Burakov laughed. "Next you'll be telling me you want tea instead."

"I hate tea."

Burakov poured two drinks, both of them large, and settled onto the sofa next to him.

"I have something to show you," he said.

"What's that?" Marcus asked.

"Have a look." He pointed to a blue folder on the coffee table.

Marcus opened it and pulled out the single sheet. He read the text quickly, then read it again, letting it sink in.

It was a day-old wire-transfer confirmation to a numbered account in a Geneva-based bank for six million dollars.

"What's this?" he asked.

"A down payment."

"You're going to have to spell it out for me."

"It's a down payment on your new life."

He had to play it for the cameras, for Burakov's masters.

"That's very generous, Vasily. I'm still working through some things before I can definitively commit."

"Your wife."

"Yeah, my wife."

"How is she?"

"Not well."

"I'm sorry. But look, Marcus, I'm authorized to tell you that a further six million will be transferred in six months' time, subject to satisfactory progress. We'll immediately enter into a debriefing mode wherein you'll meet with me under the guise of continuing to attempt to turn me. You'll tell your people that I had cold feet, but I was still in play. We require what's in your head, Marcus. We will be extremely judicious about document requests. This is how people get burned. Going forward, as long as you remain an employee or a critical consultant to the CIA, you will be paid one million per annum. Should you be discovered, we will use our best efforts to get you to Moscow where, I can assure you, you'll be set for life. If you're caught and imprisoned by the US government, we will do our utmost to trade."

While Burakov talked, Marcus tried to signal his puzzlement with a curl of the lip, a wrinkling of his brow. He understood that this was their critical last meeting on French soil, but the level of specificity of the offer was curious.

Burakov must have picked up on his confusion because he said, "The game is over, my friend. You've been working me and I've been working you, but I was never going to jump. My wife would never go for it. We have enormous families back home and to us, family is everything. And Moscow treats me well. You, on the other hand, are more untethered—your family ties are limited, you don't have close friends, and quite frankly, Langley has never afforded you the respect and position you deserve. If you had to come live in Moscow, you wouldn't have big problems making the adjustment."

Marcus put his drink down. He found himself searching in earnest for the cameras. It wasn't really important; it was something to do to quench the fire in his brain. He thought he spotted one in a bookcase, peeking out above a row of old encyclopedias.

"I know what you're thinking, Marcus," Burakov said gently. "There won't be any exfils today. My wife and sons aren't at the Galeries Lafayette today, which is saving me a lot of money. We have eyes on both your follow teams. You'll signal to them that the operation today is aborted. For now, relax. Finish your drink. Have another. Keep the wire-transfer document or commit the account number to memory. Whatever suits you best. I very much look forward to working with you in the months and years to come. I think we can be more than colleagues. I think we can be friends."

There was a vibration in Marcus's pocket. Wordlessly, he pulled out his phone and saw he had a text from his sister-in-law. He read it. It was short, only three words.

Alice is dead.

Burakov read his face and asked what the matter was. Marcus showed him the phone.

"I'm so very sorry," Burakov said.

It started as a whisper. "You're sorry." Every time Marcus

repeated it, he got louder, until he was screaming at the top of his lungs.

Burakov stood up and tried to calm him to no avail.

"You fucking bastard!" Marcus yelled. "I left her! For you! I wasn't there when she died because you fucked me!"

His hands found Burakov's neck. He was stronger than the Russian who put up surprisingly little resistance. Marcus's face turned red, Burakov's blue.

Suddenly there was a thunder of footsteps coming down the stairs and two sets of strong arms pulled Marcus away.

Burakov's security team forced Marcus back down onto his chair and urged him to calm down.

"Get a sedative," Burakov said, panting and rubbing his neck. "He's had a shock."

"I don't want a fucking sedative," Marcus said. "I want to kill you."

19

It was a reckoning.

Jim Alicante bundled Marcus onto the Agency jet and rode back to Virginia with him. His ass was on the line too, but the difference was that Marcus didn't give a shit.

A full after-action team was convening on the seventh floor, chaired by the deputy executive director, a fellow only two slots down from the director. But before they went in, Dennis Correia wanted some facetime in his office.

At first, he didn't even address Marcus. "What the fuck, Jim? How does something like this happen?"

"We misread it. He was never going to come over."

"I've got memos from both of you saying it was a lock."

Alicante said, "Color me wrong, Dennis. I've never claimed infallibility. And I don't think I used the term lock. I said it was a high probability we'd pull him into the boat."

"I just want you to know that I'm not taking the fall. This was at director-level, gentlemen. I'm told reliably that he's got his knives out."

Marcus had been looking out the window. Without changing the angle of his gaze, he said, "It's on me. I'll take the hit."

"Yes, you will, my friend. Truer words were never spoken."

Alicante objected to Correia's demeaning tone. "Go easy, why don't you?" he said. "He's going through hell."

"Oh yeah, I forgot," Correia said. "My condolences. Unfortunately, in our business, the shit keeps coming and life goes on. When we go upstairs, you're going to be asked about the wire transfer."

"What about it?" Marcus said.

"Folks will want to know whether you'll be dipping your quill. I understand you didn't keep Burakov's piece of paper."

Marcus rattled off the wire-transfer number from memory.

Correia grabbed a pen and told him to repeat it, then said, "We need to get the Swiss FIS to seize the account before the FSB claws it back or someone empties it."

"Fuck you," Marcus said listlessly.

"That's right, fuck me. What are you going to do, try to beat me up, choke me out like you did to Burakov? You're lucky they didn't shoot you on the spot, for Christ's sake. It would have caused an international incident—but only a brief one—because once the Russians passed us the video of you attacking Burakov, we would have folded like a cheap lawn chair."

"Burakov felt sorry for me," Marcus mumbled.

"I'll bet he did," Correia said. "So, are you going to do the right thing on the seventh floor with the DED? The right thing is going to be way more than saying it's on you and taking the hit. You're going to admit you fucked me over with your ineptitude and poor judgment. You're going to admit you fucked Jim over with the same—because as pissed as I am with him, he's infinitely more valuable to this organization than you are. You going to throw yourself on the mercy of the court and when the DED metes out terrible punishment with his big old paddle, you're going to say, thank you, Mother Superior, I'd like another."

"I'm not going to do that," Marcus said, getting up.

"Excuse me?"

"I'm not going to the meeting. I resign. Right here, right now. I'm done."

Alicante said, "Come on, Marcus, let's take a walk and talk this out."

Marcus extended his hand. "Jim, it's been an honor to work for you. You're one of the good guys. I'm sorry I landed you in the crapper. I've made up my mind. I'm going to stop by human resources to do paperwork. Then I've got a funeral to arrange."

Marcus had arranged a grand total of one funeral previously—his mother's. She had stage-managed his father's and as the only child, Ruth Handler's burial fell on him. It was a thin affair. She had outlived almost all her friends. A smattering of nursing-home residents and staff attended and the service was conducted by a young rabbi who had never met her.

Alice's funeral would have to be on an entirely different plane. She had an abundance of friends and colleagues stretched across the publishing industry and the local community. She also had a spiritual life that operated wholly separately from his. He was a non-observant Jew from South Philadelphia. She was a practicing Lutheran from Maryland. The last time he was in a Jewish temple was for his mother's service. Alice had always been a regular churchgoer. Her involvement with her Lutheran church in Bonn had been the single factor making her posting in Germany tolerable. Now, closeted in their house in Reston, her friends rang the doorbell, bearing food and trading stories, occasionally telling him things about her that he had not known.

At the funeral home, the funeral director asked if he wanted some time alone with the open casket before the general viewings began. He knew the question was coming, but he continued to agonize right up to the second he said yes. In anticipation of the turnout, the room was the largest in the home and it swallowed up the polished casket. The black-suited man lifted the lid and gave her corpse a practiced stare while Marcus acclimated to the sight. She looked emaciated. Had his memory failed him or had she lost a great deal more weight in the past month? He wondered if the dress he chose was appropriate. She had worn it to summer parties, but it wasn't summer now, was it? It would have been better if he had subcontracted those kinds of decisions to Alice's sister, but he and Janie had gotten into a shouting match on his first day back. Her hairstyle was way off—she'd never had a central part—and it dawned on him that he'd neglected to send a photo to the funeral director. He wanted to touch her, but he couldn't decide where. His hand hovered until two fingers, seemingly involuntarily, settled on her hard, cool cheek. He withdrew them in haste.

"What do you think?" the funeral director asked.

"About what?"

"How she looks."

"She looks dead."

"Ah, yes, indeed." After an awkward pause he continued, "I'll just make sure the preparations for your guests are complete. How long would you like with her?"

"I don't know."

"I'll come back in five minutes. How would that be?"

He felt like he was lording over her, so he pulled up a chair from the front row, engaged her at eye level, and tried to control his fury. There was a lot to be angry about, but death itself was top of mind. What a ridiculous concept it was. You go through all the turmoil and strife to make your way in life, you survive the indignities of childhood and adolescence, you struggle through the challenges of being a productive member of society, you spin a web of relationships, and then this: you end up as a cold, inanimate slab of tissue. Alice may have believed differently, but as far as he was concerned, this was the end of the line. No soul escaping to parts unknown, no continuity, no life after, only a grand nothingness.

Then, his anger turned inward. For him, it was the apex of silliness to talk to the dead as many did, but for his own sanity, he had things to say. He started by thinking the words, but when that proved too amorphous, he opened his mouth and spoke.

"Look, I made so many mistakes that I've lost count. The biggest was the last one. That's the one I'm going to have to live with. I should have been there for you. You were an exceptional woman. I wasn't worthy. I'm sorry."

The night before the funeral service, he got very drunk, and he dealt with the aftermath the next morning by pouring a hit into his coffee. The sanctuary at the Lutheran church in Reston was packed to the gills. He recognized maybe ten percent. As people streamed in, Alice's boss, the executive editor of her publishing company, sidled up to him and asked if he recognized this person or that who were coming in. Apparently, some famous authors had come to pay their respects, but Marcus hadn't heard of any of them. Janie and her husband, their children, and some of Alice's cousins from back home populated the front row. They must have all been well prepped by Janie, because they all gave him stink eyes.

The pastor, a nice enough gentleman who knew Alice well, had conferred with Marcus earlier and had told him that in the Lutheran faith, eulogies were permitted, though not required. If Marcus liked, he would include elements of a eulogy in his sermon. It was a tempting dodge, but Marcus decided to man up and take it upon himself. When Janie found out, she was apoplectic, figuring it would be one last indignation to let the scoundrel do the honors, but there was nothing she could do.

When the time came, he climbed to the chancel and grasped the edges of the altar for stability. His head was throbbing and he was momentarily distracted by the dark red electric candle by the altar, suspended within his sightline. It was a reminder of God's eternal presence and meant to be comforting, but in his state of mind, it struck him as a threat.

He looked down to her coffin and said, "Alice Carpenter Handler was the best person I ever knew. There wasn't a close second. We met at Georgetown where she lit up the campus with her smile and her enthusiasm for acquiring knowledge. She was a great college student. She became a great student of life. She never stopped learning and she never stopped loving to learn. I had a chance to speak with some of her friends and co-workers over the past few days and they all said the same thing. There was no one more beloved and more respected in her social and professional communities than Alice. It's a cliché to say that she was taken from us too soon, but, it's the truth. It's not something that any of us are going to recover from. That's not an opinion, it's a fact. As far as I know, Alice only made one big mistake in her life. She married me."

Faint murmurs made their way around the sanctuary, prompting Marcus to pause. He caught sight of Janie whispering something to her husband.

"I don't really know why she stuck with me," he said. "We didn't have children. She could have been happier with someone else or on her own. I asked her the question a month ago before I cruelly and unreasonably left her on her sickbed to go back overseas. She told me she thought about leaving me more than once, but she always remembered what we had going for us in the early days of our marriage. She hoped we'd be able to find the spark again. That didn't happen. It won't happen. I have a confession I want to make to all of you who've come to see Alice off. I didn't treasure her enough. I put myself ahead of her. The way I saw it, country came first, my career came second, she came third. Can you imagine how messed up that was? When I left her a month ago to return to my post in Paris, I had a notion that I was doing something important and patriotic, but what I was really doing was being a selfish ass. I'm going to have to live with that for the rest of my life. Alice Carpenter Handler. The best person I ever met."

When the service ended, Marcus hurriedly escaped the sanctuary for the parking lot where he smoked a cigarette beside one of the cemetery-bound limos. The plan was to share a limo with Janie, Bill, and their two teenagers for the ride to the burial. He saw Janie heading straight for him and he was prepared to take the beating. He wasn't going to fight back. Nothing she was going to say would be untrue.

"Marcus," she said after a sharp exhalation.

He flicked away his smoke. "Janie."

"You spoke the truth."

"I tried."

"I'll always dislike you, but it took guts to publicly admit you were a prick."

All he could say was: "I'm glad someone who loved her was with her when she died. That's not something I'm going to have."

Marcus reconfigured his study the way he liked it and for the next several months, he sorted through Alice's paperwork, smoked and drank, and did some professional networking. He had a government pension to fall back on and could have downsized and made do, but he was only in his mid-forties and needed to work to give himself a raison d'être and to keep himself from gutter-level drinking. One day, a call from a headhunter gave him a new trajectory.

"Ever hear of a company called Andreason Engineering?"

"Nope."

"I'll send you a package on them."

"Why?"

"They're interested in interviewing you in Chicago. They're looking for a VP of corporate security. What are you doing next Thursday?"

Marcus didn't need to look at his calendar. "I think I can make it."

When he got out of the taxi and was hit by the February wind blasting off of Lake Michigan, Marcus wondered if this was really such a great idea. They had manufacturing plants in five states, but Andreason's corporate headquarters was on the Chicago River, near Boeing, one of their largest customers.

His first impression of Mickey Andreason was favorable. He was a compact, nattily dressed man with an elegant Danish accent and perfect English. He was in his sixties, but his fitness regime and passion for some kind of nutritional regimen made him seem younger and healthier than Marcus. Mickey's lunch—his usual, he said—served up by a white-jacketed waiter, consisted of a green salad with a cloudburst of sprouts and some very small nuts. Marcus hesitated, briefly, before pressing ahead with his order of steak and fries. He was pretty sure the circumstances of his exit from the CIA were going to squash his employment chances, not his menu choices.

Mickey forked a bunch of greens and said, "You know, Marcus, it's always a pain in the ass hiring someone whose employment history is protected by layers of security clearances."

"I imagine that's so."

"But I'm a well-connected fellow," Mickey said, not as a boast but as a matter of fact. "If I don't know people directly, I know a person who knows a person. In government circles, I don't usually have to go much further than one degree of separation. As it happens, I know two people who worked with you over the years. One of them has direct knowledge of why you left the Agency."

"You know I'm not going to be able to talk about that," Marcus said. The steak was delicious. The trip wouldn't be a total bust.

"Of course not. All I want to hear is a broad-brush, no-names, no-specifics version to see if it jives with what I heard. Humor me."

He found Mickey's sparkling eyes and said, "I tried to strangle a Russian operative inside one of their safe houses."

"And why were you inclined to do that?"

"He royally pissed me off."

Mickey got caught with a mouthful of health and had to deal with it before he could explode in laughter. Executives craned their necks from other tables. They looked like they'd never seen the big boss that jolly.

"That's very good. Yes, that's terrific!" He composed himself and turned serious. "My source tells me that you went back on foreign assignment despite your wife's serious illness, and that you missed her passing because of it."

"Not my finest moment."

"Perhaps not, but from my perspective as your potential employer, it shows me that you are a mission-focused man and that you displayed a powerful loyalty to your country. Am I correct or am I missing something?"

"I think it's a charitable view of my situation."

They talked for an hour and as they did, the dining room thinned out. Mickey told him about the security challenges that Andreason Engineering faced and posed question after question about how Marcus might approach various sets of problems.

"Why don't we continue down in my office," Mickey said at one point. "I'm going to have our general counsel give you a non-disclosure agreement to sign so I can share with you some specific acts of espionage we've had to deal with recently. I want to pick your brains."

Just then, a young couple entered the dining room, the woman was pushing a toddler in a stroller. Marcus thought the little girl had the most remarkable hair that fell in ringlets around a perfectly round face. Mickey instantly sparked to them and Marcus found himself momentarily fading into the background.

"Jesper, come over here," Mickey called out. "I want you to meet someone."

Jesper Andreason was strikingly handsome and Marcus immediately recognized him as a younger, taller version of the chairman. He came over to the table, leaving his wife stranded. A waiter rescued her, showing her to a table where she sat down and discreetly began to breastfeed.

"For goodness' sake," Mickey said to his son. "Does she have to do that here?"

"Yes, Dad, she does. Elizabeth is hungry and Elena doesn't flash her tits."

"Well, your mother never breastfed in public."

"I was under the impression I was suckled by wolves."

"Very funny. I'd like you to meet our new head of

security, Marcus Handler. Marcus was, until recently, a card-carrying spook."

Marcus hadn't been aware he'd been offered or accepted the job.

"CIA?" the young man asked.

"Yes, sir."

"You don't have to call him sir," Mickey said. "Jesper may be heir apparent, but he's a long way off from taking the throne. He's only a senior manager of our missile guidance division and you're a VP, so he should be calling you sir."

"Well," his son said awkwardly, "I'll be off. I've got a late night planned, so my wife came by for lunch."

"A pleasure meeting you," Marcus said. "Your little girl is very beautiful."

"Yes, she is," the young man agreed. "She's out of this world."

Armed with a firm offer and a compensation package that exceeded his expectations, Marcus returned to Virginia to sort out his affairs. The first person he called was a realtor who came by to do a valuation and a pitch. Her perkiness and can-do spirit nauseated him, but he warmed to her when she dropped her veil and frowned at some of the problematical areas such as the haze of cigarette smoke, empty bottles of booze crowding the kitchen counters, a sink filled with crusted dishes, dirty clothes on the bedroom floor, and bank statements and estate documents scattered everywhere.

"I know this neighborhood extremely well," she said. "It's highly desirable and I think we can get a good price.

But we can't list it until the place has a very thorough clean-out. Frankly, it would show better if it were completely empty and the carpets were cleaned."

"I'm going to Chicago for a new job," he said. "Can you handle everything? I'll take my clothes, some photos, some paperwork. Everything else can go."

"We don't operate that way, but I can get you a list of people who can help with furniture sales, cleaning services, and the like."

He lit a cigarette and asked, "What's your normal commission?"

"Six percent."

"Let's make it ten percent and you take care of everything. I'm out of here on Sunday and I'm never coming back. Deal?"

She cleared her throat and asked for a cigarette. "I don't ever, ever smoke in a client's home, but four extra points is making me giddy."

20

Present day

Roberto Lumaga invaded his dreams and Marcus was not pleased about it.

He tried to shake his heavy head to change the channels inside his brain, but with every movement came a new wave of excruciating pain. And Lumaga was still there. Worse still, he began to talk.

"Marcus? Can you hear me? It's Roberto."

It wasn't a dream, it was the policeman in the flesh, but why was he here and where was here?

"I hear you," Marcus said, shielding daylight with his right hand. "What's going on?"

"You're in the hospital, Marcus. The Santo Spirito Hospital, very near to the Vatican. That's where you were taken after your accident."

He tried to sit, but abandoned the effort to pain, this time coming from his left shoulder. "What accident?"

"You don't remember?"

A nurse came in and demanded that Lumaga move aside.

She told the Carabinieri that this was the first time he had become conscious since his admission. She checked his vital signs, then went to fetch a doctor.

"I don't know if I remember or not," Marcus said. "I've been having dreams."

"About what?"

"Chasing an ambulance. Shooting someone. Those kind of dreams."

"They're not dreams, my friend. They're memories."

"The fuck, you say. I shot someone?"

"You shot two men, one in the hospital, one in the street."

"Dead?"

"Very much so. Both of them. They badly wounded the Carabinieri who was guarding the girls, a good man, I'm told. He's still unconscious down the hall."

"I really killed two men?"

"You did."

"Am I in trouble?"

"You have a friend in high places—me. You're not even going to be arrested. We've done witness statements and looked at the CCTV. We can presume you shot the man in the hospital room in self-defense or in defense of the girls. You clearly shot the ambulance driver in self-defense. Another man who was in the passenger seat came around and hit you in the head."

"He was blond."

"We don't have a good image of his face."

Marcus blinked in thought. "They were wearing masks in the hospital."

"You suffered a bad concussion. You're in the intensive

care ward. But I think it's a good sign that you're remembering these things."

Marcus looked around at the machines beeping and humming at his bedside.

"How long have I been here?"

"Since yesterday evening."

A neurologist came in and asked Lumaga to leave, but the policeman told him he wasn't going anywhere. The doctor dropped his insistence and did an examination.

"You don't have a fractured skull," the neurologist said, "but you sustained a significant concussion. There is a very small amount of bleeding over the visual centers of the brain—back here where you were hit—but it should resorb without any specific therapy."

"The light hurts my eyes," Marcus said.

"It will for a day or two. You'll have headaches for longer than that. Perhaps some flashes and dots in front of your eyes for a time. Expect some dizziness as well. When we discharge you, I don't want you to do anything strenuous for two weeks. Don't lift anything heavier than a small stack of books."

"How about lifting a bottle of Scotch?"

The doctor didn't seem to have a refined sense of humor, but Lumaga chuckled.

"Restrict your alcohol intake, please," the doctor said.

"When can I get out of here?"

"Let's aim for tomorrow. We'll need to get clearance from the surgeon who took care of your shoulder wound."

"Oh yeah, my shoulder's killing me."

"You were stabbed. There was no nerve damage and I'm

told the knife didn't cut any tendons or ligaments. In any event, I'll see you again in the morning and we'll make a final decision," he said, sweeping out.

"The girls," Marcus said. "Are they all right?"

Lumaga nodded. "Thanks to you, they are. It was extremely upsetting for them, of course, to see the terrible violence. They were moved to another floor and they're receiving psychological therapy. Of course, we've dramatically increased the level of security surrounding them."

"Who were they?"

"The two dead men were Slovakians," Lumaga consulted his notebook. "The ambulance driver was named Jakub Duris, age thirty-seven. The one in the girls' room was Matej Beno, age forty-two. They both had passports on their persons. We know they flew to Rome the day before yesterday from Bratislava, where they live. We don't know where they were staying here. The Slovakian authorities are cooperating and we should get more information about them. I think we can hypothesize that the blond man who gave you your headache is also part of this Slovakian gang, but we can't know for sure."

"What did they want?"

"We presume this was a kidnapping attempt and these men are part of some sort of criminal enterprise. The girls are internationally known. It is a matter of public knowledge that Mikkel Andreason is a very wealthy man. Hospitals— even with police guards—are not completely secure."

Marcus rubbed his eyes and asked how Mickey was taking it.

"He's like a crazed animal," Lumaga said. "He's been furiously working to overturn my directive that the girls must stay in Italy during the investigation. So far, the relevant ministers are continuing to support me. For them, it's a matter of Italian sovereignty. They don't like getting pushed around by Americans."

"Who can blame them?" Marcus quipped.

"However, I have had to accept one of his demands."

"Which is?"

"He's hired a private security group to augment the vigilance of the Carabinieri. They are already in place. It's bound to create difficult situations, but I had to make the concession for the sake of peace. You'll be pleased to know that he didn't impose his private guards on you."

"Me? Why would I need protection?"

"Well, my friend, all you did was kill two members of a well-organized, international kidnap gang. It's not beyond the realm of possibility that they will wish to exact a measure of revenge. But don't worry. I've had a Carabinieri detail assigned to you. There's a man outside your door right now."

"I don't need anyone, Roberto," he insisted.

"You'll need police just to get through the cordon of journalists. You can't believe what's going on outside both hospitals. Your heroics added to the mystery surrounding the girls and has caused a frenzy unlike any other."

Marcus was adamant. "Still, no thank you."

"Humor me. At least for a little while. I'm busy enough right now. I don't need the distraction of investigating your murder."

"I thought you were going to say something different."

He smiled brightly. "Well, maybe I'd be a little upset if that happened."

*

Mickey stopped by Marcus's hospital room that evening and did something remarkable, at least to Marcus. He cried.

When he composed himself, he said, "You saved them, Marcus, and I am eternally grateful."

"I'm glad I was in the right place at the right time."

"Major Lumaga told me exactly what you did. It was fierce. It was effective. It was extraordinary."

"It's only extraordinary because I'm not a spring chicken."

"To this truly old man, you're a young buck in his prime. I know you don't and won't talk about your operational work at the Agency, but—"

"No, Mickey, I never killed anyone before. It's not—it's not a good feeling."

"Sons of bitches deserved what they got. Lumaga says they're part of a kidnap gang from Slovakia."

"So he says."

"You don't buy that?"

"I'm sure he's right. There's just so much weirdness. It's hard to piece it all together."

"You on the mend?"

"Getting there. I should be ready to get out of here tomorrow."

"Good, good. I tried to think of something to bring you. I don't figure you for a flower and chocolates guy, so I got you this."

He took a silver hipflask from his jacket pocket.

Marcus brightened considerably. "Is that empty or full?"

"What do you think? Johnnie Walker Blue. The rest of

the bottle's in your hotel room. It's probably not strictly allowed after concussions, but I figure it's medicinal."

Marcus closed his eyes and took a hit. "You have no idea." He didn't want to admit it to himself or his doctors, but he'd been getting jittery. What better way to scratch the itch than with the nectar of the gods? "How are Vicky and Elizabeth doing?" he asked.

"Not great. They're crying a lot—not that I should talk. Their other grandparents are better with them than me. I'm not a hugger. You know that."

Marcus was actually touched by this self-aware version of Mickey. "They're Italian," Marcus said.

"That they are. Leukemia-wise, these girls are doing great. Dr. Spara says the drug he's got them on is working. He's going to let them leave the hospital on the medicine for two weeks. Then he'll bring them back for bone marrow transplants. Turns out Armando's the best match."

"Lumaga told me you hired a security company."

"Best in Europe. A bunch of ex-SAS guys in from the UK. They're already fighting like cats and dogs with the Carabinieri. But fuck 'em. If Lumaga won't let me leave the country with the kids, he's going to have to put up with some hard-core bastards on my payroll. We're decamping for Calabria as soon as the three of you are discharged. The girls want to travel with Uncle Marcus on the plane. Besides, Lumaga says you need protection too."

"That's bull."

"Your professional opinion."

"It is. Why do you want to go back down south?"

"Why not? Victoria and Elizabeth are comfortable

in their old house. Armando and Leonora will move in along with both of us. I've had one of the VPs from the security company go down there to scope out the property and he says the cliffs and the long driveway to the road make it highly defensible. They're not going to rely on the Carabinieri for anything but traffic control."

"What about the rest of the entourage?"

"You mean Celeste and Colonel Carter? They're coming too."

Marcus took another sip from the flask. "Christ, Mickey, why?"

"I know you don't like them, but I'm covering all the bases, okay? Celeste had a vision about Jesper yesterday. He was bathed in light, she said, standing in a remote forest. He was coming home."

"Elena wasn't in her vision?"

"Apparently not."

"Do you think maybe that's because she's playing to you? An audience of one?"

"I can't answer that."

"You're being selective about her visions, aren't you? You're willing to ignore her on the bone marrow transplants."

Mickey put a hand through his thinning hair. "In my business—hell, in life—I've always played the risk-reward game. Bruno Spara is a world-class hematologist. Everything he's said and recommended, I've gone back to my consultant in Chicago to see what she thinks. There's not a millimeter of daylight between their opinions. So, I'm going with the scientists over the psychic on this one."

"Thank goodness for that. And Carter? You don't want to cut him loose?"

"He's harmless and besides, he's been working with this European UFO group, CUFOM, on sightings around the time Jesper and the girls were abducted and the time the girls returned. He seems to think there may be some credible leads. What do I have to lose? The price of a hotel room?"

"Don't forget the cost of meals," Marcus said. "That man can eat."

The return flight to Reggio Calabria was crowded. Every seat of Mickey's Gulfstream was filled, thanks to the presence of one shift of the British private security guards. Mickey chartered a second plane for the other two shifts of Brits. By popular demand, Marcus sat with the girls and their omnipresent board games. It was the first he'd seen them since the attack and they were noticeably subdued.

Victoria wanted to know why his arm was in a sling.

"The bad man poked me with something sharp," was the most benign way he could think to put it.

"Does it hurt?"

"Of course, it hurts," Elizabeth interjected.

"It only hurts a little now," he said. Just about the last thing he could be accused of was having the sensitivity of a therapist, but he felt he ought to confront the obvious. "What happened in your room was scary."

"Were you scared?" Victoria asked.

"I was very scared," he said.

"I thought you were going to die," Elizabeth said, playing with her hair.

"I did too," he admitted.

"I'm glad you didn't die," Victoria said.

"Yeah, me too," he said. "I've heard it helps to talk about scary things."

"A lady came to talk to us," Elizabeth told him. "She was nice. Did she talk to you?"

"No, I talked to your granddad, Mickey, and my friend, Roberto."

"Oh," Victoria said, setting up the pieces on the board. "Let's play."

Mickey was watching from his seat by the cockpit. He flashed Marcus a thumbs-up.

Later, when they were airborne, Marcus sidled back toward the lavatory and stopped to exchange pleasantries with Celeste and Carter who were sitting together. They had boarded before him and he hadn't seen them since the incident.

"Good to see you're on the mend," Carter said. "I mean, what the hell, Marcus? This place is like the wild west. And in the shadow of the Vatican! But you're one tough hombre, my friend. My hat is off to you."

"The girls are bringing the crazies out, that's for sure," Marcus said. He pointed toward the musclemen aft. "It's good that Mickey has the resources for these guys. I'm done playing Superman."

"Well, when you're up for it, I've got some interesting info for you from the CUFOM people."

"Good," he said unconvincingly. "Later."

Celeste had been looking at him intently and she reached

out to touch his hand. "I was so, so worried about you, Marcus. They wouldn't allow me to see you."

He told her he appreciated it, then added, "I understand from Mickey that your vision factory's been busy."

"It's hardly a factory, Marcus," she said. "My visions come to me spontaneously, wholly unlike the output of a factory. But yes, I had a vision about Jesper. I saw him in a remote forest, bathed in light. He said he was coming home."

"Well, let's hope you're right," Marcus said. "That would make his father extremely happy."

His last few paces toward the lavatory were interrupted by a huge arm projecting from a bulging T-shirt.

"Just wanted to shake your hand, sir," the man said in a British accent as three other young men looked on, nodding. "I'm Tim Wheelock, team leader for CSS, Canterbury Security Solutions. If any one of my men had accomplished what you did against armed adversaries, they'd have drinks bought for them for a lifetime. Truly magnificent."

"I appreciate that, Tim. I think any one of you guys would have gotten out of the situation without a scratch." He painfully raised his arm. "As you can see, I didn't."

"Nah, you're a warrior, sir."

His shoulder throbbed and his head was still pounding. If he was a warrior, he felt like one with one foot in the grave.

Major Lumaga summoned Fabiana Odorico to his office to report on progress in the murder investigation of Ferruccio Gressani and Cinzia Rondinelli. However, she turned the tables on him, and grilled him about the hospital attack that was on front pages across Italy.

"Who would have thought that Marcus had it in him to fight like that?" Odorico said.

"Don't underestimate him," he said. "That man can drink you under the table at night then beat the stuffing out of you in the morning. Now, let's talk about your case, if you please."

"I've been working on Ferruccio's web of relationships when he lived in Italy, particularly on the 'Ndrangheta angle. Do you remember that Ferruccio's mother told me about his friendship with Marco Zuliani?"

"Sure, sure," Lumaga said.

"Marco moved to Toronto with his immediate family about ten years ago, but some of the Zuliani clan stayed in Calabria."

"Did you interview them?"

"Of course, but here's a shock for you. They refused to cooperate. They wouldn't answer one question and told me to piss off. Even the little children were abusive."

Lumaga gave her one of his deep shrugs. "Disrespect for the law starts young in these families."

"I didn't stop there," she said. "I went through the police files going back a decade, searching for any past incidents involving Ferruccio or any of the Zulianis."

"And?" Lumaga said. "With this slow build-up of yours, you'd better have something to say."

She opened a folder with a flourish. "I do. Maybe you remember this because you were at this station back then, but four years ago, a couple of bodies washed up in Algeria. They were young men from this area. One of them was Matteo Zuliani who went by Teo. The other was his brother-in-law, Gianluca Rizzo, known as Lu."

Lumaga reached for the folder. "Let me see that." He read through the file and said, "I do remember this. The bodies were decomposed and devoured by marine life, but the Algerian authorities found this gold bracelet with Matteo's name and they traced him here to Oppido Mamertina. The other boy was from the next village. Both of them had gunshot wounds to the head. We thought that this was some kind of execution carried out by rival drug gangs, but we never made any progress. We were up against the same omertà you experienced. Why do you think this has anything to do with Ferruccio?"

"Matteo was Marco Zuliani's first cousin; Marco was Ferruccio's childhood friend," she said.

"Okay, but still, this doesn't help us at all with Ferruccio's murder, does it?"

She responded with a question. "Back then, did you ever wonder how the bodies got to Algeria?"

The question sent him back to the folder. He ruffled through the rest of the investigative notes.

"Okay, I see we checked on whether they took any ferries or if they flew to Algeria. They didn't. So, they must have been thrown into the sea and floated there. We found Zuliani's car near the beach in Porto di Bagnara. What's the big deal?"

Odorico said, "I asked myself, is this possible? To float from Calabria to Algeria? Of course, I didn't know the answer, so I called a marine scientist at the Mediterranea University. He told me that if bodies were dropped into the sea off the west coast of Italy, the Mediterranean currents would carry them north then west toward Spain before they circled back toward the south and east. Eventually, a floating object could get to Algeria that way, but it would take a very long time and a body wouldn't survive the circuit without completely disintegrating."

"So, where were they dumped?"

"The professor said that based on what I told him about the state of the bodies, they must have been put into the sea off the southern coast of Spain."

"Spain," Lumaga said. "Ferruccio was in Spain four years ago. I don't know what this means, Fabiana, but I have a feeling it's important. Did anyone ever tell you that you were clever?"

She puckered her mouth knowingly. "Only my mother, my father, all my teachers, and all my superiors. You're only just noticing?"

Villa Shibui was tranquil on the inside, but beyond the gates, it was a madhouse. The media had discovered that the girls and their heroic savior, Marcus Handler, had returned from Rome and they stretched along the road for a kilometer in both directions. Carabinieri officers from Lumaga's unit stood guard at the gate, and the private CSS operatives patrolled the grounds. They piggybacked off the firearms license of a sister Italian security company, enabling the men to carry assault rifles and side-arms.

It was hot and clear and Marcus sat on the back patio with Mickey drinking morning coffee. The girls were just waking up in their beds and their grandmother, Leonora, was fussing over them. Giuseppe and Noemi Pennestrì were cooking, cleaning, and doing laundry, tending to a full house for the first time in years.

Marcus heard it before Mickey.

It was a whining noise, octaves higher than the waves. He stood and shielded his eyes.

"What?" Mickey asked.

There were two CSS men in the back garden on the morning shift. One of them was Tim Wheelock who alerted to the sound when Marcus did.

Wheelock pointed toward the bright sky, barked orders to his men via his headset, and shouted for Marcus and Mickey to get inside.

Marcus saw what Wheelock pointed at, the small drone that had climbed vertically along the cliff face and was now hovering a hundred meters overhead. Marcus made sure that Mickey went inside, and at the door, he shouted for everyone in the house to stay where they were. He didn't take his own advice and went back out where he saw Wheelock sighting through the optics of his short-barreled rifle. Three loud pops rang out and the drone dropped like a stone. It clattered onto the tile roof and fell into a flower bed.

One of Wheelock's men ran to it and poked it with his rifle before yelling, "Camera only! No explosive charge!"

Wheelock radioed for his men at the front of the property to hold their positions, but Carabinieri officers on hearing the shots, opened the gate and motored to the house, their weapons drawn. That precipitated a shouting match between the senior officer and Wheelock about discharging weapons. Mickey came outside again and demanded to know what was happening, but everyone ignored him.

Marcus was heading toward the Lucite fence at the edge of the cliff because he heard a commotion coming from the beach.

He leaned over and saw two men—who later would be identified as journalists from a British tabloid—shouting and waving that they wanted their drone back.

"Unbelievable," Marcus mumbled.

He didn't notice the man speaking into his phone standing near the journalists, and he didn't see his blond hair under his baseball cap.

"What's all the noise, Gunar?" the blond man was asked over the phone.

"Idiot with drone tried take pictures. Guards shoot it down."

"They're at the house?"

"Yes."

"How can you be sure?"

"Marcus Handler. He looking from top of cliff right at me. If I have rifle, I can shoot motherfucker in head."

21

"Can you come see me at the hotel?"

Marcus hadn't recognized the number on his phone.

"How'd you get my number?" he asked.

"I asked Mikkel for it," Celeste said.

He was alone in the living room of Villa Shibui, involved with his first after-dinner Scotch. Mickey was out, taking a walk on the beach, Noemi Pennestrì was clearing up in the kitchen, and the girls were upstairs with their Italian grandparents.

"Why do you want to see me?"

"It's very important, Marcus. Please come."

"You're going to have to try harder than that."

"I've had another vision," she said. "It's terribly urgent. I didn't know why it was so important until Colonel Carter educated me."

He heard Carter in the background, sounding like a parrot perched on her shoulder. "Tell him I've got to talk to him too."

"Colonel Carter says—"

"I heard him."

He looked out the window at the soft, evening light and

at the fresh bottle of Johnnie Walker Blue—Mickey had ordered in an entire case for him.

"Why tell me," he said. "Why not talk to Mickey?"

"He told me to go through you on everything," she said. "He values you greatly, you know."

He resigned himself to the drive to Reggio Calabria. "I'll come," he said.

He saw the two of them near the rear, but not wanting to waste time, Marcus placed his drink order with the bartender on his way. The Scotch and ice arrived before they had gotten much beyond small talk. The young waiter laughed approvingly when Marcus ordered his next round before tasting the first.

"Got to like a man who likes his liquor," Carter said, sipping a beer and munching peanuts. "Celeste told me it's okay for me to go first with what I've put together. Kind of like the appetizer to her main course."

"Entertain me," Marcus said.

"Oh, I intend to," Carter said. "Like I told you, my friend Antonio at CUFOM has been sorting through his databases at my behest, plus he put out a message to the Italian and European UFO community for any sightings that weren't previously logged. I think I've got some really compelling data to share with you. Let's start four years ago, specifically in the week preceding the abduction of the Andreason family. I've made a little PowerPoint presentation, if you'll allow me." Carter opened his laptop to the first slide, a map of Europe. "All righty," he said, "as I understand it, you don't know exactly what time the abductions occurred—could have been on the night of the twelfth or the early morning of the thirteenth." Marcus nodded his agreement and Carter went on, "This dot over Brest in France represents a UFO sighting at 10:59 p.m. Here's the video of the sighting, taken with a mobile phone camera by a teenager walking home from a friend's house."

To Marcus's eye, it was a classic, small bright light flashing through the sky type of nonsense he'd seen countless times online, each time eliciting a yawn.

The next slide had a dot over the south of France.

"Now, at 11:01 p.m.," Carter said, "an Air France pilot on descent to Lyon at an altitude of approximately eight thousand feet, radioed air traffic control that an ultra-bright yellow light flashed across his field of view at an extraordinary speed. He wanted to know if there were any missile launches in the vicinity. He was informed there were none."

The next slide had a dot over Corsica.

"At 11:03, we've got another video, this one taken by a German tourist on northern Corsica, smoking a cigar on his balcony. Here it is."

It was another fast-moving orb against a black sky, with the German providing a soundtrack of his shouting at his wife to come look at what he was seeing.

"That was the last report that night to make it into CUFOM's database," Carter said, "but look at this."

The last slide was a view of Europe connecting the dots and projecting the line across the Tyrrhenian Sea where it intersected with Reggio Calabria.

Carter dinged the screen with his finger and said, "A minute or two later, the UFO would have been right smack over their house. Now, what do you think of that?"

Marcus had already finished drink number one and was searching the room for the waiter and drink number two. "Fascinating," he said.

"Well, I can tell you're not impressed," Carter said. "Admittedly it's circumstantial, but, hell, I think it's pretty damned compelling."

"Are you impressed?" Marcus asked Celeste who had been quietly sipping at her drink. She was wearing her low-cut red dress again, and he was trying hard not to look at her chest.

"I'm not an expert like the colonel, but I find it quite interesting," she said. "I have a completely open mind. One must, in these circumstances, no?"

"Must one?" Marcus asked.

"Okay, last piece of info from CUFOM," Carter said, "and I think it's a winner too. The night the girls returned, a group of Italian university students were leaving a pizzeria in Naples close to midnight when one of them looks into the sky and sees a bright object moving fast toward the nearly full moon. By the time she whips out her phone and hits record, it's seen here, in this video as a dark object streaking across the yellow moon."

He clicked on a file and played the video.

"Now, here in slow motion, the object passes over the moon and now it's bright yellow against the night sky. You can see that it's the same color and shape as the UFOs in the videos from four years ago, and now, in normal motion, you can see it zips along at a similar incredible speed. Now, I maintain, that it is a distinct possibility that Victoria and Elizabeth Andreason were on that UFO when this was shot, just moments before they were returned to their house just up the road from here. That's all I've got, but I feel like we've moved the needle on the investigation. And while I've got you, I want to say that I still haven't gotten my interview with the girls."

"A few things have taken priority, if you haven't noticed."

"I have noticed and it's perfectly reasonable that I've gotten bumped to the back of the queue, but I just don't want to get bumped out of existence. Will you please talk to Mickey?"

Marcus breathed out a couple of yeahs. A new drink arrived and he gave it his full attention for a few moments. "So, that was the appetizer," he said. "I think I still have some room for the main course."

"Yes, okay, my turn," Celeste said, "although the colonel also has some things to say about the main course. What I find remarkable is that the two of us, a military man and a psychic have found common ground and are aligned on matters of importance. My vision this afternoon came about in the most ordinary of ways, although this is a common pattern with me. I had taken my lunch with the colonel in a small café nearby and when I returned to my room, I washed my teeth. While I was putting away the brush, I was seized by a powerful image that left me standing in front of the sink, motionless, for some considerable time. I was in a dense, dark forest, in an elevated place. It was the same forest in my earlier vision of Jesper—I told you about it on the plane. Initially, I had the sense I wasn't alone; however, I could not tell you who I was with. I most certainly did not know why I was there until the thought came to me: they are coming back."

Marcus knew what she was going to say, but he was

content to play along. He was here already. He was in a bar. He had a drink in his hand.

"Then it came to me again, even stronger," she said. "They are coming back. I was looking up at the dark, dark sky, searching for something, anything, to show itself in the blackness, and then I saw it. At first it was a tiny speck of light, like a star in a distant galaxy. Then it became larger and larger by degrees, and as it got closer, it got brighter and brighter, until the forest floor was bathed in pure light. My eyes hurt terribly and I was unable to shield them properly, so I closed them tightly. When I opened them again, I saw Jesper first and then Elena, standing close to one another, awash in white light—pure, white light. That's when another thought flashed through my consciousness. Actually, it was more like signage, telling me the time and the place. Friday night. Torriglia. Monte Prelà. Then all was normal again. I was looking into the mirror. The toothbrush was in my hand."

"What's Torriglia?" Marcus asked.

"I didn't know until I had words with the colonel. My goodness, the significance soon became apparent!"

Carter shifted in his chair and only then did Marcus see that he was wearing cargo shorts that exposed massive, hairy legs.

"I don't mind telling you," Carter said, "that I almost fell over when she mentioned Torriglia. For Italians, it's like saying Roswell to an American. It is ground zero for UFOs in this neck of the woods. I guess you've never heard of it."

"Guess not," Marcus said.

"Then you won't have heard of Pier Zanfretta either."

"Doesn't ring any bells."

"Well, Pier Zanfretta is a fellow—he's still alive as far as I know—who was abducted by aliens in the north of Italy, at Torriglia, in December 1978. More accurately, that was the first time he was abducted."

"Poor guy got snatched twice?" Marcus snorted.

"More than twice. It's a saga, to tell you the truth. Let me walk you through it, 'cause I'm sure Mickey's going to have plenty of questions. He's an inquisitive fellow, as you are well aware. The Torriglia incidents have some similarities and some differences to the Andreason case. For instance, Zanfretta wasn't abducted by Grays. They were Reptilians. On the other hand—"

Carter's mobile phone rang. He saw the ID, swore a little, and asked Marcus to hang on a second so he could take the call. He wandered off and returned with an exasperated look.

"I'm on mute," he said. "It's my daughter. Her husband, a sorry-ass turkey just got arrested. Again. I've got to deal with this, but here's a printout I made in the business center about the Zanfretta case and Torriglia. If Mickey needs to speak to me, you know where I am. Ciao, as they say around here."

Marcus took a peek at the small stack of paper and excused himself to use the men's room. When he got back to the table, another Scotch was waiting for him.

"I didn't order this," he said.

"I did," Celeste said. "I hope you don't mind."

He saw it was a double. "If I drink this, I won't be able to drive for a while."

She smiled slyly. "Perhaps, that was my plan."

He decided that it was now okay to have a more direct

look at her figure. The tight red dress and red lipstick were killers, but why was she trying to slay him? He had maybe twenty years on her, and while he was given to understand by lady-friends that he was a pretty good fifty-four, her motives were suspect. That said, did he really care? He hit the new Scotch hard and in short order, another one mysteriously appeared, courtesy of the grinning waiter.

Her room didn't seem like it had been occupied. It looked as pristine as a hotel room looks on check-in, and as he stood by the bed, swaying from the drink, the part of his brain that remained sentient told him that she had squirreled away all her personal belongings before coming down to the bar. That smacked of premeditation.

It became clear soon enough that she wanted to be the aggressor in this interlude, and he didn't put up a struggle. If it worked for her, it worked for him. In any case, his shoulder still hurt like hell, which limited his mobility. She shed the red dress the way a snake sheds its skin and pulled him by his belt buckle onto the bed. He wasn't altogether sure how competent his performance was, but before long, she was moaning and that got to him—in a good way. When they were both spent, he felt for something to cover their nakedness, but since they were lying on top of a made bed, he came up empty.

"Here," she said, kissing him on the lips. "Let's get under."

He was a little more sober now and it began to sink in. He'd slept with a woman he didn't particularly care for. No, it was stronger than that. He was deeply suspicious of her and couldn't figure out her angle. Were these visions of hers part of an elaborate scam? Was she about to hit Mickey up for a big payday? Was this new Torriglia thing a lead-up to the big ask? And why did she feed him liquor and lead him by the nose to her bed? Was that a bribe for him to convince Mickey she was the real deal?

"A penny for your thoughts?" she said. She was on her side, her head propped by an arm. He turned his neck and saw the tattoo on her wrist.

"That's all they're worth," he said.

"Oh, I doubt that. You're a man of uncommon substance."

"Good to know."

"And you're an excellent lover."

"Better to know." He was eager to change the subject. "Why the Big Dipper?"

She laughed. "My tattoo? I got it when I was quite young. I always liked the way you can use the Big Dipper to find the North Star." She ran the sharp nail of her pointer finger lightly across his chest. "You make a line from the two outer stars in the cup of the Big Dipper, then there's the North Star." She stabbed her finger into his breast, just hard enough to make him twitch. "It's important to know where the North Star is, don't you think? It centers you and guides you through life."

He didn't answer. His persistent dull headache had become a painfully throbbing one. His doctor had neglected to tell him that sex could make post-concussion symptoms worse. When he started to massage his eyes and temples, she picked up on it and took over, working the muscles of his head and neck.

"You've been through a lot," she said. "You were very brave."

"Also known as very stupid. I shouldn't have chased after the ambulance."

"I think your training took over. Mickey told me you worked at the CIA."

"People have a lot of misconceptions about that line of work. It's mostly sitting at desks and staring at computers."

"You're not James Bond?" she purred.

"I've got his drinking down to a science, but that's about it."

"I disagree. You also ravish the ladies."

"My recollection is that you were the one doing most of the ravishing."

Her laugh was small and sexy. "I couldn't help myself."

It was time to transition to an interrogation. "Why me? I'm not quite old enough to be your father, but, still."

She abruptly stopped the massage and propped herself on pillows to sit up.

"I'm sorry," he said. "Did I offend you."

"Would you mind getting me a water from the minibar?" she asked.

He was aware of her eyes on his naked body.

When he was back under the sheets, she said, "I had a complicated relationship with my father."

"We can change the subject."

"No, it's okay. We are adults. We can talk. I told you he was Lebanese, no? He was a dominant man, very aggressive in his approach to life."

"An alpha male."

"Yes, alpha for sure. When I was young, I was in awe of him—you know, the size of him, his incendiary temperament, always like a volcano about to erupt, his thick, black moustache and the way he went to work cleanly shaved and returned for dinner with heavy stubble. His life force was strong."

"And your mother?"

"A beautiful woman, especially in her youth—always quiet and reserved. They were both Christian, but she was more religious." She got quieter. "She was afraid of him. He could be brutal with her. Also, tender, but it's the brutality I remember most acutely. It was the same with me. When he was happy, when things were going well with his business, he was tender. When he had trouble with his business, he was brutal."

"Physically brutal?" Marcus asked.

"Oh, yes," she whispered. "But he didn't beat me."

He got the drift. He didn't want the confession—he wasn't a priest. But it came anyway.

"I was abused. Sexually abused. I left home when I was sixteen, but I'm afraid the lifelong damage was done. He died of a heart attack when I was twenty. It was all very difficult and tragic, especially for my poor mother who did not have a good life before or after, to be honest."

He tried to find something positive to say. "You seem to have done all right."

"Perhaps my childhood created the environment, a certain sensitivity that led to fostering my psychic abilities. In that sense, I did do all right. I have been able to earn a living, helping people, doing what comes naturally. But what I've told you is also a long answer to your question of why me? Because of my complicated relationship with my father, I've always been attracted to men who are older than me. I saw a psychiatrist some years ago and I have a complete awareness of my situation. Of course, the men must be attractive."

"I'm glad it's not just my age," he said with an edge.

"Please don't be offended, Marcus. I'm comfortable with you, so I am able to be totally honest."

"Honesty is good," he said.

"Will you tell Mickey about my vision? About Torriglia?"

"It's my job to pass along information, regardless of what I think about it. He's a grown man. He's the one paying the bills. He'll make his own decisions about what to do with it."

"Will you promise not to put up a roadblock?"

"Like I said, he makes up his own mind."

She reached over and began stimulating him. "Will you promise?"

His head was clearer now. The effects of the booze were waning.

"Yeah, I promise."

He rolled onto her and this time, at the risk of making his headache worse, he was the aggressor.

When he returned to Villa Shibui, the house was dark. The Carabinieri let him through the gate and the late shift of Mickey's private security, verified him before he could get inside. He sat at the kitchen table with a big glass of water, donned his reading glasses, and browsed Carter's printouts on the Zanfretta abduction.

On December 6, 1978, Pier Zanfretta, a twenty-six-year-old night watchman was on a routine patrol at the empty country house of one of his clients in Torriglia, north of Genoa. Suddenly, his car died and its radio and lights failed. He saw lights in the garden and, believing there were thieves, he exited the car with his pistol and flashlight. In the garden, he felt something touching his shoulder, and when he wheeled around, he saw, according to his testimony, "an enormous green, ugly and frightful creature, with undulating skin, no less than ten feet tall." Then he saw a huge triangular UFO hovering over the house and was pulled into the craft after he was blasted by a searing wave of heat. A couple of hours later, Zanfretta was deposited back at the house where he contacted his dispatch by radio, babbling incoherently about being assaulted by non-humans. When other watchmen from the company arrived, the normally sober family man was agitated and inconsolable. The Carabinieri were summoned and they discovered imprints of three-meter wide horseshoes in the frosted grass of the garden, presumably from the ship's landing gear. Their subsequent investigation found over fifty residents of Torriglia reporting a bright illumination in the vicinity of the country house at the precise time of Zanfretta's abduction.

In the midst of the media hysteria, experts were called in. Zanfretta was put under hypnosis by a renowned specialist whereby he described details of his time on board an alien craft and communicating with the giant creatures using translation devices. He was probed and examined and was told that the aliens wanted to talk to humans and would return at a later time in larger numbers.

That wasn't the end of things for Zanfretta. Back on patrol three weeks after the first incident, he was abducted again near the mountainous Scoffera Pass and was returned after some hours in a confused and agitated state. When the Carabinieri arrived, his Fiat, though bathed in cold rain, was said to be as hot as if it had been baking under a hot sun. The car was also surrounded by fifty-centimeter-long boot prints. He was once again hypnotized and revealed an account of his captivity on a spaceship, where, among other details, the aliens fired his pistol into a panel to test the destructiveness of Earth weapons. A prominent neurologist examined Zanfretta and declared that he was in a state of shock but perfectly sane.

The furor died down for several years until Zanfretta was abducted *four more times* in 1979 and 1980 in and around Genoa, firmly establishing the region as the UFO capital of Italy, and Zanfretta as an icon. But now, Marcus was skimming and yawning, glossing over the details of the remaining papers in Carter's Zanfretta file. He got the picture. Torriglia was hallowed ground for alien-abduction types.

"How come you're up in the middle of the night?"

Mickey was in his bathrobe.

"Just doing a little reading," Marcus said.

"I couldn't sleep," Mickey said. "I'm going to have some cereal. Reading about what?"

Marcus was going to tell him about Celeste's new vision and Torriglia in the morning, but now was as good a time as any. He kept his promise. It was difficult, but he played it straight, giving Mickey the facts devoid of the snarky commentary he could have interjected. Mickey munched and listened and when Marcus was done, he took his bowl to the sink and washed it out.

"I know what you must be thinking about all that, Marcus. I appreciate your being an honest reporter and keeping your opinions to yourself. This is on me. If there's even the slightest chance of getting Jesper and Elena back, it's imperative we act. We're going to Torriglia on Friday."

22

On Friday afternoon, Mickey's plane went wheels up at Reggio Calabria, bound for Genoa. On board were Mickey, Marcus, Celeste, and Colonel Carter. Tim Wheelock from Canterbury Securities had offered to send one of his men, but Mickey didn't want to deplete a shift.

In the days following their tryst, Marcus stayed away from Celeste and now, shoehorned together into the jet, he chose a seat as far away as he could. In the years since Alice died, he'd never regretted drunken one-nighters, but this time was different. When he met a woman at a bar and decided in the cold light of day that he had made a colossal error, he walked away and filed the encounter in a part of his brain where it got lost. He couldn't do the same with Celeste, at least not yet. Until Mickey was satisfied her usefulness had come to an end, he had to keep her in the frame. Hopefully, after a fruitless night atop a mountain, Mickey would send her packing.

He wanted a drink, but he supposed he was technically on duty. He got out of his seat and went to the galley where Mickey watched him pour himself a soda water.

"Surprising choice of beverage," Mickey said, snidely.

When he backtracked, Celeste was sitting on the

unoccupied cross-aisle bench from him. She was wearing a red leather jacket over jeans; it was the first time he'd seen her in anything other than a skin-tight dress.

"Hi," she said.

"Hi, back."

"Are you angry with me?" she whispered.

He told her he wasn't. Even to his own ear, it sounded like a lie.

"I think you are."

"You're free to think what you like."

She said, "What happened the other night—you may regret it, but I don't."

"I haven't thought about it. I've been busy."

"Busy with what?"

"Busy not thinking about it," he said. "And—"

"And what?"

"Drinking."

"Yes, you do like your drink," she said with a tiny laugh. "I find non-drinkers to be very dull. You are not dull. But, listen, Marcus, I don't want to make you uncomfortable. I loved being with you. I would like to be with you again. I like you very much. If you knock on my door, I will open it."

"Yours, mine, everyone's focus has to be on Elizabeth and Victoria," he said. "Nothing else matters."

"You're absolutely right," she said. "I promise to keep my wickedness under control. The girls deserve our full attention. So, thank you."

"For what?"

"For persuading Mickey to agree to come to Torriglia."

"I thought it was a bullshit idea," he said. "Mickey didn't need any persuading."

She got up and leaned over him. "You'll see, Marcus. In a few hours, you'll see."

"Just curious," he said. "That stuff about your father. Was it true?"

"Unfortunately, yes. It's all true."

When they arrived at the private aviation terminal at the Genoa airport, a van from an alpine excursion company was waiting. Mickey had hired a guide to lead them to the summit of Monte Prelà.

The guide was an extremely fit-looking fellow with a heavy black beard and a winning smile.

"I am here," he called out, waving his M. Andreason cardboard sign.

Mickey identified himself and shook the man's hand.

"Giancarlo Zanardi, at your service," the guide said. "You are perfectly on time. What a beautiful airplane, if I might say."

Mickey waved off the compliment. "Shall we go?"

The other three passengers disembarked and Zanardi looked everyone over. "You have bags to unload?" he asked.

"No, why?" Mickey asked.

"These are your clothes and shoes?"

"I don't understand your question," Mickey snapped.

"Did you not receive my email?"

Mickey sighed. "I get too many damned emails. What did it say?"

"It suggested the proper attire for hiking Monte Prelà. The trail is not at all difficult, as I told you on the phone, but your shoes are not ideal. Also, I think it will be a little cold for you, particularly the lady, at the summit late at night. Your jacket is quite thin, signora. It's a nice September evening at sea level, but in several hours, we can expect a temperature of ten degrees Centigrade at the summit."

"My jacket's nice and warm," Carter boasted.

Mickey grunted, "Well, we'll just have to make do."

Zanardi said, "My cousin owns an alpine outfitter store in Genoa. Let's go."

"We don't have time for that, do we?" Mickey complained.

"No, no, we have time. I assure you. Come, come. I am a fast driver."

Leonora Cutrì adjusted the temperature of the bath water until it was perfect, then called the girls. As usual, they wanted to bathe together. During their years in their white room they had used the same white tub, always under the watchful gaze of the Gray Woman, and their habit of washing together was not something their grandmother could not easily break.

"You're big girls now," she told them. "Big girls don't share tubs."

"But we always share tubs!" Victoria cried.

"What about you, Elizabeth?" Leonora said. "Wouldn't you prefer to bathe on your own?"

"I don't mind," she said. "We can get in together."

"Very well," Leonora said. "In you go. Do you want me to scrub your backs?"

"We can do it," Victoria said. "I do her back and then she does mine. Then I wash her hair and she washes mine."

"All right. I'll leave you to it."

Leonora hovered just outside the door, listening to their chatter. It was childish and charming. They weighed their options of things they might do before bedtime. Board games, video games, coloring, and reading were all discussed before they settled on a repeat viewing of a Disney video. They huddled on Elizabeth's bed where their grandmother dried Victoria's hair with a towel.

"What's that?" Leonora asked.

Victoria pulled down the sleeve of her fluffy robe.

"Let me see," Leonora said. She slid the sleeve up the little girl's arm and looked at the dots of ink. "Who did this?" she asked.

"I did," Victoria said. "With a marker."

"What is it?"

"Gray Lady had it," Victoria said. "I liked it."

"She had marks there?" Leonora asked tremulously.

Elizabeth said, "Yes, but it didn't look at all like that. Vicky did a terrible job."

"I did not!"

"Yes, you did!"

Leonora stepped in and told the girls not to fight. "Here, let me get your markers and some paper. I want each of you to make a drawing of the marks for me."

"Like a contest?" Elizabeth asked.

"Yes, like a contest."

"I'm going to win!" Victoria cried.

Mickey announced he was picking up the tab for hiking boots and down jackets for everyone. Celeste tried to get Marcus to smile by modeling red hiking boots and a bright red jacket, but he wasn't buying what she was selling. Colonel Carter admired a blue jacket for himself, mumbled something to the effect that it was warmer than his old one, and threw it on the counter for Zanardi's cousin to ring up. The shopkeeper commented that there were six jackets, two extra ones—a large men's and a medium lady's—but Mickey told him it wasn't a mistake. Marcus shook his head at the gesture—the old guy really expected to see his son and daughter-in-law tonight, didn't he? While they shopped, the guide was at a nearby café to buy sandwiches, pastries, and bottles of water to carry in his backpack for a late-night snack.

They arrived at the trailhead at the village of Donetta, just north of Torriglia, about an hour before sunset. As Zanardi drove, he gave a running commentary to a distracted Mickey. From one row behind, Marcus didn't think his boss was paying attention to anything the guide was saying about the geography of the region, the flora, the fauna, the local economy, you name it.

"So, here we are at Donetta," he said parking the van in a clearing. "We have been steadily climbing since Genoa and here, we are at one thousand meters. To the peak of Monte Prelà it is four hundred meters more."

"How long will it take?" Marcus asked.

"Only one hour. It will just be getting dark when we arrive, but don't worry. I have very strong torches—what you Americans call flashlights—that will make it very safe to descend when you are ready. You said you wanted to be there until midnight?"

"Yes, midnight," Celeste piped up from the row behind Marcus. He hadn't been aware she was listening.

"I'm afraid that I haven't been told why you wanted to be on the mountain at this hour."

"That's right," Mickey said. "You haven't been told."

The guide smiled broadly. "Never mind about that. I will get you safely to the summit, I will get you safely back to Genoa, and you will be tired, but happy, as you fly to Calabria on your beautiful airplane."

Leonora, ever the artist, closely observed as the girls dove into their drawing contest. They both chose black markers and white paper, but Elizabeth picked out a fine-tipped pen whereas Victoria's had a thick nub. Victoria approached the task with intensity, her tongue protruding from her lips in concentration. Dissatisfied with her maiden effort, she made a pouting noise, crumpled the paper, and reached for a fresh sheet. Elizabeth was more precise and careful, pausing frequently and looking into space as she plumbed her memory.

When both were finished, Leonora took the sheets and stuck them onto a bedroom wall with a bit of molding clay.

"Which one wins?" Victoria demanded.

Elizabeth's drawing was clearly recognizable for what it was, but Leonora was wise enough to abdicate the role of judge.

"Let me ask both of you," Leonora said. "Which one is most like what you saw on the Gray Lady?"

Elizabeth smiled confidently and said nothing. Her silence enraged Victoria who shouted, "Fine! I don't care who wins. It's a stupid contest!" She began to cry.

Elizabeth said, "I know who the winner is."

"And who is that?" her grandmother asked.

"It's a tie. It's both of us."

Victoria looked up from her pout and said, "Yes, it's a tie. That means I didn't lose."

"Bedtime, now," Leonora said. "Go brush your teeth."

While they were in the bathroom, Leonora snapped a picture of Elizabeth's drawing and sent it in a text.

The night was clear and cool as they began their ascent of Monte Prelà. The light was fading, but the need for flashlights was at least an hour away. At the trailhead, the mule track rose, gently at first, then more steeply, through a terraced meadow until they were in a sparse wood. Their guide struck a languid clip since they were in the opposite of a rush. His clients wanted to be at the summit at midnight, so even at a snail's pace, they'd have four hours of sitting and waiting. He didn't have a clue what they would be waiting for, but the man paying his fee had agreed to an exorbitant, last-minute quotation, so he would happily wait for whatever might happen.

As they snaked up the path, Mickey fell in behind Zanardi, followed by Colonel Carter and Celeste. Marcus decided it was the gentlemanly thing to take up the rear. From his vantage point, he was convinced that Celeste in her tight jeans, was purposefully exaggerating the sway of her hips.

They walked in silence until Carter began complaining about his new shoes. "I think I got a size too small," he said. "These dogs are going to be barking tomorrow morning, let me tell you."

A creature began to call from a higher elevation. It was rhythmical, high-pitched, with the quality of a power tool.

"What the hell is that?" Mickey asked Zanardi.

"It's a nightjar," Zanardi said.

"Bird or insect?"

"It's a bird," the guide said, "it's annoying, isn't it, but I'm afraid it doesn't have an off switch."

Another sound interrupted the night, the tone of Mickey's mobile phone.

He glanced at it and swore. "It's my office in Chicago. I told them not to call unless it was important." He picked it up and said, "Hello? Hello? Hello? I can't hear you! If you can hear me, call back later!"

"The reception is always quite poor here," the guide said. "Sometimes you can get one bar on top of the mountain."

"I don't care," Mickey said. "I don't want any distractions tonight."

"Look at them," Armando whispered, standing at the foot of the girls' beds. "Two angels."

His wife agreed and said, "As much as I've been with them, I still can't wrap my head around it. Gone for four years and here they are—the same as they were."

"Think about it, my dear," her husband said. "It's like a gift. We haven't missed watching them grow up."

"I suppose," she said.

"Come, let's have a little drink on the patio."

Downstairs, Armando prepared the Negronis and through the kitchen window watched Tim Wheelock walk across the back lawn to have a word with one of his security men.

"Do you think there's a chance?" Leonora asked.

"A chance that Elena and Jesper will come back tonight? Is that what you're asking?" Armando said.

She wiped her eyes with a tissue.

"If I tell you what I think, you'll accuse me of robbing your hope, so I won't say a thing."

"But Mickey believes her. They'll be at the mountain now, won't they?"

Armando glanced at the clock on the microwave and grunted. "Mickey is an optimist. He always has been and it gets the better of him sometimes. How else can you explain a sober engineer casting his lot with a psychic? Marcus doesn't believe her as far as he can toss her."

"But he went along with them?"

"He's paid to do Mickey's bidding. There's no mystery to it."

"Well, I choose to believe that Elena's going to appear on top of the mountain tonight with Jesper and I'm not going to bed until we get Mickey's call."

He handed her a cocktail. "You know something? Neither will I."

The trail became quite steep in the final half hour of the ascent, although it presented no technical challenges. The mule path was fairly smooth without many rocks or roots to trip them up. Still, Colonel Carter was loudly huffing and puffing, and Marcus found himself too winded to light a cigarette along the way. The path narrowed to a single file and cut across the western slope of the mountain in the midst of a lovely beech wood. Soon, the trees gave way to a dramatic vista and in the twilight, they could see the dark waters of Brugneto Lake.

"It's very beautiful," Celeste said, turning to Marcus.

"Another ten minutes and we'll be there," the guide called out. "The last grove we pass through will be a little dark, so you might wish to use your torches."

Finally, they emerged from the wood and the trail disappeared, replaced by an expanse of bald rock stretching the last hundred meters to the flat summit. It was nine o'clock and just past sunset. Out in the open and unprotected, the chilly wind had them all zipping up their new jackets. Zanardi had been gathering kindling along the way, and he set about starting a fire while everyone else found a comfortable enough place to sit. While Carter loosened his shoelaces and moaned, Marcus lit a cigarette and Mickey checked his mobile signal and grunted at the no-service icon.

"Come, sit by the nice fire," the guide said cheerfully, "and we will have our mountain meal. We can eat and watch the stars come out and before you know it, midnight will come. Personally, I can't wait to see why you wanted to be here tonight. Also, I have a little brandy. Who would like some?"

Marcus raised his hand.

At 11:30 p.m. the two Carabinieri guarding the gate of Villa Shibui saw a van approaching from the north. It slowed as it got closer.

The non-commissioned officer named Vaglio, a vice

brigadiere, said to his underling, a young carabiniere, "What the hell does this jackass want?"

The van had no commercial markings. It stopped in the road opposite the gate and the driver's side window lowered. A large man with long, blond hair said, "Hey, you. English? You speak English?"

"Go, go," the vice brigadiere answered in English, making a backhanded shooing gesture. "Move away."

The carabiniere lifted his hand to unbutton his white holster and edged forward.

A pistol appeared in the blond man's hand. The suppressor tube on its barrel made it look freakishly long. The shooter eliminated the threat from the younger man first.

Thwack, thwack.

The older carabinieri heard the muted percussions and saw his colleague clutching his chest and falling, but he didn't see him hit the ground before he took a bullet to the forehead.

The driver pulled on a black balaclava and turned the wheel, rolling over the body of the vice brigadiere, rocking the vehicle.

In Slovakian, the blond man said to the others in the van, "You know what they call the speed bumps in England? Sleeping policemen! Pretty funny, eh?"

He gently accelerated until the front bumper was against the gate, then gave it a little more gas until the gate cracked open, scraping the sides of the van as it pushed through.

Tim Wheelock was at the rear of the villa, smoking a cigar and chatting with one of his men when he heard over his earpiece, "Breach, breach, breach. White van. Unknown—"

"Jimmy!" Wheelock said, beginning his sprint and unshouldering his bullpup assault rifle. "Jimmy! Report!"

Including Wheelock, there were four CSS guards on duty, two in the rear, two in the front of the house. As he ran, Wheelock ordered Graham, the other rear guard, to circle around the opposite side.

Halfway down the driveway, the van stood empty. Three men in black clothing and black balaclavas lay on the grass underneath olive trees, two on one side of the drive, one on the other. All of them used identical gear—barrel-suppressed, .308 caliber rifles with bipods and night-vision scopes. The guard named Jimmy went down in the initial volley. The second CSS guard patrolling the front of the villa acquired the dark form of one of the shooters in his sights just as a round fired by another exploded his skull.

Wheelock came around his side of the house and saw a muzzle flash from the olive grove and heard the soft *thwack* of a suppressed round and a buzzing noise like an angry insect as the bullet flew past him. He started zigzagging, trying to make his way to the cover of the nearest outbuilding. Graham came around the opposite side of the house. He too saw muzzle flashes from the olive grove and he fired two-round bursts downrange. The CSS rifles weren't suppressed and his firing shattered the night.

Inside one of the guest bedrooms, Armando shut his book. Leonora had fallen asleep beside him and she snapped awake and asked what the noise was.

"I don't know," he said. "It sounded like a gun."

"The girls!" she cried, heading for the door.

"Jimmy!" Wheelock said into his mic. "Report! Marty! Report! Graham! Report!"

"On your right flank, boss," Graham said. "I see Marty. He's down. I don't have Jimmy. There's at least three shooters in the trees. I'm going to—"

The blond man was crouching behind plastic garbage bins. When Graham passed him, he rose up and executed him at point-blank range, then moved toward a side door of the house.

"Graham, come in," Wheelock said. "I lost you. Say again."

Wheelock felt a burning sensation in his forearm as a bullet grazed his skin. He reached the protective cover of the barn and began moving along its side. "Graham," he said into his mic, "if you can hear me, I'm going to move along the south fence line and outflank them."

At the corner of the barn, he paused to look through his rifle scope toward the olive grove.

A branch snapped behind him.

He had time to say, "Fuck," then died.

When the blond man entered the girls' room, still cloaked in his balaclava, Victoria and Elizabeth were bolt upright in bed, Leonora was standing between them, and Armando was clutching a portable phone.

"Down, down," the intruder said in English, pointing his pistol at the lawyer's midsection. "Put telephone down."

Victoria screamed. Leonora was too frightened to comfort her.

"Who are you?" Armando said, dropping the phone onto the rug. "What do you want?"

"No, no, I ask. Who are you?"

"We are their grandparents."

The man reached into the pocket of his black jacket and took out a roll of duct tape.

"Okay, grandparents. You have choice," he said. "You do what I say or you can die."

"What do you want me to do?" Armando said.

He tossed Armando the roll and said, "Lady, sit on chair there. He going to tape hands and feet. Tape them good. Fast, fast."

Elizabeth shouted, "No, Granddad, don't hurt her!"

"Don't worry, child," Leonora said. "He's not hurting me."

"Quiet, you," the blond man said, pointing his gun at the girl. "Okay, now go round and round. Tape lady to chair. Good man. You do good."

When Armando had her bound tight, he was ordered to sit in another chair and tape his own feet.

"Good," the man said, snatching the tape from his hands. "I finish you." He taped Armando's hands tightly and looped the tape around the chair-back and his chest several times until he was immobile. Then he ripped off two short lengths of tape and plastered them over his mouth and Leonora's.

The girls were hysterical now and the man was getting angry at the noise.

"You girls! Quiet! If you no quiet, I put tape on grandparent noses and they die—no air. You want me do?"

Elizabeth looked into the frightened eyes of her grandparents and stopped sobbing.

"Come, Vicky," she said. "Don't cry. You're a big girl and you're very, very brave."

Victoria wiped the snot from her nose with the back of her hand and her crying sputtered to a halt.

"Good. Good girls," the man said. "Come. Spaceship waiting for you."

23

It was almost midnight when Fabiana Odorico wandered into her boss's office.

"I saw the light," she said. "I thought it was only me here."

Lumaga turned away from his computer. "There's something wrong with the world when the chiefs work later than everyone else."

"Maybe it's why we're the ones who got the promotions," she said.

"Promoted at work, demoted at home," he said. "Anything going on?"

"I stayed late for a call with the Toronto police. They brought in Marco Zuliani for questioning."

"On what grounds?"

"It turns out that our Zulio is a confidential informant for them. They've got a big problem with a lot of competing drug gangs in Toronto. The 'Ndrangheta is only one of them. They've got Somalis, Russians, Albanians, Punjabis, biker gangs, white supremacists—all of them competing for turf. Zulio's been a police CI for years, dishing dirt on his rivals. He's playing the long game."

"So, what did he say about his cousin, Matteo, getting dumped in the sea as fish food?"

"Not much. He said he didn't know anything about the circumstances."

"Did they tell him that his pal, Ferruccio, got killed?"

"He said he was surprised to hear it. He told them he was a good kid who wasn't in the business as far as he knew."

"The business—meaning drugs."

"That's right. I had them ask him if Matteo and Ferruccio had anything to do with each other in Spain. He told them he didn't have any idea."

"Did they think he was telling the truth?"

"The cop I talked to, who's been running him for years as an informant, told me he thought he was evasive, but that's as far as they could take it."

"So, the Canada connection is dead."

"As dead as Ferruccio and Cinzia, I'm sorry to say."

"And the rest of the case?"

"I've got nothing. The Spanish authorities have no idea where Ferruccio's been living in recent years and no information on his source of income, which was considerable. Guess how much money they found in his bank account?"

"I hate guessing games."

"Seven eighty thousand euros. For the past five years he's made deposits—in cash—of fifteen thousand euros per month, regular as a clock."

"How is drug money so regular and uniform?" Lumaga asked.

"Good question—I have no answer. There's also nothing from the crime scene. The final forensic report is in and the killer left no traces behind. It was very professional. And Cinzia's background was completely clean. I think she took in an old boyfriend and got caught in his situation, whatever it was. It's all very frustrating. Any joy with the Andreason case?"

"No joy. Just agony. You know the Slovakians that Marcus Handler killed—Duris and Beno? I just got some alarming news from the Slovakian police. Two days before the attempted abduction at the hospital, these guys flew into Rome from Bratislava on Ryanair flight 1452. Not surprisingly, more than half the passengers were Slovakian. But Duris and Beno had something in common with six of the passengers. All of them served in the same army unit—the 5th Special Purpose Regiment. It's an elite special operations group that handles counterterrorism missions. But it's worse than that. When they were discharged, all eight of these guys went to work for the same mercenary group called Millennial Tactics, that's based in Luxembourg and sends men for hire into conflict zones, mostly in Africa, but all over the map."

"You mean there's six more of them in Italy?"

"Yes, and we don't have any idea where they went when they left Ciampino Airport and what they're doing here. I just put in a call over to Vaglio, who's in charge of the night duty at Filarete to be extra vigilant. Unfortunately, I haven't been able to reach him. There's private security at the villa also, no?"

"I was critical of Mickey Andreason for bringing them in, but right now, I'm grateful. I was just about to call the house. The Cutrìs are staying there."

Odorico waited while he rang the landline. When there

was no answer, he looked up Armando Cutrì's mobile number and tried that too. Then he tried Vaglio again.

"I don't like this," Lumaga said, getting up and reaching for his holster. "I'm going over there."

"I'm coming too," Odorico said.

He winked at her. "You can even drive."

Giancarlo Zanardi had not been wrong about the starlight. The combination of a clear, cold night and a sliver of a moon turned the Milky Way into a glorious light show. The only light pollution from the summit came from the glowing tip of one of Marcus's cigarettes and Colonel Carter's flashlight during one of his trips to a clump of bushes. When he returned to the fold one more time, he felt the need to explain that his prostate gland was the size of a kiwi fruit and that he was scheduled to have it "shaved down" when he got home.

"Too much information, Virgil," Marcus muttered.

"It's 11:55," Zanardi called out. "It's not too late to tell me what's supposed to happen at midnight," he said hopefully.

"You've shown admirable patience," Mickey said. "Let's see if you can control it for five more minutes."

"Yes, absolutely," the guide said, breaking off a piece of dark chocolate.

Carter tried his mobile phone again and complained that there still wasn't any signal. "I wish to hell I could communicate with Antonio over at CUFOM. If there's UFO traffic in the area, he's going to know it. He's got his network of sky gazers on the alert."

"Did I hear you mention UFOs?" Zanardi said. "Is that what this is about?"

"What did I just say about patience?" Mickey asked.

Celeste had been sitting on her own. She got to her feet and came over to Marcus.

"Could I have one?" she asked.

"A cigarette? I didn't know you smoked."

"I used to."

"You sure you want to start again?"

"My nerves are going wild," she said. "Yes, I'm sure."

She sat beside him and lit up.

"How long are we going to have to wait past midnight when nothing happens?" he asked.

"Something will happen," she said, closing her eyes at the nicotine rush.

Mickey's phone began to chirp with a voice mail message. He pulled it out, declared that he had one bar, and began to listen to a message from his office about a supply-chain problem. Everyone else, with the exception of Celeste, reached for their phones addictively. Zanardi's wife had left a text, inquiring when he'd be home tonight, Antonio from CUFOM sent Carter a WhatsApp asking if he'd seen anything over Torriglia yet, and Marcus saw a text from an unassigned Italian number.

Marcus, this is Leonora Cutrì. Tonight the girls told me about strange marks they saw on the wrist of their Gray Woman. It was the first time I heard about this. Perhaps they already told you but if not here is a picture that Elizabeth drew of the marks. Good luck tonight. I am praying.

He tapped on the photo to download it.

The download was painfully slow.

When the image was ready, he blinked at it in non-comprehension.

There were seven black dots in a singular array.

The Big Dipper.

The moment Odorico turned her steering wheel toward the entrance to Villa Shibui, he knew there was trouble. The gate was half open and one of the leaves was hanging, touching the gravel.

"Oh, my God!" Odorico shouted. "Man down!"

They both jumped out and knelt on either side of Vice Brigadiere Vaglio's bullet-ridden body.

"He's gone," Lumaga said.

"There!" Odorico said, spotting another body on the gravel. It was the other Carabiniere on duty and he too was beyond help.

They both drew their weapons and headed down the drive on foot. Lumaga swept his torch side to side. There was no sign of the vehicle that must have crashed through the gate, but they quickly found two more bodies, both with catastrophic head wounds.

"Canterbury men," Lumaga said. "Spread out, Fabiana. Go left, I'll go right. We need to get inside."

"Should I radio for backup?" she said.

"Yes. Do it. Ambulances too."

On the way to the house, by the barn, Lumaga's torch

found a boot. Standing over the body, he recognized Tim Wheelock, the team leader he'd liaised with in establishing the joint security protocol.

He met Odorico at the front door. She had found another Canterbury man by the trash bins.

"All four dead," Lumaga said, "plus our guys. Fucking disaster. Let's go in."

"I called in the Reparto Operativo," she said. "Their tactical team is mobilizing. Should we wait?"

"I say move now."

"I'm with you," she said.

Marcus grabbed Celeste's hand. She misinterpreted the gesture and smiled, but when he roughly yanked it toward him and rolled back her sleeve, she tried to pull away.

"What are you doing?" she asked.

"This!" he said, pointing to her tattoo. "This!"

"What about it?"

He let go and showed her his phone. "Elizabeth drew this tonight. She saw it on the wrist of the Gray Woman."

He saw fear. She opened her mouth to say something.

The door to Victoria and Elizabeth's bedroom was open. Lumaga went in first, pistol up, ready to engage a threat. Odorico was a step behind.

She flipped the light switch.

Armando and Leonora Cutrì were duct-taped to chairs. The girls' beds were empty.

Lumaga ripped the tape off Armando's mouth.

"The girls! They've been taken!" he cried.

"Look!" Carter shouted, and everyone snapped their necks back and stared into the night sky.

"Good God!" Mickey yelled.

Marcus's lips parted, but he said nothing. He raised his good arm to protect his eyes.

Celeste looked up, started to flee, then ran back toward Marcus.

The rocky summit was suddenly bathed in a blinding, pure, white light.

24

The light came first.

The sound followed.

To Marcus, the noise wasn't other-worldly. In the space of three or four seconds, he recognized the percussive *whump, whump, whump*.

"Helicopter!" was on the tip of his tongue, but he never got the word out.

A continuous deafening burst of automatic fire rained onto the mountain summit, splitting rocks and shredding flesh.

Later, when he described the moment to Roberto Lumaga, Marcus said he perceived the event in a kind of slow motion. What had taken no more than fifteen, maybe twenty seconds, played out over a much longer ribbon of time.

Carter was the first to be hit. Marcus turned toward him when he shouted, "Look!" A volley of lead tore through his torso, flaying his chest like a can opener and releasing puffs of goose down from his new blue jacket.

He saw their guide, Zanardi, tumbling off into the darkness.

And as he felt himself falling, he saw Mickey's head disappearing in a red mist.

A weight was on top of him and he found it hard to breathe. His mouth filled with fabric.

Amidst ear-splitting gunfire, he heard low-pitched grunts. Or maybe he hadn't heard them. Maybe he only felt vibrations.

Then, as suddenly as the aerial menace came, it was gone.

The summit was dark again.

Now, the only sound was the urgent call of nightjars, alarmed by the mechanical invader.

He used his good arm and shoulder to push the weight away from his face, and when there was a separation, he saw that the fabric in his mouth had been red.

He wriggled free until he was lying beside her.

"Celeste!"

When he ran his hands over her red jacket, his fingers got wet.

He heard a man shouting. It was Zanardi. "What in God's name has happened!" he cried.

The Carabinieri command station at Torriglia was a tan building with banana-yellow shutters located on a sloping street near the center of the town. Roberto Lumaga arrived there the next morning on the first flight to Genoa.

Zanardi had raised the alarm after multiple attempts on a weak mobile phone signal, and when the police and emergency services finally arrived at the summit of Monte Prelà in the early hours of the morning, all they could do was pronounce Mickey, Colonel Carter, and Celeste dead. While he waited, Marcus shivered in his down jacket and numbly chain-smoked the rest of his pack. The first thing he requested from the rescuers was more cigarettes.

Zanardi remained at the headquarters until 6 a.m. and when he was finished giving his statement, he found Marcus and put his hands on his shoulders.

He said, "I apologize."

"For what?" Marcus said. "You weren't responsible for this."

"It was my tour and it ended tragically. I should have refused to take you up the mountain in the middle of the night."

"It wasn't remotely your fault."

Zanardi hung his head, unconvinced. "Who did this?" he asked.

"I don't know, but I'm going to find out."

Marcus reached for his wallet and pulled out all his euros.

"What are you doing?" Zanardi asked.

"Someone should pay you. Mickey Andreason can't."

"Put your money away," the guide said. "I'm going home."

Marcus seemed surprised when Lumaga showed his face.

"I wasn't expecting you," he said.

"And I wasn't expecting this," the policeman said. "All of them dead."

"Except for me and our guide."

"How did you survive?"

"I need a smoke," Marcus said.

They went for a walk in the cloudy, warming air. The insouciance of the residents of the alpine town going about their routines clashed with Marcus's boiling turmoil. He developed the shakes and Lumaga lit the cigarette for him.

"I also need a drink," Marcus admitted.

"No problem."

They were outside a restaurant. Lumaga tried the door and rapped on the glass.

"It's closed," Marcus said.

"Let's see," Lumaga replied.

The owner appeared and said through the door that he was closed.

Lumaga was in uniform. "Police business," he said in Italian.

When the owner unlocked the door, Lumaga told him that this man needed a drink. The restaurateur eyed Marcus and asked if he was part of the terrible event on the mountain. Lumaga said he was and the man invited them in.

"Give him a whiskey," Lumaga said, "and don't worry about serving early."

Sitting at a small table in the rear, Lumaga repeated his question.

Marcus drank half the glass and said, "It was Celeste. She fell on top of me. She took the bullets."

"Was this a purposeful act?" Lumaga asked.

He finished the drink. The owner had been watching. He came with the bottle and refilled his glass.

"It might have been. I don't know. She started to run away, but she came back. I'll never know for sure. But she was part of it."

"Part of what?"

Marcus showed him Leonora's text and Elizabeth's drawing.

"So what?" Lumaga asked.

"Celeste had the same tattoo on her wrist."

"I don't think I noticed it," Lumaga said.

"You never slept with her."

Lumaga paused and said, "Ah, I see."

"I'm not proud of it. I was drunk and she was—how shall I put it—insistent."

"It's not my business," Lumaga said, "but what are you saying? She lured you to the mountain to be shot?"

"I'm pretty sure she did."

"Why?"

"I don't know."

"You think she was involved with the abductions four years ago?"

"I've got a lot of questions, Roberto, and precious few answers."

Lumaga asked if they could smoke, and after a gesture from the owner that seemed to say, *you're going to do what you're going to do*, he lit up and said, "I've got more questions for you to ponder, I'm afraid."

Marcus helped himself to Lumaga's pack and said, "What happened?"

"Last night, just an hour before your situation, the villa was attacked."

"Oh, God no," Marcus said, steeling himself for more.

"It was coordinated and professional. Two of my men were killed. All four of the Canterbury men on duty were killed, including Wheelock. The girls were taken. They're gone."

"Jesus. The grandparents?"

"They were left bound and gagged, but they're all right. Shaken to the bones, but all right."

"This was a coordinated, two-front attack," Marcus said. "Eliminate Mickey and me and take the girls."

"Orchestrated by Celeste?"

"She can't be more than a pawn in this."

"And Virgil Carter?"

"An old fool who got caught up in a shitstorm. Roberto, you know this must be connected to the abduction attempt at the hospital."

"I'm certain of this."

Marcus's eyes narrowed. "Certain is a strong word."

"Armando Cutrì told me that the man who bound them spoke English with a strong Eastern European accent."

"My blond friend."

"He was wearing a balaclava, but probably him. The two Slovaks you killed in Rome—we found out last night they traveled to Rome in the company of six other Slovakian nationals, all of them former members of the 5th Special Purpose Regiment."

Marcus bumbled the Slovakian when he said, "5 Pluk špeciálneho určenia."

"You know of them?"

"From my former life. They're based in Žilina. Counterterrorism group. We did some work with them. They're good. You said former?"

"Since leaving, they all went to work for a company in Luxembourg called Millennial Tactics. Mercenaries. Soldiers for hire in conflict zones. Europol raided them this morning. I don't have complete information yet, but their CEO denied they were on any assignment of his. They were a tight-knit group who all took holiday leave at the same time. Apparently, he was quite agitated and repeatedly blamed an ex-employee, a Slovakian who maintained contact with his subordinates. The guy quit the company years ago. He was a bad apple in his words, and if the head of a mercenary group talks about a bad apple, the guy's got to be riddled with worms."

"This bad apple got a name?"

"Gunar Materska. And guess what? He's blond."

"Where's Gunar been hanging his hat since Luxembourg?"

"No information yet. I've got people working on it."

Lumaga reached for his buzzing phone and read a text.

"A body was just discovered at the Genoa airport, at a private helicopter charter company."

"You're going to tell me a helicopter's missing too," Marcus said.

"Major D'Ascanio, the local Carabinieri commander, is heading there. I assume you'll want to come."

"He'll be okay with that?"

"I told him you're my partner in this. You're going to have to give him a CIA anecdote to keep him happy."

"I'll make some shit up."

Marcus offered to pay for the whiskey, but the owner of the restaurant refused to take his money.

"Lot of nice people in this part of the world," Marcus mumbled.

Lombardy Helicopter Tours had a hangar at the Genova Sestri Airport. When Marcus arrived with the two Carabinieri officers, the general manager of the company was still distraught. The four of them stood on the spot where the helicopter had been kept.

"Giovanni was my best pilot and my best friend," he lamented. "Who would do such a thing? Are you certain my helicopter was used for the attack at Monte Prelà?"

"We are quite sure," Major D'Ascanio told him. "On the way here, we got word that the French police found an Agusta helicopter abandoned in Bessans, not far from the Italian border."

"Do you have a model number? A registration number?"

"It's an Agusta AW109SP," the officer said. "Here's the serial number."

"Yes, it's mine," the general manager said. "I'll be glad to have it back, but I'd rather have Giovanni back."

"We were told there was a video camera in operation at the hangar," Lumaga said.

"I can play the recording for you," he said. "It shows the men who booked the charter. Giovanni was going to fly them to Como for the night. That was the plan. You can't see their faces well, but you can see for yourself."

"When they booked, did they leave a name? A credit card?" Marcus asked.

"I have a name. I don't know if it's real or fake. We require payment in advance. They paid via bank transfer."

"Which bank?"

The general manager said he would check, then added, "I hate to go into the office. That's where I found Giovanni."

He came back with the wire transfer details. The funds came from the National Bank of Slovakia.

The video showed two men in dark clothes, getting out of a car and parking in front of the hangar. The car was later found to be have been stolen in Genoa. A second camera showed them entering the hangar where they were

GLENN COOPER

met by the pilot who was immediately forced at gunpoint into the office. His killing took place off-camera. When the two men emerged, they opened the hangar door and manually pushed the copter through the door using its ground-handling wheels. Outside, they loaded a large duffel bag into the craft, started the rotors spinning, and took off.

"One of them is a pilot," Lumaga said. "We can find out who it is with the help of the Slovakian authorities."

"The other one must have been the sharpshooter," the other policeman said.

"He didn't have to be that good," Marcus said. "It was like shooting fish in a barrel." For a moment, his mind flashed with the image of Mickey losing a chunk of his head, and he squeezed his eyes. It was going to be something he'd have to deal with. In time.

Marcus was so tired he felt like he was sleepwalking, but there was one last task to perform before he could collapse at a local hotel. The coroner in Genoa summoned him to formally identify the bodies of the Monte Prelà victims. They had to fight their way inside through a crush of media, and although names of the shooting victims had not yet been released, nor had the calamity in Calabria been revealed, the world would soon know that the Andreason girls were once again at the center of dramatic events, because a reporter from Milan recognized Marcus and began shouting questions.

"So, this is the tattoo," Lumaga said.

To Marcus's eye, the ink of the stars seemed blacker now that her cold, bloodless skin was paper-white.

"Let me see the girl's drawing again."

Marcus showed it to him.

"What's the tattoo's significance?" Lumaga asked.

"I think she just liked it," Marcus said in little more than a whisper. Morgues, like churches, weren't places for loud talking. "She said it helped her find her North Star."

"And you believe that whatever she wore to make the girls believe her skin was gray, simply rolled up one day and exposed the tattoo?"

"I can't be sure, but, yes, I think so."

"Her ID and plane tickets were in one of these anti-pickpocket belts that is worn under the clothes," he said.

Lumaga flipped through the documents.

"When she flew to Italy—where did she say she was coming from?" he asked Marcus.

"Marseilles."

"That was a lie. She flew from Madrid."

"What the hell?" Marcus said.

"Spain again," Lumaga said. "I'm dreaming about Spain these days."

"What do you mean?"

"Sorry, it's another case. So, Celeste Bobier is at the center of this whole mess. She came here for a purpose—to subvert our investigation, to kidnap the girls and murder their protectors. We need to find out everything there is to know about her."

"I'm going to Spain," Marcus said, giving Celeste's body a last look.

"But you've lost your employer," Lumaga said.

"This isn't about a job anymore. This is about Victoria and Elizabeth. I'm going to find them or die trying."

25

The Madrid weather was depressing. It was midday and the sky was the color of mud. Rain came down in sheets. Standing under a cheap umbrella Marcus had borrowed from his hotel, he waited on the sidewalk, smoking a cigarette outside a restaurant on Calle de Gallur, well east of the city center. It had been fifteen years since he last saw Abril Segura, but he recognized her at a distance. She had always liked Burberry trench coats and she was wearing one today, but it was her determined gait that he remembered best—always leaning forward as if fighting a stiff wind.

"Oh, my God! Sweetheart!" she said in heavily accented English before exchanging cheek-kisses. "I didn't think I'd ever see you again."

"It could have gone either way," he said, flicking away his cigarette.

He studied her while she studied the menu. She had changed, but not as much as he might have thought. She was still a strikingly handsome woman—high cheekbones, narrow nose, full lips, and her figure was as sleek as he remembered. She had to be well into her sixties, but she didn't look anything near it.

"The sea bass, for sure," she said. "It's always good here. I come often. It's near work."

"We've met here before," he said.

"Have we?"

By work, she meant CIFAS, the Spanish Armed Forces Intelligence Center. Marcus spent four years in Madrid assigned to the American Embassy, and Segura was then, and remained, a senior counterterrorism analyst. They had been colleagues on a myriad of security matters, and for a time, they had been close. That was the euphemism that Marcus's wife used once when she saw them off together in a corner at an embassy cocktail party. "You and that woman seem—close," she had said.

They ordered. He told her it was good she'd kept the same mobile number. Otherwise, he would never have been put through to her desk at CIFAS.

"Cell phone numbers are like fingerprints," she said. "They stay with you throughout life." She clinked wine glasses. "So, I must say, you're looking good, Marcus."

"What a liar."

"No, really."

"You're the one who's looking good. Really good."

"I've had help," she whispered. "I have an aesthetician who is a maestro with a syringe."

"I'll drink to that," he said. "Still single?"

"Yes and no. I'm still married to the job. In the old days it was the Russians. Now it's the Russians and the Chinese and the jihadis. It never ends. How's your wife. It was Alice, no?"

"She's been gone for years. Cancer."

"I'm so sorry, Marcus. You never remarried?"

"Nope." He chuckled and said, "There's still hope for us, I guess."

She didn't participate in his laughter, but she smiled and said, "We were quite good together. I always liked younger men. There was a time when I might have thought about it. I was in love with you, you know."

"I didn't know."

"Of course, you didn't. Tell me why you're here, Marcus. You haven't been in the game for a long while. I know you didn't come to Madrid to look up an old flame, although that would be frightfully romantic if you had."

"Have you heard about the missing American girls who resurfaced in Italy four years after they were abducted?"

Her expression revealed that she knew all about it. "What does that have to do with you?"

"I'm in the middle of it, right in the goddamn middle of it."

He told her everything, like one counterterrorism professional briefing another about a complex matter. And, like the experienced interlocutor she was, she didn't interrupt him during a monologue that spanned the luncheon service. When he finished, her entrée was mostly consumed and his untouched.

"So," she said, reaching for her wine glass, "no spaceship."

"No spaceship."

"No aliens."

"No aliens."

"This woman—Bobier—she was no psychic. She was sent to deflect you. To set you up."

"It appears so."

"Did her masters assassinate her, or was she killed accidentally?"

"Hard to know. There's a third possibility."

"What would that be?"

"That she died protecting me."

She considered this and said, "You have an effect on women. You haven't eaten. Should I ask them to heat up your plate?"

"I'm not hungry."

"I'm not your mother, but you look thin. Would you like my assessment?"

"I would."

"First, I haven't got a reasonable explanation for any of this."

"Join the club," he said, tasting his steak and putting his utensils down again. He asked the passing waiter for a Scotch.

"Their abduction four years ago—it wasn't for economic gain, that is clear," she said. "Certainly, no one has advanced a theory of their age-defying years of captivity or their identical rare illnesses. And no one has advanced an explanation for their return to Italy. One wonders whether it was something that the conspirators planned, as they had to go to elaborate lengths to take these girls a second time. One thing is certain, however. The people behind this have significant resources. One only has to look at their employment of a small army of Slovakian special operators. But, Marcus, none of this has escaped you."

"We're on the same murky page."

"Has it occurred to you that a state actor is responsible?"

"I've thought about it. It's hard to come up with a state's motivation."

She shook her head and paused to look deeply at her old friend. "So, what's the purpose of my meal and your fast?"

"I need your help."

"With what?"

"Celeste Bobier. I need to know who she is and what she was doing in Spain."

"Surely the Italian police can make inquiries via their Spanish counterparts."

"They can and they are, but you'll be better and faster."

"By law, I can't investigate a Spanish national without a judicial order."

He handed her Celeste's ID. "She was a Spanish resident, but she's a French national," he said.

"Ah, you're a step ahead of me. Tell me, where are you staying?"

It was a two-star hotel in a seedy district.

"Why there? It's a dump."

"I'm paying my own way," he said. "I lost my benefactor on top of that mountain."

"I'll see what I can find out on one condition," she said. "You must agree to come to my flat tomorrow night for a home-cooked meal that you *will* consume."

He readily agreed, then took a folded sheet from his pocket and pushed it across the table.

"What's this?" she said.

"The Slovakians. I want to know if they're known to CIFAS and other agencies."

She took the paper and put it into her purse. "You're incorrigible," she said.

★

He spent the next day texting Lumaga while he strolled aimlessly in a drizzle through Retiro Park and then the Prado Museum when the rain got heavier. As he suspected, the Carabinieri and the Spanish police were bogged down in paperwork and information about Celeste wasn't flowing.

He didn't need directions to Segura's flat. It had been the scene of their assignations. The nature of his work then had dictated irregular hours and occasional all-nighters, and until Alice remarked on his closeness with Abril, he believed his affair was flying under her radar. She lived in the ritzy Salamanca district on Calle Castelló in an apartment that an ordinary government employee couldn't have hoped to possess. The first time he visited her there, he ogled its size and magnificence, and she told him that it helped to be the only child of a wealthy banker.

"You remembered your way," she said, taking his coat. She was dressed in a short and simple black dress with no jewelry. She still had nice legs.

"It's fifteen years, but it seems like fifteen days. I remembered the smell of the lobby and the funny way the elevator stutters when it's about to stop at the fourth floor."

"It's done that since I was a little girl," she said.

She took his bottle of wine with a kiss and he followed her into the kitchen where she had a bottle of a different sort waiting for him.

"You used to drink Glenlivet," she said. "It's okay for you?"

"More than okay. I'd drink it all the time if I could afford it."

"Surely, a man like you who went to work for a corporation like Andreason can buy whatever Scotch you like."

"Past tense. Worked. I've been unemployed for four years."

"But you said Mikkel Andreason agreed to pay you handsomely to accompany him to Italy. Things will be brighter for you financially now."

"He's dead and I only got a down payment. I'll be sticking to the bottom-shelf booze, I guess."

She poured him a huge measure in a crystal glass. The last woman who plied him with drink was Celeste. Abril was the kind of woman who might have found that interesting, but he kept it to himself.

"I know you want to hear what I was able to find out," she said, "but if I tell you now, you'll get distracted and you won't eat. Supper first, then business."

She had made a lamb chilindron that she ladled into large bowls at her kitchen table. The dining room seemed too formal for old friends, she said.

The stew was rich and spicy and when he asked if she came home early from work to prepare it, she said, "Two words: slow cooker. While I was saving Spain from its enemies—foreign and domestic—and finding the time to do your bidding, the chilindron was preparing itself."

While they ate, they talked about old adversaries and new.

"Do you miss it?" she asked at one point.

"Every dog has its day. I had mine."

"I know about your busted case in Paris," she said. "Everyone has one of these. I had something like this happen to me—well, maybe not so dramatic, but I didn't feel an obligation to fall on my sword. Why did you?"

"It was more complicated than a bad deal," he said. "I made a terrible decision. I should have been at home with Alice. I chose to be in the field chasing fool's gold." The Glenlivet was on the table beside a small flower arrangement. He reached for it. "It ended me," he said.

"I see," she said quietly. "Will you have some flan?"

"I'd rather have information."

She made an effort to lighten the mood. "You were a good boy. You cleaned your plate. You shall have your information for dessert. Come to my study."

She led him to a cozy book-lined room off the much larger sitting room. It had been her father's office and she'd made it hers by replacing the painting above the mantel, a gloomy, nineteenth-century still life (stored behind the love seat) with a colorful abstraction of a woman lying on her side by the contemporary Spanish artist Merello. He told her he liked the painting, which delighted her. They sat, side-by-side on the sofa, with a CIFAS folder on the coffee table. His friend's slow reveal had made him tense, and the sharp edges of the crystal glass dug into his clenched palm.

"Celeste Bobier," she began. "Thirty-four years of age. Born in Saint-Étienne, France, near Lyon. I should begin by saying that she was not known to CIFAS, Interpol, Europol, or to local police authorities in Spain or France. She had no known arrests, not even a parking ticket. By all conventional indicators, this is a person with a spotless record and a life of rectitude."

He repeated her phrase: *by all conventional indicators.*

"But," she said, "as we know, there is nothing conventional

about your case. She was educated in Grenoble as a nurse and went to work—"

"She was a nurse?" he said.

"Yes, that's what I said. She didn't tell you that?"

"No, she did not. What kind of a nurse?"

She checked her notes. "I don't know. A general sort of a nurse, I suppose. She was employed in a hospital in the south of France. I can give you the details, if you wish to find out more about this phase of her life. However, six years ago, your Celeste emigrates to Spain where she takes up a position in Madrid, as a nurse at the Hospital Universitario La Paz, which is a prestigious clinic affiliated with Universidad Autónoma de Madrid. She worked there for only one year and there, my dear Marcus, the trail runs cold. I could find no further records of her employment or residence within Spain, France, or indeed anywhere within the EU."

"Do you have anything on co-workers or superiors at the hospital? Her department?"

"Nothing on that."

"How about where she lived when she worked there?"

"I probably have that, but I didn't print it out. Why do you want that?"

"To see if I can find an old neighbor, someone who knew her."

"Of course. I can look it up when I get back to my desk."

"Don't worry. I can find it on my own. Is there anything on why she left her hospital job?"

"I'm afraid not. I can't tell you why she left her position at La Paz, whether voluntarily or involuntarily."

"So, she's been a ghost for five years," he said.

"A ghost, yes. No employment records, no tax payments, no car insurance, no bank accounts, nothing."

"I think I'm fucked," he mumbled.

"Have more faith, my friend. It's darkest before dawn. There's a little bit more I can tell you about Celeste Bobier. She was wealthy."

He had been staring absently at her patterned rug. The word wealthy snapped him to attention. "You just said she didn't have any bank accounts. How do know she had money?"

"I should have said conventional bank accounts. She had a very unconventional account. Do you remember the scandal from several years ago—the Panama Papers scandal?"

"Sure. Millions of leaked financial documents of offshore transactions in Panama."

"CIFAS was obligated to construct a database for various purposes, not the least of which was the revelation that Spanish politicians, sports figures, even members of the royal family were illegally hiding funds offshore. When I entered Celeste's name into our internal search engines, I got a hit from Panama. She's been getting regular payments into a Panamanian bank account for five years. Her account has a balance of over three million euros."

"What! Who's been paying her?"

"That, I can't say. It's not recorded."

"Can you find out?"

"That won't be easy, Marcus. There's no way to get the info through official channels."

"When did official channels ever stop you?"

She had her own drink, a small snifter of brandy. She

lightly clinked his glass and said she would see what could be done.

"What about the Slovakians?" he asked.

"No joy there, I'm afraid. None of your names ring bells. They're not on any international watch lists. They've never entered Spain. I emailed a friend at the Slovakian SIS. They are mercenaries as you said, but they aren't known to be criminals."

His phone dinged with a text from Lumaga.

"It's my Carabinieri contact in Italy," Marcus said. "He wants to know if I found out anything about Celeste."

She ran a fingernail up the inseam of his trousers. "Why don't you answer him later. I have a larger painting by Merello I'd like to show you. It's in my bedroom."

It was nearly midnight when Marcus wandered from Segura's bedroom in search of his cigarettes and more Glenlivet. He lit up on a balcony of her stately building overlooking a lamp-lit, quiet street, still wet from the earlier rain. Lumaga answered his text immediately. He was still up and was happy to talk.

Over the phone, Marcus said, "I didn't think you'd still be up."

"Not only up, I'm at the office. I'm *persona non grata* with my wife."

Marcus was half-inclined to give him cautionary advice about domestic balance, but he didn't. Instead he started to spill his newly found intelligence on Celeste.

"I'm sorry," Lumaga interrupted. "Did you say she worked at the Hospital Universitario La Paz?"

"Yeah, why?"

"Hold on, let me check my notes."

Marcus heard papers rustling and he waited, blowing smoke rings into the cool night until Lumaga came back on the line.

"While everything was happening with the Andreason case, I had another important case occupying my department," Lumaga said. "It was a double murder—an Italian boy and his former girlfriend. His name was Ferruccio Gressani. He came back to Calabria to visit this woman from Madrid, where he's been living."

"I'm listening," Marcus said.

"You're never going to guess where he used to work as a technician. The Hospital Universitario La Paz."

26

The following morning, Segura was in a pensive mood. While Marcus had a coffee in bed, she was wrapped in a silk dressing gown, preparing for her day.

"As much as I enjoyed our night, I want you to leave Spain," she said, taking a travel bag from her closet.

"Why is that?"

"I don't want you to be hurt. Or worse. You're up against a determined and well-funded adversary, whoever they are. Twice! Twice you were almost killed. You don't have the resources of the American government behind you. You don't even have a powerful employer behind you. You only have yourself."

"Not true. I have a buddy in the Italian police. And I have you."

"Stop kidding around, Marcus. This is serious. Leave this with the police where it belongs. The girls will be found."

"Their names are Victoria and Elizabeth. They call me Uncle Marcus. I'm going to find them."

She began going through her drawers and tossing clothes into her bag. "You know why you're doing this, don't you? You want to be vital again—although, if you ask me, you were plenty vital last night even with a skin of Glenlivet in you, and a stiff shoulder. Your last tango ended badly—by the way, did you know that Burakov had a fatal heart attack last year?"

"Good. I hope it hurt."

"You're guilty about Alice and it's still eating you up. You think that being the hero today is going to assuage that guilt. It won't."

"Thank you, Dr. Freud. How much do I owe you?"

"You're not going to drop this, are you?"

He swung his feet over and got his cigarettes from his trousers.

"You're not going to smoke in here," she scolded.

He got up and unlatched the French doors. "Balcony."

"Fine, but put something on. I don't want my neighbors to see a naked man."

He obliged her and sat outside at a little wrought-iron table with his phone to his ear.

Lumaga didn't sound fresh.

"Anything on your end?" Marcus asked.

"I already talked with the French police this morning. Other than a bucketful of 5.56 shell casings from a Slovakian manufacturer on the floor of the helicopter, there were no fingerprints or useful evidence. CCTV picked up a green SUV on a road near the landing site that was later recovered about fifty kilometers away. It was stolen a couple of days before. The trail ended there. The autopsies from Monte Prelà and Villa Shibui were concluded. No surprises—you know how everyone died. We've had people looking at surveillance from all the airports, all the land crossings to

France, Switzerland, Austria, Slovenia, and all the seaports for signs of the girls and there's nothing. That's it. I don't have anything more."

"I need your help with something," Marcus said.

"Of course, anything."

"I can't march into some administration office at the La Paz Hospital and expect to get personnel information about Celeste and Ferruccio Gressani. Can you go back to Ferruccio's friends and family and see if you can find out where he worked there? A department? A boss's name? A co-worker?"

"Sure. I'll try. Later."

Segura had to fly to Brussels for a NATO security conference. She offered Marcus the use of her car. Like a couple, they parted with a kiss when her driver arrived, and he retrieved the BMW from the garage underneath her building.

Fabiana Odorico returned to the pretty house with red shutters and flower boxes in Cessaniti. Manuela Gressani was expecting her and was ready with coffee and cookies. Her scoliotic spine bowed her black mourning dress and Odorico insisted on carrying the tray from the kitchen.

"Is there any news about who killed my Ferruccio?" she asked.

"Nothing, but we are actively working on it. That's why I'm here."

"Tell me," the woman said. "How can I help?"

"We need to know more about where Ferruccio worked in Madrid."

"I found the name of the hospital for you, don't you remember?"

"Yes, I have that. What I mean is—at the hospital, which department did he work in? Or if you have it, the name of his boss at the hospital."

"I don't think I know these things. Why would he tell me?"

"Did he write you using hospital stationery? Give you a hospital return address on a letter?"

The elderly woman shook her head, then asked if Odorico could pick up the tray again.

"I'm sorry," Odorico said, "did I do something to offend you?"

The woman cackled, "Oh no! We just need to go to the dining room."

Odorico understood when she turned the corner. Laid out on the dining room table was a scrapbook into which Ferruccio's mother had been pasting photos and memorabilia.

"Ferruccio's life," the woman said sadly. "From his birth to his death. What else can I do? I haven't pasted the recent photographs yet he sent me from his years in Spain. You're welcome to look at them."

Odorico sat down and munched sugar cookies while sorting through the small stacks of photos. She stopped at one of them of a young, bearded man wearing a lab coat.

"That was soon after he arrived in Madrid," his mother said. "See how handsome he was?"

"Yes, I see. May I take this?"

"I'd prefer you didn't. I don't know if I have another with such a warm smile."

"Then I'll just take a photo of it, if that's okay."

"Yes, please, go ahead. I can see why you want that one. Ferruccio never looked better."

The Biblioteca Pública Municipal Eugenio Trías was a modern public library within Retiro Park occupying two large pavilions at the site of an old zoo. Marcus tried to resurrect his limited Spanish vocabulary, but the woman at the information desk took pity on him and replied, "I'm sure it will be easier for you if I speak English."

"Yes, I'm sure it will. I'm looking for old Madrid phone directories."

"How old?"

"Modern, actually. Past decade."

"Certainly. You'll find what you want here," she said, handing him a printed floor plan with her notation.

He found the Madrid municipal phone books and began with the current year. There was no listing for Celeste. He marched back in time, year by year, until six years back, there she was. C. Bobier, 45 Calle de la Villa de Marín, #719. He gave the woman at the information booth a thumbs-up on his way out and went to retrieve Segura's parked car.

The sun was finally out and the park looked lovely in yellow light. Retirees were strolling the walkways, mothers were pushing prams, tourists were taking pictures.

He stopped noticing his surroundings.

A text from Lumaga made everything disappear.

The attached photo, Lumaga explained, was of Ferruccio Gressani at the Le Paz Hospital. In it, the young, bearded man wearing a long white lab coat, was standing in a hospital corridor in front of a sign:

Instituto de Genética Médica y Molecular

Marcus began taking long, fast strides toward the car.

The hospital complex, north of the city, was hugged by the busy M-30 motorway. The Institute of Genetics and Molecular Medicine was in its own modern building at the heart of the medical area. Marcus found the administration offices and asked to speak with the director. He didn't think his Spanish was going to cut the mustard, so he asked in English.

"Dr. Gaytan?" the receptionist asked back.

"If Dr. Gaytan is the director, then yes."

"I'm sorry," she said, "do you have an appointment today?"

"I don't actually, but it's important that I have a brief word with him."

"This isn't a patient area, sir. If you go down to the lobby, they can show you how to get to the clinics."

"I'm not a patient. It's a personnel matter I need Dr. Gaytan's help with."

"Without an appointment, I'm afraid that won't be possible." She scribbled a number on a card and handed it over the counter. "If you call this number and leave a voice message, Dr. Gaytan can decide whether he can call you back."

He could tell if he persisted on the same track that she

was only a couple of steps away from calling security. In the parking garage, he had prepared for a brick-wall moment by pulling out a relic from his wallet, an old, worn business card.

Central Intelligence Agency
Marcus Handler
George Bush Center for Intelligence
Langley, Virginia 22101

He presented it and repeated that it was urgent that he speak with the director. She looked at it wide-eyed, excused herself, and disappeared through a door. While he waited, he wondered how many laws he had just broken. She quickly returned and asked him to follow her. At a corner office overlooking hilly parkland further to the north, a man Marcus's age got up from his desk and slipped on a figure-hugging suit jacket that had been draped over his chair.

"Mr. Handler, I am Dr. Gaytan," he said. "Please come in."

Gaytan had luxuriously thick, black hair, graying at the temples and a film-star tan. Marcus never paid much attention to another man's physical attributes, but there was no denying that this was a good-looking fellow. He offered Marcus a coffee and when he accepted, Gaytan picked up his phone.

He returned Marcus's card, presented one of his own—Dr. Ferrol Luis Gaytan, director of the institute, and said, "How may I assist you, Mr. Handler? It's not every day that I get a visit from the CIA."

"I'm looking for information on one of your former employees."

"This is a very large facility with hundreds of employees, but if I don't know the individual personally, I can make inquiries within the appropriate group."

A stylish female administrative assistant materialized with the coffees and when she left, Marcus said, "Ferruccio Gressani. He was a laboratory technician who worked here about six years ago."

Gaytan frowned and said, "I don't recognize the name. How old is he?"

"The question should be, how old was he? He was thirty-two."

"He's dead?"

"Murdered."

"May I ask why the CIA is interested in this man?"

"I'm not at liberty to discuss that."

"Which can only mean some sort of terroristic association. It's important for you to know about his employment at the institute?"

"It is. And to see if anyone knows where he went when he left here."

"Then, I will find out. Let me make a call."

Gaytan called his assistant and asked to be transferred to the human resources office where he inquired after the personnel file of a Ferruccio Gressani who left employment in the time frame Marcus stipulated. Marcus sipped coffee and tried to make out the Spanish of Gaytan's end of the conversation.

"He was an Italian national? The cytogenetics lab? Who

was his supervisor? Me? It couldn't have been me. Ah, Lopez was the lab manager. Yes, I was the acting head of the lab back then. Wait a minute, I remember the boy. Yes, yes, now I remember. Yes, I refused to write a letter of reference when he left. For obvious reasons. Was there a forwarding address of any kind? I see. Look, you've been very helpful. I appreciate it."

Gaytan hung up and shook his head.

"I understood some of that," Marcus said. "I was stationed in Spain for a few years."

"Good, good, then you heard that my memory was prodded and I realized I knew Gressani. He was a charming boy, a low-level technician who operated some of our analytical instruments. Sometimes he made a joke about the similarities in our first names—Ferruccio and Ferrol. I found it a little forward, but I never paid it much attention. He was dismissed. Fired. The laboratory manager discovered a piece of machinery was missing and it seems Gressani stole it. When confronted with the evidence, he admitted the theft and returned it. It was suspected that he had a drugs problem. We agreed to not report him to the police in return for his immediate resignation. The institute just wanted to be done with the situation. His file doesn't have any information on where he might have gone. You say he was murdered?"

"In Italy."

"I see. It seems his life took an unfortunate turn. I'm sorry I couldn't be more helpful, Mr. Handler."

Marcus sighed. Another dead end. "Do you think you could steer me toward the human resources office. I've got another person I'm working on. She could have worked anywhere in the hospital. Her name is Celeste Bobier."

Gaytan's face registered his surprise. "Celeste? I knew Celeste. She was a research nurse for a short while. She was involved in clinical trials of experimental therapies on our in-patient wards. She wasn't here long, but she was a woman who is hard to forget, if you understand my meaning. She's all right, I hope—not in any trouble."

"I'm sorry to say that she's dead too."

"My God! What happened?"

"Also murdered. Again, I can't discuss any of the details."

"What in God's name is going on here?" Gaytan said, shaking his head. "Has the world gone mad?"

"What can you tell me about her?"

"Well, she was French—from the south of France, if I can recall. She was very competent, energetic, a good sense of humor. And as I implied, she was also something of a beauty. She turned heads."

"Did you know her socially as well as professionally?"

"Heavens, no! Did I give you that impression? Just professionally, I assure you."

"When did she leave?"

"I don't recall exactly. Four years ago? Five?"

"Why'd she leave?"

"My recollection is that she needed to return to France. A sick mother, perhaps?"

"You had no further contact with her?"

"None whatsoever."

"Would you have given her a reference?"

"It's quite possible. She was an excellent nurse. I can check my files."

"Do you know if she and Gressani knew each other when they worked here?"

"I have no idea about that. You're sure you can't tell me what happened to Celeste? This is deeply shocking news."

"I wish I could. Listen, could I trouble you for one last thing? Could you also check with your human resources people and see if she left a forwarding address?"

Gaytan stood and pointed to his thin, gold watch. "I have a meeting now, but I'll be happy to look into this further. I didn't see a contact number on your business card. How can I reach you?"

Marcus asked for a piece of paper and wrote down his mobile number.

"You're staying in Madrid?"

He said he was and mentioned his hotel.

"I think I've heard of it," Gaytan said with a bemused smile. "I think maybe the CIA doesn't give you a big expense account."

27

It was a short drive to Calle de la Villa de Marín. Marcus parked outside Celeste's old apartment block, a red-brick tower with stacked balconies, and called Lumaga to tell him what he had just learned.

"Incredible," Lumaga said. "Ferruccio and Celeste may have known each other."

"I'm betting they did," Marcus said. "They worked in the same institute and left the hospital in the same time frame. The question is—where did they go and who was paying them all that money?"

Lumaga added, "And what were they being paid to do? The usual way that people get rich fast is drugs. It's interesting that this Dr. Gaytan thought that Ferruccio might have had a habit. There's also his undeniable 'Ndrangheta connection. The big unanswered question is how the girls fit into this picture."

"Kidnapping to raise cash would have fit—if there'd been a ransom demand. We also don't know how the Slovakians fit into the picture. Is there an 'Ndrangheta/Slovakia connection?"

"Not that I'm aware of, but these gangsters get around. They have tentacles. What's next for you?"

"I'm outside a building where Celeste used to live. I'm going to see if I can find out where she went after La Paz."

Marcus pushed open the red gate to the courtyard of the apartment building and entered the lobby. The next set of doors was locked. He saw a man with a small dog waiting for the elevator and rapped on the glass to get his attention. The man gave him a sour look and got into the elevator. There was a large array of buzzers on the wall and he pressed 719, Celeste's old unit, but there was no response. He tried 718 and 720 with the same result, but a man answered at 717.

In his best Spanish, he attempted to say, "Excuse me, I am an old friend of the woman, Miss Bobier, who used to live in apartment 719. I'd like to speak to you about where she went to live after she left the building."

The man answered, "I'm sorry, what?"

When he tried again, the man said, "I speak English. What do you want?"

The man immediately buzzed him up.

Marcus saw the peephole darkening as the resident of apartment 717 gave him the once-over. Apparently, his appearance wasn't threatening, because the door opened, revealing an elderly gentleman with a goatee, leaning heavily on a cane. Marcus was invited into a tidy room dominated by books. Aside from the man's lounger, there weren't any chairs or sofas without stacks of books and periodicals on them.

"I apologize," the man said. "I like books more than people."

As he made a one-handed attempt to clear off a chair,

Marcus said, "I can stand. I don't want to take up your time, I—"

"Nonsense. There. Sit. Let's be civilized. You seem like a civilized fellow—for an American. I am Javier."

"I'll take that as a compliment, Javier."

"As it was intended."

"I'm Marcus."

"Hello, Marcus. Tea?"

Marcus thought it would be rude to decline, so he lied and said he'd love a cup.

He heard a stove-top kettle whistling from the kitchen and when the old man returned with one hand on his cane and one on a cup, he accepted a tea in a chipped mug. Marcus offered to get Javier's cup, but the man said no, and made another round trip.

"You have an extensive library," Marcus said. "A lot of English books."

"I was a university professor," he said. "I taught courses in comparative governments. I was a minor expert on the American government."

"My old employer."

"Oh, yes? Which branch?"

"I spent my career at the CIA."

"Really? How fascinating. You retired from there?"

"I guess you could say that. I suppose I could be called a burnt-out case."

That induced a broad smile. "The title of my favorite Graham Greene novel."

"Except I didn't have leprosy," Marcus said.

"Excellent. You are well read. Is the tea to your liking?"

"Very nice, thanks."

"Tell me, how can I help you?"

"As I said, Celeste Bobier is an old friend I've lost contact with. I know she used to live in number 719. Did you know her?"

"Not well, but I knew her, certainly. We saw each other in passing. A very attractive, young Frenchwoman who was a nurse at the La Paz Hospital, I believe. She asked about my walking because of this silly stick."

"Do you know where she went when she moved out?"

"I have no idea. We were not that close."

"I don't suppose you know why she left her job at the hospital?"

"I would not know that either. But you know, the woman immediately next door to her in number 720, Señora Iglesias, knew her better, I believe. Unlike me, she still works, but I can ask her tonight and give you a call."

"I have an American mobile number. You'll need to dial—"

"I'm sure that will be too complicated for me."

"Then I can give you my hotel number."

"Much easier," the man said.

Marcus returned to his hotel near the Quintana Metro stop and found a parking spot on the street for the BMW. It was warm, almost hot, and he left his jacket in the car when he set off, looking for a liquor store. When he returned with a bottle of Scotch and a sandwich, he stopped to retrieve his jacket and went inside.

Across the street, a big blond man in jeans and an

untucked shirt watched, smoking a cigarette. When Marcus disappeared, so did the man.

Marcus spent the rest of the day at his hotel, holed up with the bottle, watching TV and metering his drinking in case he got a call about Celeste from Dr. Gaytan or the old man with the cane. When nightfall came, he ate the other half of his sandwich and threw caution to the wind, knocking back the whiskey until he was pleasantly inebriated. At some point, he dozed off until the hotel phone rang him awake.

"Is this Marcus?" a man asked.

"Yes, who's this?" he said groggily.

"I hope I haven't disturbed you," the man said. "This is Javier from apartment 717. You know, the one with all the books."

He sat up. "Of course. No, you're not disturbing me."

"I just spoke to my neighbor, Señora Iglesias. She tells me that she spoke to your friend shortly before she left the building. She will gladly speak to you if you wish to see her this evening."

"That's fantastic. Please tell her I'll be there shortly," Marcus said.

It was nine-fifteen. Rising to his feet, Marcus realized he wasn't fit to drive. He splashed his face, brushed his teeth and his hair, and grabbed his phone. He groaned when he saw the battery was almost run down; the charger plug had been off. On the street, he hailed a passing taxi and tried using willpower to sober up.

At ten o'clock, Abril Segura, on the way home from the airport, called Marcus and got put straight into voice mail.

She tried a second time a few minutes later, then asked her driver to take her to his hotel.

Arriving, she said to the driver, "Wait for me," then changed her mind and said, "No, just drop me off. I see my car."

Mrs. Iglesias was a nice woman who seemed delighted to have an American pay a visit. She too was a passable English-speaker. She took the opportunity to invite her neighbor, Javier over and offered up slices of cake. When she asked if Marcus wanted coffee, he jumped on the opportunity to clear his head further. Once ensconced in her frilly sitting room, there was no fast escape. She was determined to give Marcus the details of both her trips to the United States before turning to the subject of her old neighbor.

Finally, he was able to interject, "I understand that you knew Celeste fairly well."

"What a beauty she was," the woman gushed. "But you know that."

"You don't see all that many redheads these days," Javier said, cake crumbs falling from his mouth onto his jumper. "It used to be more popular."

"Did she tell you why she was leaving her job?" Marcus asked.

"I believe I asked," Iglesias said, "but she was vague. It's time to move on—yes, that's what she said. I remember that because I have never moved on from anything. I have always done what I did before. I work for the municipality, you know, ever since I left school."

"Did she tell you where she was moving?"

"I remember that too. You know, her Spanish was excellent and she spoke with a charming French accent. She told me, 'I going to the live where I can see the mountains.' She said, 'I love mountains.' She said, 'I grew up near the Alps.'"

"Which mountains?" Marcus asked.

"Well, I don't really know, but I'm quite sure it was in Spain. Yes, Spain. I don't recall why I know, but for some reason I feel certain of that. Javier asked me if I had a forwarding address, but I do not. Would you like more cake?"

Marcus declined and wondered why he couldn't have been told this less than illuminating information over the phone. This spurred him to check his mobile. It was completely dead.

At the hotel reception desk, Segura was told that Marcus Handler's key wasn't in its slot, so it appeared he had gone out. She had the clerk ring the room to make sure and when there was no response, she tried his cell phone one last time. She asked the clerk for an envelope, then took a paper from her briefcase and wrote in the margin: *Sorry I missed you. Here's the information you requested. I spotted my car outside—I need it for a meeting tomorrow away from the office. Luckily, I have my spare keys. Let's grab dinner tomorrow night. OK?*

She sealed the envelope, left it at the desk, then rolled her travel bag along the sidewalk to the car.

Marcus was seven kilometers away and inside Señora Iglesias's apartment, when they heard a low, rumbling blast.

They had a brief discussion about what might have happened, before he thanked his host and managed to slip away.

His taxi driver complained that he couldn't get close to the hotel because of fire trucks and emergency vehicles blocking the road. He got out on a street several blocks behind the hotel and walked the rest of the way. When he got closer, he saw emergency services crews and police were everywhere. The smell of gasoline was in the air and small pieces of glass and metal were afoot. Whatever happened was near to where he left the BMW. He'd be mad as hell if Abril's car was damaged on his watch.

"What's going on?" Marcus asked the clerk when he got inside.

"There was a huge explosion, very close to us," the clerk said. "No one is telling us anything. If it was a gas explosion, you would think they would tell us." He shook his head and remembered something. "A woman left a letter for you."

Marcus tore open the envelope, saw the handwritten note, and rushed outside in a panic. He ran toward the fire trucks and got close enough for a policeman to stop him going further.

There was a tangled, smoking hulk of metal where he'd parked the BMW.

He tried to push through and the policeman and another manhandled him back.

"My friend was in that car!" he shouted. "For God's sake, let me through!"

The crowds grew and the sidewalk in front of the hotel was clogged with pedestrians trying to get close to the bomb site. The hotel clerk was seized by morbid fascination and for every minute he spent at reception, he spent ten outside, trying to see if he could find out what was going on.

He was away from his post when a large man with blond hair entered the deserted lobby, checked the guest list on the logged-in computer, and headed upstairs to Marcus Handler's room.

It was hours later when Marcus got to his hotel room. He went straight for the Scotch, sat on the edge of the bed, and swigged from the bottle, wishing he was the one who'd been killed. When he felt his brain numbing, he reached into his pocket for Abril's letter. He read her note again, then looked at the substance of it. It was a printout of a single, five-year-old wire transfer for two hundred thousand euros sent from a bank in Segovia, Spain to Celeste Bobier's Panamanian account.

Marcus blinked at the sender's name.

Dr. Ferrol Luis Gaytan.

Ferrol's Story

28

It was a fairy-tale place for a childhood, for what little boy wouldn't want to grow up in a castle?

And it was no ordinary castle, but a massive four thousand square meters of Gothic majesty set on fifty acres of vineyards and agricultural land on the northern foothills of the Guadarrama Mountains, with Segovia to the north and Madrid to the south.

A smaller eighth-century Moorish castle probably antedated the present structure. It was the fourteenth century when the massive walls and six towers were erected. For as long as records existed, the property had been in the hands of the Gaytan family, Spanish *hidalgos de sangre* whose nobility traced back to the mists of time, untethered by memory or documentation of origin. These immemorial nobles basked in their obscurity and, in a certain respect, were more prestigious than many other Spanish nobles who could trace their position to royal decree. Yet, the nobility of hidalgos did nothing to cement their solvency and certainly did not guarantee a wealth sufficient to maintain an enormous castle. The Gaytans were wealthy because their ancestors had been consistently successful in business. In recent centuries they were farmers, vintners, and traders.

In the twentieth century, they were merchants, lawyers, and politicians, and in the 1950s the Banco Gaytan was formed and became a leading merchant bank in Segovia and the province of Castile and León.

For a boy like Ferrol Luis Gaytan, it was pure magic. Even at a tender age, his family—his grandmother in particular—made sure that he was aware that most little boys did not live in a house with twenty bedrooms, twenty-five bathrooms, a banquet hall that could accommodate three hundred guests, crenellated ramparts with views of the mountains to the south and plains to the north, a library with ten thousand rare books, endless, spooky cellars, stables full of beautiful horses, and a small army of servants and gardeners.

His father, a banker, was seldom present and his mother was distracted by her social and charitable obligations, but his paternal grandmother, Izabel Gaytan, took care to ground Ferrol, an only child, in a measure of social awareness. To that end, she encouraged him to play with the children of servants and agricultural workers and arranged play dates and mutual sleepovers where he would spend time in their modest houses and they would come to the castle.

Ferrol's best friend was a boy his age named Hugo whose father drove a tractor on the estate. The two boys were joined at the hip and disappeared for hours on end into the vast spaces of the castle and surrounding lands. When the time came for Ferrol to enroll in a prestigious boarding school in Segovia, he complained bitterly to his grandmother that he would be separated from his friend who was slated to attend the primary school in the nearby village of Lirio. Izabel pressed Ferrol's case with her son and daughter-in-law, but Ferrol's parents were unmoved.

On no account would their son be sent to a state school and Hugo's family could not begin to afford the tuition at the boarding school. That is when Izabel made a fateful decision: she would pay for Hugo's tuition from her own purse.

"You're the best grandmother in the world," Ferrol told Izabel inside her apartment within the castle.

"And you are the best grandson," she said, gathering him up for a kiss.

"I hate Papa," he said. "I like Mama, but I love you."

She pouted and said, "You must love all of us equally, especially your father who works so hard to provide this wonderful life you have."

"But Papa and Mama didn't help Hugo. You did. And Papa and Mama are mean and angry all the time, but you are always sweet."

"I helped Hugo to help you. You are my shining star. Your parents are strict and that is a good thing. My husband whom you never knew—your father's father—was very strict and that is why your father is such a successful man. I'm an old woman and I have the luxury of being a sweet grandmother and nothing else."

"You're not an old woman!"

"I am. How old do you think I am?"

Ferrol screwed his face into a hard piece of thinking. "Forty?"

"My boy! Your parents are older than that. I am seventy years old."

"That's old."

"I know!"

The boy frowned and Izabel asked him what was wrong.

GLENN COOPER

"I don't want you to die."

She reached for his little hands. "What do you know about dying?"

"Hugo and I saw a horse die and last year we saw a cow die."

"Well, I don't plan on dying—at least anytime soon."

"Will you promise you won't?"

"That is a very difficult promise to make."

Tears formed in his eyes. "Please?"

"Very well, I promise."

At the age of twelve, Ferrol and Hugo, still good friends, returned to Lirio for the Christmas break. Both boys had grown like weeds, but Ferrol was taller and stronger. Both boys played football and rugby, but it was Ferrol who was the stand-out athlete and it was Ferrol who was, by far, the better student. In fact, Ferrol was considered by his teachers to be the finest student in his class with a particular aptitude in mathematics and science. The physical and intellectual divide that was forming between them wasn't a problem for Ferrol, but Hugo was beginning to harbor resentments. Theirs was an all-boys school, but when they were allowed to go into Segovia for an afternoon every now and again, it was Ferrol's refined, dashing looks that attracted the girls, not Hugo's coarser, darker countenance.

Over Christmas, their old boyish games of hide-and-seek in the nooks and crannies of the castle, or pretending to be knights repelling invaders, no longer held sway and they were becoming bored.

Sitting in the kitchen after the cook made them lunch, Hugo asked, "What do you want to do?"

Ferrol tossed it back to him. "I don't know, what do you want to do?"

It was chilly, not much above freezing outside, and neither of them wanted to ride the mini-tractors or horses.

Ferrol got irritated when he heard Hugo say one more time, "I don't know what to do. What do you want to do?" and Ferrol declared that they might as well tackle some of the holiday reading their literature teacher had assigned.

Hugo was wholly uninterested and told Ferrol that if he was serious about reading, then he was going home.

"Fine, go home," Ferrol said.

"Fine, I will," Hugo said, storming off.

Ferrol got a book and hurried across the big, open courtyard to the warmth of the western tower where his grandmother lived. She answered her door and with a look of delight, invited him to join her in the comfort of her sitting room with its strong log fire.

"What is the book you have there?" she asked.

"It's called, *La Roja Insignia Del Valor*, The Red Badge of Courage," he said, adding the English translation to impress her.

"Never heard of it."

"It's by an American called Stephen Crane," he said. "It's about a young soldier in the American Civil War. Our teacher assigned it."

"There are so many wonderful Spanish books," she said. "Why read an American book, especially one I've never heard of?"

"We are studying courage and valor. The soldier's name is Henry. He starts off as a coward in battle. I haven't finished it yet, but I think he's going to be a hero in the end. I'll have to write an essay."

"If you want to read about courage, you should be reading *Don Quixote*."

"How many times can you read *Don Quixote*?" Ferrol asked.

"You may have a point. Would I like this book of yours?"

"I think so, Grandmother. It's really nice."

"Well, come over here by the fire. Sit on the cushion while you read. I shall carry on with my needlepoint."

On the afternoon of Christmas Eve, Ferrol and Hugo decided to play inside the largest barn on the estate, where bales of hay were stacked for the winter. It was Hugo's father who had been in charge of the baling operation in the autumn, and all of his family, with the exception of Hugo who had already departed for boarding school, had participated in the stacking. Work horses were stabled in one end of the barn, and their shuffling and soft neighing added a soundtrack to their game. They hid behind hay bales, playing at war, shooting at each other with a pair of Ferrol's BB guns. They were separated enough that an on-target shot hurt, but didn't break the skin, and in a rare display of caution, they wore safety glasses from the wood-working shop. When they tired of getting stung by BBs, they climbed the wooden ladder to the loft and lay on a bed of hay and looked out the loading hatch to see what they could see around the estate.

After a while, Ferrol spied a girl named Mariana coming out of the milking barn. She was the daughter of one of the casual workers employed by the Gaytans, helping her mother over the holidays. Both boys knew her. She was a year or two older than them, not very bright, but exceptionally well developed for her age.

Ferrol aimed down the sight of his pistol.

"Do you think I can hit her in her tit?" he asked.

"How could you miss?" Hugo said. "They're huge."

"Come on! Look how far away she is," Ferrol said. "It's a hard shot. What will you give me if I hit her?"

"Well, I don't have any money, if that's what you're hoping for."

"I don't want money. If I hit her, you have to call me Your Majesty for a whole day. Agreed?"

"Sure. Whatever."

Ferrol took careful aim and squeezed the trigger. The BB missed and the gun wasn't very loud, so the girl didn't notice she was being shot at. The boy swore and tried again. This time the BB must have grazed her scalp, because she swatted at her hair, perhaps thinking that an insect had dive-bombed her, forgetting it was the winter.

The boys broke out laughing.

The girl heard them and looked up at the hatch and shouted at them, "What did you do?"

"He shot you!" Hugo called back.

"Come up here," Ferrol yelled.

"Why?"

"We want to talk to you."

As she headed to the barn, Hugo said, "I don't want to talk to her. She's stupid."

"You didn't call me, Your Majesty," Ferrol said.

"That was if you hit her tit," Hugo said.

"No, it was if I hit her anywhere."

"No, her tit. Come on, don't cheat."

Ferrol made a face. "I could have hit her tit with my first shot."

"She would have felt it."

"Maybe not. She's wearing a jacket."

They were still bickering when she climbed the ladder to the loft.

"What are you arguing about?" Mariana asked.

Ferrol explained his bet with Hugo and said that she could settle the matter if she bared her chest. Hugo sniggered, but she wanted to know what she'd get if she stripped off.

"Fifty pesetas," he said.

She said, okay, sending Hugo into more hysterics.

Soon, her jacket, shirt, and bra were off and both boys stared in awe at her big breasts. Ferrol's breathing got husky.

"See, I don't have any red marks," she said.

"We should check," Hugo said.

"Yes, we need to check," Ferrol said, grabbing one of her breasts.

She told him to let go, but he didn't and soon he was cupping both breasts and pushing her on her back onto the hay.

"Go away! Stop!" she said, trying to wriggle free.

She was a big, strong girl and Ferrol was having trouble keeping her still. He straddled her, but she was still bucking him off.

"Hold her down!" he told Hugo.

Hugo didn't hesitate. He held her shoulders down and

Ferrol gave her a good feel-up, squeezing her the way he'd seen the family cook squeezing melons for ripeness. This was his first time and he was getting excited.

"Keep going," Hugo said. "She likes it."

"Do you?" Ferrol said. "Do you like it?"

"No! Let me go!"

Ferrol pried open her legs and got in between them and began humping her.

With every thrust of his pelvis, Hugo pressed down harder on her shoulders and said, "Go!"

Ferrol kept thrusting, until all of a sudden, he groaned and said, "Shit," then rolled off.

"Why'd you stop?" Hugo said, letting go and allowing Mariana to get up and grab her clothes.

Ferrol felt wet and squishy in his pants and he got red with embarrassment. "No reason. I got tired of this game," he said.

Mariana started crying and Ferrol turned to damage control.

"You're not going to tell anyone, are you?" he asked.

"I'm going to tell my mother."

"I'll give you a hundred pesetas if you keep quiet," he said.

She finished dressing and made for the ladder.

"Two hundred," Ferrol said.

"Leave me alone! I'm going home."

"If you tell, I'll make sure your mother is fired!" he shouted at her as she disappeared down the ladder.

"Hey, Your Majesty," Hugo said. "That was awesome!"

★

The next day, the Gaytans were having their Christmas feast in the castle banqueting hall when the door chimed. One of the servants entered and whispered something to Señor Gaytan who excused himself. Ferrol's mother and grandmother asked each other who could possibly have come calling on Christmas and after several minutes, Señor Gaytan returned and asked Ferrol to come with him.

"What's happening?" his wife asked.

"Nothing," she was told. "Don't interrupt your meal."

Mariana's mother and father, dressed in their Sunday best, were standing nervously on the yellow and black tiles of the grand reception hall. They did not or could not look at Ferrol.

His father had always been cold to him, but now, his voice was like an ice dagger. "The Martíns have made a serious accusation against you, Ferrol. They say you violated their daughter yesterday."

Ferrol stared at the floor and denied it.

His father continued, "Were you in the hay barn yesterday afternoon?"

"Yes, sir."

"The girl, Mariana, was seen going into the barn yesterday afternoon. Did you see her?"

Ferrol played the angles in his head. It was possible that someone had indeed seen him and Hugo playing in the barn just before the girl came in.

"Yes, sir," he said.

"Are you denying that you shot at her with your BB gun?"

"I didn't do that, sir."

"Are you denying that you offered her money to touch her breasts?"

"I didn't do that, sir."

"Are you denying that you pulled her legs apart and got in between them?"

"I didn't do that, sir."

"Are you denying that this girl was violated?"

"No, sir."

His father looked astonished. "You're not denying this? Explain yourself."

He blurted out, "Hugo did it."

"Hugo touched her breasts? Hugo got in between her legs?"

"Yes, sir."

"And what were you doing while this was going on?"

"Nothing, sir. I was scared to do anything. Hugo said that he would kill me if I tried to stop him."

Señora Martín broke her silence. "My Mariana never lies. She said that Hugo helped to hold her down, but it was Ferrol who violated her."

Señor Gaytan reacted forcefully, surprising Ferrol with his vigorous defense. "I must stop you there, Señora. I don't know your daughter, but I know my son. Ferrol never lies. We are an ancient, honorable family and Ferrol is an honorable young man. It is not acceptable that he failed to intervene and he will be punished for that—by me. However, it seems to me that it is the boy, Hugo, who should bear the overwhelming responsibility for this despicable act."

"Please don't hurt Hugo, father," Ferrol said. "He's my friend."

"Go back to the dining room," his father ordered. "And say nothing of this to your mother or grandmother."

Señor Gaytan invited the Martíns into his study to continue the discussion. Negotiation was his lifeblood and he dominated the brief proceedings, interrupted only by Mariana's mother repeating that she believed her daughter's version of the story and Mariana's father repeating that he demanded justice for the girl. These were poor, simple people coming, hat in hand, to the castle of the lord of the manor and the banker was quickly able to come to an economic solution. One hundred thousand pesetas was a trivial amount to Gaytan, but a fortune to Mariana's parents. For that sum, they and their daughter would keep silent about this incident forever and Mariana's mother would be allowed to continue her milking job at the farm.

"What about the boys?" Mariana's father said. "Are you saying that they will escape punishment?"

"Oh, no, they will be punished, of that you may be sure."

Ferrol's punishment was confiscation of his BB guns, a one-month suspension of his allowance that he relied on to purchase extra sweets at school, and a fiery lecture from his father.

The banker raged, "You realize that I know the truth in this matter, don't you?"

"Yes, sir."

"Do you know what you did wrong?"

"Lied, sir?"

"I don't care about lying to these peasants but lying to me is the worst thing you can possibly do. What else did you do wrong?"

"Touched the girl?"

"I don't care about that either. I care about your getting caught. Use your head in the future, not your pecker. Don't fool around with simpletons like this girl who goes running to her parents. Do you understand me?"

The boy understood perfectly.

Hugo's punishment was harsher by far. Señor Gaytan's estate manager paid a visit to his house informing the family that Hugo's boarding school fees would no longer be paid and that his father was dismissed, with immediate effect, from his employment as a tractor driver. All of them were banished from the estate.

Hugo bitterly denied being the main perpetrator, but his cries fell on deaf ears and his father beat him within an inch of his life.

For Hugo and his family, it was the blackest of Christmases.

29

Over the next year, Ferrol excelled in school and solidified his place as the brightest and most popular student in his form. His teachers praised his abilities in mathematics and natural sciences and on his thirteenth birthday, he declared to his parents and grandmother that he would be a famous scientist one day who would find a cure for cancer or some horrible disease. He hardly cared about Hugo's absence and didn't ask what had become of him. As far as he understood, his family had moved from Lirio to another village some distance away. He suspected that his father had told his mother about the incident, because from that day forward, she was colder and more aloof than before, but much to his relief, he detected no change in his grandmother's behavior.

By the next Christmas, he was taller, physically stronger, and immensely self-confident. Señor Gaytan had been on a business trip to New York City and the entire family didn't gather until Christmas Eve when they hosted a gala dinner for the employees of the bank inside the grand banqueting hall. Ferrol had been obligated to wear his best blue suit. He was fighting off boredom at the family's table when his grandmother delighted him with the request that he accompany her back to her apartment.

"I'm feeling quite tired, Ferrol," she said. "Could I tear you away?"

"With pleasure," he said, grinning.

In her kitchen, she set the kettle on the stove and made piping-hot mugs of instant cocoa that they sipped by the fire.

"These parties are dreadfully dull," she said.

"I thought I was going to die," Ferrol said.

"That's what old ladies say, not young boys. Don't feel obligated to stay with me. Do whatever you fancy."

"I fancy staying with my grandmother."

She laughed lightly. "You've just given me my best Christmas present," she said. "The last time I was in Segovia, I bought myself a new jigsaw puzzle. I haven't even opened it yet. Would you like to start it with me?"

"What's the picture?" he asked.

"It's the Swiss Alps. It's three thousand, mostly white pieces!"

Ferrol kicked off his shoes and removed his necktie while his grandmother changed out of her gown into her night dress and bathrobe. Then the two of them spread the pieces on the large table she used for her puzzles and began sorting the straight edges. She became tired first and retired to bed. He kept going for another hour, then trundled off through the dark, cold corridors of the ancient castle, skirting the remnants of the Christmas party, until he was under the warm covers of his bed.

★

It was 3 a.m. when a figure dressed all in black made his way toward the castle past the bare orchards, the stables, and barns. He had been walking for hours in the frigid air and he was shivering. The castle loomed in total darkness. Because he knew his way around, he went straight for the northern wall of the keep that housed the main family residence. Señor and Señora Gaytan's bedroom suite was above a large reception room on the ground level. Above them on the second floor, was Ferrol's bedroom.

He had a backpack, which he removed and zipped open. Inside was a wine bottle with a smelly rag stuck into its neck. He had thought of everything. In case he couldn't find a suitable rock in the darkness, he had brought one with him. Without a second of hesitation, he threw it through the largest ground-floor window, struck a match, and lit the gas-soaked rag.

He threw the bottle as hard as he could through the broken pane of glass and moved closer to witness the blast with his own eyes, but he had the misfortune of striking a brass lamp right by the window. The Molotov cocktail exploded and the resulting fireball shot through the hole in the window, engulfing his head in flames. He took off, wailing into the night.

The petrol bomb caught the heavy draperies, the furniture, and the millwork. The flames quickly spread beyond the reception room to the hall where they caught ancient tapestries and climbed. Thick smoke began billowing upwards, filling the castle keep. Señor Gaytan was the first to wake, coughing and sputtering. He roused his wife, opened a window, and through it, he screamed for Ferrol to wake up. Then he made the terrible mistake of opening the bedroom door where a wall of fire in the hallway hurtled toward the open window.

Ferrol dreamed he heard someone shouting his name from somewhere far, far away. He dreamed that a herd of wild horses was running across the roof. He dreamed someone was choking him.

Then his eyes snapped open and all he could see was a terrible, rippling orange light where his windows should have been.

One of the estate workers in a cottage on the grounds heard agonizing screams and when he investigated, found someone rolling on the frosty grass, his face blackened by fire, his hair singed to the scalp. That's when he saw the flames licking out the windows of the castle and raised the alarm with the corps of firefighters.

When the firemen arrived, the deputy head of the brigade who was driving behind the ladder and pumper trucks, slowed at the sight of a solitary figure walking down the private road. He recognized the boy who was dressed only in boxer shorts. He bundled him into the car and he threw his jacket over him.

"Young sir, are you all right? Are you hurt?"

Ferrol coughed and stared glassy-eyed into the darkness. "The fire," he said. "The fire."

Juan Prieto, Señor Gaytan's personal lawyer, sat with Ferrol and his grandmother in her tower apartment. It was a week after the fire. All of Ferrol's clothes had been lost to smoke or flames and he was wearing some rough togs donated by an estate worker. Lawyer Prieto was an efficient man who got down to business after a bare-bones display of condolence and commiseration.

"In the event that your father and mother died at the same time, his will stipulated that you, his only child, would be the sole heir to his estate. I will be receiving a full report from your father's accountancy firm in the next several days, but my understanding is that you will inherit a considerable sum, no, a very considerable sum. Even after inheritance taxes, you will be one of the wealthiest men in Segovia."

Ferrol had no more tears. Dry-eyed, he said, "What about grandmother?"

"You don't have to worry about me, dear boy," she said.

"Señora Gaytan is correct. She has been provided for—for life—by her late husband's estate. Fortunately, while the main residence areas of the castle are renovated, this wing is entirely inhabitable. I assume you will return to your boarding school after the funerals."

"I haven't thought about it."

"Of course you will," his grandmother said. "I will supervise that which must be done here."

Ferrol got up and looked through one of the narrow tower windows. In the harsh sunlight, he had a direct view over the courtyard of soot-blackened masonry.

"I want to see him," he said.

"I don't think that's advisable," Prieto said.

"I didn't ask your opinion. Please make the arrangements."

The lawyer nodded and gave the boy a look of approval, as if to say, you'll be all right—like father, like son. "I'll see what I can do," he said.

*

There was a Segovia policeman sitting in a chair outside the hospital room. When he asked the boy his name, the policeman nodded and said he was expected, but that he needed to check with the nurses before entering. At the nursing station, one of the nurses told him what to expect and set him a limit of five minutes.

Hugo's face was wrapped in gauze stained with weeping serum from the third-degree burns. There was a patch over the eye that had sustained cornea damage. A breathing tube through his nose bypassed the thermal injury to his trachea, and delivered oxygen to his lungs.

He saw his visitor and tried to look away, but Ferrol got so close he couldn't avoid him.

"Why did you do it?" Ferrol demanded.

Hugo stared back at him with that one eye.

"Was it because you got kicked out of school?"

Hugo stared and nodded.

"Was it because your father lost his job?"

He nodded again.

"Did you want to kill me too?"

Tears formed in the good eye. He nodded to that too.

"You got what you deserved, didn't you? Blown up by your own bomb, you fucking idiot."

The bellows of the breathing machine whooshed away. A radio on the windowsill was on low, tuned to a pop music station.

"But I don't think you got enough. My lawyer told me that after you recover, you'll probably be sent away to some kind of hospital for crazy kids for a few years and then you'll be released. My parents are dead. If it wasn't for my grandmother, I'd be an orphan. You know what I think? I don't think you got nearly enough."

Ferrol turned up the radio and reached for one of Hugo's hands. The boy must have misinterpreted the gesture because he gently squeezed back, but Ferrol had other ideas. There were leather restraints and straps attached to the bed that were used at night to prevent him from pulling out the tube while he slept. He slid the restraint around his wrist and tightened it. Hugo fought back when Ferrol tried to restrain his other wrist, but Ferrol was strong and determined.

Ferrol spoke directly into one of Hugo's ears. "I, Ferrol Luis Gaytan, hidalgo de sangre, do hereby sentence you to death."

With a twist, he separated the breathing tube from the connecting hose and covered the end with his palm.

Hugo began to thrash and pull at his restraints, but the music drowned out the rattling bed and the beeping alarm of the breathing machine.

When his body was still, Ferrol reattached the hose and turned down the radio.

He exited the room and coolly told the policeman, "I think you should get the nurse. My friend seems to be having trouble breathing."

For the next eight years, Ferrol returned to the castle every single holiday. When other wealthy young men were spending their summers touring European capitals and North America or yachting in the Mediterranean, he remained devoted to his increasingly frail grandmother. At the age of twenty he was a busy medical student at the Autonomous University of Madrid, but while he studied, he monitored her health from afar. Izabel Gaytan's medical issues were myriad in her last years. Arthritis limited her mobility. Atrial fibrillation led to heart failure. Dizziness led to falls and broken bones. She was a proud woman who wouldn't consider going into a nursing home and fortunately, Ferrol had the resources to allow her to stay at the castle in relative safety. There were nurses around the clock, physical therapists, cooks, and cleaners. Ferrol even arranged for a hairdresser to come to her apartment and a semi-retired priest to say Mass for her. Her mental faculties were undiminished and the high point of her week was the Sunday afternoon phone conversation with her grandson.

Ferrol got the call he had been dreading while he was in the anatomy lab, dissecting the thigh of a cadaver. According to one of her nurses, his grandmother was deteriorating and didn't have long. With the permission of his dean, he hopped in his Porsche and sped north.

When he arrived, she was propped upright on four pillows to ease her congested heart and receiving oxygen via a face mask. Her eyes were closed and sunken into her skeletal skull. He went to take her pulse at a wrist with skin as thin as rice paper. It was hard for him to feel the thready, irregular beats.

"Is she unconscious?" he asked the nurse.

"She's sleeping. She's been sleeping a lot. Per the doctor's orders I've been giving her small injections of morphine every four hours to ease her heart. Only a milligram at a time. It makes her sleepy, but you can wake her."

He moved his grip from her wrist to her hand and gave it a gentle squeeze.

"Grandmother," he said. "It's Ferrol."

She opened her gummy eyes and as the nurse dabbed at the secretions, she managed a smile. She tried to talk through her mask.

"I'm going to take it off," he said.

When the nurse objected, he dismissed her. "Leave us. This is between me and my grandmother."

With the mask gone, she said in a breathy rush, "Ferrol—"

"Yes, I came. Of course, I came."

"Good. It's good," she said. "You came."

He sat beside her and leaned in close. Feeling her limp hand in his, he began to cry.

In a halting cadence she said, "No. Don't cry. It is—my time."

"You're all I have in this world."

"I didn't want—to die until you were—a man," she wheezed. "You are—a man now."

"I don't want you to go," he said. "I don't want you to ever die."

"We all die—dear boy."

His voice was thin and dry. "I'll be all alone."

"But I want to die now."

He dried his eyes with his free hand and shook his head.

"You say no," she said. "I say yes. The syringe—there. All of it. Please."

He let go of her hand and inspected the syringe. It was loaded with ten milligrams of morphine.

"If I inject all of it, you'll go to sleep and you won't wake up," he said.

"It is—what I want. It is too hard—to live."

"Are you sure?" he asked.

"I am sure. Please."

His hands shook as the needle neared the injection port of her intravenous line. He punctured the membrane and pushed the plunger to the hilt.

"Thank you," she said, closing her eyes.

He kissed her cool forehead. "I love you, Grandmother. I'll love you forever."

"I love you too," she said. "Do not be sad. You will have—a wonderful—"

He knew what her last word was going to be, but it never crossed her lips.

30

No one was surprised when Dr. Ferrol Gaytan was named the Director of the Institute of Genetics and Molecular Medicine at La Paz. There had been an air of inevitability about the promotion ever since the young, rising star turned down offer after offer of academic positions at other universities throughout Europe and the United States. "Madrid is my city," he would say, "Spain is my country."

By the time he was forty-five, his curriculum vitae was as thick as a novella with two hundred journal publications, countless plenary lectures, and a dozen chapters in medical textbooks. He employed thirty people in his lab and commanded millions of euros in sponsored research grants. Early in his career, he gravitated to the field of molecular genetics where the study of the function of chromosomes and genes at the molecular level promised treatment for genetic diseases. He threw himself into fundamental work on childhood conditions such as sickle cell anemia, beta thalassemia, and cystic fibrosis and conducted clinical trials on the pediatric ward.

His principal lab was a large, open-plan space with rows of benches and hoods, crammed with analytical instruments.

However, some years after he took control of the institute, he awarded himself another smaller lab down the hall and plucked a single technician from the main lab to work there. The small lab quickly took on an air of mystery. The people in the main Gaytan lab had no idea what the new one was for and the young tech who moved over to staff it wasn't talking. His reticence was especially remarkable because he was known as a gregarious motormouth, albeit a non-fluent one. Spanish wasn't his native language and he butchered it in a genial sort of way. When his co-workers cornered him in the canteen or the toilets he smiled and said, "The general has sworn me to secrecy and I'm a good soldier."

The lab quickly became known as the Gaytan skunkworks.

When Dr. Gaytan visited the wards to see one of his clinical trial patients, the female nurses noticed. He had a reputation. The handsome, wealthy bachelor was a notorious womanizer and because he seemed to spend most of his evenings and weekends on the La Paz campus, the hospital and his institute were his happy hunting grounds.

His patient on this day was an eight-year-old Senegalese girl with severe sickle-cell disease who had recently been dosed with a gene therapy medicine of his own design. He entered her room with his entourage of junior doctors and medical students and repaid her bright smile with his own.

"How is my favorite patient in the whole wide world?" he asked, pulling the privacy curtain.

The small girl was all skin and bones. "I'm good, Doctor," she said.

"Are you eating lots of tasty food?"

She said she was.

"When are your mother and father coming to see you?"

"Soon."

"Good. I want to speak with them to tell them how you are doing, which is excellent. I'm going to use big medical words with my colleagues now. Is that okay?"

"Yes, Doctor."

He addressed his entourage. "So, little Khady received her stem-cell transplant a week ago. We transfected her own hematopoietic stem cells with the normal copy of the HBB gene using a viral construct we developed in our lab. Then we infused the stem cells intravenously. They naturally home to the bone marrow where they should already be producing normal hemoglobin. We'll draw blood today to see how her peripheral red blood cells look and whether they have the new gene. Where's the nurse? I want the blood drawn now and hand-delivered to me."

The nurse, who was with the other patient by the window bed, parted the curtain and said in French-accented Spanish, "Here I am, Doctor."

It was no easy feat looking sexy in the shapeless scrubs worn by the pediatric nurses, but this young woman managed to do just that. While most of her fellow nurses chose scrubs a size too large for comfort, she opted for a size too small and her voluptuous figure was very much on display. And while the majority of nurses eschewed makeup, she did not, and her red lipstick set against her olive skin could stop traffic. A couple of female medical students exchanged knowing smirks, as if to say: *We know your type, lady—could you possibly be more obvious?*

For his part, if Ferrol missed a beat the first time he laid eyes on her, it was a well-concealed half a beat.

"I'll need two red-top tubes and one green-top," he said. "Do you know where my lab is?"

"No, Doctor," she said.

"It's in the Institute of Genetics. Do you know where that is?"

"I'll find it."

"Good. I'll be in room 611. Have you drawn Khady before?"

"I haven't. I just transferred to this floor, but I am very, very gentle. She will hardly feel it."

Ferrol nodded and said to the young girl, "So, Khady, tomorrow I'll be asking you how well Nurse—" he sought out her identity card, hanging on a ribbon that bisected her ample breasts "—how well Nurse Bobier did."

Room 611 was the mystery lab. Ferrol was working at a bench and he swiveled at the knock on the door. Celeste Bobier smiled and held up a small plastic bag containing three tubes of blood.

"Were you very, very gentle?" he asked.

"Of course."

"And Khady will give you a good report tomorrow?"

"Almost certainly. I have excellent technique."

Ferrol's young technician was working away, preparing some reagents at another bench.

"Leave the tubes with him," Ferrol said.

The technician promptly inserted the tubes into a centrifuge and set them spinning.

"You're French, aren't you?" Ferrol asked.

"I am. From Lyon."

"Why are you here, if I could ask?"

"Well, it's a good job in a top hospital in a beautiful city. Are these sufficient reasons?"

He nodded vigorously, sending a lock of black hair onto his forehead. "The best reasons, I'd say. It's amazing really. Here we are in one of the best medical centers in Spain and only one-third of the people in this room are Spanish. We have—" he looked at her badge again "—Celeste Bobier from France and my technician, Ferruccio Gressani from Italy. One has to love the European Union."

He followed her out into the hall, watching her hips.

"Nurse, do you have a minute?"

She turned before he finished the question, seemingly aware she was being tracked.

"I might even have two minutes," she said.

"It's short notice, but I wonder—"

"Yes, I'm free for dinner tonight."

"How did you know?"

"Maybe I'm psychic," she teased.

He folded his hands across the front of his long white coat. "Is that so?" he said.

"That, plus the girl talk. I was warned about the dangerous Dr. Ferrol Gaytan."

"I thought you just arrived on the ward."

"Word travels fast."

One thing led to another and Ferrol decided to play the castle card; it was his way of sealing the deal with a new girlfriend. They usually went limp at the sight of the fortress walls, the towers, the battlements, but Celeste's reaction amused him no end.

"Welcome to Castle Gaytan," he said.

She raised her sunglasses and replied, "I was expecting something larger."

"I'll have to take you to the Alhambra for our next date."

A female housekeeper hugged him at the door and told him she'd have their bags taken up.

"The usual?" she asked, eyeing the long-legged woman in a tight, red skirt. It was just loud enough for Celeste to hear.

Ferrol told her, yes.

"What's the usual?" Celeste asked him a moment later.

"Adjoining rooms."

She saluted the suit of armor in the reception hall and said, "I should like a tour."

"With or without champagne?"

"With."

He took her to the library first, a vast dark room that required tall ladders on iron rails to scale the highest reaches. He told her there were ten thousand volumes, many priceless, and that one night, many years ago, the fire brigade saved it from fast-spreading flames. When she asked about the fire, he demurred and moved her onto the banqueting hall, where she craned her neck to look at the ancient tapestries and taxidermy and a huge heraldic crest of family Gaytan.

"This is where you have your intimate dinners for a few hundred of your closest friends?" she asked.

"The last time this hall was used was when I was twelve years old."

At the entrance to the western tower, she asked what was behind the door.

"My grandmother used to live here. I don't allow visitors."

"You must have been close to keep it as a shrine."

"You're very perceptive," he replied.

At a stone staircase that plunged into darkness, she asked whether there were dungeons.

"The dungeons are long gone, but I can show you where they used to be."

He hit the lights and they descended into the coolness of the subterranean space. There was a rabbit warren of rooms and he showed her some iron fittings sunk into an exterior stone wall where, legend had it, medieval prisoners of clan Gaytan were shackled. In another area there was a large stack of drywall, pallets of tiles, unassembled cabinetry, and assorted building materials.

"What's that for?" she asked.

"Just a small hobby of mine," he said.

They ascended and went to the main living quarters. After the fire, twelve-year-old Ferrol had his lawyer hire the finest craftsmen in Castile and León to rebuild the ravaged wing to its original medieval glory. He had a sense that as the new master of Castle Gaytan he would need an appropriate place to reside when he was in attendance.

"This is your room," he said. Her overnight bag was at the foot of the bed on a bench. "There's a bathroom through there."

"What's that door?" she asked.

"My suite," he said.

"Is the door locked?" she asked.

"It doesn't have to be."

★

Celeste opened the door.

She was wearing only the skimpiest bits of red silk. Ferrol switched off his book-light and watched her closely as she approached the bed.

Now, the only light in the room came from an antique crystal kerosene lamp on his desk, a calculated bit of ambiance.

"I hope I'm not disturbing you," she said.

"Does it look like I'm disturbed?"

"I don't know you well enough to say."

He patted the bed. "Come, get to know me better."

He was his usual amorous self and it wasn't until the small hours when they fell asleep in each other's arms.

Celeste awoke to thrashing and yelling.

Ferrol was flailing about. Frightened moans rose from deep within his chest and emerged from his throat as low, shuddering screams.

"What's the matter?" she said, freeing herself from his grasp.

When he didn't answer, she turned on her bedside light and saw his eyes were shut. She prodded him gently, then harder, and when he kept thrashing, she got close and tightly wrapped him in her arms, cooing and soothing him with her voice and her lips.

Suddenly, he stopped and was quiet. His eyes opened with a look of utter confusion.

"Was I?" he asked.

She kissed his forehead and his eyes. "You're okay now."

"I should have warned you."

"Tell me, what's the matter?"

"Night terrors. They're called night terrors."

"Children have this."

"They started when I was twelve. They never went away."

"The fire."

"I said you were perceptive," he said.

"Would you like to talk about it?"

"I never have."

"But I think you've had women in your bed before. You never told any of them?"

He reached for a bottle of water on his table. "No."

"I think you'll tell me," she said.

He ran a finger up her belly. "Why?"

"Because you've never met someone like me."

He told her. He told her about waking in abject fear to a room ablaze, about learning from the firemen in the dead of night that he was an orphan. When she asked why Hugo had done it, he gave her a version of a poor boy's pathological resentment toward the rich, then surprised himself when he slid into a retelling of how he visited Hugo in the hospital and snuffed out his life.

"Maybe it wasn't the best start to a career of saving lives," he said.

"He deserved it," she said, simply. "When did the night terrors start?"

"A month after the fire."

"They come every night?"

"No, but they're quite frequent."

"What are you afraid of?"

"Ah. The big question. I'm afraid of the jaws of the final beast."

"I'm sorry, I don't understand."

"When I was a boy, my favorite author was the American Stephen Crane, who wrote about the horrors of the Civil War—you know, the North versus the South. It's what he called death—the jaws of the final beast."

"We're all scared of death, aren't we?" she said.

"For me, it's all-consuming, forged in Hugo's fire. But I should say that it goes beyond fear, because the fear turns to anger. When I lost my parents, my only family was my grandmother. She succumbed to old age when I was in medical school. I desperately did not want her to die. I did not want to be all alone. It made me so angry that she had to leave me. I still get angry when one of my patients dies. Anger and fear are my daily bread."

"What about love?"

He didn't answer, but said, "I have a dream I'd like to share with you."

"I'm ready to hear it."

"In the morning. Now, I want you again."

She lay back and took him in her arms. "You can have me whenever you like."

31

Ferrol was standing at a drafting table lit by a high-intensity lamp inside his dark basement. He invited Celeste Bobier and Ferruccio Gressani to review his blueprints.

He had been confident for a long while that eventually Gressani would join him in some shape or form, but Celeste had dropped into his lap in a manner could best be described as *deus ex machina*, for surely none other than the gods could have manufactured someone as perfect. He needed an able nurse, he needed a willing partner, and as a bonus, he got the company of a beautiful and sexy lover. But Ferrol was a cautious man. It had taken two decades of work and planning to come to this point and he was not going to jeopardize his project, and perhaps even his liberty, by making rash decisions.

Could these two be trusted?

He knew that loyalty—initially—could be purchased. He had plucked Gressani from his main research group and transferred him to his skunkworks lab because he liked his enthusiasm and hard work, but more than that, the young man possessed a certain openness and naivety that Ferrol believed he could exploit. In the process of grooming him, he invited Gressani for a coffee where he probed his background. He learned that he was an ambitious fellow who had grown up in a working-class household where there was never enough money. The opportunities in his small town, and indeed his native area of southern Italy, were limited. Growing up, his role models for success weren't the plumbers, carpenters, and shopkeepers in his village, but the young men with flashy cars and girlfriends and pockets stuffed with five-hundred-euro notes who made their money in the drugs trade. Perhaps if he had been born into one of their families, he would have become one of them.

At school, he was friendly with an 'Ndrangheta boy named Marco Zuliani who, when he was trying to decide what to do with his life, tried to persuade him to join his crew. But Gressani knew that as a family outsider, he'd never advance far, and besides, he didn't have the disposition or intestinal fortitude to be a gangster. So, he followed his natural aptitude and interests and became a laboratory technician. After several years without raises at his lab in Reggio Calabria, he followed the money and took a higher-paying position in Madrid, even though it meant fracturing his relationship with his girlfriend, Cinzia.

Ferrol, on hearing his story, pounced like a cat tired of merely playing with his captured mouse.

"You've done an excellent job in the 611 lab, Ferruccio."

"Thank you, Dr. G," Gressani said.

"More than that, I've come to have faith in your willingness to maintain confidentiality. As you know, for a variety of reasons, the work we're doing in 611 is secret and sensitive."

GLENN COOPER

Gressani nodded. Ferrol had told him that leaks could enable his academic competitors and interfere with future patent claims. "I think the project I'm working on is exciting. I feel like I'm making a contribution to something that's really important," he said earnestly.

"That, it is," Ferrol said. "How would you like to take your participation to the next level?"

Gressani's open face was like a child's. "I'd be very interested."

"The next phase of our work won't take place at the hospital. I'll be building a lab elsewhere."

"Why?"

"I want more secrecy and less bureaucracy. You have no idea about the hoops I have to jump through to do my work at La Paz."

"I can imagine."

"If you join me, you'd leave La Paz. I would pay you off the books, in cash, so you wouldn't have to worry about taxes. You'd also have free accommodations and meals and you could keep your apartment in Madrid for weekend visits and the like."

"The new lab would be nearby?"

"Not far. North of here."

"Would I get a raise?"

Ferrol offered a movie-star smile. "Are you sitting down?"

Gressani was, indeed, sitting. He leaned closer in anticipation of a nice number. What he heard was so nice he almost jumped out of his chair to embrace the man.

"Fifteen thousand a month? Are you kidding me? Tax-free?"

"That's my offer."

"When could I start?"

"Some of what we do won't be entirely legal."

Gressani didn't miss a beat. "I asked when I could start."

Ferrol engaged Celeste in a similar discussion, but in her case, it played out over a weekend at Castle Gaytan, mostly in his bed. She too had come to Madrid, chasing the higher wages the hospital was offering for highly qualified nurses, and she too had grown up in modest circumstances. Her role in his enterprise would be more critical than Gressani's and he would pay her more. He wasn't prepared for the strength of her negotiating skills, but he wasn't put off by them. It only made him want her more.

Without divulging the exact nature of her employment, he offered her two hundred fifty thousand euros per year, free of tax.

"That's a great deal of money," she replied, her skin glistening from lovemaking.

"I have confidence you'll be worth it."

"You're a wealthy man," she said.

"I am."

"And your project isn't going to be legal, is it?"

"Strictly speaking? No."

"What would be the consequence of being caught doing whatever it is you intend to do?"

"For me—disastrous on all levels," he said. "For you? Probably not disastrous, but certainly not good."

"Not good, as in jail?"

"I would think so, although I am extremely careful. That won't happen."

"So careful that you're offering me a lot of money to work for you after knowing me for less than a month?"

He laughed. "I have good instincts about people and besides, I feel I've had an intense introduction to Mademoiselle Celeste Bobier."

"Double it," she said suddenly. "Half a million a year. And I want it paid into an untraceable off-shore account."

He grabbed her ass with both hands. "For me, the way you negotiate is extremely sexy," he said.

"Do we have an agreement?" she asked.

"I think we're very close."

Now, with the three of them gathered in the basement, it was time for Ferrol to open his kimono further.

He pointed to his architectural plans and said, "Here's where the lab will be. Ferruccio, this will be your lair. It will have all the equipment that the 611 lab has and more. State of the art. Celeste, here is your office. This is my office. The canteen will be here. Storage for medical supplies, here. Storage for food, here. You'll live upstairs in the castle proper. Ferruccio, you've seen your apartment in the south tower."

"It's fantastic, yes."

"And Celeste, you've seen your accommodations."

It was Ferrol's private, opulent suite of rooms.

"They are quite adequate," she said with a naughty smile.

She touched a long fingernail to the largest space on the blueprints. Although unlabeled, the icons for beds, sink, toilet, and shower tipped it as living space. "What's this for?" she asked.

"It's for our patients," he said.

32

Ferrol's laboratory took almost a year to build. Due to a caution bordering on paranoia, he refused to hire local men for the work; wagging tongues were an unacceptable risk. He used a Swiss architect, a German general contractor, and skilled Turkish workers who lived in buildings on his estate. To ensure that local Castile and León officials were in the dark, he paid his general contractor a large bribe to do the work without permits. With Ferrol obligated to spending most of his time in Madrid, the supervision of the project fell to Gunar Materska, his estate manager and head of security who had been with him for years. He was an imposing, scowling presence whose rudimentary Spanish and English was matched only by his rudimentary sense of humor. Gunar did nothing to ingratiate himself to Celeste or Ferruccio Gressani. Both of them were thoroughly intimidated by his hulking ways and lupine stares and they avoided him when possible.

"He scares the shit out of me," Gressani told Celeste one day over lunch in the castle kitchen.

"Me as well," she agreed.

"Where do you think he's from?" he asked.

"Ferrol told me he's Slovakian. He used to be some kind of a soldier."

"Why'd Dr. G hire him?"

"He doesn't trust the locals."

"I wouldn't be surprised if he's murdered people," Gressani said.

"I wouldn't be surprised if he's raped people," she added.

"Possibly both," Gressani concluded.

The contrast of transforming the dank, ancient space where medieval Gaytan lords kept their wine and their feudal hostages, to gleaming labs was startling—with passage through a set of security doors, five centuries vanished. Celeste joked that she needed sunglasses to work there because of the gleaming whiteness of every surface. Ferrol even chose ceiling fixtures that delivered a high-Kelvin, pure white.

White is the color of progress, he would say, the color of cleanliness, the color of life.

Celeste and Gressani left their hospital jobs and were on Ferrol's personal payroll during the construction project. During the week, Ferrol remained in Madrid supervising his mainstream research and joined them in Lirio on weekends to work through experimental protocols for what was to come. Gressani found the isolation of the castle and the absence of a social life somewhat boring, but Celeste enthusiastically assumed the role of lady of the manor, bossing around the domestic staff to whom the basement was strictly off-limits, and luxuriating in the opulence of medieval finery. When the underground lab was finally complete and the construction teams were gone, Ferrol had his cook prepare a celebratory dinner, laid on in dramatic fashion in the vast banqueting hall.

Ferrol sat at one end of an impossibly long dining table with Celeste to his right and Gressani to his left.

Lifting a glass of vintage champagne, he said, "This is the end of one phase of my journey and the beginning of the next. We have demonstrated in animal experiments that my techniques work. It's time to take the giant leap. With your help, we can achieve what has only been dreamed of before. A toast! To us! To a long and healthy future!"

Celeste's red lips stained the rim of her glass and she rubbed his inner thigh under the table.

Ferrol patted her hand and said, "Ferruccio, the next job will be yours and yours alone. I'm depending on you to get it done."

"What can I do, Dr. G?"

"You know people I do not know. People from your home, the criminals, the 'Ndrangheta. I want you to reach out to these people. I'm certain they can get us what we need. They'll want a lot of money. I'm not a fool—I will negotiate. However, I'm prepared to pay whatever it takes."

Next to sex, weightlifting was Matteo Zuliani's greatest pleasure. He regularly injected a cocktail of anabolic steroids and testosterone, and as a result, he often had to cut the arms off of T-shirts to accommodate his bulging muscles. It was a hot, muggy July night and as he waited outside his brother-in-law's house, he was sweating heavily. The job tonight was straightforward. He had done these kinds of things before. However, this one was different in a delightful way. For this job, the payment was guaranteed, two-thirds in advance, a third on delivery.

Gianluca Rizzo was a natural choice for his partner. He was a good soldier who worked hard, he had a decent attitude, and he was determined to curry favor with Matteo's father. As someone linked to the Zulianis by marriage, not blood, he knew he'd be judged only by his productivity and earning power.

Zuliani got impatient and knocked on the door. Rizzo answered, somewhat flustered.

"What the fuck's taking you so long?" Zuliani asked.

"Sorry, Teo. I'm trying to figure out how much to pack?"

"We're not going on holiday, for Christ's sake. Just bring a fucking toothbrush, Lu."

"When are we going to be back?"

"I told you. This time tomorrow night. Now, go kiss my goddamn sister and let's go."

He heard his sister calling out, "When's he going to be back?"

"Tomorrow fucking night!"

"Does he need a jacket?"

"It's the middle of the fucking summer!" he yelled.

"He said he's going to be on a boat."

"Hey, Lu, did you give her all the details of the job?" Zuliani asked.

"Just that we're going to be on a boat."

Zuliani began walking back to his car. "I'm starting the car and I'm leaving. You'd better have your rear end in the passenger seat or you're going to be in deep shit."

They drove down from the hills toward the sea.

After a while, Rizzo asked, "So, how do you know about this family?"

"A friend of mine hangs out in a bar in Favazzina. An

old guy comes in there all the time. He and his wife are caretakers for a villa owned by some Americans who come here for the summer. He's always going on about how rich they are and that they've got these nice little girls. I checked the place out two weeks ago, before the family arrived. They don't have cameras, there's a security system, but it wasn't on."

"How'd you know?"

"I hopped the gate and climbed a drainpipe up to the first floor where a window was a little bit open. Open windows mean there's no alarm set."

"Yeah, smart."

"So, I'm in the house and in one of the closets on the ground floor, there's the alarm panel that's got a sticky note with the alarm code and the gate code and a bunch of duplicate door keys. Can you believe how stupid these fucking pricks are?"

"Unbelievable."

"This place had everything we needed. They were busting my balls telling me this couldn't look like a break-in."

"Why?"

"How the fuck should I know? They paid enough. Whatever they say, right?"

"You got the money?"

"Yeah. I gave it to my father. He's happy as shit. He'll pay you out when we get back."

Near Villa Shibui, they put on balaclavas and gloves to finish the journey. Zuliani hopped out and punched in the gate code. Then he slowly drove down the gravel drive and parked by the barn next to the family cars.

Zuliani tugged on the slide of his pistol and told his

brother-in-law that it was only for an emergency. "Remember," he said, "no violence, no blood. We can scare them, but we're not allowed to hurt them. Come on, let's do this."

It was two in the morning and the house was dark.

Zuliani used the spare house key he had stolen. He was prepared to disarm the alarm at the touch-panel in the hall, but the panel didn't beep.

"Upstairs," he whispered.

He led Rizzo to the open door of the master bedroom. There, he turned on his LED torch, barged in and flooded the bed with blinding light.

Jesper and Elena Andreason awoke at the same time and both let out cries of alarm.

When Jesper threw off the bedspread, Zuliani used some of the few English words he knew, "No, stop, gun, gun." Then he told Rizzo to hit the lights.

"What do you want?" Jesper said, staring into the barrel of a pistol.

"Get clothes."

"Give them money to leave," Elena said through sobs.

"I don't have much cash," Jesper said fearfully, "but you can take watches, jewelry, our cars. Just don't harm us. Please."

"Not money," Zuliani said, not fully understanding Jesper's plea. "Get clothes."

Elena spoke to him in Italian. "You don't know what you're getting yourself into. My father-in-law is an important American businessman. My father is a big lawyer here. If you get the fuck out now, you'll be safe. If you kidnap us, you'll be running until you're caught and then you'll be in prison for the rest of your life. Think carefully."

"Whoa! Your accent! A local girl and not bad-looking either. Get dressed now or I'll take you into the bathroom and bend you over the sink. I'm not fucking around."

When Jesper and Elena threw on clothes, Rizzo zip-tied their wrists behind their backs and sat them back down. Elena's shouts and cries were grating on him so he told her if she didn't shut up, he'd shoot her husband.

"What did he say?" Jesper asked.

"He wants me to be quiet or he'll shoot you."

"Maybe you should," Jesper said.

"Where's the other one? What's he doing with my daughters?" Elena asked Rizzo.

"Nothing. We promised not to hurt anyone."

"Who'd you promise?" Elena asked. "Who are you doing this for?"

"One more word and we'll break the promise."

Zuliani crept into the girls' bedroom and took out the stoppered vial he'd been given from his pocket. They were tucked in, sound asleep. He followed his instructions, leaned over each bed, and with the medicine dropper, delivered a few drops into their mouths.

He waited the five minutes and tested the effect of the drops by flicking each girl hard with a finger. When they didn't wake, he put one of them under each of his huge arms and called for Rizzo to bring the parents.

When Elena saw the two limp figures, she screamed, "What have you done to them!"

"Nothing," Zuliani said. "They're asleep. I gave them medicine so they wouldn't be frightened. I'm a nice guy."

The four Andreasons were bundled into the back seat of Zuliani's car. Rizzo put hoods over the parents' heads and they drove off, after locking the front door and closing the gate.

It was a short drive to Porto di Bagnara where north of the marina, on a desolate stretch of pebbly beach, a tender boat had been dragged onto the shore. Zuliani parked on an access road, carried the drugged girls as before, and had Rizzo wrangle Jesper and Elena.

Gunar was waiting on the beach with a boat driver, his blond hair flapping in the warm wind. With a penlight, he checked to make sure the girls were alive.

"No problem?" he said in English.

"Yes, yes, no problem," Zuliani said.

Gunar gestured toward the sea and barked, "We go boat."

The large motor yacht, a sixty-footer, was anchored a kilometer offshore, and once everyone was onboard, and the tender secured, the captain took off to the west at full throttle.

While Gunar was putting the Andreasons below decks, Zuliani went to the bridge and tried to ask the captain a question, but the little English he knew wasn't sufficient for the task.

In Spanish, the captain asked, "You speak Spanish?"

"No Spanish."

The captain shifted to Italian and said, "I speak more Italian than you speak English. I learned from charter passengers. What are you asking me?"

"How far are we going?"

"About seven hundred fifty nautical miles. At this speed, about twelve hours to Spain."

"Is that where we're going?" the young man asked.

"You didn't know?"

"No one told us. You're going to bring us back?"

"That's what I'm being paid to do. We'll get some fuel and return to Italy this time tomorrow night. We have a couple of crew bunks below you and your friend can use for sleep. There's food in the galley."

"Where's that big blond guy from?" Zuliani asked. "He looks like his face is going to fall apart if he smiles."

"I don't know a fucking thing about him. I don't know a fucking thing about you or the people you brought on the boat. And I don't want to know, okay?"

"Up now. You come."

Zuliani and Rizzo woke to the command. They had been asleep for a couple of hours on narrow bunks.

"What the hell?" Rizzo mumbled in the dark. "What's he want?"

Gunar was in the doorway, blotting out the light from the corridor.

"Come now," he repeated.

"I think he wants us to come," Zuliani said.

"What's going on?"

"I guess we're going to find out."

They clamored up the stairs where Gunar was waiting for them in the main salon. He tried to hand Zuliani a small revolver.

Zuliani wouldn't take it. He used his best English and reached into his waistband, "Don't need. Big gun. See?"

Gunar persisted. "Little gun—twenty-two—little blood. Less to clean."

"What's going on, Teo?" Rizzo asked in Italian.

"I think this guy wants us to shoot someone."

"We didn't sign up for that, did we?"

"We were paid for a snatch job, that's all."

"Tell him."

Zuliani tried his hardest to get the point across, but Gunar said, "Part of job. You paid lot of money."

He led them out to the stern deck where Jesper and Elena were seated on a bench, hoods over their heads, zip-ties still binding their hands.

Above them on the bridge, the captain turned up his playlist.

Elena was sobbing, Jesper was silent, his chest heaving.

Elena snapped her head off her chest when she heard Rizzo asking Zuliani in Italian if he was going to do it.

"Do what?" she cried. "What are you going to do?"

"Nothing," Zuliani said, shooting Jesper in the head.

Elena started screaming. She stood up and blindly ran forward, bumping into the wall that was Gunar's chest. He pushed her back onto the bench where she made contact with Jesper's body.

"Kill me but don't hurt my babies!" she screamed. "Please, not my babies!"

"Will you please shut the fuck up," Zuliani said, firing into her hood.

Gunar took the revolver back and pointed the Italians to two piles of anchor chain.

"Wrap them good. No one find."

The afternoon sun was blazing hot when the yacht made port in Valencia. It was a busy marina and Gunar told Zuliani and Rizzo to stay inside the boat, out of sight.

Gunar carried two duffel bags down the dock and into the parking lot where a large camper van was idling with the air conditioning on.

"Let me see them," Ferrol said. "Are they okay?"

"They okay," Gunar said. "Had to give more drops when they almost wake."

Ferrol eagerly unzipped the bags, but when he saw fair skin and golden-brown hair, he became alarmed.

"These aren't Italian children," he said.

"Kidnappers say they American," Gunar replied.

"No, no, no. They're supposed to be Italians. Poor Italians."

"I don't know, boss," Gunar said. "They took mother and father too. We dump them in sea."

Ferrol clasped his head in his hands and told Gunar he wanted to talk to the kidnappers. They left the girls in the cool camper in their unzipped bags and boarded the yacht.

"You sure you want them see you face?" Gunar asked.

"It won't matter," Ferrol said. "Make sure the crew stays on the bridge. I don't want them to see me."

Ferrol spoke five languages. Italian was one of them. Zuliani and Rizzo were stuffing themselves on thick sandwiches in the galley when he entered and demanded, "Tell me about the two girls. Where did you find them?"

"Who are you?" Zuliani asked.

"I'm the one who paid you," Ferrol said.

Zuliani yawned and told him that a friend heard about these kids in a little place called Filarete and when he checked the house out it was perfect for all these reasons.

"What was the house like?" Ferrol asked.

"A beautiful villa. Unbelievable. I've never seen a place so big and so nice."

"So, this was a rich family."

"Very rich. Money coming out of their asses."

"And they're Americans, I understand."

"Well, the mother was Italian. Calabrian, for sure. I guess the father was American. What does it matter?"

Ferrol was seething. "You were supposed to get me poor children. From the slums. Low-profile, where the media attention goes away quickly. I know you were told this."

Zuliani got red in the face. "You don't know what the fuck I was told, okay? You wanted two kids less than ten years old, you got two kids less than ten years old. Don't be busting our balls. Now, give us the rest of our money. And since we're talking to the big cheese, you should pay us for shooting the parents. That wasn't part of the deal. That should be extra."

Ferrol put up his hands and said, "All right. You boys delivered. Gunar, give them their money. I paid you a fortune. It's enough. Have a good trip back to Italy."

Gunar passed them a tote bag and Zuliani told them to wait while he dumped it out on the table and had Rizzo count it.

On the dock, Ferrol told Gunar, "This is bad for us. Rich Americans, for Christ's sake. This is going to be big news all over the world. We're going to have to be extremely careful. Go talk to the captain. Tell him the bag of money you gave those boys is for him. Tell him to feed the fish some Italian food."

33

Victoria and Elizabeth woke up in a gleaming white room, each on a soft bed with a white pillow and a white duvet.

"Where are we?" Elizabeth said.

Ferrol had been watching from his office on closed-circuit cameras.

"Celeste," he said through an intercom. "Suit up. They're awake."

They had drilled for this moment, but now they were faced with last-minute linguistic changes. They had planned on Italian-speaking kids and Celeste had spent a year learning Italian to the point where she was semi-fluent. Gressani, of course, would have had no issues. With two so-called American kids with an Italian mother, they didn't know what language or languages they spoke and Gressani's English was basic, at best.

While Celeste got prepared, Ferrol thought back to the day he introduced her and Gressani to this small part of his larger plan.

*

He opened the box and said to them, "When you work with the children, this is what you'll wear."

They took it as a joke, something to lighten the mood, but he was serious. The full-head latex masks were in the plastic bags of a high-end Hollywood prosthetics company. The labels described them as: **Alien Latex Mask, UFO, Extra-Terrestrial, Grays.** They were gray, hairless, and skeletal, with huge black eyes, small black mouths and tiny black nostrils. There were matching latex gloves in another bag.

"Try them on," Ferrol said. "You remember when I took measurements of your heads? Now you know why."

"Is this a prank on us, Dr. G?" Gressani said.

"It's not a prank."

Celeste pinned her hair into a bun and stretched the mask over her head.

"Voila," she said, her voice muffled. "Would you like me to wear this in bed tonight?"

Gressani cracked up, but he stopped at Ferrol's dirty look.

"You'll be wearing disposable white jumpsuits over your clothes and white shoe covers, so all they'll see is your heads and hands.

Celeste peeled her mask off and told him it was hot inside.

"You'll get used to it," Ferrol said.

"Tell me why we're doing this?" she asked. "I understand the need to protect ourselves from identification, but there are more comfortable ways to shield our faces."

"You know how careful I am. I've thought through all of this," Ferrol said. "We can't predict everything. Chaos theory tells us that the unexpected can and will happen. In the event that we decide the children must be released, there can't be any way for the police to make a connection to people or places. These will be young, impressionable children. They will be asleep when they are taken. They will be drugged in transit. They will awaken in a windowless, white room. They will be greeted and subsequently cared for by the two of you who will appear as alien beings. They will be told they have been taken to a spaceship for study. If and when they are released, they will tell the police what they experienced. From what I've read about alien abductions, a great many people will believe them. It's incredible how gullible people are. Forty percent of people believe in aliens. Twenty percent say they've seen a UFO. People who claim they've been abducted become celebrities. What the children describe will confound any investigations."

He leaned back in his reclining desk chair with a look of self-satisfaction.

"Isn't there a problem with your plan, Dr. G?" Gressani said. "I'm going to sound like an ordinary Italian boy and Celeste with her French-Italian accent—well, you know how she sounds. Even children will recognize our voices as coming from regular people."

Ferrol's answer came in the form of a bag he retrieved from a desk drawer. He opened it and gave each of his compatriots a small black box and a headset.

"Electronic voice changers," he said. "You'll clip the boxes inside your white suits and wear the headsets under the masks. I've adjusted the faders to give a distortion level that I would describe as a huskier version of the creature in *E.T.*"

Gressani wanted to try his out, but Celeste appeared distracted.

"I'm troubled by something you said."

"What's that?" he asked.

She unpinned her bun, let her red hair fall down her back, and said, "You said, if and when they are released. This shocks me. We can't hold them forever. They'll need to be returned to their families. I know that kidnapping innocent children is quite barbaric. All of us accept it's the only way to advance something that will benefit mankind, but these aren't laboratory animals to be sacrificed at the end of an experiment. They are children."

While she spoke, Ferrol nodded professorially and replied, "I couldn't agree with you more. I misspoke. When they're released, I meant to say. I don't know how long the work will last, but when we've reached a clear, definable endpoint, we will return them to Italy. Understood?"

She was about to say something when Gressani began jabbering in a distorted, robotic voice.

Celeste was ready.

It took a loose, shapeless suit to obscure her curves and a rubber creature mask to hide her beauty.

"You look perfect," Ferrol said. "I know you're nervous. We're all nervous, but we've rehearsed this countless times. We're ready. Be a good nurse. Make them comfortable. Do what you do."

She started to talk, but she had already activated her voice distortion. Annoyed, she reached through her suit for the off button.

"What should I say about their parents? Were the parents asleep when they were taken?"

Ferrol remained impassive. He knew Celeste would discover the lie soon enough—he had already seen early news reports from Italy about an entire family who had gone missing. Later, when she and Gressani saw the news themselves, he would blame the kidnappers for lying to him and express great remorse for their terrible and brutal actions. He would tell them he made sure that Gunar made the thugs pay. For now, he needed her to be reassuring and reduce the girls' stress as much as possible.

He said, "I was told their mother and father are fine. Make sure you tell them that. The men who took the girls from their beds were very quiet. They told me the parents didn't wake up."

She nodded her gray, alien head, and activated her voice changer.

Ferrol watched through his monitor and only when he began gasping for air, did he realize he'd been holding his breath.

Victoria let out a high-pitched scream and scuttled over to Elizabeth's bed when Celeste entered. The two girls held each other and cried.

"Don't be afraid," the mechanical voice said. "You are safe. I won't harm you. Please tell me if you understand me."

Both girls had their eyes closed. It was Elizabeth who opened hers first and said, "You sound funny."

"To me, *you* sound funny."

"Where are we?" Elizabeth asked.

"On a spaceship."

"Where are Mommy and Daddy?"

"They are asleep in their beds."

"When they wake up and we're gone, they'll be upset."

"We whispered in their ears not to be worried. They know you're safe."

Victoria's eyes popped open. "What's your name?" she asked.

"We don't have names."

"Then what shall I call you?"

"You may call me your friend."

"Why are we here?" Elizabeth demanded, suddenly feisty.

"We wish to learn about human children. You can teach us many things."

"But I want to go back home!" Victoria shouted. "I don't like it here. I want my mommy."

"You will be happy here. My job is to make you happy."

"How?" Victoria demanded.

"We have all the Earth games and toys and videos and books. We can make all your favorite Earth foods. I will sing songs and play games with you. I learned English, your language, so I can be a good companion. You were in the country of Italy. Do you speak Italian too?"

"A few words," Elizabeth said, "*Ciao. Mangia. Ti amo.*"

"Very well, we will speak in English. You must be very hungry after your long journey. What would you like to eat?"

"I want macaroni and cheese and an ice cream sundae," Victoria said.

"I'm not hungry," Elizabeth said.

"You must eat."

"I said, I'm not hungry!"

"I will bring you food anyway. Through that door is a bathroom. It is just like your bathrooms on Earth. That chest is filled with clothes. Later, I will show you all the toys and games. You will love it here. I will love you and soon, you will love me."

Celeste returned to Ferrol's office and before she could do or say anything, he told her that he had called up the meal request to the upstairs kitchen.

Her knees buckled as she removed her mask and Ferrol had to spring up to stop her from falling. She began to sob.

"No, no," he said, "you did perfectly. It's okay. They're okay and you're okay."

"We've done something terrible," she said. "I knew, in my head, that this was wrong, but you're so fucking persuasive, I went along with it. Ferruccio and I have become members of your cult. That's what this is—a cult. Seeing those precious little girls—I don't know what to do now. Oh, God."

He tightened his embrace and kissed her sweaty ear. "Listen," he said, "this is a completely normal reaction. The shock will wear off soon and you and Ferruccio will be all right. You'll see how happy the girls will be. They won't have a care in the world. They're young. They'll miss their parents for a while, but that will fade. Believe me. I went through this myself. We'll all keep our eyes on the ultimate prize. We are going to change what it means to be human. We are going to remove humanity's greatest fear. Goddamn it, Celeste, we are going to conquer death."

Ferrol waited a week for the girls to acclimatize. During that time, he dealt with the inevitable internal crisis when Celeste and Ferruccio saw the news that Elena and Jesper Andreason were also kidnapping victims. He felt like

GLENN COOPER

a firefighter, putting out flames that kept flaring from smoldering hotspots. The irony of the analogy did not go unnoticed, for it was in this very castle where his journey began, that night long ago when a twelve-year-old lost his parents and nearly lost his own life to fire.

When his fractious colleagues settled down, he decided it was time for the first blood-draw.

"I don't want them to become scared of me," Celeste said. "They're just building up a rapport with Gray Woman. That's what they call me. I think Ferruccio should do the first draws."

"But you're better at it than me," Gressani argued.

"There are going to be a lot of blood tests," Ferrol said. "They won't get a complex about them if the first ones go smoothly. Celeste, you go first. When the time comes for infusions, we'll put them to sleep with barbiturates. But I don't want to have to do that every time we draw blood."

In a month, Ferrol was ready.

Gressani had been working in Ferrol's skunkworks lab, so he was well versed in the objectives and techniques. When Celeste became part of the team, Ferrol had to initiate her. One night, he brought her to his study off the castle library and wrote a word on a whiteboard.

Telomeres.

"Do you know what they are?" he asked like a stern professor.

She said she didn't with the look of a girl who hadn't done her homework.

He noticed and softened his style. "There's no reason you

should. Don't worry. I'm going to teach you everything you need to know."

He bent over her chair and kissed her forehead, and if some might have seen this as patronizing, she didn't. She smiled gratefully and reached for his hand.

He returned to the board and began drawing illustrations. "Telomeres are the pieces of DNA that cap the ends of chromosomes. They prevent damage to the chromosomes that naturally occur with aging. However, these telomeres are also susceptible to damage, and as the cells in our organs divide, the telomeres get shorter and shorter. Every time they divide, the telomeres shorten, until the cells cannot divide any longer and they die. Think of telomeres as the clocks inside of cells, ticking down to cell death. Now, here's the important observation: some people have a genetic tendency toward longer telomeres and they live longer. Let me repeat—they live longer. People who live to a hundred or more have markedly longer telomeres than everyone else."

His passion began to crest. "Celeste, listen, the holy grail is finding a way to lengthen the telomeres inside our cells and to defeat aging. Telomere scientists have been working on anti-aging approaches for years and some have shown modest success in extending lifespan of mice by twenty percent, thirty percent. But here's where it gets interesting. I've developed a radically different approach to everyone else in the field that stops aging in its tracks! Fruit flies live no more than fifty days. My fruit flies are still alive and buzzing about their jars five years after treatment. Mice live for two years. My mice are as sleek and healthy as adolescents eight years after treatment. I've cracked the code, Celeste. I can stop aging. I can defeat death."

His excitement was infectious. "Who else knows about this?" she asked. "Surely, you've published your results."

"Only Ferruccio knows. I've told no one. I've published nothing. I've funded all this work from my own pocket. I've needed to keep it a secret because I knew where this was heading."

"To humans," she whispered.

"Yes, of course. I didn't want to draw any attention. I'm not boasting, but if I were a conventional scientist, there'd be a Nobel Prize for my work. I console myself in the knowledge that what I want to achieve is far more important than a trip to Stockholm. The chance of ever getting scientific and ethical review boards to agree to human experiments is zero. It will never happen in our lifetimes."

"What are the risks?" she asked.

"I think they're small, but people will worry about unintended consequences like cancers. Proving the negative would be impossible. My research would be blocked. The only way to do human studies is to do them myself. Here. With you and Ferruccio."

"But who would volunteer to be your guinea pigs? Are you going to entice people by paying them a lot?"

"Here is the dilemma, Celeste. You can measure the length of telomeres, but that's only a surrogate observation for the true measures of anti-aging. The best, of course, is the extension of lifespan. That's impractical. It takes too long in humans. The second-best measure is to see if a person stops aging. This is more practical than looking to lifespan, but determining if, say a forty-year-old man has stopped aging, might take a decade or more to be sure. No, the only realistic way of knowing if my techniques work within a reasonable length of time is to do the experiments on young children. In a few years, one can know."

"Children," she gasped. "Holy mother of Christ. You can't be serious?"

"I'm very serious."

"How will you get children?"

"We'll talk about that later." His voice rose like a Shakespearean actor. "First, let's talk about what it will mean for mankind to defeat that which all of us fear— decrepitude, degenerative diseases, and death. Let's talk about that."

Ferrol asked Gressani to tutor Celeste on the experimental techniques. One day when Ferrol was in Madrid, they took a walk through the orchards and fields, and the young man explained how the work was done.

"Everything begins with blood," he said. "We draw blood and in the lab, I isolate the immune cells, the T cells. Using a cocktail of growth factors and chemicals that Dr. G perfected, I turn the T cells into cells called pluripotent stem cells. These are immature cells that can mature into all the cell types in our bodies. Then I insert a gene into them that Dr. G discovered, that prevents telomeres from getting shorter. It's actually better than that. It makes telomeres get longer. Dr. G calls it his Methuselah gene. So, now we've got the stem cells with the Methuselah genes and we're ready to use it as a therapy. You can't just inject it back into the animal or a patient or whatever. You've got to wipe out the bone marrow first, so all the old stem cells don't counteract what the new ones are supposed to do. We pre-treat with chemotherapy to destroy the old stem cells, then infuse the new ones. Then, all the stem cells and eventually,

GLENN COOPER

most of the cells in the body will have the Methuselah gene and super-long telomeres. And there you have it—maybe not immortality, but maybe you'll live for two hundred, three hundred years if you don't get hit by a car."

Celeste kicked at some rusting iron sticking out of the plowed field. It was an old horseshoe. Who knew how long it had been there?

"Have you wrapped your head around what we're going to be doing, Ferruccio?"

"You mean using children?"

"Yes, children."

"Dr. G has done all the animal experiments. This is ready for humans. He's explained it to you. Children are the only fast way to see if it works. I mean, it stinks and I'll probably have nightmares, but maybe in the future we'll be seen as pioneers. Maybe even heroes. In the meantime, he's paying us a lot of money. I wonder, is he paying you more than me? I mean, you have to sleep with him. I don't."

"Go fuck yourself, Ferruccio," she said, and she headed back to the castle on her own.

34

Ferrol was in his basement office, reviewing validation data from the laboratory instruments that Gressani would soon use to process the girls' blood cells. Celeste was next to him, mapping out menus and recreation schedules to keep the girls healthy and active. One video monitor was trained on the girls who were sitting on their beds, drawing with colored pens. A small TV on mute was tuned to Antena 3, but when Ferrol saw a chyron announcing a press conference regarding the kidnapping in Italy, he reached for the remote and turned on the sound.

Celeste looked up and both of them watched a tall, distinguished man in a tan suit standing in front of the iron gates of a villa, addressing the media.

"My name is Mikkel Andreason. This will be in English. I'm sorry I don't speak Italian. I am the father of Jesper Andreason, the father-in-law of Elena Andreason, and the grandfather of Elizabeth and Victoria Andreason. My beloved family was taken from their holiday home here in Reggio Calabria. All of them they are missing. We don't know who took them or why. What I do know is that I want them back immediately."

"My God," Celeste cried, "What have we done? You said the parents were left alone. You lied!"

Ferrol didn't reply. He watched until Mickey turned back toward the villa without taking any questions, then muted the TV.

"I didn't lie. I didn't know until later," Ferrol said, frowning deeply. "We have to keep our eyes on the bigger picture. All of mankind suffers from the tyranny of sickness and death. Every single day, millions of people suffer from the loss of family and friends. What we will do here can change everything. If we are successful—and I believe we will be successful—we won't have to say goodbye to our loved ones just because they've reached their eighth or ninth decade. The perspective of mankind will change. We'll live longer, work longer, play longer, love longer."

"I know," she said over and over, as if trying to convince herself.

Ferrol's mood darkened. "The only unanticipated problem is that the idiots Ferruccio got to do the job ignored their instructions. I wanted children from a poor family without the means to keep the case in the public eye. We got the opposite. A billionaire, God help us! I want to do something. As a precaution."

"Do what?"

"I want you to write this Mikkel Andreason a letter. I want you to say that you're a psychic who's had a vision. You'll say that in your vision, the girls were on a spaceship, abducted by aliens with gray skin, et cetera. You'll offer to help."

She had a nervous habit of twirling her long hair around

a finger, and she was doing it now. Twirl, release, twirl, release. "Why would we do that?"

"Because if we decide to abort our mission prematurely, for whatever reason, or when the mission is completed, I want to make sure that as many signposts as possible point to alien abduction to reinforce the story the girls will tell."

"A crazy letter from a psychic will do that?"

"One more brick in the wall. That's all. Listen, you want us to have options, don't you?"

"What do you mean?"

"The more we can rely on the alien story to deflect the police away from Spain, the less likely we would even contemplate the unthinkable."

She stood and pointed an accusatory finger. "You wouldn't dare hurt them, Ferrol."

"Of course not. I just believe in options. I'll compose a letter to send to Mikkel Andreason at his offices in America. They'll get so many letters from sick and deranged people, they'll take no action. They'll file it away. I want you to write out the letter on stationery and sign it."

"But not with my real name!"

"No, no, it will have to be your real name. In the most extreme of all the scenarios, it might be necessary for you to make yourself known, to actively make sure an investigation is steered toward gray men from outer space. You would have to use your real name. These things are too easy to check."

"I'll never show myself like that," she said. "I won't do it."

He got up and drew her close. "Don't worry. The odds

of having to show yourself are a million to one. Those are good odds, no?"

A year passed, and then another.

They all had their own rhythms.

Victoria and Elizabeth talked and played games and read books and wrote stories and watched videos, some of them educational to keep their minds active and learning. When they tired of their old videos and games, Gray Woman produced newer ones beamed, she said, from Planet Earth. When Ferrol and Celeste worried they weren't getting enough exercise, mini trampolines appeared and indoor badminton and football sets. For the most part, they remained healthy. Their only significant illness occurred during their first weeks of captivity, following chemotherapy to wipe out their bone marrows for the stem-cell transplantations. For a fortnight, they had nausea and diarrhea, fever and chills, and Celeste's competence as a nurse got them through.

Gressani ran laboratory tests, checking on the function of the new line of stem cells, transplanted into the girls and measured the length of their telomeres. He kept meticulous records in case, miracle of miracles, Ferrol ever published a journal paper on a research project that broke a thousand laws. But Ferrol wanted everything documented for posterity. As Gray Man, Gressani split care and feeding duties with Celeste and divvied up night call, which consisted of keeping a video monitor at their bedsides in case of a night-time emergency in the white room. He played games with the girls and watched enough videos with them. To make himself comfortable, he ordered a beanbag chair and dragged it into their room.

"Look at Gray Man!" Victoria said, the first time they saw him with the chair. "He's going to sleep!"

On his off-hours, he also watched a lot of football on TV and a lot of porn on his tablet and obsessively admired his growing bank balance. To better communicate with the girls, he improved his English. And every Sunday he called his mother in Italy, inquiring if she liked the latest gifts he'd sent.

Celeste had many of the same duties, although she was the one who closely monitored the girls' health and recorded their weight, height and vital signs. While she and Gressani both bonded with them, he was more of a pal; she was more of a mother. If she had to pick a favorite, it was Elizabeth, who was smart and feisty and rarely seemed gloomy or depressed. Victoria was more petulant and defiant and she was the one who cried longest for her mother, but by their first anniversary, neither talked about their past lives.

When Ferrol was away in Madrid at the La Paz Hospital, as he was most weekdays, Celeste ruled the roost. The domestic and estate staff—with the exception of Gunar—looked to her for routine decisions. If she ever heard the cook or one of the maids whispering to one another about the trays of food that Celeste or Gressani took to the basement, she asked if they wanted to be reported to Ferrol. Gunar, was always patrolling the grounds and interiors of the castle, but Celeste stayed out of his way as much as possible, although sometimes, she caught him staring at her like a hungry dog. When Ferrol was back on weekends, she shared his bed and, increasingly and utterly, she fell in love with him.

Ferrol maintained his double life with skill and energy. During the week, he ran his hospital laboratory, churning out data and publications on his mainstream research and fulfilling his administrative duties as the head of the institute. Without Celeste's knowledge, he led a parallel social life in Madrid, dating a string of beautiful women and entertaining them at his apartment. When he returned to Castile and León on Friday nights or Saturday mornings, he fell back into his domestic partnership with Celeste and lavished her with all the attention she craved. But his true passion was studying Victoria and Elizabeth. He watched them endlessly on video monitors and pored over Gressani's weekly datapoints to the point of memorization.

Early into their third year of captivity, Ferrol returned to the castle one weekend, eager to test some new software. He shut himself in his office and, after an hour, called upstairs for Celeste.

Her hair was still wet from a bath. "What couldn't wait?"

"I bought some software from the Netherlands that police departments use to age photographs of missing people to see what they might look like over time. It confirms what we've been suspecting for a year now. The problem is, there's too much bias in our own observations. We desperately want to believe our own eyes, but we don't want to be led down the garden path." He clicked his mouse and the computer awoke. "Here is a photo of Victoria from the first week she came here. I've used the software to age her two years—age four to six. Here's what six-year-old Victoria should look like. Here's a photo of her from this week."

"My goodness, look at that," Celeste said.

They all knew the girls looked little different to when first arrived. But, seeing the Victoria as she ought to look at age six was a light-bulb moment. Her older face was longer, thinner, her nose more narrow, her lips less full.

"Show me Elizabeth," she said.

The age-rendered Elizabeth was even more dramatic. Ten-year-old Elizabeth was no longer a little girl. She was becoming a young lady.

"It's working, Celeste," he said. "We've seen the way their telomere length is still super-long and rock stable. With this, I'm convinced now, more than ever, that it's working."

"Then we can take them back, right? If we know it's working, we can let them go. Their parents are dead, but they have grandparents."

Ferrol wouldn't hear of it. "It's out of the question. It's far too early. We have to see if the effect persists. We've got to check their telomeres and cell function over time. I know it's two years, but it's still early days. Have patience. I'm sure this is working, but we need so much more before the next phase."

She noticed that her hair was dripping on the floor and got a paper towel.

"What next phase? You never talked about a next phase."

He bent over, took the moist towel from her, and threw it into a hamper.

"The next phase involves you, Celeste, and it involves me."

35

Twenty months later—three years and eight months since the girls were taken—Ferrol declared that he was finally ready for his "next phase" and it came when things in the basement at Castle Gaytan were nearing a breaking point.

They no longer needed software to know the girls had stopped aging. The girls too had become self-aware, but they were satisfied with the explanation from Gray Woman and Gray Man that humans in space didn't get older. But for Celeste and Gressani, enough was enough. This had gone on far too long and Celeste, as their spokesperson, beseeched Ferrol to let the girls go.

"We can't take this anymore," Celeste protested. "You're in Madrid most of the time and we're stuck here. We can't leave for more than a day or two. We can't go on holiday. We have to watch these poor creatures every minute. We're zookeepers, that's what we are, and they are animals in a cage. Ferruccio and I are going crazy and I think the girls are too. They're listless. They don't want to play like they used to. Victoria cries in bed every night. She doesn't even know why she's crying. Enough! Please!"

They were in his bedroom. He poured himself another glass of wine and said, "Listen to me, Celeste. We're almost there. This can stop at five years. It's critically important for my future work to study the telomeres in the cells that divide the slowest. Ideally, I'd want to sample heart muscle cells that turn over exceedingly slowly, but I don't have the technical expertise to do a heart biopsy. The next best candidates are fat cells which divide every eight years. It's quite easy and non-invasive to biopsy fat. I've done the calculations. Five years is the minimum time to get usable data from fat cells. Then, we'll be done. Then, we can send them back."

"That's too long, Ferrol! It's not just me. Ferruccio feels the same way."

"Let me tell you why we need the time," he said, approaching her. "We need the fullest set of data to inform the next phase—to predict what we can expect in the future."

She resisted his embrace. "No! You always think you can tame me with a hug and a kiss. Tell me what you're talking about. What is this next phase you're always hinting at?"

"Sit down," he said. "Have some more wine. Please." When she was settled into one of his overstuffed chairs with a full glass in her hand he said, "I love you, Celeste."

She shook her head lightly, as if she had misheard. "You've never told me that before."

"Maybe it's taken me longer than it should have to realize it. I'm not a person who does introspection. Maybe, I'm a little blocked."

"Not a little, Ferrol. A lot. It's understandable. What happened to you when you were young was horrible."

"I don't want to look back," he said. "I want to look forward. I'm no longer a young man. In the best of

GLENN COOPER

circumstances, how long will we have together? Twenty years? Thirty?"

"It's enough," she said.

"No, it's not. We'll get old. We'll get sick. We'll die. Me first—this is a statistical probability—then you. I don't want to die, at least not for a very long time. I don't want you to die. I want to carry on living and working and loving you. Here's the next phase. I want both of us to have the treatment. I'm telling Ferruccio tomorrow to begin preparations. I'm going to be transplanted first. You'll take care of me while my bone marrow is suppressed. Then, if you agree, you'll go next and I'll take care of you. We can stop time, together. We can live as we are for a hundred years more, two hundred. Who knows how long? We can cheat death. Will you take the journey with me?"

Her lip trembled and the trembling spread in waves to her whole body. She said one word in reply. "Yes."

Ferrol, Celeste, and Gressani marked the fourth anniversary of the girls' captivity with a special dinner of suckling pig and grilled vegetables served in the banquet hall. The restive feelings of past year had been replaced by the frenetic pace and excitement of the past four months. Ferrol and Celeste now had genetically altered stem cells circulating and dividing inside their bodies. Ferrol's procedure had gone smoothly. Celeste's had not. She developed sepsis when her bone marrow was at its peak of chemotherapy suppression, and had it not been for Ferrol's skills and devotion, she might not have survived. Now, they were both strong and happy. Prior to the transplants, Gressani concluded that his leverage had never been higher and he got Ferrol to double his salary, so his mood had vastly improved too. And the contagion even spread to the girls. They seemed happier and more active. Ferrol had gotten them stationary bicycles, and they raced each other every day.

Sated on roast meat, they were waiting for the cook to bring out dessert when Celeste glanced at the display on her phone, a live feed from the white room that she covered with a napkin whenever the cook came in. She noticed something and removed herself to the far reaches of the hall to turn up the sound.

She heard screaming and began to run.

She had never donned the Gray Woman costume so quickly. Ferrol and Gressani hurried to the basement with her and both of them watched the monitors as Celeste went in.

"Vicky is bleeding!" Elizabeth cried. "Help her!"

Celeste brought gauze with her and she tried to staunch the flow of blood from Victoria's nose.

"What's going on, Dr. G?" Gressani asked.

"I don't know," Ferrol snapped. "Suit up and give them chocolate milk with barbiturates. I want to examine them."

By the time Gray Man entered, Elizabeth had a nosebleed too. She became hysterical and ran into the bathroom to check herself in the mirror.

Ferrol picked up the image in the bathroom camera and said to himself, "What the hell is happening?"

Hours later, Ferrol raised his head from his microscope and delivered the verdict. The girls were still sleeping, a deep barbiturate sleep, their noses packed with gauze.

"I'm not an expert, but I think this could be leukemia."

"Both of them?" Celeste said.

"The blood smears look identical," he said, rubbing his eyes. "There are a lot of immature white cells. I'm not sure what type. I'm going to have to do some research."

"How is this possible?" Celeste said, fear catching in her throat.

Ferrol pushed his stool away from the bench and got up. "Both of them sick simultaneously. The only explanation is their stem cells. We must have activated oncogenes. I'm going to have to do some research."

"Stop saying you need to do research!" Celeste cried. "You said the treatment was safe!"

"For four years, it was," Ferrol said, weakly.

Celeste was on her way to a full-blown hysteria. "I want you to remove my stem cells! I don't want them inside me anymore."

"Calm down. Let's go upstairs and get some brandy."

"I don't want to calm down! I want the cells gone."

His words spilled out in a gush. "Come, let's all go to the kitchen for brandy and dessert. I'm going to run back to Madrid in the morning. They need platelet transfusions. I'll get compatible platelets from the blood bank. I'll figure out what kind of therapy they need and get the right drugs. This will be okay. We'll get through this. I'll learn the techniques to study their oncogenes. Once I know what went wrong, I'll be able to develop a solution. Don't worry, Celeste. You won't get sick."

Gressani was the only one who remained calm. He shook his head and said, "I'm sorry, Dr. G, but I think the girls need a specialist. This is serious. They could die."

His lit fuse touched powder and Ferrol exploded,

shouting so loudly that Celeste and Gressani tried to shush him for fear the sound might penetrate the white room.

"They are not going to die! No one is going to die!" he screamed. "They are staying right here. It's not open to debate. I need to study them to find out what to do. Now, come upstairs and have some fucking dessert!"

Ferrol was gone for three days. While he was in Madrid, he called Celeste every few hours for status reports. They were still bleeding, she said, but it wasn't catastrophic. He told her he was making progress. He had the platelets. He thought he knew the kind of leukemia it was. He was working on procuring the drugs to treat them.

When he finally returned to the castle, he hurried inside with a cooler box of platelets and a bag of medicines. He found Celeste in the kitchen, having a cup of tea, with a wan and peculiar look.

"What's wrong?" he demanded. "How are they?"

She didn't answer and that unnerved him.

"Tell me, goddamn it!"

"I think we should go downstairs," she said.

He hurried ahead of her and reached his office first and looked at the monitor.

"Where are they?" he said, scanning the white room. "Where the hell are they?" He switched views and looked at the bathroom camera feed. The only off-camera area was the toilet stall. He said, "Are they hiding in the toilet?"

Celeste was rigidly standing behind him. She said dully, "No, Ferrol, they're not. They're gone."

He wheeled around panic-struck. "Gone? You mean dead?"

She spoke mechanically, without emotion. She was all cried out. "They're not dead. They're gone. Ferruccio couldn't take it anymore. I couldn't take it. They're sick. They needed to be seen by specialists. They needed to go home. It was his idea, but I didn't stop him. He waited until the night before last when the staff went home and Gunar was asleep. He drugged them and carried them to his car. He said he could make the trip to Calabria in twenty-six hours if he drove straight through. Gunar saw Ferruccio's car was gone. I told him that he was taking a few days off. Ferruccio's going to stay with his ex-girlfriend, Cinzia, a few days. He's worked out what he wants to do. You and I need to work out what we're going to do."

He had been listening, but he'd also been thinking, thinking fast and thinking hard. He wanted to howl. He wanted to pummel her. There was a pair of scissors on his desk. He wanted to bury them in her chest.

His cell phone buzzed with an alert.

He glanced at it and fumbled for the TV remote.

"What?" she said. "What's happening?"

A Spanish television anchor was talking rapidly, saying something about breaking news from Italy. The shot changed from the studio to a sunlit plaza in front of a Carabinieri station. An officer was standing at a podium bristling with microphones.

"My name is Major Roberto Lumaga, the commanding officer of the Carabinieri station in Reggio Calabria. I'd like to make a statement and then I will take a few questions. We can confirm that there has been a significant development in the case of the Andreasons, the American family who disappeared four years ago from their holiday villa in Filarete. The two girls, Victoria and Elizabeth Andreason, have been returned to the villa. Both of them are being evaluated by medical doctors at the Morelli Hospital. At this time, we have no information about the location or the fate of their parents, Jesper and Elena. The girls have obviously been traumatized and we are interviewing them slowly, in stages, so as not to put them under unnecessary stress. Their Italian grandparents and American grandfather are with the girls and are assisting in their recovery."

Ferrol slumped into his chair and buried his head in his hands.

"It's over, Ferrol," she said, putting a hand on his shoulder. "It will be all right. Ferruccio's not going to say anything. He's not going to tell anyone about us. He's going to take his money and start over in South America."

He brushed her hand aside.

"It's not over," he said. His voice had the hardness of cold steel. "Do you love me?"

"Yes, I love you."

"Then why did you betray me?"

"I didn't betray you. I helped Ferruccio help Victoria and Elizabeth."

"No, no, no, it was a betrayal. But you can redeem yourself. We are going to get them back. You are going to help me get them back. They don't need a specialist. I have the medicine to treat them. I need to study them. I need to understand why they got sick. You don't want to get sick, do you, Celeste?"

"Of course, I don't, but—"

"No, no, listen to me. Don't speak. You're going to help me. If you don't, I'll have no choice but to kill myself. I'll kill myself in front of you. I'll do it in a brutal way. You know I don't want to die. You know how much it scares me. If you love me, you'll save me. Will you save me, Celeste?"

She crumpled to the floor and began to sob. "I love you. You know I love you."

"Then will you save me?"

"Yes," she said, raising her head. "I'll save you."

36

Present day

At 5 a.m., Marcus was just beginning to sober up in his Madrid hotel room. His empty bottle of Scotch was in the trash receptacle. He hadn't slept a minute all night; he couldn't get Abril's face out of his head. She was dead because of him. The bomb had been for him. He'd been pacing around his little room fully dressed, shifting from the chair to the bed and back again, waiting for daybreak so he could channel his anger into finding Victoria and Elizabeth. And getting revenge.

He was finishing shaving when he thought he heard something from the street below. He parted the curtain and recognized the black and gold insignias on the sides of the tactical vehicles. A serpent intertwined with a warbird. The GEO, Grupo Especial de Operaciones. The special operations group of the Spanish National Police were here, and it didn't take a genius to realize they were here for him.

He grabbed Celeste Bobier's wire transfer and shoved the

sheet into his pocket, gathered up his phone and wallet, put the Do Not Disturb sign on his door, and slipped out.

He knew the drill. They'd be flooding both staircases and the elevator. He couldn't get past them. The best he could do was hide. He took the closest staircase and ran down one flight to the mezzanine level. There were a couple of dingy meeting rooms, but there was no place to conceal himself. He found an unlocked service closet with stocked shelves and an empty laundry cart, which he quickly filled with towels and bed linens before climbing in and covering himself. He waited.

Police in green uniforms and ballistic vests wielding SG-550 assault rifles banged on his hotel-room door. When there was no answer, they used a pass key. It only took seconds to satisfy themselves that the small room was empty. The squad leader had them fan out for a wider search of the premises. Soon, an officer was entering the service closet. Marcus heard the crackle of the radio, saw faint light filtered through the canvas of laundry cart, and held his breath. A few moments later, it got dark and quiet again and Marcus exhaled into a dirty towel.

He didn't want to climb out before the police were gone, but he didn't want to stay too long, lest an employee come for the cart. He settled on two hours as a sweet spot and it was the longest two hours he'd ever weathered. When he finally got out, he stretched his cramped legs and took the stairs to the basement where he heard a couple of employees inside a service manager's office. He headed in the opposite direction toward an exit sign. A short run of metal stairs took him up to a deserted alleyway behind the hotel.

He avoided Calle de Alcalá. It was likely still crawling

with police investigating the car-bombing. Instead of using the Quintana Metro stop, he took a meandering route to the Cartagena station and rode the Metro to Tres Olivos. It was rush hour and he was grateful to be packed like a sardine in perfect anonymity. It was only a short walk from Tres Olivos to the La Paz Hospital. He already knew his way to Ferrol Gaytan's office. What he didn't know was what he was going to do when he saw him. Would he do a dance or go right for the jugular? Would he use words or fists?

Gaytan's young receptionist immediately recognized him.

"The CIA man," she said.

"You remember me," he said. "I need to see Dr. Gaytan."

She gave him an eye-roll. "I don't suppose you have an appointment."

"Actually no, but please tell him it will be brief."

"It will be extremely brief," she said, "because he isn't here today."

"I see. Do you know where I can find him?"

"I'm sorry, I wouldn't know that."

"Do you know when he's expected back?"

"Again, sir, I have no idea."

"Could you check with someone? I really need to find him."

She reluctantly excused herself and disappeared in the back. When she returned, she informed him that no one knew his whereabouts and that all his appointments had been canceled for the next several days. She gave him an office number to call and leave a voice message, telling him that the doctor was usually quite diligent in checking his messages. He could see the relief on her face when the phone rang and she could tactfully disengage. However, he was still standing at the desk when she finished her call.

"Look," he said, "I'm sure you have his home address." He winked. "You know I'll be able to find it—I'm with the CIA. But you'll be saving me a little time if you just give it to me."

"You don't have to be in the CIA to find it," she said. "I know for a fact it's in the Madrid phone book."

She called up a page on her computer, wrote something on a piece of paper, and handed it over with a forced smile.

Twenty minutes later, a taxi was dropping him off on a leafy, residential street in the Chamberí area outside an elegant building with wrought-iron balconies. Gaytan, it appeared, wasn't hurting for money. Marcus rang for Flat 4, the top floor apparently, and leaned on the buzzer when there was no response. Frustrated, he tried Flat 3 and Flat 2, and finally got an answer at Flat 1. The woman on the intercom only spoke Spanish and he did the best he could.

"I'm a friend of Dr. Gaytan. He asked me to come."

"He's not here," the woman said. "I saw him in the garage last night putting bags in his car."

"Do you know where he went?"

"I don't know. Goodbye."

There was a small park a block away, and in the shade of a tree, Marcus smoked a cigarette, and pondered his next move. He switched his phone back on and saw there were five missed calls from Roberto Lumaga.

Lumaga answered at the first ring. "Christ, Marcus! I've been trying to reach you all morning."

"I've been busy."

"I know all about it."

"How?"

"I got the alert this morning. Europol has issued a European Arrest Warrant for you on behalf of the Spanish authorities. You're wanted for the car-bomb murder of a woman named Abril Segura, an employee of CIFAS."

"She was a friend of mine. The bomb was meant for me."

"Of course, I believe you," Lumaga said, "but they found some plastic explosives and a detonator under the mattress of your hotel room."

"That's horse shit. I'm being framed."

"There's more. Because of the warrant, the Carabinieri up in Genoa want to question you for the shooting on the mountain."

"More horse shit."

"Yes, yes, of course."

All of a sudden, Marcus realized that this call was a problem. A CIFAS analyst was dead. The intelligence services would already have his mobile number. He was broadcasting his location.

He talked fast. "I need your help, Roberto. I know who's behind this."

"Who?"

"His name is Dr. Ferrol Luis Gaytan. He lives in Madrid."

"But how—"

"There's no time. Are you at your computer?"

"Yes."

"See what you have on him. He's not at his apartment in Madrid."

"Okay, hold on."

The phone in his hand felt like a traitor. He looked around nervously at the bench-sitters and the fit young man in a track suit, standing nearby, talking loudly into his phone. Seconds added up, a minute.

"You still there?" he asked.

"Yes, yes, coming," Lumaga said.

"Hurry."

"Okay, I've got your man. He's a big scientist, the director of an institute in Madrid."

"Yeah, I know that part."

"He's wealthy, it seems. Old money. Rich family."

"Police record?"

"I don't have access to that."

"You're not on a law enforcement site?"

"Wikipedia Spain."

"For fuck's sake. I could have looked it up myself."

"But you didn't. This is interesting. When he was a boy, he lost both his parents in an arson fire at their castle."

"He's got a castle? Still?"

"I don't know. It's called Castle Gaytan, so maybe, yes."

"Where is it?"

As Lumaga answered, Marcus heard sirens.

"Near Segovia. A village called Lirio."

"I've got to go."

"Wait—"

Marcus got up and dropped the live phone into a municipal trash can.

Lumaga kept listening. He heard police sirens getting louder and louder as they descended on the small park.

"Well, well, Marcus Handler! I wasn't expecting to see you so soon, or even again."

Marcus was back at Calle de la Villa de Marín standing at the door of the old professor's apartment. With Abril gone, this gentleman was the closest thing he had to a friend in Madrid.

"Javier, it's good to see you. I need your help."

"Come in. I'm just making tea."

Marcus was brutally honest. As the old man sipped his tea, he told him what he hadn't told him before—that he was looking for the famous missing Andreason girls, that a woman at CIFAS who had been helping him was murdered, that he was wanted by the police, that he was innocent.

"I believe that I am a good judge of character," Javier said. "I choose to believe you. How can I help?"

"I need to get to Segovia. They'll be looking for me at the train stations. All the car rental agencies will have my details by now. Do you have a car?"

"I do. It is hardly ever used. I do not even know why I keep it. The insurance is crazy for a piece of steel that does not move. Once a month I go to the garage and start it, for the battery, you see. I think you are a good man. I hope you find these poor girls. Take the car and may God keep you safe."

37

Marcus parked Javier's car in the center of Segovia and visited a few shops until someone was able to tell him the location of the nearest store for hunting supplies.

The San Cristóbal Armory, a short drive away, was a small shop packed with hunting and fishing gear. The proprietor grunted at his customer and kept checking a catalogue resting on a display case. Marcus went for a rack of paper maps and chose one that was detailed enough to show not only the village of Lirio, but the location of Castle Gaytan.

"Can I see those binoculars?" Marcus said in Spanish.

"American?" the shop owner asked.

"I am."

"Then I speak to you in English, okay?"

"That would be good, thank you."

"I was in army," the man said. "We had NATO exercises. I had American friends. I visited my friend in California."

"California's great." He had a look through the German binoculars and said he'd take them. Behind the owner there was a wall-rack of shotguns. "You've got a nice selection," he said.

"Some nicer than others," the owner said.

"What's your nicest?"

"This one," he said, reaching. "The Benelli Super Vinci pump-action. I can take or leave Italians, but I can't deny they make an excellent shotgun."

"May I?"

Marcus pumped it and visually inspected the chamber to make sure it was empty, while the proprietor nodded his approval at his safe handling. He felt its balance point and sighted down the long barrel.

"How much?" he asked.

"One thousand six hundred. For a nice American gentleman, one thousand five hundred."

"I'll take it."

"Fantastic. I'll just need to see your license."

Marcus said, "That's going to be a bit of a problem."

"No license, no sale. This is Spain, not America."

"There was a fair amount of dust on this gun," Marcus said. "How long have you had it?"

"I was a younger man." He patted his big gut. "And thinner."

"I'll take it off your hands for three thousand."

"I don't want to go to prison," the man said, moistening his lips with his tongue.

"I don't want you to go to prison either."

The prospect of a huge windfall was making the fellow breathe fast. "The no-license price is five thousand. Cash. No records."

Marcus winked. "With the binoculars?"

"Binoculars, map, shells—sure."

When Marcus returned from a bank with the cash, there was a closed sign on the door. The owner unlocked it, let him in, and counted the cash.

"Wait here," the man said, taking the gun with him.

"Where are you going?" Marcus asked.

"Give me five minutes."

Marcus heard loud grinding from a back room and figured out what was happening.

When the owner returned, he said, "No more serial number and looks like my camera stopped working, the piece of shit. You were never here."

"You're right. I was never here."

"I'm not going to read about you in the papers, am I?"

Marcus said, "Stick to the sports pages and you'll be good."

He left his car at the trailhead parking lot and from a vantage point on a hiking trail a hundred meters up the Guadarrama Mountains, Marcus focused his new binoculars. From this elevation, the earthen-brown, stone castle looked squat and massive. He could see a long drive from the main road that passed through vineyards and orchards before ending at the castle entrance. There were several vehicles parked in front of the main structure, but he couldn't see any people. He had a loaf of bread, some cheese, and a large bottle of water, and he kept his hunger and thirst at bay while he maintained his surveillance.

An hour passed by and doubts crept in.

He had no idea the girls were here. He had no idea whether Gaytan was here. He had just dropped five thousand euros, an uncomfortably large chunk of change, on an illegal gun. Did he think he was going to be charging in like Rambo? For the moment, all he could do was keep observing and figure out his next steps. He was a man wanted for murder who couldn't exactly expect the Spanish police to be sympathetic to a request to raid the home of a prominent doctor.

He put down his water bottle and lifted his binoculars when he thought he saw something moving on the roof. It was a man walking the ramparts. He didn't appear to have a weapon, but he too had binoculars he was using to scan the grounds. The sun was high in the early-afternoon sky and because his position was due south, he thought his lenses wouldn't be glinting.

A sentry had to be a sign of something going on inside.

Then he saw something that short-circuited all his carefully considered and rational thought.

Up on the ramparts, a second figure came into view.

Marcus recognized that face and he recognized that blond hair.

He tossed his food aside. *Victoria and Elizabeth, I'm coming for you*, he thought, *and God help anyone who stands in my way.*

For a man who prided himself on his analytical abilities, Marcus's mind was blank as he sped down the estate road. Then one inconsequential thought crept in that almost made him laugh. It involved that sweet man, Javier, and his old car. He would try not to wreck it.

Through the windshield the castle loomed large.

He saw the rifle on the ramparts and began to weave. As he cut the wheel to the left, a bullet pierced the right side of the windshield where his head would have been. His view was blighted by spidered glass, but he saw a large barn to his left and floored the gas pedal. He heard rapid-fire pops coming from above. Another round caught the car roof as he braked to a skidding stop behind the safety of the barn.

He grabbed the shotgun and got out of the car, making his way around the barn until he had what he thought was a protected line of sight to the castle entrance. It turned out not to be as protected as he hoped, because the rooftop shooter fired and chipped some stone from the barn wall, just to his right. His own shot didn't require much skill. He simply pointed toward the roof and let the buckshot do the rest. It plinked the upper walls and crenellations and sent the shooter ducking for cover.

He started running.

The massive main door was festooned with ancient iron hardware. He made it there without catching more fire, and racked another shell into the chamber of the Benelli. The motion was agony for his injured left shoulder.

The huge door creaked open.

A rifle barrel poked out, then an arm, and a shoulder.

Marcus was hoping the next thing he saw was blond hair, but the shooter's hair was brown.

When Marcus pulled the trigger, the brown turned red.

He racked the gun again, grimaced, and stepped over the body into the entrance hall.

Out of the corner of his eye he saw a threatening shape, but it was a silver suit of armor with a lance. The afternoon was bright, and it took a moment for his eyes to adjust to the darkness of the hall. There were large dimly lit rooms to his right and left and a sweeping stone staircase ahead.

He heard a voice he recognized.

"I am going to come downstairs, Mr. Handler. I am not

armed. I would appreciate not being shot. Are you going to shoot me?"

Marcus called back, "Let me have the girls and no one else needs to get hurt."

Ferrol appeared at the top of the stairs holding his hands in the air. Marcus was struck by how calm he appeared in the face of blood spreading across the yellow and black tiles of his hall, and having a shotgun pointed at him. Either he always wore a sports coat at home, or he was a cool enough customer who'd gotten himself properly attired for a guest after the alarm was raised.

Ferrol took a couple more stairs and said, "Please put the gun down. Would you like some coffee? We can sit and talk. You might be interested to hear what I have to say."

The room to his left appeared to be a library.

There was a flicker of movement and Marcus yelled, "Tell the man on my left that he's got three seconds to throw down his weapon or I'll shoot you."

"You in the library! Do as he says!" Ferrol shouted.

A pistol slid over the tiles.

Then he heard Ferrol shout, "Don't shoot him!"

Marcus was about to say that he wasn't going to shoot if the man showed himself, but Ferrol wasn't talking to him.

He was talking to the blond man who shot Marcus in the head.

One moment it was pitch black and the next moment it was phosphorous white. Everything was pure and luminous in every direction he turned his head.

He tried to focus through the worst pain he'd ever felt.

When he tried to close his right eye, the pain got worse and the whiteness persisted. When he closed his left eye, things got black again. Confused, he tried to reach for his face but his arms were tethered at his sides.

His voice was his own but it was so thin and dry he didn't recognize it. "Help. Help me."

A small face appeared over him.

Then another face.

"Uncle Marcus!"

"Am I alive?" he heard himself ask.

"What a silly question," Victoria said.

"Did you come to rescue us?" Elizabeth asked.

"If I did, I didn't do a very good job. Where am I?"

"Don't you know?" Victoria said.

"I can't remember."

"You're with us," Victoria said. "On the spaceship."

38

Marcus used his good eye to look around the white room, and painfully craned his neck to see what was behind him. There were cameras at each corner of the square chamber.

Elizabeth's head reappeared over him. "What happened to your head?" she asked.

"I wish I knew."

"Does it hurt?"

"I'm afraid it does."

"Bad Gray Man told us to give you water," she said. "Would you like some?"

"Yes, please."

"Vicky, bring it here," she told her sister.

Elizabeth placed a straw in his mouth and he sucked at it hard.

"Thank you. Who is Bad Gray Man?"

"He's the new one. He wasn't here when we were here before. Gray Woman and Gray Man are gone."

Victoria said, "He's really mean. He shouts at us. He won't play with us. He just brings us food and then leaves." She began to cry. "We don't want to be back on

379

the spaceship. We want to be with Granny Leonora and Grandpa Armando."

"I must have come to find you," Marcus said, struggling to remember, the pain in his head unbearable. "Are you all right?"

"We're not having any more nosebleeds," Elizabeth said. "I suppose that's good."

"Could you undo these straps on my wrists?" he asked.

Elizabeth shook her head. "Bad Gray Man told us that if we did that, he would hurt us very badly. He said he's watching us."

"It's okay, sweetheart, I don't want you to get hurt. I think I need to rest for a few minutes," Marcus said, the pain and drowsiness getting the better of him. "Don't let me sleep too long."

Marcus woke with a jolt to the sound of his stretcher ratcheting higher. He opened his unbandaged eye. A gray, alien face with large black eyes was staring down at him.

In a distorted voice, it said, "Get onto your beds and stay there."

"Don't take Uncle Marcus!" Victoria shouted.

The distorted voice shouted, "I said, go to your beds!"

The stretcher began to move. It stopped at a door and the gray alien stepped around, took a white plastic card hanging from his neck, and waved it at a wall panel. The door opened and Marcus was wheeled through.

He looked up at ceilings and doorway headers and side to side at laboratories filled with instruments. He came to a stop in a room that looked like an office. There was a desk, shelves with black notebooks, a stainless-steel cabinet with narrow drawers, and a TV on the wall with a five-window view, four of the white room with the girls on their beds, and one of the bathroom.

Then he saw the gray head again. Gray fingers partially unzipped the front of the white suit and two gray hands pulled at its hairless scalp. The mask came off and Marcus was staring into a sweaty, familiar face.

The man removed his gray latex gloves, then his headset, which he unplugged from the distortion box on his belt under the white suit, then the card around his neck.

"Do you know who you are?" the man asked.

"Marcus Handler."

"Do you know who I am?"

It took him several seconds to place him. His thoughts were moving like molasses. It came in stages—Madrid. The hospital. The institute.

"Dr. Gaytan. Ferrol Gaytan," Marcus said.

"Okay, good. Do you know where you are?"

He tried to remember but couldn't. "Are we in Spain?"

"Do you know what happened to you?"

He thought hard, but nothing came.

"No."

"You're a mess, Mr. Handler. You were shot. My man was about to shoot you squarely in the back of your head, but he flinched when I yelled at him to stop. The bullet entered behind your right ear and took a shallow course along the side of your head, exiting at the corner of your right eye. I think your eye is intact, but I'm not certain. I am not an ophthalmologist or a neurosurgeon. I don't have any x-ray or scanning equipment here. I have no way of

GLENN COOPER

knowing whether you've had bleeding in your brain, but it's a distinct possibility. It's the second time you've had head trauma. Like I said, you're a mess. I tended to you the best I could and put you in with the girls so I could keep an eye on you while I saw to the problems you've caused."

"My head hurts."

"I'm sure it does."

"What goes on here?"

"It's called science, Mr. Handler. It's called improving the human condition."

"I've got another word for it—"

Ferrol cut him off. "I don't care what you say and I don't care what you think. You're insignificant. The only thing I want from you is to tell me if anyone else knows about me. Were you working on your own or were you communicating with anyone?"

"I don't remember."

"Are you lying to me?"

He was telling the truth. "I don't know. It's not a lie if I can't remember."

"What's the last thing you do remember?"

"Can I have water?"

Ferrol got a bottle of water and put it to his lips.

"The last thing you remember," Ferrol repeated.

He dug in and tried to unearth something from the black depths. Then, it came to him. The smell of gasoline, the bits of metal and glass. Abril. "The bomb," he said. "I remember the bomb."

"The police say you were the bomber. They're looking for you."

"It wasn't me."

382

"What if I don't believe this was your last memory?" Ferrol said.

"I don't remember anything after that."

"You're saying this, but I need to know if it's the truth. I need to know if you told anyone about me. I need to know if I'm safe. If you're lying, I'll hurt the girls very badly. I need them alive, but that doesn't mean they can't be put through pain."

His rising anger made his head hurt even more. "Are you a monster?"

"You would be the monster for lying when you know what I might to do to them. I only need the truth from you. Then you can rest."

"Rest? You mean kill me?"

"Rest means rest."

"I swear. I don't remember if I told anyone about you. I hope I did."

Ferrol went to his steel cabinet and slid open one of the drawers. "It's possible you're telling the truth. You might have retrograde amnesia from the trauma. I'm going to give you Decadron, a steroid to reduce swelling in your brain. We'll try again in a few hours."

Ferrol unbuckled the straps on Marcus's left arm, poked a vein with a butterfly needle, and injected a dose of Decadron. When he turned away to discard the syringe, Marcus used his untethered hand to reach for the plastic card Ferrol had left on the side of the mattress with his headset, mask, and gloves, and shoved it under his thigh. Ferrol buckled his wrist again.

"I'm taking you back now," Ferrol said, reaching for his headset.

Marcus wanted to distract him enough to forget the keycard.

"Celeste," he said.

Ferrol forced the latex mask over his head and said, "What about her?"

"I was there when she died."

"She was useful. She got you onto the mountain. Everyone was supposed to die, including her. She was a loose end, like Ferruccio Gressani. She meant nothing to me," Ferrol said. He zipped up his suit, pulled on the gloves, and began to wheel Marcus back to the white room.

There was a knock on the office door and Gunar came in.

"Sorry. You busy," he said.

"I'm just putting him back."

"What he say?"

"Nothing useful."

"You want me make him talk?"

"I gave him a drug. Maybe later. Mr. Handler, anything to say to the man who shot you?"

Through his good eye, Marcus saw blond hair and a smirking mouth, and said, "Fuck you."

"Seems appropriate," Ferrol said.

"When you done, come up, please?" Gunar said to Ferrol. "Need to talk about bring more men to Spain."

Ferrol pushed the button on the box under his suit and in a distorted voice said, "I'll be right there."

As Marcus was wheeled back through the laboratories, he tried to remember if he'd told Roberto Lumaga or anyone else about finding Gaytan. He couldn't even remember where he was or how he'd gotten here. He didn't know if help was going to come. He was badly injured, but there was only one person he could rely on, and it was himself.

Inside the white room, Bad Gray Man told the girls to remember they'd be punished if they undid Marcus's restraints, then left him on his stretcher.

When they were alone, Elizabeth asked if he was thirsty. Ferrol had left the stretcher higher than before and she had trouble reaching him with the glass. As she rose on her tiptoes, she slipped and splashed his face with cold water.

It went up his nostrils and made him gasp.

"I'm sorry, Uncle Marcus! I didn't mean to do that!"

"It's all right, sweetheart. Don't worry."

"Vicky, get a towel," she said, and the little girl scurried to the bathroom.

"Come close," Marcus whispered very softly. "Are you a brave girl? Answer me in your tiniest whisper."

"I think so," Elizabeth whispered in his good ear.

"Will you do something very brave for me?"

"Yes."

"I want you to unbuckle my wrist straps."

"Bad Gray Man said he'd hurt us if we did that."

"He won't. It's just a threat to scare you. I want to take you back to your grandparents, but first, I need you to help me."

"We're in space. What can you do?"

He wanted to set her straight, but the only thing protecting them was Ferrol's ability to release them none the wiser.

"I can drive the spaceship home," he whispered. "Here's your sister. Tell her to be very, very quiet, then undo the straps."

39

Lying on the stretcher, the pain was unbearable.

It was worse on his feet.

He made it through the gleaming labs to a door that took him to a cool, medieval basement of stone walls and dimly lit corridors. Along the way he found a broken ax handle and used it as a cane. He hobbled up a run of stone stairs, and at the top, he unlatched a heavy wooden door and slowly pushed it open.

He was in a long hallway.

He had to rest.

The dizziness he felt climbing the stairs was getting worse. He might have to throw up.

His lack of depth perception wasn't helping. In the distance, he made out faint voices and as he crept closer he saw a kitchen. A little further down the hall, there was a large cabinet filled with crockery and he used it for cover.

He heard Ferrol in English, say, "No, keep them all on the roof."

Gunar replied, "Take three days for more men. Till then, don't have enough guys for big raid."

"We don't know if a raid is coming. We don't know if Handler told anyone where he was going."

"Okay. Getting dark now. Need to bring guys night-vision goggles."

"I sent the servants away for the night. I'll be upstairs. I'll question Handler again in a couple of hours."

Footsteps headed in opposite directions.

He waited until both sets had faded away, peered into the empty kitchen, then took another wider, grander corridor, this one lined with oil paintings and tapestries, until he was in a huge entrance hall with a floor of yellow and black tiles and a suit of medieval armor. A massive stone staircase swept to the next floor.

He almost fell on slippery tiles smeared with mopped blood and he wondered if he had anything to do with it. By the door, a shotgun stood on its stock. He traded his ax handle and when he picked it up, it seemed vaguely familiar. There was at least one shell visible behind the receiver shell-latch.

He started up the stairs, using the weapon to steady himself.

He reached a wide hallway carpeted with a long oriental runner that dampened his footfalls. There were closed doors on either side of the hall, but further along, there was an open one. Drawing closer, he heard a TV.

Ferrol came out of his bathroom, lay on his bed, and reached for the tablet on the bedspread. He glanced at the white-room feed. The girls were on their beds. He looked closer and spread his fingers to increase the magnification. Handler's stretcher was empty.

He sprang up and grabbed the walkie-talkie on his desk.

"Gunar! Handler's escaped! Get down here!"

Marcus turned the shotgun from a walking stick back into a weapon.

He heard Gunar's reply come through. "Coming, boss," followed by, "Fuck! Choppers!"

At the doorway, Marcus saw sheer curtains billowing at the open windows. The evening breeze carried the sound of rotor blades.

Gunar grabbed a rifle with a night-vision scope and scanned the skies.

He acquired the lead helicopter in his sights, a Eurocopter Tigre emblazoned with the black and gold serpent and warbird of the Grupo Especial de Operaciones.

Gunar shouted to his men in Slovakian, "Engage!"

The helicopter opened up on the castle ramparts with its nose-mounted thirty-millimeter turret.

The weapons officer had an excellent screen-view of Gunar's blond head poking through a crenellation and directed a long burst into it.

At the first volley, Ferrol ducked away from the window.

The heavy automatic fire overhead was deafening.

Marcus shouted over it, "Looks like I did tell someone I was here."

Ferrol turned looking like a trapped animal. His wild eyes darted about and settled on the kerosene lamp on his desk.

"Put it down," Marcus shouted. It was hard keeping his balance. His headache made him want to scream.

Ferrol didn't put it down. He poured kerosene over his

head and splashed the rest on his sweater. Then he grabbed a butane lighter.

"Don't do it!" Marcus yelled.

Ferrol backed toward his bathroom door.

The firing stopped outside.

Marcus could hear helicopters landing.

Ferrol said, "My parents died in this room, many years ago. They died by fire. Since then, I've had a mortal fear of fire and a mortal fear of death. I thought I could cheat death. I was wrong."

"Put the lighter down."

"My notebooks," Ferrol said. "At least my work will live forever."

He flicked the lighter and erupted in a fireball.

As he fell backwards into the bathroom, Marcus heard him screaming.

"The beast! The beast! The final beast!"

Marcus dropped the shotgun and tried to pull the bedspread off to suffocate the flames.

But, as he was tugging at the heavy fabric, he felt an explosion go off inside his head.

At a great distance, Marcus heard a familiar voice.

"My friend, can you hear me? Please, can you hear me?"

Opening his unbandaged eye felt like the hardest thing he had ever done. It wanted to stay shut, to keep him cloaked in darkness. He was lying on a rug. His bandage was soaked through. Blood was pouring down his shoulder.

"Roberto," he said, weakly. "Did I tell you I was here?"

"Yes, of course. If only I could have arrived sooner. My God, look at you."

"Give me a cigarette."

Lumaga helped him sit against the bed. He lit a cigarette for him and put it between his lips.

A Spanish GEO officer emerged from the bathroom and gave Lumaga a thumbs-down.

"That's Ferrol Gaytan in there?" Lumaga asked.

Marcus didn't answer. He closed his eye and in the darkness, he saw someone standing in the distance.

"Marcus, please stay with me!" Lumaga said.

The cigarette dropped away. "The girls are in the basement," he whispered. "It's all in the notebooks."

Something curious was happening. As it got darker and darker, the figure standing there got brighter and brighter until Marcus recognized her.

"Alice," he said in a voice that Lumaga couldn't hear. "I wasn't there for you, but you're here for me."

40

Six months later

"Come, let me see you!" Dr. Spara exclaimed. "How are my two favorite patients?"

Victoria and Elizabeth bounced into the doctor's examination room at the Bambino Gesù Hospital and gave their Bruno Bear the hugs he demanded. Leonora and Armando Cutrì followed them in and shook Spara's hand.

"So, we're coming up on their six-month anniversary of their bone marrow transplants," Spara said. "How have they been?"

"Full of energy," Armando said.

"Their appetites are very good too," Leonora said.

"How's their Italian coming along?"

Elizabeth answered in Italian, "We speak like natives!"

"Like natives, eh?" Spara said.

"I'm an Italian girl!" Victoria exclaimed.

"Of course, you are," Spara said in English. "Come on. Up on the scales. You know the drill. Height and weight."

Spara did his measurements and wrote down the results.

"Tell us, Professore," Armando said.

"I'm pleased to say that each of them has grown two centimeters."

Leonora began to weep.

"Why is Granny crying?" Victoria asked her sister.

"I don't know," Elizabeth said. "Are you sad, Granny?"

"No, dearest ones, I'm not sad. Just give me a minute."

Her husband followed her into the hall and gave her his pocket handkerchief.

"They'll get old and they'll die, like all men and beasts," she said, drying her eyes. "At least they're in God's hands now, not the Devil's."

About the Author

GLENN COOPER is a Harvard-trained infectious diseases physician who became the CEO of a large public biotech company in Massachusetts. He sold his company in 2009, about the time that his first novel, Library of the Dead, was published. He has been a full-time writer ever since, with fourteen top-ten bestselling thrillers published in thirty translations, and eight million copies sold.
@GlennCooper www.glenncooperbooks.com